Praise for the historical novels of
Diane Haeger

"Spectacular. . . . Haeger explores the fascinating, rich, exciting, and tragic life of Henry II's beloved. . . . Lush in characterization and rich in historical detail, *Courtesan* will sweep readers up into its pages and carry them away."
—*Romantic Times*

"In Haeger's impressive Restoration romance, King Charles II and his mistress . . . leap off the page. . . . Charles and Nell are marvelously complex—jealous and petty, devoted yet fallible. Haeger perfectly balances the history with the trystery."
—*Publishers W*

"Set against the vivid descriptive detail of P
vere, Haeger's tale of how the ring cam
Raphael masterpiece resonates w
macy of epic love stories. . . . This
vored as the wonderful historical tale   *BookPage*

"Lush . . . [a] rich yet fast-paced story."
—*The Historical Novels Review*

"With her wealth of detail cleverly interwoven into a fabulous plot, Diane Haeger has written a triumphant tale that will provide much delight to fans of historical fiction and Regency romance."
—*Affaire de Coeur*

The Secret Bride

IN THE COURT OF HENRY VIII

DIANE HAEGER

NEW AMERICAN LIBRARY

New American Library
Published by New American Library,
a division of Penguin Group (USA) Inc.,
375 Hudson Street, New York, New York 10014, USA
Penguin Group (Canada), 90 Eglinton Avenue East, Suite 700, Toronto,
Ontario M4P 2Y3, Canada (a division of Pearson Penguin Canada Inc.)
Penguin Books Ltd., 80 Strand, London WC2R 0RL, England
Penguin Ireland, 25 St. Stephen's Green, Dublin 2,
Ireland (a division of Penguin Books Ltd.)
Penguin Group (Australia), 250 Camberwell Road, Camberwell,
Victoria 3124, Australia (a division of Pearson Australia Group Pty. Ltd.)
Penguin Books India Pvt. Ltd., 11 Community Centre,
Panchsheel Park, New Delhi–110 017, India
Penguin Group (NZ), 67 Apollo Drive, Rosedale, North Shore 0632,
New Zealand (a division of Pearson New Zealand Ltd.)
Penguin Books (South Africa) (Pty.) Ltd., 24 Sturdee Avenue,
Rosebank, Johannesburg 2196, South Africa

Penguin Books Ltd., Registered Offices:
80 Strand, London WC2R 0RL, England

First published by New American Library,
a division of Penguin Group (USA) Inc.

First Printing, April 2008
3 5 7 9 10 8 6 4

Copyright © Diane Haeger, 2008
Readers Guide copyright © Penguin Group (USA) Inc., 2008
All rights reserved

▣ REGISTERED TRADEMARK—MARCA REGISTRADA

LIBRARY OF CONGRESS CATALOGING-IN-PUBLICATION DATA
Haeger, Diane.
The secret bride : in the court of Henry VIII / Diane Haeger.
p. cm.
ISBN: 978-0-451-22313-5
1. Mary, Queen, consort of Louis XII, King of France, 1496–1533—Fiction.   2. Great
Britain—History—Henry VIII, 1509–1547—Fiction.   I. Title.
PS3558.A32125S425 2008
813'.54—dc22   2007042219

Set in Simoncini Garamond
Designed by Elke Sigal

Printed in the United States of America

For Alex, my joy, with all my love

Acknowledgments

$\mathcal{I}$am especially indebted to Steven J. Gunn, Professor of History at Merton College, Oxford, England, for so graciously sharing his extensive knowledge regarding the life of Charles Brandon; to the staff at Hampton Court Palace for the generosity of their time and detailed information regarding a Tudor palace; to Frederic J. Baumgartner, Professor of History at Virginia Tech, for his assistance with details at the Court of Louis XII; to Elizabeth Haeger, truly the strongest person I know, you really do guide me daily; to Marlene Fried, for graciously reading every word I write; to Kelly Costello for her enduring friendship beyond anything I could ask; to my amazing literary agent, Irene Goodman, and my editor, Claire Zion, who both had a vision for and belief in this book and supported it every step of the way; and finally to Fran Measley once again, who has brought so much joy and encouragement to me this past year, there are no words to say what that has meant. You are extraordinary.

The Secret Bride

Chapter One

The ever whirling wheel of change; the which all mortal things doth sway.

—*Edmund Spenser*

April 1502, Eltham Palace

A collection of columbines, sweet peas and lilies of the valley clutched tightly in her hand, Mary dodged through the rows of apple trees in the orchard, chasing butterflies out behind the palace. Jane skittered just behind as they crossed the flagstone path, edged with rich moss, that bordered the new tiltyard the king had constructed. The spring wind carried their dresses out behind them like billowing sails, all beneath a broad azure sky. The royal nursery at Eltham was tucked deeply into the lush countryside outside the city, near Greenwich, where Henry VII's children, and their companions, were being brought up in an idyllic moated brick castle blanketed in emerald ivy, far from the complexities of court. The princess Mary and Jane Popincourt, sent from Paris to speak French with the children, dashed past the moat, where swans glided over the surface of the water, which that day was smooth as glass. Each bird wore a badge loosely about its long graceful neck emblazoned with the Beaufort insignia. It was the crest of Mary's powerful grandmother, the determined woman who had helped her son win the war that made him Henry VII. It was then, in the front courtyard, that Mary and Jane both heard it—whispered words, uttered by a servant.`

"Poor, dear Arthur! Poor Katherine!" The sound of weeping followed.

Not understanding, Mary dashed up the steps and through the entrance toward the twisted staircase, with its carved, polished banister. Jane followed, their smiles falling by degrees. Upstairs, they walked through the oak-paneled gallery, hands suddenly linked. Jane was like a sister to Mary since her own elder sister, Margaret, was being prepared to be sent to Scotland as the bride of King James. It was a political match, made by ambassadors, that greatly pleased their father but left Margaret fearful and sad, the fun gone out of her in preparation for her royal duty. Poor Margaret, Mary always thought, made to marry a man of the advanced age of twenty-nine, one who had already been married and widowed. Yet her turn would come soon enough. She too was the daughter of Henry VII. But Mary refused to think of that yet—at least until she turned eleven.

Beyond the door, the entire house was in an uproar. Mary could hear the faraway sound of more weeping, but those servants who moved around her carefully avoided her gaze. The few who did catch her eye bore unmistakable pity in their expressions. Jane and Mary exchanged a glance.

"What's happened?" Mary whispered, fingers splaying

across her mouth, her other hand tightening with Jane's. As it always did when anything was wrong, Mary felt panic rise and a need to find her brother strongly follow. Henry would know what had happened and how to fix it. He would know what to do.

Mary broke into a run toward the cavernous great hall, with its intricate hammer-beamed roof, rows of oriel windows, minstrels gallery and grand stone fireplace. She knew Henry would be there wrestling just now. But by the time she found him, her brother was surrounded by servants, all silent. He was standing still as a stone in their midst, tall and slim, his chin-length red-gold hair plastered with sweat against his forehead and cheeks.

Beside him stood his friend Charles Brandon, who was older, taller, auburn-haired and somber-eyed. In spite of the fact that both of them were covered in perspiration from the contest, their linen-shirted chests still heaving from exertion, the color had completely drained from her brother's face. Mary paused near the door, surveying the scene for a moment, her heart pounding. The flowers slipped from her hand and fell into a little pile of stems and petals at her feet. As she drew near, then stopped before him, Henry met her gaze and his pale green eyes misted with tears.

"It's Arthur. He is dead," Henry said, with a quiver in his voice that Mary had never heard from her carefree brother before.

While their eldest brother, Arthur, had always been weak, she never imagined that England's heir might actually die. At eight, she thought little of death and tragedy, especially living the idyllic life she did in the country, surrounded by endless emerald hills, water-meadows and streams, well protected from the harshness of court life.

Only four months ago Arthur, at age fifteen, had been married off to Katherine of Aragon, daughter of Queen Isabella of Spain, with whom he had been betrothed since his infancy. The match had been made in order to secure the alliance between their two countries. But Katherine at seventeen was pretty and sweet enough, and Henry and Mary both liked her. Arthur had seemed happy with her too; his tenuous health had seemed strengthened by their union, in spite of his youth. But all of that was over now. Gone in a moment. The world would change for everyone, but most especially for Henry, who she could see had only just now fully realized that he would next be King of England.

Then, to her surprise, Charles Brandon, and not her brother Henry, extended his arms in that odd, silent moment, and drew her against him in a comforting, fatherly embrace. The feel of his lean, muscular torso pressed against her own flat child's chest startled her, in spite of her grief. The sensation was a shock to a girl who was not yet even nine. Until that day—that moment exactly—she had never thought of Charles as anything but her brother Henry's friend and companion.

At eighteen, Brandon was older than them both—there by the grace of the king, who had installed him at Eltham as a debt owed to Charles's father. William Brandon had fought nobly beside the king at Bosworth Field and lost his life there. His mother had died in childbirth, leaving Charles orphaned, and two siblings, a sister and brother, left to distant relatives to care for. But the family had made sacrifices which the king meant to honor. Henry VII was many things; most especially he was loyal to those who had shown loyalty to him, and so Charles Brandon had been chosen as a companion for his son.

With Arthur and Katherine away establishing their own court in Wales at their father's command, Brandon had quickly become Henry's closest friend just as Jane had become Mary's. In spite of the difference in their ages, the boys were well matched, not only in athletics, but in their sense of humor, and Henry watched and sought to learn everything from an older Charles's remarkable effect on women.

Many was the time Mary had sat at dinner in the great dining hall with her sister, Margaret, and Jane, watching Henry and Charles wager how quickly Charles could entice a particular girl more rapidly. Most often, Mary observed Charles win out, which only made Henry push himself the more. Henry was a natural and graceful athlete and he excelled in everything—tennis, archery, the hunt, dancing— and he was learning from the master about flirtation.

Realizing the way she was shivering in Charles's arms, Mary pulled away from him and cast a glance at Henry. "What are we to do?" she asked, wiping her own tears with the back of her hand.

"We are to do nothing."

"What of Katherine? She must be so sad and afraid, all alone now."

"I imagine the king will send her back to Spain, believing she has failed her family."

"But Arthur's death is not her fault!"

"Of course not. But only if by some miracle she is already carrying an heir will she have accomplished her family's goal."

He and Henry both smiled wryly at the thought of Arthur fathering a child and she found it shocking, especially when Arthur was dead and Katherine, with whom she had laughed and danced the branle so happily not a month before, at Richmond, would need to return to Spain suddenly in dishonor and shame.

"Oh, come now," Charles remarked, seeing Mary's expression. "We only hope to put a bit of a brave face on a horrid tragedy."

"And how difficult for you is that?" she asked tautly, sounding much older than her years. "Now your dearest friend will next be king. Arthur barely knew you, and what he knew he did not much like. But my brother Henry adores you. It seems to me great fortune for you in the tragedy of another."

"*Mary!*" Henry charged. "I understand you are upset— we all are. But you really must apologize for such words."

"I will not," she stubbornly declared, tipping up her chin with a defiance like his own, which ran so thickly through her blood that she could not have tamed it. "Charles is arrogant and selfish and I do not like him."

"Yet *I* do. And it is I whose command you shall be made to follow soon enough."

"You can command my compliance, Harry, but never my heart!"

"Would you prefer I leave the two of you alone so your sister can insult me in privacy?" Charles moved a step nearer, his normally arrogant expression suddenly decorated with challenge.

"Stay where you are," Henry shot back, despite hearing

the nickname she always used to soften him. His own defiance was as sharp as hers now. "My sister was just leaving, so that she does not risk embarrassing herself further."

"But Harry!" Mary heard herself cry out. Her anger was swiftly undone at the thought of losing her brother's affection for that of a mere friend. Insecurity rose up within her as a flood of tears clouded her eyes. "You would choose him over me? I am your sister. Your Mary!"

"And Charles is my friend. The two of you must come to an understanding as we are all bound to be together for a very long time to come—particularly after I am king."

Hearing his harsh tone toward her at that moment was like a slap in the face. Mary bolted from the room, her eyes so full of warm tears that she could barely see her way as the skirts and petticoats of her brocade dress rippled out behind her. Charles Brandon was someone to be feared and respected, for he had a place in Henry's heart that he stubbornly meant to retain. Realizing it fully then made her feel as if she had lost two brothers that day instead of just one. But she would never take for granted Charles Brandon, or his power over Henry, ever again.

Henry came alone to her bedchamber not quite an hour later, knocked, then let himself in. She was sitting within the window embrasure, arms wrapped around her legs, her profusion of red-gold curls loose on her shoulders, meeting the silver medallion at her chest. She was gazing out across the green expanse of hills and valleys as he sat down beside her and took up both of her hands. They looked startlingly alike: their hair, the square shape of their faces, the pale green eyes with long light lashes and the small rosebud lips. Neither Margaret nor Arthur looked like them, which was one of the many things that had bonded them. They sat together quietly for what felt to Mary like a very long time, both of them pretending to see all that was before them beneath the cloudless sky.

"You know you are always first in my heart, my little Mary," Henry finally said very gently. When she met his gaze, his face was so full of that irresistably boyish charm she wanted to cry all over again.

"I know it not," she pouted, tears still filling her eyes.

"It was only the shock of things. Forgive me, do you?"

"I will always forgive you, Harry," she replied on a teary sob full of relief a moment later. "I can't quite believe it will just be the two of us left as soon as Margaret marries. That makes me feel so sad."

"I'll always take care of you, Mary, you know that," he declared in the almost fatherly, protective voice that she loved. He wrapped his arm around her then, pulled a handkerchief from his doublet and patiently wiped her eyes. "Someday, when I am king, we will rule England together. Will that not be grand? You will have no time to be sad then."

"What about your queen?"

"Her as well, of course. But I could not rule without *you*. That would be unthinkable," he mused. They both refused to acknowledge for the moment that one day she would likely leave England in some political arrangement their father would make, as he had for Margaret and Arthur already. Marriage would be the first duty for them both. But right now they were children, and they could ignore the future. At least in this little world of their own making at Eltham. "And one of the very first things I am going to do when I am Henry VIII is name a great ship after you . . . the *Mary Rose*, I will call it, and it will be the most spectacular ship in my fleet."

"I do like the sound of that."

He always knew how to make her smile, she thought, even if their conversation did seem horribly disrespectful to Arthur. "But, in the meantime, you really must learn to like Charles better, Mary. Beneath the lionesque exterior he has the heart of a lamb. If you look for it, you will see it as I do."

"I will try," Mary resolved on a tearful little hiccup, her lower lip turned out. "But only for you, Harry."

Henry smiled at her and chucked her gently beneath the chin. He had a way with her—and she with him—that no one else did. "Splendid. Because I could not bear it if we were really angry with one another, especially with all that is about to happen," he said with a weary little chuckle, and Mary could not help but feel the enormous weight of the future in that sound.

Their brother's funeral was a great state occasion, costly and somber. He had died on the second of April and had lain in state until St. George's Day, on the twenty-third of that month. The king was devastated by his elder son's death. Like Mary, he had not allowed himself to believe that Arthur might actually die. Margaret, Henry and Mary were taken to Ludlow Castle to participate in the somber procession. It was to culminate at the great Worcester Cathedral, with its towers and pointed spires and massive stained-glass window, on the banks of the Severn River. No one was surprised that a foul April day blanketed the procession in cold, gray rain.

Stricken by the same sweating sickness that had killed Arthur, Katherine was too ill to attend her young husband's funeral. The king and queen would attend the funeral, but would enter the cathedral privately. They were too bereft to ride in the procession. It was therefore left to Henry, Margaret, Mary and their grandmother Lady Beaufort to hold their heads high and show the dignity of their line to those who, three and four people deep, lined the muddy, rain-soaked roads. The people had come to pay their respects to a prince who had been loved and respected by everyone in England.

The children rode white palfreys in a somber cadence behind the queue of bishops, abbots and priors who followed a cart draped and canopied in black velvet, drawn by four sleek Italian coursers. Despite the crowd, the only sounds were the muffled clop of horses' hooves in the mud, the jangle of harnesses, the tolling of church bells and the soft echo of weeping. There was an unending procession behind Mary, Margaret and Henry, lords and ladies cloaked in black satin or velvet. In spite of the thick black mourning attire, the cold, windy rain seeped through their cloaks and beneath the brims of their plumed hats and headdresses.

As she rode, Mary tried to ignore the constant rhythmic drip, drip, drip of raindrops from the frame of her black gabled headdress as they fell into her eyes. She was glad for the rain, which helped to hide her tears. She had been wiping them away until her grandmother shot Mary a reproachful glare from eyes that were deep-set and commanding. The family matriarch was as religious as she was stern. Her expression reminded Mary they were Tudors, victors in war, and meant to suffer with the greatest dignity and grace no matter what they felt inside. They were above all other things to be gravely royal. Mary learned that lesson well in those days just before her eighth birthday, not only from her grandmother, but from watching her brother Henry work hard not to shed a single tear, and succeeding.

When they finally entered the cathedral, Mary saw the plain wood coffin was surrounded by torches and beeswax candles all blazing beneath banners embroidered with the royal coat of arms for both England and Spain in a soaring nave lavish with marble and medieval carvings. The bishops, gowned in copes of rich velvet, stood beside a grand collection of stone-faced abbots and priors. A choir of children in the gallery above them, wearing white surplices, looked, Mary thought, like little angels come to bear poor Arthur up to heaven.

The requiem sermon felt to her as if it lasted an eternity. She sat motionless in the dank, musty-smelling cathedral chilled to the bone and biting her lip until she could taste her own blood so that she would not cry again, but the somber scene was almost too much for her to bear. She could hear her mother's quiet weeping from the seats in the row ahead of her. Henry sat on one side of Mary, staring straight ahead and unmoving, and on the other side of her was Thomas Wolsey. Their father's robust almoner, with his fleshy face, black eyes and hawkish nose, seemed always to be about these days. Now he reached over and put his large hand atop her own and squeezed ever so slightly. The compassionate gesture surprised Mary yet brought her an odd comfort, and she did not pull away. She turned to look up at him after a moment but he did not meet her gaze. Like Henry, he sat staring straight ahead, fixed on the ancient ceremony being carried out before them. Still, she thought, she would not forget this small kindness.

After their elder brother's coffin was lowered into the deep pit prepared before them all in the church nave just below the altar, it was covered over with rich cloth of gold that had been sewn with a cross of white silk—a blanket for eternity, Mary thought. She was frightened by the endless ritual of Arthur's burial when the staffs and rods of his household were broken. The rigid, snapping sound was like bones breaking, and it echoed across the vast cathedral, just before they were cast into the grave and his body was lowered away forever from those who had so dearly loved him. Down into the earth, buried away forever. Gone. One day forgotten.

Choking incense clouded the cold, hollow nave, along with the sounds of a somber *Te Deum*, and it darkened her heart. Arthur, sweet gentle Arthur, with his shining eyes and the dusting of freckles across the bridge of his nose. Arthur, whose laugh had been sweet and light, and still full of as much innocence as hers. It would be forever gone from all but for her fleeting memories. No more jests. No more hope of a future with all four of them grown, powerful and united, as they had so often childishly decided they would be. Nor would he be buried in London or Richmond, or anywhere she could ever easily visit to ease a sister's heart. He would be alone here in Worcester, so far from court, far from those who had loved him. At that moment, that felt a devastation. She may be a princess and a Tudor, but she was still a little girl.

Even after midnight, all of the images, sounds and memories of the day moved through her mind, and Mary could not sleep. She lay fitfully beneath her red velvet canopy, the curtains drawn around her bed. She could hear the fire in her room cracking and sputtering to embers. As she listened, she heard two of her ladies who had begun to whisper in the alcove just beyond the crimson velvet curtains. Their tone was hushed, yet urgent. Carefully, she pressed back the bedcovers, then the curtain, got out of bed and very quietly tiptoed toward the sitting room.

"Poor little Katherine suffers the sweating sickness now as well?" Lady Guildford was asking on a sigh. "It is said that Queen Isabella is demanding the girl's return to Spain the moment she is recovered."

"Not if the king can find a way to keep her here once she recovers. He is determined to do that, for if she goes, that vast Spanish dowry goes with her."

"I heard it whispered that now he wishes to marry her to the new Prince of Wales, so that he can maintain the alliance with Spain—and keep her Spanish purse."

"The pope will never permit such a scandalous thing. The Bible clearly directs no man to lie with his brother's wife."

"Unless perhaps he was too young to lie with her himself?"

"Would His Highness argue such a point?"

"For the riches of Spain I should think King Henry would argue it to the death."

"Sad little princess," Lady Guildford sighed. "Good only for the purse she bears."

"And the princes she yet might bear for England."

She may be a princess meant to be a queen, Mary thought, yet poor Katherine was no better than chattel. Mary remembered how the sweet Spanish girl had struggled so nobly with her English, broken and charming as it was, just to please Arthur the last time Mary had seen her. Now that same girl was being bought, sold and now bartered. She leaned forward on her toes and pressed her hands against the wall, but abruptly the women stopped speaking. She could hear skirts rustling, then the tap of shoe soles across the wood floor. Princess or not, the punishment for eavesdropping would be severe. Lady Beaufort ran the royal nursery with precision, and no deviation would be tolerated. Thinking only of that, Mary spun away and dashed through a small, rounded side door to her dressing room and out the servants' entrance into the long, torchlit gallery—and headlong into Charles Brandon. As she collided with that same long, lean chest, Mary realized he had with him a companion who was clinging quite tightly to his arm. In a glance she saw he was with the widow. The one about whom everyone gossiped.

Margaret Mortimer was tall and attractive, but noticeably older than Charles—thirty-eight to his eighteen years. She had heard Henry and the Earl of Northumberland's son, James, speaking about it that morning before the funeral procession. She knew that Charles intended to marry Lady Mortimer for her family's fortune. This was in spite of his having been first contracted to marry Margaret's younger and beautiful niece.

"Be not too hard on him," Henry had laughed that morning when she had told him the gossip she had heard. "Marriage really is the only way for poor Charles to rise above his modest circumstances. He will get her houses and land, and Lady Mortimer will get a young, virile man in her bed."

"That is vulgar."

"That is the dirty side of life at court," he had countered on a wicked laugh. "And the life you will know only too well before you are ready, if you insist on hiding around corners and eavesdropping."

Hearing the cause of his ignoble ambitions had done little to make Mary like Charles Brandon any more than before. To a child, her brother's exceedingly handsome friend seemed self-serving and shallow. Just as he looked now, she thought as she gazed up at him.

"Ho there, my little lady Mary." Charles laughed deeply, stopping her with his arms and pushing her back to regard her. "Should you not be more properly attired for a midnight stroll?"

"Should wisdom not counsel you to speak less condescendingly to the daughter of your king?"

"Point taken." He nodded, his smile broad and confident. Mary felt like an awkward child in her nightdress and cap, just as she often did in his company. Glancing at Margaret Mortimer in her elegant blue silk dress with white sarcenet sleeves lined with fur, and a gable headdress, she fought a childish burst of jealousy. "My most humble apologies to you," he added, bowing deeply, almost reverently, which seemed a small condescension of its own.

Only then did Mary realize that she had been so entranced

by this eighteen-year-old upstart swaggering and smiling before her that she had not heard the footsteps approaching
from behind. It was not Lady Guildford, as it might have
been, but the queen, who was returning with a collection of
her ladies from supper in the great hall. There could not be a
worse circumstance. Mary could feel her mother's reproving
stare like heat on the back of her neck as Charles once again
bowed deeply and Margaret Mortimer made a proper curtsy.
Mary let the fear invade her as her heart pounded. A girl of
any age at court was not to be out in her nightclothes—least
of all a child-princess whose virginity and honor were the
highest prize.

Her mother's voice was sharp. The heavy fragrance of her
ambergris perfume swirled around her, along with the scent
of burning candles, which glowed, flickered and danced from
the iron braziers on the wall. "Mary . . ."

"My lady mother." She curtsied deeply now, trembling as
she did, and sensing her mother's displeasure.

Elizabeth of York had been a wonderful role model for
her daughters and had patiently taught them the importance of
their heritage and duty. And since Margaret had become betrothed to King James, the queen had seemed especially at
peace with her life. That was, until Arthur's death. Now both
the king and queen seemed brittle, both pale shadows of
what they had once been. The happiness was gone from them
both. All that remained seemed to be a shallow sense of obligation that moved them through their duties.

Oddly, while standing in the glare of her mother's cold
stare, Mary's mind flitted to a joyful memory. It had been a
warm summer day when the queen had held her hand and

taken her daughter alone to her private chamber. Together they had laughed and ate jellies and sweets and her mother had set her on her lap to teach her how to embroider a rose. Her sweet scent of lavender water encircled Mary like a warm embrace, as she patiently guided her daughter's tiny hand through the fabric on the hoop before them. *That's it, my heart . . . like that . . . just like that. . . .*

She stood before Mary now in a tight-bodiced dress of mourning black, the square-cut neck hung with a chain of gold and pearls. She offered no smile, no sign of affection. She was surrounded by her ladies and Mary's frighteningly stern grandmother Lady Beaufort, all of whom wore black as well. The kind softness she remembered was gone now.

"What have you to say for this?" her mother now asked.

"I—well . . . my lady mother, I truly thought that I—" She heard herself stammer out sounds for words, the kind of spineless response she knew the queen despised. Elizabeth of York, Queen of England, had, along with the king, survived what would later become known as the War of the Roses, and she respected conviction and purposeful speech above all else. She had learned in her own childhood not to suffer weakness at all.

"If Your Highness shall permit me, I must entirely take the blame," Brandon said, suddenly intervening. "Embarrassing as it is to admit, the lady Mary heard my companion and I, not a little drunk, I am afraid, outside her chamber door. The child only came to bid me not to disturb her ladies, who were retiring, and to be quiet so that she too might sleep. Both Lady Mortimer and I were asking her indulgence when Your Highness came upon us just now."

Mary looked over at Charles Brandon, unable to mask her shock at what she thought was his smooth and believable response.

"Someone nearly grown asking indulgence from so young a child—and in the dark of night?"

"Your Highness's daughter has a keen sense of propriety and a most caring nature. Alas, yes, the fault is mine, in the dark of night."

"Odd that you would notice a child's nature when you are so entirely turned toward *maturity*, Master Brandon."

"The influence of His Grace, Prince Henry, has enhanced my discerning eye to all manner of things, Your Highness. Unfortunately, it has done little to increase my sense of moderation."

Mary watched her grandmother assess him critically in the awkward silence that followed as candles flickered in the wall braziers around them, casting them all in shadows and golden light. The awkward moment stretched on, her mother's and grandmother's expressions both softening at last. Mary thought angrily that there was probably no woman Charles Brandon could not sweeten. "You appear to owe my daughter a debt of thanks."

"Indeed I do." He smiled charmingly, his smooth cheeks dimpling. "And I was in the midst of paying that debt."

"Is that true, Mary?" the queen asked, still with a hint of suspicion sharpening her tone, and a single thin eyebrow raised, as she always did when she was attempting to discern truth from fiction.

"It is, my lady mother," Mary replied, head held high,

eyes trained on the queen, her tone so convincing suddenly that she nearly believed the lie herself.

"Then Lady Guildford, see my daughter back to her bed. Just so she is not tempted to assist any other poor unfortunate soul who might lose his way in the dark of night."

Mary's attendant, Joan Guildford, ruddy-cheeked and hearty, nodded to the queen but Mary still did not break her gaze. Conviction was of more value to the queen than nearly anything else. As Lady Guildford pressed Mary's small cold fingers into her warm fleshy hand, and finally turned to lead her away, Mary caught a last glimpse of her mother. In Elizabeth's reserved smile she was certain she saw what seemed a tiny hint of pride in her younger daughter. That moment would have lived on in Mary's memory as a small sweet victory had her mother not died in childbirth a few months later. As it was, Mary was left with a great guilt for having deceived her mother so boldly on the very day she had buried her eldest child. But worse than that guilt was the knowledge of how effortless it had been, and what she had learned from succeeding.

Taut and ready for a fight, Henry stormed into his own chamber, pushing past the green-and-white-clad Yeomen of the Guard who stood at attention, gilt halberds and silver breastplates poised beside them—past the courtiers, rooms and gentlemen ushers, esquires and pages there waiting just to serve the future king. He startled his entourage of young cultured friends, all Gentlemen of the Privy Chamber, who sat playing primero, waiting for him, as he sent the heavy oak door back on its hinges crashing with a thud against the wall.

It was 1505, and Henry was now living at Greenwich Palace. Mary was at Eltham, and the king was at Richmond. The queen had died in childbirth a year after Arthur. His closest friends—Charles Brandon, Edward Howard, Thomas Grey, who was Marquess of Dorset, Thomas Knyvet and the Guildford brothers, Edward and Henry—all looked up and then each laid down his cards.

Henry's rooms at Greenwich were suitably elegant, with grand Flemish tapestries warming the walls, heavy oak furnishings, a ticking clock, and the Tudor coat of arms in the colored windowpanes beside them. The rushes upon the rich floor carpets were strewn daily with herbs to help sweeten the stale air. At this hour, their scent was still strong.

"Have I any news from court?" Henry called out to no one in particular, slumping into one of the chairs. "Or from Croyden?"

Croyden Palace was the residence, on the shore of the Thames in London, where Katherine of Aragon had been made to wait in seclusion during her recovery, and while the king negotiated her return to Spain now that she was widowed. There was a notion among some of his privy councillors, the Duke of Buckingham primarily, that to maintain relations and keep her sizeable dowry, His Highness should consider a marriage between Katherine and his new heir. For his part, Henry had begun to allow himself the dangerous desire of wanting that more than anything. Waiting for his father's decision had, of late, begun to consume his emotions and his life.

But the problem was complex. The avaricious king did not desire only the power of such a match. He desired the additional riches that he might obtain from it. Before he would even seriously consider such a controversial match Henry VII was bent on making certain he could retain the massive dowry Spain had paid before Katherine's first marriage. Queen Isabella had balked when the English ambassador proposed this, and so the English king had decided to be every bit as obstinate. A fortnight prior, in order to secure the Spanish wealth he wished, Henry VII had forced his son to sign a formal protest vowing never to marry Katherine, in order to press the pope and to show him that the control was not entirely his. While they also waited for word from the Holy Father on the matter, the protest signed had been lorded over the Spanish ambassador, Don Gutierre Gomez de Fuensalida. It was a high-stakes game that Henry truly wished his father to win.

"Thus far, there is no word, Your Grace." Only Brandon was brave enough to reply as the clock beside them chimed the hour. He sat impassively in a dove gray velvet doublet and padded trunk hose, long legs sprawled before an octagonally shaped table inlaid with Italian rosewood.

"It is obvious why the Spanish are resisting," offered Thomas Knyvet, the tall, likeable, equally red-haired son of an earl. "Even if the princess's first marriage to your brother is annulled by Rome and a dispensation is granted, Queen Isabella knows your father is under no obligation to provide for her daughter and her retinue of servants, which leaves them vulnerable as the negotiating drags on."

"But what the devil is taking my father so long to decide

what it is *he* wishes?" Henry barked, standing and beginning to stalk the room again. "Either he will have me marry Katherine or he will not."

Edward Howard, short and more stout than the others— a son of the powerful Earl of Surrey, who was one of the king's closest aides—glanced over at Henry. He was trying to determine if it would be wise to speak next. Henry could be a good friend, but he already had an infamous temper. Now that he would next be sovereign, even his dearest friends were mindful of that.

"We heard that he has sought counsel on the matter from His Holiness in Rome; he also awaits a formal response from Spain about the dowry. You know His majesty will never let you marry her without a papal approval," Knyvet said carefully.

Henry stopped and slammed his fist angrily onto the card table. "They are saying she bedded with Arthur as their excuse to deny me. But she did not. Katherine told me herself. He was too weak. And a marriage that was never consummated is no marriage at all."

Edward Guildford, tall and slim, with a long, straight nose and an unruly mop of dark hair, exchanged a glance with his brother, who was built like a small bear.

"Would you dare to call Katherine a liar, Thomas?" Henry raged at Knyvet, his voice thundering across the broad, high-ceilinged expanse of his chamber, his handsome face suddenly compressed into a red, angry frown and the rest of his body tensing along with it.

"Never, Your Grace. I only meant that in four months'

time, four months of days and nights, it seems only likely that—"

In a response so swift and powerfully fluid that no one saw it coming, or had time to prevent it, Henry clutched the collar of Thomas Knyvet's finely braided blue velvet doublet, drew him forward across the table and pelted him across the side of his face with a fist so powerful that he collapsed in a heap upon the tabletop, and the spray of cards went flying all around. As the others scrambled to restrain him, Henry's coiled body unwound on Knyvet as he unleashed his angry fist a second time, clipping his nose, then a third time, until Charles Brandon and the much larger Edward Howard drew him back and restrained him at the elbows.

"Your Grace," Charles intervened, trying to calm his friend's steadily growing temper. "He meant nothing by it. Surely you see that."

Henry's chest heaved with exertion as his breathing gradually slowed. "Arthur was a weakling. It did not happen between them!"

"Of course not, Henry."

"The pope will concur with what she and her duenna are saying they shall state in writing," Edward Howard chimed in. "That is the wish of everyone, Your Grace."

The tone of friendship behind the statement calmed him. Feeling placated, Henry sank into the chair again and put a hand through his hair.

"Are you all right, Thomas?" he finally asked, though with a note of defensive anger still lingering in his tone.

"No harm done, Your Grace," Thomas replied as he

straightened his collar and cuffs. "I should not have spoken as I did."

"No, you should not have."

Henry studied Thomas Knyvet for a moment. He was a likeable boy of seventeen, who had been a companion of his since they were all very young. Thomas himself was betrothed to the powerful Earl of Surrey's daughter. Edward Howard, who had leapt to his defense, was like a brother. The ties in this court world were strong and complex for them all.

"Make no mistake, any of you, I wish to marry her," Henry said now, his thick, auburn brows drawn together and a muscle flexing along the side of his square jaw. "And I mean to do just that. One way or another, Katherine shall be my queen and the mother of my sons. And of those there shall be many."

"Of course, a nursery full, Your Grace," Charles echoed. "Because His Holiness will give his blessing *and* the dispensation to a union between you. He shall be counseled that he shall have no reason not to. And Queen Isabella will see that the bond she wished between Spain and England then is the same one she wishes now."

Henry felt the relief of encouraging words spoken by friends, and saw not the self-promotion in it. If asked, he would have confessed himself that he did not understand why he already felt himself in love with Katherine, and he wished one day to marry her. He thought at times that perhaps it was that one time last summer that had changed everything. There had been a match of shuttlecock, and then they had all been dancing in an afternoon's disguising. The moment when everyone tore off their masks, Katherine had been the one before him, older, experienced, a boy's fantasy. There had been a speck on her face and he had brushed it away gently with a fingertip. She had been near enough that he could feel her shiver. He had known there was a connection between them even before then. But that had sent a response through Henry's young body like nothing else ever had. At first, it was only pity he felt for so beautiful and spirited a girl being tied to his sickly brother, then caught in this political limbo. But those feelings had grown into a sense of protection, which turned more quickly than he could have imagined to love.

"You shall dance at my wedding one day, all of you," Henry declared with the cocky assurance of a royal youth, son of a king, just before a suddenly affable smile showed his teeth.

"That is truly the girl you want, Henry?" Charles asked him.

"Forevermore," Henry replied with the greatest conviction.

Chapter Two

If a man shall take his brother's wife, it is an unclean thing, he hath uncovered his brother's nakedness, they shall be childless.

—*Leviticus*

February 1507, Eltham Palace

Following the queen's death, Mary did not see Henry or his companion Charles Brandon for nearly a year. Indeed, even in the ensuing four years, their reunions were sporadic and brief, brought about only during short, formal visits and at Christmastide. Following their sister Margaret's delivery of a son to the King of Scotland, Henry VII directed his son to live mainly at court in Richmond and Greenwich so that he might be more actively shown the duties of a king, and prepared for the marriage that Henry VII and Queen Isabella were at last arranging between his son and her daughter, Katherine. Yet they waited still for the papal dispensation as Katherine and her train of Spanish ladies maintained that her first marriage had never been consummated with a young and weak husband. They had been forced to send signed and witnessed statements to Rome.

Mary had no idea Henry and Katherine actually wished

to marry each other. Henry had never spoken to her of it. But she understood that what Lady Guildford had said that night was true: the marriage was to be desired because there was political and financial advantage to it. The events in those years deprived Mary of the last bit of family in her life. Instead, she followed the events of court by learning to listen, to gossip and to eavesdrop, all things she was learning to perfect.

While she dearly missed her favorite brother in those long months apart, one person she did not long to see was Charles Brandon. His behavior, especially in the past year, not only had been all the gossip at Eltham, but it had caused the king who loved him some embarrassment and more than a little concern. While Charles had gone on to marry Lady Mortimer, the older woman with whom Mary had seen him in the corridor that night, he managed to make the poor woman's niece pregnant beforehand. The girl had subsequently given birth to their daughter.

"How can anyone be so vile?" Mary asked her lady-in-waiting, Lady Guildford. Along with Jane Popincourt; the governess, Elizabeth Denton; and Anne Howard, Lady Oxford; Guildford (the woman lovingly called "Mother Guildford" for the place she now occupied in her young heart) now attended the princess exclusively. When news of Brandon's scandalous situation had reached them, Mary was shocked by it. They sat playing a card game, mumchance, at a small inlaid table, and chattering about this newest turn of events. Sheltered like this so far out in the countryside, Mary still found eavesdropping and gossip to be the most enjoyable of all the pastimes.

"He is only like every other man, Mary."

"Certainly not any man I would ever have," she declared with a prim naïveté that made the older woman laugh. Joan Guildford, tenderhearted widow of Sir Richard, Controller of the king's household, brought a reassuring comfort to a young girl with no mother.

"Oh, you would be surprised," she put in, her smile slight now and twisted as she cast down an ace. "Charles Brandon is ambitious *and* incredibly handsome—a lethal combination for any woman."

"Not for me. That sort of man would never win me."

"You need not worry about who would or would not win *you*, child," Lady Guildford responded patiently, her smile becoming more sedate now. "Your father has much greater things in mind for you than marriage to an orphaned renegade who is intent on nothing so much as his own pleasure."

In truth, the king was at that very moment negotiating another strengthening alliance between England and Spain, with Mary's betrothal to the Prince of Castile, grandson of the emperor, and nephew of Spain's Ferdinand and Isabella. It mattered to neither party that Prince Charles was five years her junior. Her future was planned and well beyond her control. It was her duty. Her heart and her dreams were unimportant.

"I think men who lust after women above all else are horrid," she stubbornly added.

"Then you think me a horror as well, do you?"

The sudden voice, rich, deep and familiar, had come from beside her chamber door. Mary turned to see her brother, Henry, standing in the doorway, magnificently tall and slim, grown at least a foot since she last had seen him. He was dressed now in a pale blue doublet, puffed trunk hose and a crimson cape edged in silver thread and bordered with jewels. His riding boots were high black leather with silver spurs, the tips caked with mud. His wardrobe had definitely improved with his position, she thought with a little smile, no mean feat in a kingdom as frugal as their father's. Henry's hands were on his hips, and his smile was confident and full of pride. That had not changed. Light from the wall of windows played through his tousled red-gold hair and his mossy-green eyes glittered. She sprang from the chair, toppling it behind her as she dashed across the room and bolted straight into his arms, feeling so happy at the unexpected visit that she thought her heart would literally burst.

"Why did you not send word that you were coming?" Mary beamed, twining her arms tightly enough around his neck to choke him.

"And miss that expression on your pretty face?"

Henry twirled her around, then kissed her cheek. As he gently set her down, Jane Popincourt and Lady Guildford both moved forward from across the room and curtsied deeply.

"I wanted to surprise you."

"Well, you've done that. But what are you doing here?"

"I have come to escort you to court actually, for the cele-bration."

"To court?" Mary gasped, her face breaking into a smile. "Does the king know you are stealing me away?"

"He commanded I escort my lovely sister who is grow-ing up too quickly and beautifully to go alone. And in truth

I believe he feels badly for you now with Margaret off in Scotland married and—" He meant to add, "and with Arthur gone," but he stopped short of saying it. "—And you out here with no one else," he said instead.

She caught a glance then between Henry and Jane, a slight smile from each to the other, but she quickly averted her eyes. An attraction, was it?

"What I mean is, you have no other family out here, in spite of what a comfort I am certain dear Jane here is to you."

Jane Popincourt had been with her so long and they had shared so much that she was like her family, but Mary knew what he meant, and she loved him the more for it. They both still felt keenly the loss of Arthur and Margaret, and both knew their bond was strengthened because of it. In spite of her governess, Elizabeth Denton, Lady Guildford, a full suite of other attending gentlewomen, a wardrobe keeper, a doctor and a schoolmaster, Mary often felt alone here and she had become anxious for the excitement of the life she knew her brother lived now without her at court. "What are we meant to celebrate?"

"The triumph of diplomacy: you have been betrothed to the emperor's grandson. The marriage has, at last, been formally agreed upon."

"I know well it is my duty. I have always known it." She began to smile, but with an incredulous shake of her head. "Yet it is still difficult to imagine such a little boy as my husband."

Henry met Mary's smile with his own as if they were two girls gossiping rather than the future King of England and his very important sister. "It was the promise from Maximilian which Father was after. He is England's indelible tie with Spain no matter what happens with Katherine and the dispensation from the pope. Your actual marriage, of course, shall keep until Charles is a man. Father is overjoyed, Mary. It was the first time I have seen him smile in a very long time as he told me it was all agreed to. He wants to see you. He wants us to be together, what is left of us, as a family."

Mary had heard the servants whispering that the king had not been well recently, grief having become like a disease that was slowly consuming him, causing him very quickly to waste away. He never really had recovered from Arthur's death, nor the queen's after that. Mary wanted to see him as well. She wanted to be with him, and with Henry—to dance with them, and ride with them, and be a part of their lives again. More than that, she had long wanted to be a part of the activity and excitement of court. Finally now she would be allowed that—and the celebration to which she was being taken was in her own honor. She could not think of a better surprise. England needed to maintain the delicate balance of power amid the dangerous rivalry between the Holy Roman Empire, Spain and France. So sheltered had she been that it was the first time in her life she felt the importance of her role in maintaining that . . . and the reality hit her then. Mary had an opportunity to shape history—not only her own but, as the sister to Henry VIII, England's history as well.

Mary sat perched on the edge of her bed strumming the strings of her lute with studied intensity, yet she was not really playing a tune. Jane, Lady Oxford, Elizabeth Denton and

Lady Guildford moved about the chamber gathering up her things in preparation for the journey to Richmond. A collection of trunks lay open around the room all smelling of the lavender sprigs her mother once fancied. In them were a brocaded velvet petticoat, robes, bonnets, and her best gown of blue and gold silk. There were several pairs of velvet winter gloves and a jeweled girdle chain that had once belonged to her mother, as well as jewel chests and two pairs of soft leather shoes. They were gathering only the things that would be good enough for court. . . . *At last, the royal court.* But Mary's mind was a million miles away from all of it. She was anxious to leave Eltham, yet she was frightened at such a change as well. As uneventful as her life here had been, she was still young and this existence had been safe. Henry had warned her that court life would change her forever.

As Jane arranged one of the open chests already stuffed with coverings for cupboards and carpets, Mary glanced around the royal house she had called home. The rooms were always slightly drafty, even with a fire blazing, the upholstery on her chairs was faded, the wall tapestry near her bed slightly fraying, and the paint on one of her plaster walls was peeling. Still, there was the warmth of reassurance here. At Eltham, she knew what was expected.

Jane came and sat beside her suddenly as Lady Guildford, Mistress Denton and Lady Oxford left the room. It was a moment before she spoke as a late winter wind battered the bare branches of a tree against her windows.

" 'Twill be all right, you know," Jane said, her French words soft and reassuringly lyrical. "Your brother will be right there with you to show you what to do."

"Life at court will change me. It will change us both, Jane. It has already changed Harry."

She smiled gently. "But he is being taught to be a king—and now he looks the part. So some changes really are for the best."

Mary looked at her for a moment. Jane was a pretty girl, coming into her full beauty now. "Do you fancy him then?"

"Who wouldn't?" Jane giggled in surprise at the question. "Every girl here fancies the Prince of Wales. I do believe he is the handsomest man in the world."

"And *I* do believe you are a silly chit." Mary laughed with her. "It is only Harry, after all."

In spite of what Mary knew, she could not imagine her brother in the way Jane saw him, and it made her laugh even trying to consider the boy with whom she had grown up as the object of any girl's fantasies. She expected him to do his duty to marry and settle into his role getting his queen with an heir. But politics had changed things, and would likely change them again so that just who his queen would one day be—Katherine of Aragon, or someone else—was still the subject of much speculation and debate across England and the world.

The Brandon family estate in Southwark across the Thames, just beyond London Bridge, was suitably grand. His uncle having inherited it, Charles was nothing more than a visitor there. Charles felt his stomach seized by a familiar knot of envy as his horse cantered past the brick-pillared gateway adorned by the family crest, then came to the end of the long gravel pathway. Wearing a costly riding coat of brown leather, welted in blue velvet and lined with lynx fur, he pulled the reins just before the front door. He sat astride a gray gelding, borrowed from the Earl of Essex, from whom he had found favor as his esquire. It was the sort of position he had worked toward for years, a position of power through affiliation.

Charles had achieved much in his time among royalty through ambition and drive. He was also, along with several other young courtiers, a member of the Company of the King's Spears, of which Essex was lieutenant. It was an expensive affiliation requiring sums of money Charles did not possess, but membership in it was absolutely essential if he meant to continue his rise at court. After losing his parents, Charles believed he had been given one very powerful opportunity by the king, and he was absolutely driven to make something of that, and of himself.

Earlier in the year, through his ever deepening friendship with Prince Henry, Charles was also made an Esquire of the Body, a highly regarded position in the king's privy chamber. It was another key rung on the ladder of courtly success, as it was a ranking among the gentry that set him one rung below knighthood. But with all of the promise so tauntingly at his feet, Charles did not possess even the worth of estates required to make him eligible to receive the honor. It was a reality that frustrated him, and only made him want it the more. Marrying the wealthy, older Lady Mortimer had been the sole means of acquiring even some of the funds that were so essential to merely exist among earls, dukes and princes at court but it had not brought him enough property.

He leaned forward now on the pommel of his saddle and exhaled deeply, trying not to think too much about all of that. He had come to this area of Southwark alone. The errand he was on was degrading and he did not wish or need to make it in polite company, as there would be pleading involved.

Finally, Charles swung his leg over the saddle and leapt to the gravel-covered ground. He gave the reins over to a waiting stable boy who knew him well but paid him little mind as the impoverished nephew of the master of the manor. Sir Thomas Brandon's own position at court was great, as a prominent counselor to the king, yet he had little inclination to assist his ambitious nephew.

Charles stood in the entrance hall, richly paneled in oak and hung with tapestries. He was left there to cool his heels intentionally, he knew, in order to keep him in his place. Sir Thomas had introduced him at court when he came of age, and that was all he intended to do. Charles squeezed his leather riding gloves and fought the mounting frustration. If there had been any other way out of his current dilemma he would have taken it.

What felt like an eternity later, a stone-faced groom formally announced, "Sir Thomas will see you now."

Charles knew the tall, spindly-legged man, William Fellows, as the gentleman who virtually ran the estate, yet Fellows always treated him like a stranger. He treated Charles precisely as his own uncle always had.

The room into which he was finally shown beside the entrance hall was formal and suitably elegant. One wall was taken up with a large black-oak sideboard with exquisitely polished silver plate on display. A clock hung on the wall beside it, and nearby stood a long table hung with fringed green cloth and several high, leather-covered chairs. Charles sank into one of them and exhaled again even more deeply. His wife would be furious if she knew he had come here again, hat in hand. She possessed ample wealth for them both and could clothe him appropriately enough for the gentrified circle, in the rich silks and velvets and the latest hats and chains. But this was very different. His wife would not understand. The money about which he had written his uncle this last time was not for him. It was for Anne and the children, in whom Margaret had little interest, for Anne had no tie at court and thus could do nothing to elevate Lady Mortimer's stature. In spite of his commitment to his wife, Anne was still Charles's first priority, and for her he would do anything.

Thomas Brandon entered the room a moment later with long, labored strides. He was a middle-aged, heavily overweight man with sagging jowls and thick black brows that merged in the middle and gave him a serious countenance. He was wearing a predictably dour black velvet long coat with ermine mantle and cuffs.

"Charles." He nodded blandly as he approached.

"Uncle." Charles nodded in return.

"I would ask what brings you here but I can assume it is the *only* thing that ever brings you to Southwark."

Charles steadied himself. It was always the same volley, which elicited the same need to restrain himself. "You know very well what my request is to be used for."

"So you do maintain that Anne's needs remain great. Yet I wonder . . . another doublet, is it truly? A new jewel, perhaps a fencing lesson? Or is it Italian lessons now? The need to keep up never ends, does it?"

"Nor does the desire. Yet as a Brandon yourself, you should know that well, Uncle."

"More avaricious than ambitious, are we now?"

"Feel free to see them as equally as you like. So, will you give it to me then?"

"Because you are my brother's son, and only so, I shall consider a loan to you—not a gift."

"As always, you are too kind."

There was a tense little silence. "I shouldn't think you will want to tell your wife about this."

"Our dealings do not concern her."

He smiled strangely and leaned back in the chair. "Ah, in spite of how you insist on playing the game, Charles, everything a married man does concerns his wife, or should."

"Not this."

"Very well. I shall honor that," he said on an irritated sigh. "But you know people talk, especially those at court. And your wife, as well as mine, does attend the queen."

"Then, Uncle, see that your wife knows nothing more of this than does my own."

Thomas steepled his hands as his elbows balanced on the carved chair arms. The ermine cuffs spilled back from his wrists as he considered the request. Charles knew that he enjoyed drawing this out as long as he possibly could. "And just why should I do that when this is not the first time you have come to me for funds—nor, I presume, will it be the last?"

"Because I am the dearest friend of the next King of England, the current king is an old man—and I have learned well from *my father's brother* about greed *and* about self-preservation."

Thomas Brandon was apparently at a loss for words after that, since he stood and went out of the room to fetch the money his nephew had written to request from him.

The next morning, as a thick white fog swirled at his ankles, Charles ducked down to pass through the low doorway in the cozy bedchamber of a little country house not far from London Bridge. The house was comfortable and stylish, yet a far cry from the family estate his uncle had inherited. A toddler sat before the fire on the rush mat–covered floor, playing with a stick and ball. Another child, a slightly older boy, with hair in gold ringlets, handed his mother a cup of Anjou wine as Charles drew off his gloves and approached them. A serving girl curtsied awkwardly to him, remaining near the door.

Seeing him, her clear blue eyes brightened and she almost smiled. "You've come after all," his sister, Anne Shilston, said on a sigh.

Charles sank into the chair at her bedside and took up her hand. "I told you I would," he warmly replied, his lips curved into a patient smile that no one but Anne ever saw. "You should learn to believe me by now."

"It just gets so lonely out here with you away at court."

He patted the little boy's head and smiled affectionately at him. The contrast between his fine velvet doublet and the boy's more modest linen shirt was stark to him in the cold morning light of his sister's bedchamber. A moment later,

Charles drew a wound piece of cloth bearing a small bit of marzipan from a pocket in his doublet. The boy smiled broadly, knowing the ritual with his uncle, snatched it greedily and popped it into his mouth.

"You did not forget!" he said, smiling as he chewed the prized confection.

"Such a doubting family I have," Charles chuckled. "Have I ever let the lot of you down?"

Born a Brandon, Anne had been pretty once, not all that long ago. But the smallpox had all but ravaged her face and caused her husband to abandon her. That he had later died, leaving her widowed, Charles knew was of little comfort. She was left a widow, and far from the beauty she'd once been. There had been three of them once, Charles, Anne and Thomas Brandon. But their elder brother had died several years earlier, not long before Arthur's death, thus, the comparisons to Arthur, Henry and Mary never escaped him.

The house in which his sister Anne lived was a charming old timbered building from the last century, with a thatched roof and a bright little flower garden in front. Before it was a white gate with an arch covered with fat vines. Modest certainly, but comfortable enough for one who had never stepped into the absolutely lush splendor of the royal court.

Charles sat now surrounded by the tokens of a life that was comfortable but not extravagant. There was a feather bed, rather than a pallet one, covered over not with fustian sheets, but with linen, and enclosed by faded velvet curtains from a generation ago. Beside it on a tabletop was a small collection of books, a candlestick in a pewter holder and an old jewelry casket. The room was warmed by a large rush floor mat and a writing table. They were all costly articles placed throughout the house in order to make his sister's life a bit easier.

"You are looking much improved since I was last here," Charles finally said.

"*They* are recovered," she replied, glancing over at her children, neither of whom was wracked with coughs any longer or threatened by the looming specter of death from the bout of the smallpox that had infested their home when she became ill a year before. "That is all that matters to me."

As an abandoned mother with little to offer a prospective second husband, Anne's life was focused on her children. Charles had not always been fair to women except for her. He knew that. His liaisons at court were not about love but survival. But he believed he could redeem himself with his sister. He could bring her comfort, security and company, yet he could not make her want to get out of bed or be seen by anyone but himself.

"So are you feeling well?"

"Well enough. And you needn't have brought us more, Charles. You have been too generous as it is, and I know that it takes every last shilling you have to exist amid all that opulence."

"With my help, you do better," he countered, showing great calm. He took out a leather purse full of coins and laid them on the table. "When was the last time the doctor was here?"

"Two days ago."

"Did he give you something more for the pain?" he asked, knowing perfectly well that she no longer suffered from anything so much as disappointment and hopelessness.

"The pain is less," she said with a smile.

A moment later, the maidservant who had remained near the door came to take the children to the nursery, and Anne and Charles fell swiftly into the deep, easy rhythm of a brother and sister. It was the same one he had seen between Henry and Mary many times. Anne smiled at him more broadly all of a sudden, and then linked her hands in her lap.

"So now, good brother, give me news of court."

He bit back a smile of his own. "Court *and* my wife?"

"Just of court. You know I do not like your wife. She has a sour temperament and an equally icy disposition, to which I shall never grow accustomed."

"Margaret is a good woman, Anne. I have done well by her."

"And doubtless she by you—the handsome young husband she can parade around by the neck like a Christmas goose."

"We both profit by our marriage. She is under no more illusion in it than I. But then, we have been over this all before." He patted the top of her hand gently and then prepared, like always, to regale her with some fanciful story of a life that was so vastly different from her own it could divert her attention from her own dismay. "So tell me, what would you like to know of court this time?"

"Very well then, let me think." She perked up a bit, forgetting her own situation in the reflection of a trusted brother's kind smile. "What do you hear of the celebrations for the new little prince of Scotland?"

"There has been more feasting and merriment this past

fortnight than ever anywhere before. But it is still difficult for me to think seriously of little Margaret as a mother."

"All right then, who wears the prettiest dresses at court? Is it still the Countess of Oxford?" she asked in a gossipy tone.

"The Earl of Surrey's daughter is a sow, short, squat and exceedingly impolite."

"That is not at all how you described her last time."

"Well, that is certainly how she seems now."

"Which means she refused you?"

Charles paused for a moment, then laughed. "Twice."

"Then she clearly has no taste in courtly lovers."

"You always did know the right thing to say." He drew his sister forward from the spray of bed pillows and embraced her. There was something warm and reassuring about her. Her lack of expectation was something he encountered from no one else in the world. He found, however, that the longer he spent at court the more he began to want it dearly in his own life. And he wanted it with someone other than his sister. But he could not tell Anne that. Not when he had spent so much of his energy convincing her that he was content in his marriage to a coldly domineering woman like Margaret Mortimer, and hoping that a way out would one day soon present itself. Although he had no earthly idea at the moment where that path might lie.

Two days later, the royal barge bearing Henry, Mary and her household neared London on a damp day, the chilled English air seeping through her sable-lined green Florentine velvet cloak and gabled hood. The mist off the Thames rose up and swirled through her thin silk hose and around her slippered feet. Henry and Mary rode at the head of a long train of royal barges, all of them lacquered in Tudor green and white. Their own bore the royal standard, which fluttered above them in the breeze as twenty-one oarsmen in matching green and white livery silently rowed toward Richmond. Jane Popincourt, Lady Guildford, Lady Oxford and the governess, Elizabeth Denton, were sitting just behind them, each cloaked in velvet and rich fur.

They passed the time talking of anything and everything as the barge cut through the slightly choppy water. Henry confirmed for Mary the gossip she had already heard, that in spite of all the debate, work by the ambassadors and even the papal dispensation he and Katherine had eventually received, the king had subsequently lost interest in the whole idea of the two of them marrying and was, even after everything they had gone through, in the process of terminating the betrothal altogether. She also learned from her brother that Thomas Wolsey had been key in the decision making. The king had just appointed him his personal chaplain, so Wolsey was ever at the king's side. Henry and Mary both liked him, and he was a great foil to their dour grandmother. The Countess of Richmond had installed herself at court and taken over many of the queen's duties, ruling for her son where she believed he could not. Mary was not so excited to see her grandmother. Where her mother had once been loving but firm, the Countess of Richmond was only firm.

"How will you feel if you do not marry Katherine after all?" Mary asked him as the wind tousled his hair.

"If not her, it will be some princess or other to whom our father shall tie me."

"Have you waited so long that you care nothing for poor Katherine any longer?"

He laughed at her. He was almost sixteen now and had endured the convolutions of this betrothal for several years already. "Poor Katherine is wealthy beyond measure, Mary, and she has become quite pretty now, actually. She shall do fine, no matter what happens."

"Will you not miss her?" she pressed, undaunted, having thought there might be something excitingly romantic in what her brother felt. "She has been in our lives for so many years I have long thought of her as a sister to us both."

"Precisely. And how many men in the world—especially kings—long to marry one of their sisters?" he asked, his laugh fading to a smile.

Mary felt her father's arms around her a curious, rather than a pleasant, sensation. She was not accustomed to her father's affection. The king had long been prone to fits of unreasonable anger, and at one time or another all of his children had been victim of that. He had fought physically with Henry for no logical reason, and many times brought Margaret or Mary to tears, neither of them having any earthly idea what they had done to displease him. Being called to his chamber had always been a cause for fearful anticipation. In spite of her long absence, today was no different.

Swirling around them in the warm and welcoming chamber, as they stood together before a grand fire blazing away in the hearth, was the familiar woody mix of musk, leather and sweat, but as they embraced Mary sensed something more. She smelled age, she thought, and futility. Both had their own particular aroma on her father now and it caused her fear to fade. They had not been close, but the king seemed to want a connection with her now. The very day she and Henry arrived at Westminster Palace he had summoned her alone to his bedchamber, to sit with him in two leather chairs, studded with hammered nails, beside the massive tester bed, his heraldic emblem sewn with gold thread into the silk behind him. The grand, slightly austere chamber was warmed by a wood fire and two charcoal braziers, which drew the worst of the chill from the air. The table beside him was littered with books, including one special volume, Froissart's *Chronicles*, that had always been spoken of as his favorite. It detailed great battles in which the kings of France were vanquished by the kings of England. Beside it was a small miniature of the queen, set in silver, and a dagger he always kept with him, once used at the Battle of Bosworth Field, where so many dear to him had died. On the walls around them were mural paintings of Old Testament battle scenes he loved to study. Beneath that sat a large round ship's chest covered with strips of iron and black leather. It was a room full of meaning, Mary knew. A room full of things that defined him.

She remembered that he spent much of his time here now, remembering his glory days, when he was wild and strong—a warrior in the field, not a king on a throne. Mary glanced around now at the remnants of his life and was filled with sadness for him. The fear was all but gone.

She sat now playing with the king's fuzzy little monkey, Solomon. She had always loved the pet and forgotten how much. The little nut brown creature would sit on her lap and eat chunks of dried fruit from her fingers, then nestle into her arms like a baby. His fur was soft, his eyes wide, and she was the only one, her father said, he had never bitten. He was dressed up like a court page, poor little thing, in a blue and gold velvet doublet and tiny little puffed trunk hose. Mary stroked his ear as her father sipped a silver goblet of wine and laid his head back against the chair that sat facing her own.

"So then, my Mary, tell me, are you pleased to be making such an important match for us all?" he asked her in that husky voice that had once only sounded of authority and power, but now revealed a steadily worsening illness.

"If Your Majesty is pleased, then I am also."

"A proper response to your sovereign: learned and delivered tolerably well," he declared, then looked directly at her, his heavily lidded eyes leveled in a challenge. "Now, child, this second time, speak not to your king but to your father."

"I know him not well enough to be pleased," she answered honestly as a log tumbled from the fire grate and the sparks and flames flared, lighting the coat of arms in the colored windowpanes beside it.

"But you have seen his portrait, and you have read his letters?"

That much was true. Henry had brought with him to Eltham two letters nearly eight-year-old Prince of Castile had written to her—doubtless with help—talking of his life, his interests and his pleasure at the news that they were one day to be married. By his portrait and his words, he seemed a bland child, his life as circumscribed as hers was here in England. Mary's first response had been pity. A warm sort of understanding that had begun to feel like acceptance had followed. There was certainly no eagerness to tie herself forever to this boy-prince she had never even seen, in the way Arthur had done with Katherine, and Margaret had done with James. But she knew she could not alter her father's will.

"I shall grow accustomed to the arrangement," she replied as dutifully as her Tudor lineage had trained her, while the little monkey on his jewel-studded chain nipped for attention at her sleeve.

"You know, Mary, I did not marry your mother for love either," he confided, on a heavy sigh. "Yet I grew to love her so deeply and profoundly that there is not a single day or night that goes by—nor shall there ever be—that I shall not miss her sweet laughter, her wise counsel or her nearness to me as I fall asleep. It comes to me and forever shall with a painful longing that cuts into my very soul. And I shall have that hollow place in my heart each and every night for as many days remaining that I draw breath."

Looking at her father, seeing the profound sadness she had never seen fully before in his ruddy, wizened face, and how it had aged him, Mary felt the prick of tears at the back of her eyes. She stroked the monkey more attentively to try to distract her own sadness at the loss of that same woman, and to help her to stay strong enough not to cry before the king. One did not do that. She had learned it well enough the day of her brother's funeral.

"I miss her as well."

"Your marriage will be a brilliant one, and you can be as happy in it as you decide to be," he declared, his own blue eyes glistening brightly with tears he would not cry, for he was stronger than she would ever be. "She favored this alliance for you, you know. We spoke of it many times."

Shadows from the firelight danced on their faces, not alike yet similar in their stony gaze and the ability to set their jaw in determination. "Does anyone like us ever marry for love?"

Her father lifted his head from the back of the chair and studied her for a moment before a weak smile broke across his face. "Ah, so very much your mother's daughter, aren't you? Stubborn and so very idealistic. She would have dearly loved to know you when you are older. She wagered that you would be quite a firebrand."

"Is Katherine not firebrand enough for Henry?"

Her father smiled patiently at her. "Perceptive *and* beautiful—just as your mother was."

"Is that why you have canceled their marriage?"

"I am not a foolish man. I have not dragged my heels in this without reason. I have always known Henry was different. Stronger. Your brother must make a strong match, Mary. The consequences of the wrong queen for someone extraordinary like Henry would plague him—and this country— for a very long time to come. No matter what he thinks he feels for her, Katherine is not the one to rule England for a lifetime with him."

Although Eltham was a royal palace, framed by the lush greenery of a forest, life there could not compare to the vibrant existence at court. At Richmond, where the king and the Prince of Wales were both installed, there was a powerful energy and an excitement Mary could actually feel. Days were vibrant and alive. In a continual hum of activity, servants moved about carrying silver trays, polishing the carved arms on chairs, and the long walls of paneling that led to the vast warren of halls and receiving rooms, or dusting picture frames and preparing for yet another massive evening banquet. Clerics strolled the corridors, speaking in low tones with one another about the latest intellectual debate. Collections of lords and ladies moved about in velvet, fur and jewels that rivaled anything she had ever worn, the ornate hems of their gowns clinging to gleaming intricate parquet floors.

Though she was a king's daughter, her mother had always economized with her. As she was the elder daughter, Margaret's wardrobe and jewels had always been seen to first, as had Arthur's wardrobe above Henry's. She was a fourth child and a daughter at that, not particularly important. She was surrounded by the very best of everything now. The foremost intellectuals in England moved around her daily. Erasmus, visiting court from Rotterdam, walked past her that first afternoon as she returned from prayer. He was speaking with his good friend Sir Thomas More. In their black velvet robes and flat velvet berets, they spoke of Sir John Cheke's recent treatise on the education of male youth. She later passed the Spanish ambassador, Fuensalida, heatedly conversing with the Duke of Buckingham. In an open doorway, after they had passed, she paused to watch her father's favorite court painter, a stout elderly Italian named Volpe, finishing a portrait of Henry.

She lingered for a moment, happy to be back in the company of her brother. She watched him standing in the center of the room beside a chair covered with velvet, his hand casually positioned on the chair back. Next to the artist Katherine stood, completely transfixed, observing his skilled hand dabbing paint onto a brush and then onto the half-finished portrait. Her back was to the door and she did not see Mary. Katherine did not see anything but Henry.

She is in love with him, Mary thought with surprise, everything important revealed then in her eyes. What great misfortune it would be to have come to care for someone whose whole heart was beyond one's ability to attain. Henry was wild and handsome, with England at his feet—and he knew it. Katherine was a widow some six years his senior who was offering herself up without a chase.

He saw Mary standing there then, and he smiled broadly. The painter muttered something in Italian and turned away in a little huff of irritation at the sudden distraction.

"Mary," he exclaimed, his voice rich with happiness. "Katherine, look who is here."

Katherine turned around then and smiled sweetly at Mary. Her face had changed, maturing into something lovely, Mary thought, just as he had said—smooth olive skin and prominent black eyes that bore long lashes. Now at the age of twenty-one, her lips were full and her nose was just long enough to suit her.

She opened her arms to Mary and smiled warmly as they embraced. "It has been a long time," she said in an English that was still charmingly accented with her native Spanish. Mary would have liked to practice her Spanish with Katherine, but Mary knew that the king frowned upon that. She had been made an English bride to Arthur, he stubbornly declared, and she would remain an English princess.

"Ah, but it is good to see you."

"I have missed you," Mary countered with utter sincerity.

"Much has happened while you were at Eltham."

"I have heard that," she replied, smiling just a bit more broadly. Katherine glanced over at Henry then with what Mary clearly saw was open adoration. Her instinct had been correct. Mary's heart warmed to Katherine then, as did her sense of pity for what would become of her friend now that the king had called off the marriage. "We have much to catch up on."

"Shall we walk?"

"As long as we leave Henry behind," Mary chuckled, linking her arm with Katherine's and moving out into the long gallery lined with Tudor portraits framed in ebony and accented in scrollwork silver. "I need to hear *everything*. And I have a feeling you will not speak a word of truth if my brother is around."

Mary had been given a new gown upon her return to court, an exquisite thing sewn of rich brown velvet with a low, square neckline and miniver sleeves. Ropes of gold chain and pearls hung from her neck, and a gold pendant was suspended there as she dressed for her first royal banquet. At her waist she wore one of her mother's jeweled girdles, and from it a gold filigreed pomander hung. She glanced down to see her grandmother's diamond surrounded by pearls glittering brightly on her first finger. She felt every bit a royal daughter on the very cusp of womanhood.

Jane and Lady Guildford marveled as well at the apartments allotted to them. They were large and very grand, with three tall leaded windows with camfered molding and hung smartly with blue sarcenet curtains held up on iron poles and rings. The chamber was appointed richly as well, with sturdy carved and crisply upholstered chairs, inlaid tables and chests, and warmed by Turkish carpets. The whitewashed walls were smooth and fresh, and decorated with Flemish tapestries and artwork from Italy.

Jane helped Mary dress early that evening, and they chattered happily, as Jane was to be her companion for the banquet. The messenger who had come from the king said he did not wish Mary to be alone for the evening. He did not think it safe for her to attend unaccompanied where anything could, and frequently did, happen. To Mary, the prospect of attention from handsome, licentious courtiers was frightening and exciting all at once.

The grand banquet that night was attended by nearly four hundred guests. Ten courses were served on gleaming gilt platters piled with wild boar, loin of veal and delicate lark's tongue. The tables upon which they were placed were covered with crisp white damask, strewn with flowers and herbs and topped with cups, goblets, ewers and finger bowls. And at the center of the king's table sat a roasted peacock, its plumes artistically reattached in an impressive display. The king's coat of arms in the colored windowpanes glittered down onto the candlelit tables, and from the gallery above, a consort of musicians serenaded the guests. Ladies of the court sat around Mary, arrayed in tight-bodiced gowns of crimson velvet, emerald satin and cloth of gold, all with chains and pearls at their waists and throats.

Mary danced and danced, and she reveled in the gazes

and whispers of several of the young and very handsome men of her father's court. Most of them were sons of dukes and lords, all privileged, all desirous of her attention. After a time, she was called upon to take the lute to entertain the company. It was Mary's best instrument and she was pleased to have so grand and important an audience after playing only for the servants at Eltham. Having all eyes on her was like a potent drug that made her heart race.

As she began to play "My Own Soul," she glanced over at the king sitting in his grand throne at the head of the room, hands curled over the chair arms, his head against the leather back. He was nodding off as she played. She was hurt at first. Insulted as well. But then she saw the old man before her, not a king, but a father, who had lived a long and complicated life, who was frail now . . . with a small measure of time left that was slipping swiftly away.

A feeling of sadness struck her, potently mixing with the elation she had felt only moments before. The king would die one day and then there would only be Henry left. He would be the new energy and the power for England. Henry was even taller now, handsome and commanding—a striking presence. Where their father was stoop-shouldered and gaunt-faced, haunted by time, her brother bore himself already as a king, one with more than a passing interest in a particular girl.

She watched Katherine and her brother huddled together deep in conversation as all the music, servants and the other courtiers swirled around them. They seemed cocooned in a little world of their own. Mary had watched him with several girls as he entered adolescence, but she had never seen him this way. Katherine smiled at him and he blushed. She averted her eyes. They looked at one another. Giggled. Mary thought it like a romantic little dance. Henry was clearly taken with their brother's widow, and it was far beyond what he had revealed to her on the barge up from Eltham. To care for someone in that way seemed a fantasy to her.

With the years since Arthur's death, Katherine's clothes had become increasingly threadbare and tight-fitting, as her body changed but her circumstances did not—an unsettling result of the dispute between Spain and England over her dowry, which Henry VII stubbornly refused to return. While the two sovereigns haggled over the details of her first marriage contract, which did call for her substantial dowry to be sent back to Spain with her, she had to rely on the Spanish ambassador to buy her what she needed, only the most basic of necessities, for he had to pay for them himself. What money poor Katherine was allotted was required to pay the retinue that had remained with her in England. Principal among them was Katherine's stout duenna, Dona Elvira, who seemed never to be far from Katherine's side, along with her husband, Don Pedro Manrique. There was also Maria de Salinas and the small, sharp-eyed Spanish ambassador, Don Gutierre Gomez de Fuensalida. In addition, the two monarchs haggled over the inheritance that she was to receive, a steady income, as the Dowager Princess of Wales. While they argued, Katherine remained a virtual hostage, having no idea whether her future lay in England or Spain. But by the expression in Henry's eyes, Mary knew what it was her brother wished.

Mary realized then why he had wanted her there, why he

had ridden all the way to Eltham to make certain she would join him. He wanted to tell her he had fallen in love with Katherine. She sank back in her chair, unable to take her eyes from the two of them. She was not so young that she did not realize the ramifications for a girl who had already given her whole heart to him, but then had her betrothal forever terminated.

"Do they not make a handsome pair?"

The voice belonged to Charles Brandon, who was suddenly sitting beside her, taking up the chair of a dinner guest who had gone to dance a lively saltarello. Charles held a silver wine goblet in hand and bore an easygoing smile as he surveyed her. She turned with a small start and looked at him. He had changed since she had seen him last Christmas, Mary thought. He was even more magnificently handsome now, if that were possible, dressed in a blue velvet doublet and sleeves slashed with gold cloth. But she believed him to be such a horrid womanizer and flirt that she could never admit her attraction to him, even to herself. Just that morning she'd learned that, less than a year into his marriage to Margaret Mortimer, Charles was looking for a way to have it invalidated. *Consanguity* was the term for having a common ancestry with one another, and Charles was going to prove it between himself and his wife. Distastefully, Mary noted that he was not likely to return Margaret's houses or her land along with her freedom. Apparently he planned to marry his wife's niece, Anne Browne, who was also the mother of his child.

As Mary looked at him now, she saw that his hair was a shade darker than Henry's, more auburn now than red. He still wore it long over his ears, and he had a mustache now and neatly trimmed beard. It all made his eyes even more prominent than before.

It also made him look older, certainly more dangerous. At just twelve to his twenty-three years, she was too young, and he was certainly too dangerous for her even to have had the thought. She knew that Charles was married and that he was now a man not only with a past, but with a child, by a woman who was not his wife. Even though Mary had long known the details, his actions were still unseemly, no matter how ambitious he was, or how incredibly handsome.

"Since the marriage is canceled, they make no pair at all, sir," she coolly replied.

"And yet you see with your own eyes that still they do wish to . . . pair."

She lowered her gaze upon him, angry for the liberty he took and for the familiar way he spoke to her. "Do you encourage the king's son to behave as you do with women, sir?"

He chuckled at that, as if her words had no impact. "The prince is his own man, my lady Mary. He shall do quite as he pleases, and already does, I assure you."

"Not with Arthur's wife, apparently."

He arched an eyebrow and his eyes glittered in the candlelight. He was slightly amused. "Are you so certain? By the looks exchanged between them, he may well ally England with Spain with a dozen little royal babes."

"You are smug and vile."

"And *you* are beautiful when you are angry."

"I am young and betrothed to the emperor's heir. And you are old—and married."

He made as if to grip his heart, but still laughing. "Ah, the little lady Mary wounds me like a much older woman."

"What good fortune for me I have the wit and not the years."

He tipped his head back and laughed but there was so much activity, so much laughter and music around them, that no one even noticed. He took a long swallow of wine then and slapped the goblet back onto the table. "Will you watch me at tennis tomorrow?"

"Have I a choice?"

"To cheer for me, yes."

"I shall cheer only if you should fail."

"Ah, my lady Mary is every bit as headstrong as her brother. And extraordinarily lovely for one so young," he said, still more amused by her words than insulted. "No wonder he finds you so companionable."

"I still cannot say the same for his taste in friends."

Charles Brandon lingered. Tonight was her night to shine and she had done that. "It is good to be clever, my lady. It is a better thing, however, to be wise. I see it is in that distinction that your youth fails you." Then he bowed just slightly. "A pleasant evening to you."

Mary could not sleep that night for the thoughts of Katherine and Henry, and what was to become of her Spanish friend if she was made to leave England. Mary's young heart went out to Katherine every time she thought that she was in a foreign country, unable to fully speak the language and completely at the mercy of others. Mary had seen quite clearly this day that Katherine was in love with Henry, and it made her believe that they belonged together. As new as she was to court, she had no idea then that life could not ever be that simple, particularly for a Tudor who was about to become a king.

Conversely, the great foolishness of youth made her scoff at the hubris of Charles Brandon, a young and obscenely handsome man who she was certain could not know the first thing about hardship, longing or love. She was wrong about many things that night.

Chapter Three

March 1509, Richmond Palace

As the trumpeters sounded a regal fanfare, Mary sat in the king's banner-draped viewing stand in the tiltyard, flanked by Jane and Katherine. A mild afternoon sun shone down upon them and was cooled further by the gentle breeze that ruffled the long bell sleeves of their dresses. Mary's was an exquisite creation of blue damask edged in velvet with ivory silk ribbons. The breeze quickly cooled the perspiration that lingered between breasts that, now that she was nearly fifteen, were prominent. Despite the fashion, which was to flatten them beneath a painfully tight-fitted bodice, she was proud of her newly shapely, and rapidly changing, body. She regularly glimpsed the looks she received now that she was at court and she was beginning to feel the absolute power in beauty.

Down on the dust-churned field, Charles Brandon waited

next to joust and Mary was angry with herself when she realized that her heart had begun to beat a little more quickly at the prospect. They saw one another regularly, as he was almost always in Henry's company. But he was a married man—now for the second time—and she still believed him to be a conceited renegade and an opportunist. She still did not like him well, in spite of how incredibly handsome he undeniably was. As his sleek black charger, caparisoned in shimmering silver, was led onto the field Jane began to giggle behind her hand. She leaned toward Mary.

"Now there is one to whom I would refuse little."

Mary stiffened and began to twist the lace at the end of her long sleeve. "He is married, Jane."

"And so?"

"Jane!" Mary forced back a smile.

"We shall both be married off forevermore to men with whom we do not wish to bed. Why not at least *have* a man once—and wildly—before we do? I hear the act itself is very like dying . . . that is, if you actually learn to enjoy it."

Mary could scarcely believe her ears as she watched Charles ride toward the king, who sat only a few feet from her. Showing his respect, he nodded deeply and deferentially. She knew Jane to be winsome and flirtatious, and she had certainly seen her attraction to Henry, but she had never before actually considered her so comfortable with the game of seduction. It both frightened and excited her to have a friend like that, who might well become her partner one day in some most delicious adventure.

She glanced over at Katherine then, sitting with her sour-faced duenna, Dona Elvira, and found her Spanish friend gazing in doe-eyed silence over at Henry, who sat beside the king. The difference between her two friends was so comical that she felt a giggle work its way up from her throat. Pious Katherine and wanton Jane. She pressed a hand over her lips but it was too late to stifle it. One moment more and Jane began to giggle as well, and they leaned in together, thick as thieves in some grand unspoken jest—until the king's stern mother leaned forward from the seats behind them and pinched Jane's shoulder. They had no idea that the morally pious Countess of Richmond had been listening.

"Guard," she flatly yet chillingly commanded, still pinching Jane's bare skin until it brought tears to her eyes. "See Mistress Popincourt to Lady Guildford's charge until tomorrow."

"But, my lady grandmother, please," Mary pleaded, trying to intercede, albeit in a weaker voice than she would have liked. "The festivities, the banquet! She shall miss them all!"

"Prudent to have considered *that* before Mistress Jane chose to put voice publicly to her most impure and inappropriate thoughts." She flicked her hand dismissively and her velvet sleeve fell back from her bony wrist. ". . . Behaving like the strumpet one assumes she shall quickly become."

"Forgive me, my lady," Jane sputtered obediently. But the king's mother sat back stiffly in her chair and gazed down onto the field. That would be the end of it. She was silver-haired and matronly, but Mary knew the Countess of Richmond was a powerful force with which to be reckoned. No one had ever changed her mind once she had made it.

As two of the king's guards moved a step nearer, Jane rose and excused herself to keep Mary from embarrassing herself more than she had done already. As Jane stumbled out onto the steps, the countess called out a final directive.

"And you are to advise Lady Guildford that Mistress Popincourt is to be soundly enough flogged so that she shall not again speak so vulgarly."

After the jousts, Mary attended the banquet meekly as she had been expected to do. She waited what felt like an eternity for her grandmother to drink enough wine, then begin dancing with the Earl of Northumberland so that she could slip away undetected. By the time Mary found Jane, she was alone in just her shift and stockings, lying on her bed in the small chamber next to Mary's own. There was darkness but for moonlight that shone like a beacon through the window. Still Mary knew Jane would be awake. She lit a candle lamp and set it down onto the table beside Jane. Her face was red and swollen from weeping and her wide blue eyes were brightened with tears as she lay on her back looking blankly up at the ceiling.

"I am so sorry," Mary whispered, aching for her friend.

"Not half so sorry as I. I'll not be caught again. I'll be more careful because I mean to live my life at court by my own rules. I believe I shall begin by seducing your brother the first moment I have a chance."

"I would rather you didn't."

"I shall make my own happiness in this world. And so should you!"

"All right," Mary said. But she did not mean it. At least not back then.

Mary spent her days that first year of 1509 at court primarily in the company of Jane and Katherine, the three of them being heavily supervised in embroidery, dancing, French, cards, etiquette and music, by the Countess of Richmond. While Katherine never spoke of her feelings for Henry during those long, mainly mild winter days, heading toward spring, both she and Jane could see them in her every look and glance. The sad romance of it all made them pity Katherine, knowing that if something did not happen soon, she would be forced to return to Spain, and the king could not be bothered even to be civilized toward her.

"What is it between you and Katherine?" Mary asked Henry one mild afternoon as they strolled together beneath a clear broad sky. They moved evenly out through the privy gardens, between the neatly clipped hedgerows, where the yew trees had been formed into the fanciful shapes of animals for the king's pleasure. They were with a large group of Henry's friends, including Charles Brandon, Thomas Knyvet and Jane, who ambled a few paces behind them, giving brother and sister a moment of privacy.

"Katherine is my good sister, as you are, and she is in need of kindness just now. That is all," he equivocated, glancing back at her, but she saw him catch Jane's eye instead. Mary turned around as well and saw Katherine, who had seen the little exchange. But she only turned and spoke in a whisper to Dona Elvira—too proud to acknowledge it.

"That is all?" she repeated on a note of disbelief.

"Very well. You always could see through me," he conceded a moment later, with a toss of his head and a crooked half smile. The pale sun highlighted the red-gold strands in his tousled golden hair, and his eyes glittered at her with absolute sincerity. "I do care for her, Mary. I care for her a great deal. And she cares for me. But the king is immovable on the notion of our marrying now. And he means absolutely to see her returned to Spain."

"You actually wish to marry one who was, for a time, chosen for you?"

"Peculiar as that seems."

"Then it is a great tragedy."

"Rather, it shall be a gloriously romantic tale *if* I can think of a way to stall her return."

She understood then. Her brother was stubborn and, like her, generally most wanted the things he could not have. Strangely, though he could have had any girl at court, Henry seemed far more interested in securing a wife than a paramour.

"Father *is* unwell."

"And *you* are the very picture of strength and health."

"The old die away as the young come to full bloom. Just like you, sweet sister. Just look at the beauty you have become already," he declared with a strangely easy smile, touching her cheek with a long finger that bore a gold and ruby ring that had once belonged to Henry V, famous for the battle of Agincourt. "There are grand things in store for the two of us, Mary."

"You shall be king and I shall be chattel," Mary said with a sudden frown.

Henry laughed in that robust way, deep and full of spirit, that she loved. "Ah, no. When it is my turn, I suspect I shall make you a queen."

"You told me once you would keep me here with you. Name a great ship after me."

"That was a childhood fantasy. Surely you knew that. But there will still be a ship. And perhaps some wonderful king to give you to."

"I am betrothed to the Prince of Castile and you well know it," Mary shot back, angry that her brother should toy with her in that way when she had no control over anything in her life, yet the world would one day belong to him.

"The only thing constant, my Mary, is change."

They walked a bit farther, out past the octagonal wooden pavilion and the little lane of fruit trees, pear and cherry, beyond. But they were close enough still to hear the lute player who had begun to strum a tune for the others back beside the splashing stone fountain.

"I need you to show me a kindness."

"Anything," Mary replied.

"Do you have a dress with which you could part? One of those exceptionally pretty new ones I have seen you wearing here at Richmond?"

She glanced at Katherine, surrounded by her sober-looking group of Spanish attendants, and knew that what she had thought before was true. The once elegant green silk dress she wore now almost daily, lined with brocade and ornamented with exquisite dark Spanish lace, had become noticeably frayed at the hem and sleeves, and the bodice was increasingly threadbare. It looked oddly out of place on so regal and proud a girl as Katherine. Still, her thick waves of black hair were done up meticulously away from her soft rounded face by Dona Elvira, as if Katherine were Queen of Spain. Thinking about what she was being forced to endure because of her own father, Mary felt angry, and defiant. Like Henry, she wanted to do anything to help her, and keep Katherine with them.

"Which would become her most?" she asked her brother. "You have but to choose. Anything I have is hers."

A smile broadened his face and she saw that happy, carefree Henry reemerge, the one she adored. "I owe you a great deal, my Mary."

"You do at that! But one day I shall find a way for you to repay me," she said, smiling in response. Of course she had agreed out of devotion to them both, and she did not mean he actually owed her anything. At least not then.

Two days later, Mary watched Jane burst out of the maze suddenly, as though someone had pushed her. Jane was out of breath, her pale hair wispy and springing out in random places from her small French hood. In the shallow silver of afternoon light, Mary was close enough to see that Jane's nose and cheeks were flushed pink, her delicate lips were chapped, and she was smoothing out her skirts.

Mary had been walking with Lady Guildford out near the pond, and past the stone urns newly filled with bright pansies and forget-me-nots on a day that was cooler than the others. Not seeing them, Jane paused. When Mary took a step toward her, prepared to speak, Lady Guildford clutched her arm firmly, drawing her back.

An instant later, Henry emerged from the maze. He paused as Jane had done, but for only an instant. He glanced both ways, and then went on in the opposite direction, not seeing his sister. Everyone by now knew Henry was in love with Katherine. This, whatever it was, could only bring Jane heartbreak.

"Leave it be, child," Mother Guildford counseled as Mary moved again to go to her friend.

"But I—"

"Some things are better left unseen."

"But I *have* seen it! Jane will need my counsel."

"Best to wait, child. She shall need your shoulder more."

Suddenly, as Mary looked back, Jane did see her. The eyes of the two friends met, neither of them able to remember any longer being without the other in their lives. The only sound in that awkward instant was of the splashing fountain, and a soft breeze as it stirred the fabric of her small headdress.

Was it pure girlish rebellion that had led Jane to something so foolish? Or did she really believe that Henry could actually care for her? They said physical attraction was strong enough to make a young girl believe it was love, but Jane had always seemed wiser to Mary than to have given in to that—a girl more certain to find a future of her own making. Would Jane Popincourt, with the sweet laugh and the vulnerable smile, ever be content as a royal mistress when she had yet to find her own true love, the way the two of them had always dreamed? They were yet all so untested by life, Katherine, Jane, Henry and herself.

"Why would he do that to her?" Mary heard herself ask, without turning back.

"Men are a different breed, child. And a prince who shall be king is something altogether different even from that. They are entitled."

"As he believes he is entitled to with Katherine?"

"That as well. He will need that strength one day to rule. So do not be too hard on him."

"And will he need the hubris that goes along with it?"

"I suspect he shall indeed."

"But what of Jane?" Mary pressed, her heart aching for her friend.

"She is expendable. As are we all. Except, perhaps, you. No one shall ever be able to use you in that way. Remember, your father is king."

"My life is not my own to make."

"No, you have been raised to know that well enough," she answered patiently. "But if you listen well, mistakes are not yours to make either. There will be people to counsel and guide you in every aspect of your life. You should find some comfort in that."

And boredom in it, Mary thought. Having other people guide her life all the way through, at this moment, seemed like the very worst thing in the world.

They walked slowly back into the house, the servants they passed dropping into perfunctory curtsies and bows as they passed. Mary rarely noticed the required business of life. It just had always been there. Like the rules. And she had broken so few. Only now had the reality of that begun to seem the littlest bit stifling to her after having watched Jane do something on her own that was entirely, utterly wrong.

Jane stood washing herself until the bare skin of her breasts were red and raw, and her hand began to ache from how tightly she held the cloth within her fist. She could wash away the feel of his touch, but never the memory of it, nor the knowledge that when he had the power to do so, Henry would marry Katherine of Aragon. She had seen them together only moments after they had left the maze, and the reality of the place Katherine had in his heart ripped through Jane, searing and lethal. He had told Jane he loved her, and even though the words were spoken in passion's heat, Jane had allowed herself to believe him. Foolish, foolish girl . . . what everyone else thought was what she now believed. She was a fool. When he was king, Katherine would share the best parts of him—his crown and his heart. She had had not one prince of England, but two. How could one girl have fortune smile down upon her in so grand a way when another marched in the darkness of love's shadow?

She squeezed her eyes shut, feeling violated and empty. *It is your own fault . . . you allowed it to happen . . . wanted it to happen . . . all of it.* Be careful what you wish for, her father had always said. And she knew, only now that it was too late, just how true that maxim was. But it did not matter anymore. Nothing did. Not her body, or her heart. *Might as well give it to the next highest bidder when the time comes. Might as well get something for my troubles. . . .* Something to ease the humiliation that had begun already to eat at her very soul.

"Jane?"

She turned with a start and saw Mary standing behind

her. Mary, so elegant, Jane thought. Even as young as she was, her beauty was astonishing, and her face was alive now with concern. Jane loved Mary with a devotion that always surprised her. She could not recall a time when they were not the dearest friends, did not know everything about one another, even finish one another's sentences. Yet the one thing that did matter to Jane, a thing Mary did not know, was that she was darkly envious, not only of Katherine, but of Mary as well. They had the lives she would never have—the future and the men. A dark little part of herself hated the king's daughter for the very different futures that lay before the two of them.

But when Mary advanced, Jane only smiled, feeling tears flood onto her face. Both girls moved to speak. A moment later both of them realized that words were not necessary between them as Jane collapsed like a child, and Mary held her in her thin arms until she stopped weeping.

Mary watched Katherine stand in the elegant, furniture-stuffed expanse of Mary's wallpapered privy dressing chamber inside Richmond Palace before an audience of Dona Elvira, Maria de Salinas, Jane Popincourt, Lady Oxford and Joan Guildford. The dress Katherine wore—Mary's dress—fit her exquisitely, and suited her far more than it ever had Mary. It was fashioned of crimson satin, with a black velvet petticoat and brocade oversleeves, which she had now ornamented with pearls. She wore a matching pearl-studded coif with a black velvet fall. The colors perfectly complemented her hair, face and skin. Henry would be so pleased. For the first time in weeks, Mary watched Katherine smile as she regarded her own reflection in the looking glass of polished steel, that thick onyx hair drawn sleekly back, so that her dark, almond-shaped eyes dominated her face.

"It is far too lovely a thing," she said so softly that Mary almost did not hear her.

"Not for the Queen of England—and my sister."

"You have been a good friend to me, Mary, but you know well I am only Dowager Princess of Wales, to be returned to Spain any day."

Mary smiled at her supportively, feeling much older than her years for how she was being trusted and made a part of things. "Not if my brother has anything to say about that. He loves you, Katherine, and he shall be king. Then everything will change."

"I only hope there will be time," she replied, in English still so thickly laced with her Spanish roots that it was often difficult to understand her. "But I do love him too, with all of my heart."

"That is a good quality in a wife, so that we might bring many fine young sons into the world with ease," Henry declared as he stood, unexpectedly, in the doorway. They all turned to him admiringly, but he was looking at Katherine as if she were the only one in the room. Mary's brother was so commanding now, tall and fit, clothed in a bold blue riding cape, edged in silver, an embroidered and braid-trimmed doublet, trunk hose and soft leather boots. Behind him, Henry's friends Thomas Knyvet and Charles Brandon stood with smiles.

Mary nodded to Lady Guildford, who gently drew her arms around Jane and Mary in response and led them, with

Henry's friends, out into the long oak-paneled corridor so that Henry and Katherine might have a moment of privacy. It was all so romantic, Mary thought, absolutely obsessed with eavesdropping on their exchange, and frustrated beyond belief that she was being barred from doing so. As everyone stood collected in the corridor, talking in low tones about how well matched they were, even the normally stoic Joan Guildford, Mary stealthily slipped back near to the door, which still stood open. She glanced to see her brother was already holding the Spanish princess tightly in his arms. They were standing near the mullioned window, where the sun cast a buttery halo of light upon them. She pressed her hands against the doorjamb and leaned nearer, wanting to take in every romantic word.

"My dearest wife," he called her in a husky tone before he pressed a gentle yet sensual kiss onto her lips. "I have missed you. But you know how the king, not I, keeps us apart."

"I do know it, and I pray to God on my knees with each and every rise and fall of the sun that there is a way for us, Hal," she said, calling him by the nickname that was hers alone for him. "When first I came here, I despised England for taking me away from Spain and my family. Then I hated it the more when I could not return after Arthur's death. . . . Now I praise England with every fiber of myself, for it is the place that you are. It is the place I long with my whole heart and soul to remain."

Mary knew she should not be witnessing so intimate an exchange, but she could not help herself. She felt her own knees weaken at the depth of Katherine's love for her brother, at their intensely murmured words . . . at the underlying passion between them. Would she ever know something so powerful herself? And if she did, with whom would it be? she wondered, as her own adolescent fantasy flared in her mind, then took hold. Certainly not the boy from Castile, with his long, gaunt face, jutting chin and owl eyes. Even a portrait painter set to flatter could not hide that.

"Did your mother never warn you about eavesdropping?"

Charles Brandon's deep, firm tenor startled Mary, coming so close to her ear that she could feel his breath. Mary spun back to see him standing there with that same half smile as always, lighting his impossibly handsome face—the smile that made her angry for the confidence it bore.

"Did your mother never warn *you* not to be impertinent?"

"My mother died when I was born, my lady, just after my father."

By my faith! Of course. She had known that. It was why he had been brought to court by their father in the first place—why Henry said Charles struggled so hard to find his place, by marrying, and attaining ever more grand positions, because he had been left nothing and he knew he must make his own way in order to remain at court. The year before, in 1508, he had married his second wife. It was all so tawdry, no matter how handsome, or ambitious, he was, or how unfortunate his beginning. Still, Mary would never admit it, but Brandon challenged her, and it was great fun sparring with her brother's friend. Even if he was older and too dangerously experienced for it to become anything more.

"Well, I am greatly sorry that she was not there to teach you an adequate supply of manners," Mary said more haughtily than she had intended. Yet she let it stand.

"Not half so sorry as I, my lady Mary," he responded, dipping into an overly exaggerated bow that forced her to bite back a smile.

"I should like to meet your new wife one day, yet it seems you keep her well away from our happy functions here at court. Why is that?"

"My wife prefers a quiet country life, my lady."

"And the company of your child?"

He met her gaze directly, powerfully, as if he could answer Mary's challenge with a single look alone. "She is a suitable mother."

"I should hope a friend of our future king would select no less."

Suddenly, she realized he had completely distracted her from Henry and Katherine, as he had meant to do all along. Yes, he was older, wiser—and he irritatingly reminded her that she was still only a girl. He could control her any way he liked—toy with her, even, and Mary did not at all like the realization of that.

"Will you attend the banquet this evening?"

"What difference could that possibly make?" she bid him with an angry flare.

"I am told you dance a tolerably good saltarello. I only thought I should like to see for myself."

"See what you like." Mary fought the powerful urge to stick her tongue out at him, since he taunted her as the untried adolescent anyway. "And it is not tolerably good—I dance a brilliant saltarello. Tell me, Master Brandon, how would we here at court find your wife's saltarello?"

"She does not dance at all, my lady."

"A pity for a man like you, who seems so fixed on finding women who can meet him on *every* level," Mary replied haughtily. She heard Thomas Knyvet and Jane stifling chuckles behind her. She knew then that they had been listening and that she had scored a point. While she had lost several sets to this handsome braggart, at that particular moment, she believed she had at last won the match . . . and she reveled in the triumph of that.

Chapter Four

I have no fear but when you heard that our Prince, now Henry 8th, whom we may call our Octavius, had succeeded to his father's throne, all your melancholy left you at once. What may you not promise yourself from a Prince with whose extraordinary and almost Divine character you are well acquainted.

—Lord Mountjoy to Erasmus, 1509

April 1509, Richmond Palace

*W*hen the leaves were only just a new and fragile green on the branches of the twisted oak trees that framed Richmond Palace, and a month after Henry had privately assured Katherine that she would one day become his wife, Mary's brother became King Henry VIII. Mary was fourteen years old on that chilly spring day and he was nearly eighteen. He was magnificent, handsome and bursting with determination to change her life and his own. Yet it was not the confident, carefree Henry whom Katherine found alone on his knees in the royal chapel, hands clasped and head lowered, late the next evening after the king's funeral. She had been accompanied there by her constant Spanish companions, Dona Elvira, Maria de Salinas and Ambassador Fuensalida.

When Mary, at the back of the chapel, saw them together, she shrank back yet remained close enough to hear them. Eavesdropping now seemed almost second nature. Seeing Henry, Katherine turned and nodded to each of her servants. Dona Elvira's expression was of warning as Katherine motioned for them to leave her. But Fuensalida, a hunched little man of years with thin silver hair and a neat mustache and beard, gave a response that was full of understanding.

"We shall wait for you in the corridor," he murmured to her in Spanish. Then, in a fatherly gesture, he touched her shoulder, nodded and silently led Dona Elvira unhappily back out of the chapel.

Mary could see Katherine draw in a breath. She could see that Katherine's love for Henry, and her pity at seeing him like this, was suddenly an overwhelming sensation. *God grant her the ability to speak the right words to him now*, Mary silently asked. *Let her be the wife to him, and the helpmate, Harry so desperately needs.* Katherine knelt on the cold stone floor beside Henry, touching his arm only briefly before she lowered her head like his. Mary knew it was the first time Katherine had ever seen this jovial, handsome prince shaken to the core as she had. Publicly, Henry was the picture of confidence and good humor, but the strain of awesome responsibility that lay ahead of him was easy enough to see, for one who loved him as desperately as she did. It was another moment before Henry looked over at Katherine and spoke.

"So much of my family is dead. . . . Am I to be next? Or will it be Mary?"

For a moment, Mary could see by her expression that Katherine could not find the words they both knew Henry wanted to hear. She drew in a breath and said a silent prayer. "It is the Lord's will to take us when He chooses. But you and Mary are both young and strong. Neither of you is like Arthur. And your mother, God rest her soul, died honorably at the birth of a child."

He looked at her then, his pale green eyes shining with unshed tears, and his face gone deathly pale. "I need you, Katherine."

As Henry VII lay so newly buried at Westminster, England's place in the world's balance of power was tenuous at best. Louis XII in France had formed the League of Cambrai with the Holy Roman Emperor Maximilian. Henry VII had not wanted to be involved, which made England vulnerable. Mary knew well that Katherine, the daughter of Ferdinand and Isabella, understood perfectly how true that was, and she knew Katherine's greatest desire was to help. Her own father had been counselor and lover and friend to her mother, understanding her role in a way no other could. In spite of once telling Mary that she despised the cold, graceless country in which she had found herself, Mary could also see that Katherine now had fallen wildly in love with its new king.

"I shall always do anything Your Majesty asks of me," she softly replied, and Mary saw the heat rise in her smooth cheeks as his gaze settled powerfully on her. He took up Katherine's hands then and held them tightly as Mary's heart beat wildly watching them—envying that kind of devotion. "If it helps to know this, I love you."

"I have known it all along," he replied as just a hint of a smile warmed his face before it disappeared behind the more troubled expression.

Katherine reached up to touch the line of his jaw. In the silence that followed Mary watched her blush and lower her eyes. Mary knew that Katherine felt a little foolish suddenly for having opened her soul to him so willingly. But she could see that she had no other choice. Katherine loved him with all of her heart, and she wanted him to know it. She would not allow herself to believe that what he meant by needing her was that, with her, he wished to secure England's place in the world. It must be, she knew, far more between them than that. Poor Katherine, Mary knew, would wait forever if she needed, to hear him say it. That vulnerability was the part of love that scared Mary quite to death.

Late the next afternoon, Katherine, Mary and Jane sat together on a stone bench in the rose garden, with Dona Elvira and Lady Guildford, as a brightly dressed Italian acrobat tumbled on the lawn to entertain them. The gardens around them were full of other courtiers strolling together, and laughing, others playing dice or chess at tables set up beneath the shade of lacy evergreens, all filling the environment with the easy pleasure Henry defined as his own distinctly new court. As the acrobat began to juggle three small blue balls, and Henry came upon them, hands clasped behind his back, Mary read a letter from her sister, Margaret, in Scotland. Wolsey, in his cleric's long pleated coat and wool hat on a stiff band, was beside Henry, wearing that same fatherly expression that he nearly always had for Henry and Mary.

"What says our Meg?" Henry asked as he stood before them, hands on his hips. He may have been her brother, but he did look particularly magnificent that day, Mary thought, wearing an exquisite honey-colored velvet doublet with slashed decorations of crimson satin, jeweled fingers and a stiff, flat cap trimmed with a feather and broach.

"She is with child again." She smiled up at him, full of hope for their sister's future.

"They do say third time is the charm."

"Pray God this one survives," Wolsey chimed with sudden piety, making a pyramid with his hands.

Their poor sister had suffered much as the Queen of Scots. While King James lavished clothes, furs and jewels upon her, he was notoriously unfaithful and had a collection of illegitimate children. She had lost his first legitimate heir after an entire year of life, and last summer Margaret had held her little daughter only once before she died as well. Now her husband was disappointed in her, and angry with Mary's father—and by extension now, with her brother, the new king, for not aligning with the league. It had strained the relations for which Henry VII had surrendered Margaret in the first place.

"It seems so unfair to blame Margaret for not yet giving him a son," Mary said.

"Nonsense. It is her duty," Henry coldly countered.

"The babies were both ill," Mary volleyed, feeling anger ignite within her, replaced swiftly by indignation. "That can hardly be a wife's fault."

"That is a wife's only real purpose—to bear strong, healthy sons. If they are not, then the fault lies with her."

Mary glanced over at Katherine, but her expression was unreadable. She would make no stand. She loved Henry too much to go against him in anything—so Mary stubbornly did it for her. "Her *only* purpose? It is not to love and support her husband, but only to breed for him like a mare?"

"Rather basely put, sister, but, yes, exactly that. And if there is love additionally, it is all the better."

He said it so matter-of-factly that time, so without malice, that she was shocked. She had been so innocently raised at Eltham on romantic tales of squires and knights and fair damsels. Henry had been raised on duty and political importance above all else. Again Mary glanced at Katherine and saw just a hint of worry in a tiny wrinkling of her brow, and the ever so slight way she pursed her lips, but that was all. She was too proud to reveal herself more than that.

"This is far off the subject of why I am here," he said, looking at Katherine as he advanced toward her. As he neared, she stood. "I have something I would like to say to you privately."

Her furrowed brow smoothed above a weak smile as she stood. Then she took his hand and they went alone down the ordered brick path toward a wooden pergola covered in vines. The fact that he had brought Wolsey, his personal almoner in charge of giving food and money to the poor on the king's behalf, was lost on none of them.

"What is happening?" Mary asked the cleric.

"He is going to marry her, just as he has been vowing for months, and he is telling her now. The privy council has advised it to keep strong our tie with Spain."

"But you know him, Wolsey, and you care for us both," Mary said, looking into the fleshy face with its blotchy complexion and endearingly reddened hawkish nose. "Did *you* advise it?"

"It is what the king wishes, and so it is my wish for him as well."

"But privately, as a man of God, do *you* believe in this marriage? Do you believe, as Katherine defends, that her marriage to Arthur was never consummated? Must we not all believe that in order to support them?"

His expression, usually so warm and jovial, changed, hardened then. "I will do nothing to dissuade His Highness from his wish to make Katherine his bride, no matter what I privately believe. That would not be prudent, nor, my lady, would it be effective."

"But surely, Wolsey, you see that my brother is new at his role and needs the counsel of those he can trust."

"He has you for that, my lady Mary."

"And what does he have you for, Wolsey?"

"Hopefully to become his chancellor one day. And perhaps, after that, if prayers are to be answered . . . cardinal."

Mary had, until that day, believed entirely that her brother and Katherine were meant for one another, and the most romantic thing in the world would be for them to find a way to marry. It was a child's view of the world; being at court, she had slowly come to see that now. A marriage, when it happened, would be a political match first and foremost, and a means to an heir.

Her destiny was no different. Mary was a little girl no longer, and she resolved to remind herself more often of that.

Chapter Five

Time to pass with goodly sport our spirits to revive and comfort;
To pipe, to sing, to dance, to spring with pleasure and delight
To follow Sensual Appetite.

—Henry VIII

June 1509, Greenwich

As if in defiance of his father's command against it, Henry VIII and Katherine were married less than two months after the death of Henry VII. The ceremony was a quiet one in the Church of the Observant Friars at Greenwich, but all across London church bells pealed joyously for the union. Katherine had waited in England for seven long years to become a queen, and when she and Henry were crowned a fortnight later at Westminster Abbey, she was twenty-three years old; Henry VIII was eighteen. For a blissful time, no one reminded either of them that she was Arthur's widow, or that the word in Leviticus had expressly forbid their marrying.

On the day of the coronation, Mary rode through the lavishly draped streets of London, the gray cobbles covered in yards of cloth of gold and decorated with tapestries and embroidery. Dressed in scarlet and ermine, she rode a white palfrey that cantered evenly just behind the new king and queen. They were shaded by a pavilion of purple velvet and a valance of gold, all of it embroidered with *H* and *K*. Henry's own crimson velvet robes were sewn with diamonds and emeralds and he wore a baldric of rubies across his chest so that, with his now towering height and square jaw, he was set apart as something almost divine to the people of London. Sweet Katherine beside him in a litter wore shimmering white satin, her hair long and loose to her waist as she gazed up adoringly at him. Mary was surprised that day that just behind her, it was Charles Brandon who rode beside her grandmother. The position, she knew, was an intentional gift from Henry to his friend—as if he were a part of the royal family.

They passed a collection of local priests standing along the street, each holding up a gleaming cross in their honor. She turned to acknowledge them with a nod and Brandon caught her eye. Recently made Warden, chief justice of all the royal forests, and Marshal of the King's Bench, the tall, broad-shouldered Brandon rode in his silver-appointed saddle, smiling broadly. Yet in his expression there was something more than polite acknowledgment as their eyes met. Mary felt a shiver turn her skin to gooseflesh. He was the most handsome man she had ever seen, although she would rather die than admit it, even to Jane. His wife was expecting their second child. When he nodded to her again, Mary simply turned away. No matter what Henry believed of his friend, Mary was determined not to like him . . . at least not too much.

"You wished to see me?" Mary asked as she lingered just inside the door of Katherine's chamber after the ceremony.

The new queen stood at the window, wringing her hands, her expression darkened with worry. Her dress was regal, elegant, no longer a remnant of the former court, nor something Mary had cast off. This was a fur-trimmed overgown of topaz velvet with a tight bodice to show off her pretty waist. Her hair was loose and long, as only a virgin—or a queen—could wear it, pulled away from her face and crowned by a simple band of pearls.

"I so wish to be a good wife to him, Mary," Katherine said in her halting English. "I want it more than my life."

"Then of course you shall be. You are already a spectacularly lovely queen."

"Perhaps you will think me odd but I want to be everything to Henry. I do so love him."

Mary smiled. "I can see that. And so can my brother. He is fortunate to have you."

"You do not look down on me since I married Arthur first? I know how much you loved him."

Mary and Katherine had never spoken about Arthur, but it had been there between them, a silent barrier, and it was a stigma with which Katherine lived every day, in the whispered words from those who still believed her marrying Henry could portend only bad things.

"You would have been a wonderful wife to my brother if he had lived, I know that," Mary said gently, then she took Katherine's hands and squeezed them with genuine affection.

"Will you promise to be honest with me?"

"Always."

Katherine hesitated for a moment. There was a little

silence and Mary watched her tugging at the lace on her sleeve in a nervous gesture. "In your heart, do you believe I can be all that he needs?"

Mary thought of Jane and Henry as she had seen them that day in the maze, and while he did not show more than a passing interest in all of the beauties who had flooded the court since his coronation, the words of her father and her grandmother still resonated in her mind. *No matter what he thinks he feels for her, she is not the one to rule England for a lifetime with him. . . .* Mary loved her brother, but she loved Katherine as well and she simply could not hurt her like that, no matter how the truth might also have protected her. Along with Jane Popincourt, Katherine of Aragon was the best friend she had.

"I believe you alone are the helpmate and the great love Henry is going to need. And you will need to be strong to bear his many sons."

"The Lord could offer me no greater honor," she replied, full of conviction.

Late that afternoon, as the sun began slowly to set, Westminster Hall was bathed in shimmering, luminescent pink light that came up from the snaking waters of the Thames, then filtered in through the long bank of windows. There was a grand coronation banquet in the splendidly decorated great hall, with sumptuous course after course brought in: veal, venison, fish and cheese, jellies and nuts, each borne forth by liveried stewards, to the regal sound of a trumpet fanfare. Two hundred gentlemen-at-arms stood guard as Mary sat with the graceful, honey-haired Countess of Oxford to her left and, curiously placed beside her to the right, Charles Brandon. They sat at a long, linen-draped table on an elevated platform with the new king and queen, their grandmother, the Duke of Buckingham, and the Earl of Surrey. The entertainment, a disguising as they dined, was grand and elaborate. That night, as a continuation of celebration of the marriage, two grand mountains were wheeled in, one representing England, the other Spain. The English mountain had been decorated lushly with greenery and topped with a court beauty, who wore flowers in her hair and smiled. The mountain representing Spain was barren, strewn with rocks and yet jewels, to represent the wealth Katherine had brought to them from her presumably spartan world. The gasps and ovations were precisely the reaction Henry wished from his new court, so vastly different from his father's frugal one, and he laughed out loud at the presentation.

Dancing followed and the royal musicians had been instructed to play only the brightest tunes, for a young and athletic new king who loved to dance and show off his kicks and turns in spirited branles and saltarellos. Many of the songs had been written by Henry, for whom music had long been not only a hobby but a tonic. As they sat watching, Mary soon felt the pull of Brandon's steady gaze upon her. As usual, his wife was nowhere to be seen at court. She heard the music for a volte begin but, for a moment, she did not recognize it for how closely he sat, and for how strongly the heady scent of his musk was swirling around her. Brandon was not speaking, only giving her that sideways glance which she could feel powerfully upon her.

"Dance with me," he finally bid her, although through

the laughter and music around them, she was the only one who heard. Mary glanced around, certain he had requested the company of the Countess of Oxford or perhaps the Marchioness of Dorset beside her. But his glittering eyes, she saw, were settled on her and only her.

"Dance?"

He bit back a smile. "That *is* what one customarily does at these things, and my lady Mary does a tolerably spirited volte, if I remember correctly."

"Spirited enough to keep pace with you."

He was still smiling. That alone irritated her. "Nearly so anyway."

She wanted to resist. She certainly meant to. Henry would not be pleased to see his older, married companion paying such attention to her. Yet suddenly for Mary there was something a little wild and slightly dangerous in returning the flirtation, after a lifetime of being protected. Mary finally felt, now that her father too was gone, like being just a little bit dangerous herself.

"Very well." She nodded, pushing back her chair and standing with a flourish, then tipping her chin just ever so slightly into the air. "The volte it is. But mind that you do not step on my toes."

"And *you* mind that you do not entirely step on my heart, for you shall soon reach an age where you very easily could," he declared, that mischievous smile never fading, as he placed a hand on his chest dramatically, then stood beside her.

They shared two dances after that, the volte and then a tourdion, and Mary completely forgot herself in the pure fun of the formal turns, sweeps and bows. The only men with whom she had ever been allowed to dance were Arthur and Henry back at Eltham during the long hours of dance instruction, the sour-faced instructor looking on critically, clapping his hands to help them keep time, and just to annoy them. Now, in this dizzying whirl of laughter, dripping candle wax, music and forbidden attraction that had taken control of her, Mary's hand met Charles's own. They dipped, then bowed, they nodded and laughed, then were back linking hands again. His hand was large and warm and powerful against hers, and Mary began to lose herself entirely in the rhythm of the music and his commanding gaze upon her. The air was quickly thick and warm and she felt little beads of perspiration work their way down beneath the velvet of her bodice. She reveled in all the new sensations—the freedom and the power, the heat and the attraction. In spite of the crowd, she felt as if they were the only two dancing . . . until a discordant commotion drew her attention to the crimson-draped platform upon which her grandmother Lady Beaufort had been seated, and where she had just now collapsed.

Outside Lady Beaufort's apartments, they paced the long, paneled hall, lit with torches in iron wall brackets, late into the night. Charles Brandon remained among the party who had come there to wait news of her condition. The fact that they waited at the other end of the very corridor where Charles had once defended her to the queen and Lady Beaufort was not lost on Mary. Despite the circumstances, she could not help gazing at him with new eyes as a man who seemed clever, dangerous and magnificent. Henry and Katherine had gone inside with the doctors, so outside Mary waited in silence with Edward Howard, Thomas Knyvet and Jane Popincourt. The great Lord High Steward, the Duke of Buckingham, had for a time lent his support, but near midnight he and the Earl of Essex had gone to bed.

In an elegant dress of blue velvet trimmed in gold, with a twisted rope of gold and pearls at her waist, Mary slumped wearily back against the oak wall paneling, arms crossed. She could not help watching Jane and Knyvet, the slim and slightly gangly courtier who was married to one of the Earl of Surrey's daughters, Muriel, and thus was as dangerously off-limits to Jane as Henry had been to her. Their own little silent dance of flirtation around the others was taking place nevertheless.

Henry had wounded Jane, Mary knew that. Now she seemed to want to hurt herself with someone else. Mary wanted to speak with her friend—she must. Henry was a king; he could do as he pleased, hurt whom he pleased, without penalty. Knyvet would not have that excuse when he wounded her.

Her thoughts were stopped by a waiting woman who opened the door and motioned to Mary with a nod to enter. She exchanged a little glance, first with Jane and then with Charles, both of whom fell silent, but Charles nodded encouragingly to her. Henry and Katherine were waiting for her with Wolsey in the small withdrawing chamber, beside the hearth. The swish of her skirts was the only sound as she entered. The fire was slowly dying, the embers glowing a soft bright red.

"Is she—?"

"She is resting. Yet she wishes a word with you," Wolsey said when Henry did not seem capable of speaking.

So many deaths, Mary thought. Arthur . . . her father . . . her mother . . . Margaret's babies . . . And she was not quite prepared now for the potential of another. Still she stiffened, forcing up her own Tudor resolve, and moved purposefully toward the bedchamber, where a ring of waiting women stood around a heavy oak bed with a thick, high claret-colored tester above it, fringed in gold. A single candle lamp burned on the table beside it. Her grandmother's eyes were closed and she looked pale and frail. Her thin gray hair, which she never freed publicly from her collection of English hoods for the youthful vanity she refused to abandon, lay spread long on the white linen pillow now behind her head. The patchwork lines on her face were evidence of the determined woman who, with a singleness of purpose, had seen her beloved son from the battlefield to the throne. Mary sank onto the stool beside her bed and when she extended her hand, her grandmother took it.

"You were always my favorite," she said softly and more affectionately than Mary had ever heard before, "but, if called upon, I shall deny that with my last breath."

Mary smiled. "I never knew that."

"You were not meant to."

"You are looking better, Grandmother."

"Oh, nonsense, child. I am dying. To one another, let us call it what it is, shall we? And let us too be honest about other things." Her faded gray eyes opened more widely then and Mary could see the urgency in them. "Be careful of Brandon, child."

"Charles Brandon?"

"I am an old woman but not a foolish one. There is something between you. Yet giving in to it would mean only heartbreak."

"He has a wife, Grandmother."

"And soon you shall be wife to the Prince of Castile. You have too great a future to sully it with someone like Brandon, you know. It would ruin much for the king, your brother."

Mary felt the rise of stubborn resistance at the thought of an unseen, untried boy like the Prince of Castile gaining not only her maidenhead, but her body and her passion for the rest of her life. "Henry got the wife he wished."

"The wife he believes, for the moment, he wishes," she corrected.

"You believe he was wrong to marry Katherine?"

"He will outgrow her."

She heard the echo of that last private conversation between her father and herself in his chamber that afternoon like a dark cloud in her mind.

"Your father was my son, and he became a wise ruler. You will have lost the benefit of his counsel now, and soon you shall lose mine."

"I will not disgrace you, Grandmother, nor the memories of my father and mother," Mary said with absolute conviction. Even so, an image of Charles Brandon as they danced, the musky scent of his skin, his eyes, flashed before her, his face smiling brightly in her mind. "I will marry the Prince of Castile."

"You will follow your destiny."

"You do not believe it will be him?"

"Loyalties and alliances for our kind do change. Until it is done, it is not fated any more than Henry's marriage to poor dear Katherine. Take care with that knowledge and act accordingly."

"I shall," Mary said. Not because she believed it. But because she had no other idea how she was meant to reply.

When Lady Beaufort finally fell asleep, it was nearly dawn. Jane was to accompany Mary to the apartments they shared, but when Mary looked for her she saw her friend had mysteriously disappeared. So had Thomas Knyvet. The coincidence was not lost on Mary. Especially when she stumbled across them closeted behind the pillar of a curved stone archway locked in a passionate kiss. Mary was confused by it, as well as by her own growing feelings for Charles Brandon. Henry would be furious if he had any idea at all that his married friend had not only flirted with her but that his young, innocent sister had returned the gestures. Wishing her not to be unaccompanied at such an hour, Charles had waited for her out in the corridor and now insisted on escorting her back to her apartments. Not wanting him to see Jane and Thomas, she readily agreed. The court had retired and they were alone as they walked, which brought Mary a sudden sensation of freedom to speak as she wished.

"What is your wife like?" Mary surprised herself by asking, as torch after torch lit the path before them.

"Anne is a good woman."

"Is she quite beautiful?"

"Quite."

"Why do you never bring her to court?"

"She prefers the simplicity of the countryside, my lady."

"And *you* prefer the simplicity of her absence?"

Brandon chuckled. "Such wit does amaze me in one so young and untested."

Her face made a little frown. It was not the response she had expected. She did not like how he used the difference between their ages to make her feel inferior. "How do you know I am so untested?"

"Innocent beauty, my lady Mary, is difficult to disguise."

"You believe I am beautiful?"

They turned into a second corridor, her cadence matching his, before he responded. "Beautiful and innocent. A lethal combination for a man like me."

"A married man, do you not mean?"

"I mean, at least a man who is wise enough to realize that you are a jealous king's prized little sister—one he must nurture and protect in order to keep her the treasure that she is." He was smiling as he made her a deep bow. They had stopped before a window and the first hint of morning fell upon them.

"Until he trades me for a greater prize."

"Crudely put . . . but something like that." His smile faded by a degree before he said, "And thus, I shall bid you good night."

She had thought he might kiss her. Foolishly, like a little girl, she had even stood there preparing herself for it as if, like a fairy tale, it was possible. But she watched him walk away. *May God forgive me the sin,* she thought. But she had wanted him to do it. At least then, like Jane, she would know what passion was, before she was forced to marry the homely boy from Castile, and surrender the rest of her life to duty.

Two days later, and only two months after the death of her son, Lady Beaufort died. Her passing marked the end of another era. It also left the new young king and his beautiful blossoming sister entirely unchecked and on their own. For the first time in their young lives, only money, power and the pursuit of pleasure lay before them.

Chapter Six

*The new king is . . . a worthy king and most hostile to
France. . . . It is thought that he will indubitably invade
France.*

—A Venetian diplomat

April 1510, Richmond Palace

By spring of the following year, Katherine was
pregnant. Henry was in love with his wife, and overjoyed at
the prospect of a son. Everything in England was changing.
Henry VIII's newfound prowess had led him toward an ag-
gressive new stance in all things. In addition to the extravagant new court he ruled, and his own young privy council he
had worked to put in place, Henry had his own fresh political
opinions. Where his father, after a lifetime of battles, had
striven for political neutrality, Henry wished to make his own
mark dramatically on the world stage. The way best to begin
making his mark, he believed, was by attacking France and
reviving the tradition of England's claim to the Angevin Empire, fought over in the now mythical battle of Agincourt.
While he sought counsel from his military advisers, moving
progressively toward that goal, he quietly sent a small delegation to Italy to purchase military weapons and armor. He was

not a king to be ignored, and he meant absolutely for his to be different from his father's dreary, ritualistic court.

Around him always now were musicians, minstrels, jugglers or some form of entertainment to cheer his friends. And in this exciting new world, Mary reigned along with her sister-in-law, presiding over banquets and disguisings, and even the joust. She reveled in the attention and praise she received, not just for her beauty, but for her quick wit and sweet laugh. All but forgotten amid the activity was the unseen Charles of Castile, the now ten-year-old boy to whom Mary was still formally betrothed. His grandfather Maximilian had continued to drag his feet concerning the match for the remaining years of Henry VII's reign, and things had not changed. But Mary refused to consider that, or him. The future as his wife seemed bleak at best, and she was too busy enjoying her role as the king's beautiful sister. Beyond that she did not wish to think.

She glanced at the door of the queen's chamber, fluffed her skirts and bit back a smile, sitting in a tall chair covered in a rich new tapestry fabric from Flanders. Mary knew what was meant to happen next. Jane and Mary sat in a circle embroidering and gossiping with Katherine, Dona Elvira, Maria de Salinas and Lady Guildford, late one morning after a banquet, as rain blanketed the sweeping emerald pastureland around Richmond. It chilled the stone walls through the plaster and the tapestries meant to warm them. Abruptly, a group of men burst in unannounced. Frightened, Katherine sprang back, toppling her chair. The mysterious men entered the chamber in a swirl of forest green velvet cloaks, hoods and masks. Their daggers, crossbows and gleaming cup-hilt rapiers were drawn in mock offense. Robin Hood and his merry band was being played out dashingly for the new queen's entertainment, though she did not know it yet. This was a complicated ruse the king and his friends had designed to please Katherine in the long last stage of her pregnancy before her lying-in began.

Mary saw that Katherine's expression at first was one of panic, and then pleasure, when she heard Henry's laughter and realized what was happening. Dona Elvira, too severe for anyone's liking, stood in absolute fury, trying to object, but she was drowned out by the laughter and delight of the other ladies of the queen's circle.

Henry did love her, Mary thought as she watched them, and he delighted in making her happy. She had seen it in a dozen different ways since he had made her his queen. Playing every bit the dashing character in his costume and mask, Henry gently drew her to her feet and embraced her. Mary saw Thomas Knyvet do the same thing with Jane, with whom an open flirtation had continued in the year since the coronation. It seemed on the surface light and fanciful. Only she knew differently. Everyone began to laugh as the women became willing captives in the mock kidnapping. The musicians of the king's privy chamber, the lutist, trumpeter and sackbut player, then entered the queen's rooms. As they struck up a tune, Henry laughed at Dona Elvira, who was standing in the corner, hands on stout hips, still protesting.

"This is an outrage, Your Highness!" she sputtered in thickly accented English. "You must leave the queen to her rest at once."

"Not until we have had what we have come for! A dance

and to make pastime with the lovely ladies surrounding you! And you, Dona Elvira, may dance as well if you like."

A moment later, Mary felt an arm from behind hook around her waist, and a voice seductively whisper to her, "Come silently, my fair lady Mary, and no harm shall come to you."

Mary knew, without looking, that the smooth, deep voice belonged to Charles Brandon. He had made something of a habit of sneaking up on her. She felt her heart quicken at the thought, and she struggled to wipe away the sickeningly eager smile turning up her mouth in response. She had not seen him since before the death of his second wife, who had been lost in childbirth. Widowed or not, Charles was still completely unsuitable for her in any way. She knew that would be Henry's stance. Lady Guildford's position as well. Yet something powerful still drew her to him, as it had since she was a very young girl. He remained her adolescent fantasy. Yet since the passing of Lady Beaufort, and his genuine kindness to her, it had begun to feel like something more. There was certainly no one else like him at Henry's court. And her newfound independence within that world gave her all the more reason to want to explore that . . . no matter what Lady Guildford, or her brother the king, would have thought.

There would not be much time left that was her own.

Feeling in control of this singular comic moment, and remembering all of that, Mary spun around to face him. Like Henry, Charles stood before her caped in green, a black mask over his eyes, making him look the more dangerous and tempting. But his wife's death, Mary could see, had matured him, sculpting him into an even more magnificent young man. His smooth face was more angular now, his lean body more boldly muscular, shoulders seemingly more broad.

"I shall put up no struggle, my lord," Mary replied, willingly playing the role and biting back an amused smile as she looked up at his masked eyes.

Before either of them could speak again, the outlaw band drew the collection of ladies down the corridor, a sweep of velvet skirts and olive green capes. They continued outside toward what they boasted was Sherwood Forest. There the king had arranged entertainment and an extravagant meal of gingered fawn and veal pie laid out on gleaming silver beneath a broad, fluttering green and white silk canopy. Only then did the costumed men remove their eye masks, revealing not only the king, Brandon and Knyvet but the Earl of Surrey's two sons, Thomas and Edward Howard, as well as Thomas Grey, Marquess of Dorset.

After they had all dined and been charmingly entertained by Henry's new fool, Will Summers, musicians, who now accompanied the king everywhere, began to play for their pleasure. But before leaving, Henry himself took up the lute with a proud smile and began to play a tune he had just written for Katherine.

> *"Youth will needs have dalliance,*
> *Of good or ill some pastance;*
> *Company me thinketh best*
> *All thought and fancies to digest . . ."*

"I was sorry to hear of your wife's death," Mary leaned over and softly said to Brandon as Henry sang.

"It happens that way at times when there is to be a child."

"Yes, it happened that way for my mother," she shot back, feeling a hint of irritation. "You are very cavalier sometimes, Master Brandon."

"And unalterably insensitive at times, as well. I was very fond of Her Highness, the late queen. My true and humble apology."

She studied him for a moment, trying her best to decide which was the real him. "I like you far better, Brandon, when you are yourself like this."

"Alas, do not let me fool you. The other is myself as well. The one that keeps me from harm with the most tempting court beauties."

"You told me once last year you thought that I was beautiful. What do you think my good brother, the king, would say to that?" she asked with a taunting sort of pleasure, feeling the weight once again of her newly blossomed beauty and power.

"I think he might have my head on a pike on the Tower Bridge, if he thought for even a moment I meant it in any way but the most general form of flattery, my lady Mary."

"And is that only how you meant it, Master Brandon?"

"But of course." He smiled, his cheeks dimpling, as he skillfully took back command of the conversation, no matter how well she thought she played the game. "One in my tenuous position would be most unwise to put attraction before ambition."

"You are the king's dearest friend. That would seem to render your position not tenuous at all."

"And yet we all but you, my lady Mary, serve at the pleasure of the king. I like my place here and I have worked long and hard to attain it."

"Do you like that place better than you favor the king's sister?"

"Indeed, I must. You shall be a princess of Castile soon enough and I shall be left to remember our pleasant conversations and your lovely smile."

"You are very smug, Brandon, and deft with a turn of phrase."

"Well *you* told *me* once, my lady, that you were young and betrothed to a grand prince, while I was old and married. You will learn one day that maturity does have its advantages."

She stomped her foot churlishly and shot him an angry stare, reducing her almost instantly, she was sure, to the little girl he had once met, but her Tudor anger overpowered her will just then. "I do believe you are the most frustrating man I have ever known."

"I shall delight in that compliment only when you are old enough to have known more men than me."

"The king would be most angry with you if he knew you were toying with me like this."

"And he would be most angry with *you* if he knew you were attempting to blandish *me.*"

"You flatter yourself."

"And your childishness puts us both at risk."

"Then perhaps you should not have spoken to me in the first place, or commanded my partnership in a dance."

"Rest assured, I shall remember your rejoinder the next time."

"Indeed you should."

Mary caught a glimpse just then of Jane and Thomas Knyvet beside her and realized that they had heard every word. But Mary did not care any more this time than she had the last, although she had tried to maneuver the situation as deftly as she had seen it done here by others. Charles Brandon was a handsome, charming and eminently irritating master. And she was out of her league with him. Still, she could not chase his image, nor their exchange, from her mind all that afternoon and into the evening. She watched him at a distance at dinner in the great hall as he dined a little too closely to Lady Oxford, then danced one too many times with her as well, laughing and talking as if Mary did not exist.

Widowed and therefore free to behave as he pleased, Charles Brandon was every bit the same center of attention with the ladies at court as she was with the gentlemen. She found that evening, however, that the attentions of every one of them annoyed her, and she sat alone beside Jane, refusing every invitation to dance.

"There's no use in it, you know," Jane finally remarked to her in French. They sat together with dishes of uneaten figs, watching the wax from a dripping candle before them puddle onto the white table linen. "He is an impossible scoundrel, certain to marry again the moment he finds a woman with enough money, and therefore destined to break your heart."

"Your situation is that much different?"

Jane leaned back in her chair and took a swallow of wine, pretending to watch the dancers, among whom were Thomas Knyvet and his wife, Muriel. Mary saw the agony in her friend's expression and instantly regretted her tone. "Do you actually love him?"

"I shouldn't like to think," Jane answered. "It was a harmless flirtation only with Thomas, in order to make your brother jealous, but a flirtation gotten wrongly out of hand."

"He only ever saw Katherine back then, with his stubborn desire to marry her," Mary said, trying to soothe Jane amid the deafening din of laughter and the constant strain of music. "I don't think he ever knew how you felt, Jane."

"How I shall forever feel for him, you mean?"

She was truly lovely, Mary thought, looking at the strained expression on an otherwise flawless face, with its softly freckled skin and clear blue eyes. And her life was unfettered by any duty to which she was born. She was certainly worth much more than she could get by loving married men who could never give her back the love she so generously bestowed on them. Mary would never tell her but she envied Jane, and the future which lay before her if she made the right changes.

"Foolish love. Do not make the same mistake, Mary, with a man whose heart shall forever be unavailable to you."

"You needn't worry. Brandon is arrogant and too distastefully smug."

"And incredibly handsome, ambitious and smart," Jane countered.

"Well, no matter. I would never give a man like that my heart—nor any other part of myself, for that matter, mainly because he believes all women are his for the taking, and I am not to be used like that."

"*I* would not turn him away."

Mary shot her a concerned stare. "I thought you were hopelessly in love with the king."

"I am. But *he* is in love with his wife."

"Sir Thomas, then?"

"Favor of one's wife appears to have reached nearly epidemic proportions just now at this court," Jane said cleverly, then she sighed as they turned back to watch the king, Katherine, Thomas and petite, slim Muriel Knyvet, all dancing happily. And Charles Brandon, who had just changed partners yet again.

"What do you mean, he is stalling?" Henry shouted, his temper flaring. The king's Gentlemen of the Privy Chamber were removing his morning costume and replacing it with a doublet with puffed black sleeves, slashed and embroidered with pearls, and trunk hose, as he stood hands on his hips, his expression one of rage. "Mary is the loveliest, most desirable bride to be had! And Maximilian is still dragging his feet, as if he would be doing *me* a favor in accepting her?"

"It is true, Your Highness," Brandon carefully confirmed.

Along with the Earl of Surrey and the Duke of Buckingham, Charles had just spoken to the English envoy, Christopher Bainbridge, newly returned from Austria. It was decided by the king's closest advisers, after much private debate, that the highly offensive information would be best delivered to the king by his dearest friend, and those of his father's former privy council that Henry trusted most. A collection of minstrels played melodically in the corner as the group spoke, but the musicians went unseen and unheard by a sovereign who was angered at the emperor's continuing insult to his beloved sister.

"So whatever the equivocal response, he is in reality declining the marriage between Mary and that simpleton son of his upon whom I am graciously bestowing the greatest court beauty in England?" Henry sputtered in disbelief.

"Not declining, Your Highness," Buckingham carefully reported. "He is simply continuing to refuse a commitment to the details."

"God's bones . . . that pompous, arrogant fool bastard . . ." He stomped the floor, his square, handsome face blazing with indignation. "*By our lady*, either he wishes the alliance or he does not. Take a stand! Mary shall not endure such insult much longer."

"Respectfully, Your Highness needs the alliance that betrothal signifies."

"I *need* no one, Buckingham. *I* am King of England."

"And, if Your Gracious Highness shall permit the observation from a trusted friend of your father's, you are a new player on the world stage, where alliances are absolutely key," Thomas, the Earl of Surrey, intervened, risking everything the Howard family struggled to maintain in defense of a man who was his rival.

Henry stopped, then shot them both a contemptuous stare in response. There was a moment of disquieting silence. The cadence of his words slowed, becoming lethal. "Yes . . . *if* I shall permit you. That is the question."

"My absolute loyalty to my king would force me to speak only the truth."

"Very well, Buckingham, go on then!" He swatted at the

air very suddenly, as if there were a particularly bothersome insect between them, and the ruby on his finger glinted in the noonday light. "I shall permit you, but brevity, my man! Brevity!"

Buckingham coughed, then moistened his suddenly dry throat. "Maintain the betrothal a while longer, Your Highness. But make no commitment on your own. You will need the alliance if you decide to strike out against France. Once Louis XII has surrendered, then reevaluate where best you can utilize the princess Mary."

The door opened with a click and a low squeal. Footsteps echoed in the tense silence. Suddenly, Wolsey was hovering over them, his face blanched. He was fingering the heavy silver pectoral cross at his chest, a nervous gesture.

"It is the queen, sire. Her Highness has been delivered of a child this past hour."

"But I was sent no word that she was gone to childbed!"

"It was sudden, Your Highness. It would be best if I accompany you to her chamber. We can speak of it as we walk," Wolsey said.

Later that afternoon, Charles followed Henry as he led his great white bay at a gallop past a little stream and through the lushly forested, shadow-dappled hunting park behind Richmond Palace, hunting stag. Like the king, Charles loved the thrill of the wind in his hair, the mossy, damp earth beneath him, and the freedom it brought. It was a particular freedom he had sought and found as a boy when the stranglehold of courtly expectation and the need for ambition had threatened to choke the life out of him. Charles had needed that freedom to breathe then, just as Henry did. Charles understood the pressures of his friend as he sought to decide, not only about whether to invade France, but whether to break Mary's betrothal once and for all. But mostly, he knew that Henry was trying to understand the death of his first child, and what that meant for him, and to the future of England as well.

Henry had told him that he could not force himself to remain with Katherine more than a few moments at a time these past few days, driven away by her gut-wrenching sobs and the murmured Spanish prayers echoing from Dona Elvira, Maria de Salinas and Ambassador Fuensalida. The three of them sat hunched in the shadows of the corner near her bed, all holding tight to their rosaries and fingering the beads. It was all so intolerably somber, so dripping with a futility that he despised. This child—this dead child, meant to be a son—had been far more to him than an heir. To Henry, and to everyone, the child had meant the end of what many believed a curse on the house of Tudor for having married his brother's widow. *God must be angry,* Henry had whispered to Charles so many times in moments of private trust. *I am meant to be punished . . . Katherine as well.* Henry had counted on this child, their son and heir, to prove everyone wrong. Instead, Katherine had delivered him a stillborn girl.

Henry pulled the reins sharply. His horse reared then snorted as he leapt onto the ground and thundered into a stand of trees. As he knew he would, only Charles Brandon had confidence and concern enough to dismount as well, and follow behind him. Safely alone, Henry kicked the trunk of a tree, unleashing a pent-up fury that frightened Brandon but even more, he suspected, did it frighten Henry himself. Henry clearly could not accept this. . . . This was defeat! *Your next shall be a fine son,* Charles had heard Dona Elvira promise Henry through her tears. That wretched Spaniard, Charles thought, with her optimism!

But no matter what strange circumstance had brought them together, or how angry he felt now, Charles knew Henry did truly love Katherine and, God willing, the queen would give him and England a living son to put an end to the gossip and innuendo. He could do it. He could do *anything.* He was, after all, king.

They stood alone in a small clearing, Charles behind him, the other riders lingering, still on horseback, a few yards away. Henry kicked at the fallen pine needles and dried leaves around them. "What do I do now, Brandon? I am so angry . . . so full of rage!"

"Of those given much, much is expected, Harry."

"*You* are quoting the Bible to me?"

"Sorry. It was all I could think of at the moment."

One heartbeat, then two. Suddenly, Henry tipped back his head and began to laugh, a great sound up from his gut. He clipped Brandon across the shoulder with a muscular palm. "You always could make me laugh, Brandon. Well, let's just make certain *you* never leave me. I find, quite surprisingly, that I cannot quite do without you around me."

Charles had never wanted anything more. Ambition was the thing. Power was the rest of it. How could there be anything better in all the world than staying at Henry VIII's court, and making himself indispensable, forever?

Chapter Seven

If thou wouldst get a friend, prove him first.

—Apocrypha 6:14

May 1510, Greenwich Palace

A month later, Mary stood in the courtyard wearing a man's riding hose of dark blue velvet and matching doublet with silver slashing. Her hair was tucked under a boy's velvet-trimmed hat, and she was holding smooth kid gloves as Knyvet, the Guildford brothers and Charles Brandon began to assemble, and their horses were brought up by grooms from the royal stables. Uncertain what to say when they realized who she was, no one spoke to her at first. An awkward silence descended upon the steadily growing group, which now included the Duke of Buckingham, the Earl of Surrey, Surrey's son Edward, and the king.

Mary watched Henry assessing the situation, and looking back and forth to each of them, then begin to chuckle as his own Spanish jennet was brought forward, a gift to him from the emperor. "What, gentlemen? You have never seen a lady before?"

"Not in a man's riding costume," Knyvet quickly replied with an earnest smile.

"She looks a far sight better in it than most men," Brandon quipped in such a solid and certain tone that all of the others turned to look.

Henry slapped his friend hard across the back. "That's the spirit! You're just the sort Mary needs in her corner. I shall have to remember that. My sister wished not just to ride and look beautiful, but to hunt as we do, and so she shall."

"I wished to be away from the endless embroidery and gossip, and the king is an accommodating brother," she amended, smiling at him.

"There is plenty of gossip on the hunt, my lady Mary, though not perhaps the sort to which you would be accustomed."

"Even better," Mary laughed happily. "I wish to hear absolutely everything I am not meant to."

"We shall all see what we can do," said Brandon, with a solicitous nod. "That is, *if* the king pleases."

"Whatever Mary desires. I have no secrets from her," Henry replied firmly, with a nod of his own toward her.

"Preposterous . . . ," someone grumbled. But she no longer cared who said it. Her brother, her best friend, was King of England, she reminded herself. She was his favorite. And she would do precisely as she pleased from now on.

Mary rode harder and faster than the others after that, challenging herself. Horses' hooves thundered out across a meadow carpeted with tall grass and bluebells, Mary in the lead beside Henry, with Charles close behind them. The wind blew the length of her red-gold hair out from her cap, and she gripped the horse's flanks hard with her thighs in a sensation that was as exhilarating as it was cold. She wondered, as they rode toward the hunting forest behind Greenwich Palace, if the Prince of Castile would be as accommodating with her whims as Henry was. Would he laugh with her and sing with her, and include her in every aspect of his life if she wished? She knew from Wolsey that the emperor was still dragging his heels on the final approval of the marriage, and secretly Mary was glad of it. She had no desire at all to leave this new and exciting life for what was certain to be an existence of dreary obligation and subservience in the unknown world of Castile.

But she was determined not to think of that as the group of royal horses thundered closely behind and Henry, in black velvet with shining silver studs on his doublet and gilded stir-rups, smiled happily over at her. This life was perfection just as it was and she meant to keep it, and her power, until the very last day before she was given over to a man she did not want.

After they had cornered the stag, seen it killed, then washed their hands in rose water, they ate a light meal of capon and pears in honey wine. It was served by a vast as-semblage of footmen, attendants' pages, carver, sewer, all of whom waited on them with silver dishes, ewers, gold salt-cellars and glass goblets. Amid the sweet strains of the lute, Mary walked across the Flanders carpet and onto the leaves and pine needles among the mossy trees and low-lying ferns of the lush forest. Charles Brandon followed her.

"So then is it all you hoped for, my lady?"

Mary looked up into his face, dappled in light and shad-ows shining down through the heavy evergreen branches.

"Would it surprise you if it were?"

"May I say everything about you surprises me?" he replied in a voice that was suddenly and surprisingly seductive.

"Good. I adore the hunt. And Henry always says that everything in life is more exciting when there is an element of surprise."

"Your brother is very young to be so wise."

"Perhaps that is why God saw fit to make him king. He is committed already to keeping people from expectation."

"Does his sister share his commitment?"

She smiled. "The king and I share most everything, Master Brandon, including our taste in friends."

"I am very pleased to hear it, my lady."

"Mary!"

The king's booming voice cut between them at that moment, calling to her from the clearing. They walked the few feet back to where tapestry-draped tables and chairs were gathered near a fire. The king's minstrels were playing softly to entertain them.

"What do you think of the song?" Henry asked.

"It's a lovely tune."

"I wrote it for Katherine and my son. It shall be a boy this time, Mary, I know it. I have a good feeling about it."

The queen was newly pregnant again. Mary felt a shiver work its way up the length of her spine but Henry was distracted by a joke Thomas Knyvet was telling. She had, in fact, had a dream that the child was to be another girl, and that it was stillborn. In a fury of disappointment, Henry—in dream's twisted reality—had his wife murdered because of it. Until this moment, she had entirely forgotten the gruesome scene her mind had conjured. Sensing her unease, Charles placed a hand very casually at the small of her back as he looked at her.

"Are you all right? Suddenly you've gone very pale."

"It is just a dream I remembered suddenly."

"More of a nightmare, by the stricken expression on your face."

"It sits heavily within me, like a premonition," she replied, not hearing the jokes and laughter being bandied back and forth between the king's friends.

"I find myself rather hoping it does not involve me."

There had actually been another dream. Two nights before, Mary's mind had conjured a strangely erotic scene where Charles had kissed her passionately in a way she as yet could only imagine. Even so, that dream, how he had looked, felt . . . tasted . . . had seemed every bit as real as her nightmare of Katherine and Henry. But she could not tell Charles that.

"No," she said. "In the main, it was about the queen— about the child."

"I see."

"I am not certain why, but I am afraid this one is not meant to survive either, and Henry is so counting on a son."

"He is, at that," Charles somberly agreed.

"I just don't know what it shall do to him if they are forced to bury this one as well."

"I've never told another person this," he began in a tone that only she could hear, "but I dreamed something oddly similar not long ago. . . . I could see the child dead. . . . I could see Henry raging with anger . . . and the queen . . ." His words trailed off as Mary leaned nearer him. "You will need to be there for him if we are both right. He will need you more than anyone else."

How very odd, Mary thought, that two people connected by the same man, but not to one another, should have the same dream about him. She knew that Charles was right. Her relationship with Henry was like no other, and the king depended upon her even above his own wife. She tried not to take advantage, knowing that, but there was great power in his dependence upon her. As they stood together pretending to watch Edward Howard now try his hand at joke telling, a memory from that morning came to her.

"I am going with you today," she had said to Henry, speaking the declaration with all of the conviction of royalty and of a man.

"I am going hunting, Mary," he had chuckled at her indulgently.

"I am well aware of that, and I wish to go along."

As he slipped on his long leather gloves, he smiled at her as if he were indulging a petulant child. "You know that while observing men at the hunt is one thing, hunting itself is not a woman's pastime."

"And you know perfectly well I am not like most women. Another afternoon of gossip and embroidery hoops will surely do me in. I need some excitement, Henry, please, I bid you."

"Is there not enough of that for you in keeping Mistress Popincourt from Thomas Knyvet's bed? I do think his poor wife has begun to suspect that little crime. Quite delicious to watch from my vantage point, but not at all pleasing for the two poor women involved, I am sure."

"You know about that?"

"Of course I know." Henry had laughed louder in that increasingly bold way that was his since becoming King of England.

"Well, I wish it were enough entertainment but it is not. Remember, unlike you, I am making up for lost time. And I am not like most women," she stubbornly declared in a voice that came out sounding more spoiled than defiant.

"How well I do know that! And at the end of the day, you know perfectly well that I can refuse you nothing. See that my dresser finds you a suitable ensemble. We ride within the hour."

"Well," said Charles, bringing her back to the moment, "are we to keep our dreams a secret?"

Her heart missed a little beat, pulled by dreams and fantasy, but then she managed a reasonably confident smile. "What we speak about," Mary said then, "shall go no further than the two of us, Master Brandon. You have my word."

His funds were low once again, and the cost of splendor— pageant finery, jewelry and jousting armor—on par with other courtiers was simply staggering. Not unlike the cost of supporting his two daughters, his sister and her children. It was a never-ending struggle no matter how much his various positions paid him. So, grudgingly, Charles had made another trip to Southwark to request a new loan from his very unsympathetic uncle—just enough to keep everything and everyone going.

The vile truth of the matter was that he had little shame when it came to doing whatever it took to survive at court. He had just enough ambition to imagine that one day, if he waited long enough—if he was clever enough and a good enough friend to the king—Henry might actually bestow a title upon him. Ah, nobility . . . respect. His own money, without conditions or strings . . . To walk with pride among men who had never known the despair of poverty. A dream, perhaps, yet he would continue to search for a way to make it a reality.

He cantered his grand sorrel-colored stallion alone down Bankside, an area that, although not far from his uncle's mansion, was a million miles from its manicured hedges, stone columns and stately surroundings. In the distance, the skyline of London was dotted with dozens of protruding church spires and chimneys, a gray haze above that. This area of Southwark, full of shadowy corners and dark alleyways, was lined with bawdy houses that were washed in white paint, to separate them from the more reputable businesses established along the same route. Charles pulled the collar of his cloak around his neck against the night chill rushing now up from the river as he glanced at the working girls in their mismatched creations of garishly bright taffeta, ribbons and bows. Obscenities echoed from the darkened alleyways around them as he stopped before the Unicorn. It was a place he had visited before, and likely would again.

Thomas Knyvet and Edward Guildford waited in rough-hewn chairs, each with a girl on his lap, as they did on the first of every month they were in London. The low-ceilinged place was filled with smoke and the odor of spilled ale, and brightened by a glowing amber from the flames licking the inside of the mammoth stone hearth before which they sat.

"Tonight we celebrate!" Knyvet declared, raising his hand in greeting to Charles.

"Isn't much for men like us to celebrate in a place like this."

"Ah, but that is where you are wrong, my friend! Low entertainment is not without a certain charm from time to time."

Thinking of Jane, Charles laughed. "I might have thought *you* would have had your hands full just now, Thomas."

Edward Guildford ran a hand through his dark curls, laughing too. "As our good king would say, there is always room for one more. Especially when it comes to women!"

"Not our good Henry," Charles countered, taking a tankard of ale. "He is still hopelessly in love with the queen."

"Last time I looked, love had little to do with this," Knyvet quipped as he kissed the stout, ruddy-faced girl in torn purple taffeta perched on his lap.

That was true enough, Charles thought. It always had been for him anyway. Why his feelings for Mary were so different he was not certain. Yet they were. And she had made him want to be different, in spite of the fact that she was a young royal . . . and there could be absolutely no chance of anything ever between them. He had come here tonight to try to escape the reality of that, and the images of the forbidden princess who plagued his mind and his dreams. He slumped more heavily into the chair as if it could swallow him up, then took another mouthful of ale and let it numb his tongue. Hopefully, his mind would follow. He did not want to think about his uncle . . . or money or even of Mary just now. The girl on Knyvet's lap smiled at him, and Charles leaned over to touch a coil of her curly, tawny-colored hair. It felt like little coils of steel. Better, he thought, that nothing in this place would remind him of Mary tonight.

Chapter Eight

*A prince should therefore have no other aim or thought,
nor take up any other thing for his study, but war and its
organization and discipline, for that is the only art that is
necessary to one who commands.*

—Niccolo Machiavelli,
The Prince

January 1511, Richmond Palace

Henry had determined to go against his father's plan and wage war with France. Hostilities commenced with the help of his father-in-law, Ferdinand. Initially, England and Spain joined with the pope, ostensibly to protect the papacy and recapture the former papal territory of Bordeaux. Ferdinand also assured Henry that if he would help him regain Navarre, Spain would assist in the return of the Aquitaine to English possession. All of the members of the Holy League would gain, and Henry VIII would soundly establish himself on the world stage.

The efforts, however, went anything but according to plan.

While Ferdinand did manage to reclaim Navarre, at a key moment his troops left the English to fend for themselves. The disaster that followed was predictable. In order to solidify his other alliances, Henry's own father-in-law callously blamed England's defeat on Henry's inexperience and extreme youth. Henry was humiliated.

Tempering the defeat—and Henry's unwarranted anger at Katherine for her father's betrayal—Katherine gave birth a second time, on New Year's Day. This time she gave Henry the son he needed and for which he longed. The child was christened Henry, Prince of Wales. Henry called for a great celebration, in spite of Wolsey's counsel against it. Katherine as well feared angering God with premature boasting, but Henry's joy would not be put down.

In the streets across England bonfires were lit in celebration. Once again the deep resonant sound of church bells rang out, though this time it was with joy and not sorrow that they pealed. A tournament was staged at Richmond, and courtiers, servants and ambassadors spoke excitedly of nothing else for days. Henry would ride in the role of Sir Loyal Heart. First, however, Charles Brandon would joust against Thomas Knyvet.

In the tiltyard, Mary sat beneath a gilded arch, and above a hanging cloth of gold emblazoned with the intertwined letters *H* and *K*, castle gargoyles glaring down on them. Transformed by time at court and by her heritage, Mary was now a striking beauty. Her skin was flawless, her features were delicate, and her green eyes were wide and bright. She smoothed her richly ornamented dress of yellow satin with gray fur at her lap, then touched a wide gold medallion at her throat, aware of the gaze of more than a few men upon her. Beside Mary, Jane, Muriel Knyvet, Anne Howard, Lady Monteagle and the ever-present Lady Guildford were all chattering. Yet

Mary was keenly aware of the attention she drew now when she went out like this. Sons of dukes, earls and lords watched her every move, clambered to dance with her and whispered to one another or smiled at her whenever she did even the least little thing out of the ordinary. Every day now, she commanded attention. Yet all Mary saw and thought about, with increasing frequency, was Charles. And as he now entered the lists, he again captured her complete attention.

Charles wore a full suit of gleaming gilt armor and feathered plumes on his helmet as he cantered out onto the field a moment later with Knyvet, amid the pealing blare of trumpets. Brandon's plume, not coincidentally, was the same bright yellow as Mary's dress. The crowd erupted in applause for Brandon, who was the most dashing and victorious combatant next to the king himself. Mary herself was cheering wildly, until Lady Guildford shot her a reproachful stare above her own more polite applause.

Then Henry entered the field in tooled armor that glittered beneath the mild noonday sun. A forest green plume danced atop his helmet, as he led his horse to the stands amid a thunderous ovation to where Katherine proudly sat. Visor up, Henry nodded to his wife, paying homage to the mother of his son as he offered her the tip of his lance, to which she tied her own Tudor green silk scarf. He clutched at his heart in response and the crowd erupted again. Henry VIII was a consummate showman, Mary thought as she watched the exchange.

For Katherine, however, it was something more. In her every glance and gesture, Mary could see her pure adoration for her husband. It was the same thing that motivated Katherine in everything.

Lance after lance was broken as the afternoon wore on. The score was at a tie in the final run as Brandon now had the unenviable task of facing the king himself. Spectators from the outlying villages who had paid to stand behind the barricade cheered wildly with each blow, mesmerized by the contest. Mary strangely thought of the Prince of Castile again. As she watched the magnificent man battling her brother, she wondered if he ever jousted or could even wield a two-handed sword in a tournament, as she had seen Brandon so brilliantly do many times before. She knew she was being childishly romantic, and unfair to keep making comparisons, but she could not help it. Charles had been her childhood fantasy and that desire had followed her unchecked into womanhood. She wanted him to win. Secretly, she cheered for him against the king, loving the dangerous betrayal in that.

"Careful, Mary. You are staring," Jane whispered.

"At Brandon?" she asked Jane, who had leaned over to her and begun to giggle behind a raised hand. "That is ridiculous."

"It is. Yet still you are."

Jane Popincourt was seventeen now and as proud as Mary of her own clever tongue. Like her royal friend, she had matured into a beauty, yet with features less delicate than Mary's and golden hair more thin than lush, eyes more intense than brilliant. Jane fluffed her skirts and glanced back down onto the field.

"Do you suppose anything less than every single soul

here has noticed that Brandon's plume matches your dress exactly? What are the odds of a coincidence like that—being a coincidence?"

"Brandon would do nothing like that."

"He is not married now. And I have seen the way he looks at you."

"Well, *I*, at least, am betrothed."

"Perhaps not for long to the Prince of Castile. Master Knyvet has told me that the king has begun to consider other suitable husbands for you. Besides, I was not implying anything like a real marriage between the two of you."

Mary shot her a scowl. "That is vulgar. Just because you indulge in scandalous liaisons does not mean I am one to do so!"

"Ah, do not be too critical of that which has gone untried."

They had lived together for so long, nearly all of their lives, that they spoke with one another like sisters. And as a sister would, Mary knew Jane's heart. Jane was not happy as an occasional mistress, yet somehow it seemed she had begun to convince herself that there was self-protection in denying the truth. As drawn as Mary was by the idea of a dangerous love like the ones Jane entertained, she was afraid of it. Her virginity was as prized as she was, and she had been raised to know it. It was one thing to dream of Charles Brandon, even to fantasize about him. But even Mary knew that was all she could ever have of him.

The deep sound of thundering hooves brought her back to the moment as the combatants charged their horses across the vast yard toward one another in a swirl of dust and heavy leveled lances. Mary held her breath. The crowd fell silent as Brandon and the king rode at a full gallop. In an instant, so sudden that there was a gasp from the crowd, the king's lance plunged at Brandon's heavy breastplate, knocking him off his horse and into a cloud of dust. Mary fought the sense of alarm and an overwhelming urge to lunge over the balustrade to reach him. But she clutched Jane's hand instead, holding it in a death grip as everyone waited for Charles to move, or at least give some sign to show them that he was still alive.

"He is a strong man. He will be fine. You will see," Jane murmured in French as several of the yeomen rushed onto the field toward him.

After what felt like an eternity, Charles sat up on his own, lifted his visor and waved to the crowd. As he turned to her, Mary could see that he was smiling.

He had sprained his wrist and had the wind knocked out of him, Brandon cavalierly explained as the king's physician nodded to Mary and then excused himself from the bedchamber. Mary stood with Jane at the foot of Charles Brandon's bed in which he was propped by a spray of silk pillows. As everyone else listened to a performance in the great hall by a soloist newly arrived from Venice, Mary had brought him a dish of candied fruit tied with a cloth and white ribbon. It was an offering to wish him good health but the gift was truly meant just to give her an excuse to see him.

"You jackanapes! You took that blow intentionally!" Mary determined suddenly as she looked at him, eating a sugared plum.

He looked up at her, a smile forming on his lips. "I have no idea, my lady Mary, what you mean."

Jane smiled now too, nodded and then silently withdrew to the other side of the room. When they were alone, partially hidden by the heavy velvet bed curtain, Charles took another chunk of fruit and popped it into his mouth.

"Have some with me?" he bid her with his clever smile.

"I shall grow fat if I do."

"Ah, I would love you, pretty lady Mary, fat or lean, weak or strong."

She looked at him critically. "You *love* me, Brandon?"

"I should think any man who had ever seen you would love you quite unconditionally."

"Ah, there you go again spouting lines worthy of a great romantic play."

"You think me insincere?"

"I think you far too polished at court pleasantries."

He bit back a smile and ate a third piece of fruit. "Yet not insincere?"

There was a faint frown suddenly between her brows. "I don't know you, Brandon."

"You know me well enough to have worried after my health, and to have brought me a confection."

She was uncomfortable suddenly. His gaze was too deep, his voice too honeyed to be as sincere as she wished it to be, and she had cared too much about his health. She knew then she should not have come. She felt childish and defensive. "Only a court pleasantry, at which I clearly need improvement. You mock me, I think."

"Nothing could be further from what I wish to do."

As a reflex, she turned, glancing behind herself for Jane, but she could not see her. "I have made an error in coming here."

"You only err by leaving."

Since she was close enough now and they were alone, he took her arm and pulled her near. The attraction between them flared. Very gently, he reached up, cupped her chin in his palm and pressed a kiss onto her mouth. He lingered for only a moment, then pulled away, but his eyes never left hers.

"Did you speak so smoothly to each of your wives, Master Brandon?" she asked breathlessly as her lips burned.

Mary could see that she had cut him with that. She saw his reaction in the way his mouth tightened and the small muscle flexed along the side of his jaw. But he was strong and bold and he would not be insulted, even by the king's sister. His eyes narrowed in the silence as he studied her, and his next words were clipped.

"Neither of them was a spoiled innocent. That much I can say with conviction. Each accepted me as I am, my lady. It is why they were my wives. Acceptance of who I am when I love someone means everything to me."

She wanted to say she was sorry if she had offended him. She meant to say it. Yet the words, as she tried to speak, would not leave her lips. When everyone else around her at court made her feel beautiful and above reproach, only Charles Brandon made her feel unsure—in addition to everything else. A moment later she turned and walked to the door, where Jane stood waiting.

"I am glad you are feeling better, Master Brandon. I am

pleased that your injuries will not keep you from the next tournament tomorrow."

It was the only thing she could think of to say in the suddenly tense moment before she walked out the door of his apartments. As they strode down the long gallery, with tall windows facing down into the gardens below, Jane glanced over at Mary, who was pounding her heels noisily into the wood floor with each step.

"If I did not know you so well, I would say you were changing your mind about Brandon, actually coming to care for him."

"But you *do* know me better," Mary said a little too quickly.

❖

"The king has a right to be told about that," Buckingham loftily declared, striding boldly in black and silver between Wolsey and the Earl of Surrey as they passed Mary and Jane going the other way.

"It would be a grave misjudgment," the cleric calmly countered. As usual, Wolsey's words were succinct and pointed, made slightly less lethal by his charmingly rotund appearance, and the affable tone he took as they strolled the paneled corridor.

"I agree with Buckingham. His Highness has a right to know what is going on right beneath his very nose," replied Thomas Howard, the distinguished-looking, silver-haired Earl of Surrey. He had seen the cleric's expression and the way he had so judgmentally shaken his head as the two girls had emerged alone from Brandon's apartments. Daylight or not, going there had been a daring move—even for the king's very indulged sister.

The Earl of Surrey had been at court for a long time, and he knew how to wait like a fox for the spoils of someone else's kill. The ruthless nature that possessed his soul seemed to have branded his appearance as well with a sharp elongated nose, small black eyes with dark arched brows and steel-gray hair. He was taut and fit for a man of his age, a contemporary of the previous king, and there was nothing he despised more than a gluttonous opportunist like Thomas Wolsey, whom he was forced to befriend. The Earl of Surrey believed Wolsey had worked for nothing he had received. Rather he cajoled, manipulated and banqueted his way to power, taking advantage of a young, immature and pleasure-loving sovereign.

Wolsey was exceedingly distasteful, the earl had determined, himself having struggled mightily for power and place. Wolsey's rise was almost as meteoric as Charles Brandon's, and Thomas Howard believed he simply could not survive the competition for most powerful place from two sources. Wolsey's Achilles' heel lay in a blind greed he was certain the king did not see. But the Earl of Surrey saw it. Wolsey believed he helped Brandon with Mary, she who was most dear to the king. But the Princess Mary was a willful little thing, far too driven by pretty gowns and dancing to have the slightest notion what was best for her. That could never be Charles Brandon. The earl had seen Wolsey ingratiating himself with her recently. After today, he knew why. This was a battle now for highest place of influence with the king, when Thomas Wolsey had thought it merely a smooth rise to elevation. No one could outfox the Earl of Surrey—even if he had to align himself with Buckingham to triumph.

"Is it that he has a right to know," Wolsey asked then, "or more that *you*, my lord, have an ambition to elevate yourself by making a harmless girl's flirtation into more than it can ever be?"

"My ambition is to seek the truth in all things," Buckingham disingenuously declared.

Wolsey shrugged, his chin doubling and his mouth turning down as he did. "My advice is that you both leave it alone or you shall live to regret it."

"A man of God threatening an earl and a Howard?" Surrey asked.

"Only a wise old friend reminding you that the king's sister will marry the Castile boy. But she is young and willful, as most privileged adolescents are, and this one has England at her feet. My lady Mary is finding the first true power of her beauty, and you must admit there really is no one among us like Brandon on which for her to test her power. But however you find their harmless little flirtation, Henry will believe her, not you."

"I know not how you can be so cavalier."

"I am realistic, not cavalier. There is no one the king loves so well as his sister, and no one—even among us—he trusts so much as Brandon. Surely my lord of Surrey is wise enough to know what they say often happens to the messenger?"

They came to the foot of a staircase, then took the steps together, Wolsey climbing each more laboriously than the fit and trim earl, and Buckingham silently a pace behind. "In my experience, His Highness values loyalty above all other things, even trust."

"A wager, to be sure," huffed the wizened cleric.

The day was made for celebrating, clear and full of sunlight. The azure sky was a broad canvas for the scudding clouds, and flocks of blackbirds passed across it. Above them grand tents of yellow and blue striped silk fluttered on the vast lawn behind Richmond Palace. First, there had been an intricate disguising—an allegorical play in which Henry and Mary played the lead parts. Henry was costumed most grandly as Zeus and Mary was the Greek goddess Athena, drawing the rest of the court in amid laughter and shouts of support for their performance. They reigned happily over the production, which included complicated scenery and a stage that had been constructed complete with a working fountain and a mulberry tree.

They then led dancing once the disguising was over. Mary took the prominent place by her brother's side as they began an intricate pavane, and then a lively branle, in which only a few of the most well placed joined. Katherine had become increasingly fearful that any sort of activity or court illness could harm her son, so she rarely attended any of the entertainments, preferring to remain with him in the nursery at Richmond. Here, the best dancers at court, brother and sister, were well matched, and Mary had no rival for attention as the crowd of elegantly dressed onlookers watched and applauded wildly after each dance.

In spite of the carefree air, the looming specter of war was lost on not a single member of King Henry's court. After the humiliating defeat for which Ferdinand still blamed his inexperience, Henry was determined to be victorious on the battlefield against the French. He would, he declared, finish what he had begun. But for now, the king and his closest group of friends laughed and danced and sipped claret from tooled silver goblets in the warm afternoon sun.

"So, tell me, sister," Henry began as they danced theatrically, both aware of the eyes upon them, both reveling in the attention, "how would you feel at the prospect of cancellation of your betrothal?"

Mary looked at her brother, and smiled for the benefit of the court. But privately, she said, "I had heard whispers you were contemplating such a thing, but I thought it only a bit of the idle speculation of which our court is so fond."

Henry laughed and kicked with impressive height. The crowd applauded. His reply, however, was said with a note of frustration. "Maximilian is a stubborn prig in this. He believes me too young and untested, and he is trying to make me look the fool because of it. I may be young, but I mean to prove him wrong."

"Have you another arrangement in mind?"

"There have been suggestions put forth, and if things do not shortly improve I will be forced to consider them more seriously."

They turned again, her blue dress swirling along with the kaleidoscope of other colored skirts twirling around her. Then they bowed to one another, as the other dancers did. "So tell me, my wise young sister, with all the world at your feet, who might you advise me to consider?"

"You seek my opinion on such a matter?"

"I shall deny it boldly if called upon to declare it, but it is your opinion alone that means the world to me, as no one else's at court could—not even Katherine's." He smiled. "But then you already knew that."

The question put forth, her mind conjured only an image of Charles Brandon. It remained there, stubbornly bright. Henry so favored his friend that he had recently bestowed upon him not only the vaunted title of Knight of the Garter, but he had made him a Gentleman of the Privy Chamber, which left little doubt of his steadily growing influence. In addition, there were few appropriate, other unmarried suitors on the world stage from whom to choose at the moment. She had once heard the old, widowed French king, Louis XII, proposed, but that seemed absurd for many reasons. For one thing, the war with France was imminent, which thankfully rendered that match unlikely. As brother and sister laughed and danced, Mary's mind dared to admit a small glimmer of a fantasy to dress up the vision before her: if she did marry Charles Brandon she could remain beside her brother at court as helpmate and companion. And had he not just said he trusted her like no other? Now that their father was dead and Henry was in control, could he possibly have thought better of losing her? At that moment, her life could not have felt more perfect. All of that whirled now in her head and she felt a happy laugh burst up from her heart as everyone watched them dance.

"Of course I am not well versed enough in court matters to advise the king," she said with a broad smile, as if she had cleverly just figured something out, "but perhaps you would find favor in a selection that would keep me a bit closer to you than Castile."

"Nothing would make me happier, my Mary."

When the dance ended, he bowed to her, and she curtsied. He kissed one cheek, then the other. Mary could not help it, looking up into his eyes: she was overjoyed. Now if she could only convince Charles Brandon to think of her as more than a risk to be taken, her life would be absolute perfection.

As everyone changed partners, Thomas Knyvet, tall and smoothly handsome, dressed as he was in dove gray silk, bowed to her next. Mary had always liked Thomas. She knew he and Muriel were a match, not a marriage, and so she could forgive his attraction to someone beautiful like Jane. She only pitied the toll it was taking on her friend, whose heart was being worn away a little more each day that she maintained her status as secret sometimes mistress.

"Wolsey tells me you are to captain a ship against the French," Mary said as they joined hands, then bowed.

"We sail at week's end, my lady."

"I wonder, in your absence, who you shall miss the more," she asked archly, which made him laugh. Everyone at court was accustomed to wit, and Mary could spar with the best of them. "Be good to her, Thomas. She deserves better."

She saw a small glimmer of a smile as his glance automatically cast about for Jane. They saw her at the same moment and Mary saw her return Thomas's smile. Jane was sitting beside Lady Monteagle, with her slim, lined face and deep-set olive-colored eyes. Both women were on fringed stools beside one of the turned poles that held up the fluttering canopy.

"You have been a good friend to Jane," Thomas Knyvet said sincerely.

"As she has been to me. You know I have counseled her to quit you."

"As well you should." He smiled evenly, not undone by her admission. "She deserves a husband of her own."

"On that we agree, Thomas. And if you hurt her, I do swear I will never forgive you. Nor shall the king. Still, do take care of yourself out there, will you? You have more than most men to return to."

Although spoken lightly, her words held an underlying sincerity few of their conversations ever had. She had known him for a long time and cared for both him and Jane. Edward Howard came upon them then, wearing a jovial smile himself and a rich doublet of blue velvet laced with silver thread. Court companions since birth, Knyvet and Howard were inseparable. Howard was not as handsome as Knyvet or Brandon, being short and stout, but he was every bit as quick with a phrase and half again as clever—like money, wit was an essential commodity to thrive at Henry's court.

"So I amend that to *three* by whom you shall be missed, and to whom you absolutely must return," Mary said as Edward bowed to her.

"We captain companion ships for the king, my lady Mary. I shall be out there right beside Thomas against the accursed French."

"Perhaps you should just stay out at sea, Thomas," Mary

joked. "That would certainly solve the problem you have back here."

"It would at that. I shall, as always, consider my lady Mary's sound advice."

She laughed. "At the very least, send a shot across to them for me, and for Mistress Popincourt as well, will you, Edward? Just to remind you both that we—and all of the complications of this happy court—shall be right here waiting for you when you return."

"Brandon and I shall send one for you as well, if you like," Henry Guildford happily offered as he came upon them in an easy stride, holding a silver goblet.

Mary felt the shock of sudden surprise. "Brandon is to go to sea as well?"

"Together, we are to captain His Highness' newest vessel, manned by the most elite force. It is a high honor."

He was right about that. The privilege Henry had bestowed upon them all was clear, but Charles Brandon felt it most particularly for the disadvantage with which he had begun life and how far he had risen at court through Henry's grace and favor. Involuntarily, Mary found herself surveying the crowd, looking for him. Seeing her as she did, Guildford leaned forward, cupping a hand around his mouth in a gossipy, just slightly feminine manner.

"He has gone to Southwark, my lady Mary. Rumor has it, there is a woman he visits there, though no one at court knows quite who she is."

Hearing it, and knowing Charles Brandon, the revelation did not surprise her. "Where would you hear such a thing?"

"You know his uncle, of course."

Everyone at court knew Thomas Brandon, the ambitious braggart who had control of what Brandon fortune there was. "Yes, I know him," she said coolly.

"At archery two days past, Sir Thomas Brandon could not help boasting that he has great things in store for the family through his nephew. Since Charles has used marriage to elevate himself before, we all assumed it has something to do with the mysterious woman in Southwark."

Mary felt a breeze across her face, cooling her childish thoughts and fantasies. Charles had a destiny, and obligation. So did she. Of course there would be another woman, and another and another—until Charles had the power he craved.

"Are you unwell, my lady? You've gone pale," Knyvet asked, pulling her back to the moment.

"Someone fetch her a chair," Guildford barked in a panic, and the vestiges of her fantasy snapped completely and were gone. She was actually glad now that he was going away, going to sea. It really was for the best.

"I am perfectly fine." She swatted at them just as Henry always did his servants. "I just lost my balance for a moment, that is all."

Muriel Knyvet had heard every word because no one had even looked or bothered to see that she was there. Not even her own husband. She had long suspected Jane Popincourt of corrupting Thomas. But having the proof of it had still been a death blow. Now she wanted to kill someone else. She wanted to kill Jane . . . and Mary, for knowing about it and telling her nothing. Each unmistakable word was like a flame burning, consuming her heart, a heart that had only ever been given to Thomas. She had loved him all of her life. Her soul now as well twisted, burned . . . turned to ashes. Yes, him most especially. She wanted Thomas to die . . . to burn with her . . . to turn to the pile of ash he had left her in for the unpardonable sin of having fallen out of love with her. The pain was blinding.

Crying and only now realizing it, Muriel dashed at the tears on her face, her rust brown skirts trailing through the grass as she walked alone away from the tent—away from the laughter, the lies, the rivalries and the deceptions. *Damn you, all of you,* she thought darkly, knowing that the only one who would ever perish for this—the only one who already had—was herself. Hearing about her own husband as she had, Muriel cared nothing at all that she was pregnant. Because it was Thomas's child alive within her, a child she knew he did not want, and she would rather face death than live the rest of her life raising it now . . . now that he loved someone else.

Less than two months after his birth, the son and heir who had brought hope and freedom from the past to Henry VIII, died suddenly at Richmond Palace. At the candlelit midnight burial in Westminster Abbey, the king sat stone-faced beside his sobbing wife. He was bereft at the loss for all his son had meant, but Henry had learned well as a child to make no show of his grief, and this occasion would be no exception. As king, he must be stronger than that. Stronger than everyone.

Chapter Nine

Men flourish only for a moment.

—Homer

August 1512, the English Channel

Standing commandingly on deck of the *John Hopton*, sea spray moistening his face, Charles grasped the wet railing as the sleek new four-masted warship he captained was heaved and pitched into another, and then another, blue-black wave. A flock of gulls flew overhead. In his captain's coat made of green and white damask, he was drenched with saltwater, and his beard, which he had not bothered to trim, had grown long.

Beneath him in the hold and at their posts around him on deck were amassed the most elite of the king's fighting men, proudly wearing the same Tudor colors as their captain. Bearing gunpowder, wooden chests full of pikes, muskets, saltpeter, and provisions of beer, flour and salted beef, they had navigated through a choppy sea raging with storms, waiting to attack. Around him, the water, full of foam and waves, was teeming with other warships preparing to attack the steadily approaching French fleet. On one was his friend Thomas Knyvet. On another was Edward Howard, Surrey's son, whom Henry had named Lord Admiral. Charles looked out at each of the ships, buffeted by the wind, both with masts and banners emblazoned with the king's crest. He should have been comforted by the nearness of his two dearest friends as he prepared for what lay ahead. But Charles's mind was full of another thing.

Mary believed he intended to marry again. Thomas Knyvet had told him of that conversation with Edward Howard the day before they set sail about a woman in Southwark. Charles had done nothing to correct the impression he knew Mary had. He had been a fool, even for a moment, to let his mind and heart suggest to him there could be a future with the king's sister. He knew his silence would put an end to those fantasies on his and Mary's part. Ambition was one thing. Absolute madness was quite another.

Suddenly, in what felt like a moment, everything shifted. He had seen the French ships approaching for the better part of an hour. Knyvet's ship, the *Regent*, was out in front, vulnerable against them. There was a shot then that ripped through the mist and sea air. A volley of them followed between the French and English ships as they weighed anchor next to one another. Charles felt something then. A premonition? It was an ominous sensation that forced words up from his solar plexus, an order shouted out through the wind.

"Full sail, steady on course!"

If Howard's ship joined with Knyvet's, they could more boldly attack the larger French vessel and be done with it. The idea seized him with little time to see it through.

Another volley of shots rang out, then a sudden violent explosion on the French ship. There was a ripping burst of color, light and sound so powerful that it tore through his chest right to his heart with a force that sent Charles hurling onto his back. The spray-slick deck around him was peppered with debris, wood and fiery cinders, raining down like crimson snow. Charles realized the hold of the French ship must have been stuffed with gunpowder. The water and the waves were quickly littered, and the air was filled with the haunting, plaintive cries of men burning to death. In a moment that twisted before him with color and the acrid scent of burning wood and human flesh, Charles cried out as he watched in helpless agony as the fire that raged aboard the French ship jumped across to the *Regent*, caught hold and began to spread through it, ignited quickly by the English ship's own store of ammunition and gunpowder. Edward Howard, Lord Admiral, stood at the bow of his own ship, which had come alongside Charles's vessel. Both men, captains, friends, stood mere feet away, helpless to go to the aid of the *Regent* or their friend Thomas Knyvet.

The cries went on, screams of terror and agony, breaking through pandemonium and blinding horror, as both Brandon and Howard shouted at their crews to dive into the wreckage-strewn water and search for survivors. Smoke from the burning overtook them completely as Brandon directed his own crew to help him aboard the Lord Admiral's ship, anchored just next to his own. He wiped the tears away from his blackened face with the back of his hand and drew in a deep breath to try to steady himself as he walked toward Edward Howard, who stood frozen, staring at the still burning massive wreckage of two ships before them.

Charles approached him slowly as the admiral's crew carefully pulled three badly burned men onto the deck. Watching with horror, Charles very cautiously put a hand onto Howard's shoulder. But his old friend seemed not to feel it.

"It's not your fault," Charles murmured. "You could not have known."

"I am Lord Admiral . . . I should have known."

A thick gray smoke enveloped the ship completely now, hiding them from all but each other, and the stench of burning flesh was so strong that Charles was forced to cover his mouth and nose. But short, stout Edward Howard stood completely unmoving as the call from a dozen voices for bandages and fresh water rose up over the continuing cries of agony. Even as Charles gave the order to draw up anchor, Edward Howard said nothing else other than the single phrase he had already uttered.

"God help me, I should have known. . . ."

News of the gruesome death of Thomas Knyvet, and the rest of the *Regent* crew, swept through court. The shock of it extinguished the optimism of the new reign. The romance of war was quickly replaced in the minds of sheltered courtiers with the gritty reality of battle. The ladies in Mary's apartments were sympathetic to grief-stricken Jane, but there was little public comfort they could offer, since Muriel Knyvet was lady to the queen.

Thinner now than ever, pale and gaunt, Muriel wore widow's black, and Jane avoided her. At night, Mary held Jane as she wept, Mary alone knowing the truth—that someone else's husband truly had cared for Jane—and she felt the horror of the last words she had spoken to Knyvet herself. *Perhaps you should stay out at sea. . . .*

"I wish I had died with him. . . ." Jane keenly wept, safe in Mary's tight embrace that first night after hearing. "God take me . . . I feel as if I am already dead."

They lay together deep beneath the down-filled blankets and enclosed inside the tapestry draperies of Mary's bed, and Mary held her friend like a small child. Her own guilt was extreme, as if her words alone, those last few, had changed his fate. But that was foolish. She knew it. And in the moment, she felt a certain fading away of her youth and maturity begin to take its place. She had been so bound by the desire to grow up at court that, until now, Mary realized, she had embarrassingly done only the opposite, consumed as she had been by dresses, dances and flirtation and other trivial things. She had been childish. She stroked Jane's forehead tenderly now and heard a rustling of fabric beyond the doors. Servants were speaking in hushed tones. Let them talk, Mary thought, uninterested for the first time in eavesdropping. She was meant to be here with Jane. In spite of how they came together, Jane had loved Thomas, and Mary's heart went out to the pretty young girl at Eltham who had run through the gardens with her those many carefree years ago.

She was bleeding to death.

Thank the Lord God. . . . At last, an answer.

Muriel Knyvet lay motionless in the bed she had shared with Thomas, listening to the piercing wail of the newborn infant and very slowly feeling the life drain from her body. She had refused food for days, refused the doctor's potion to slow the bleeding. This was her answer. She had not looked at his child, had not touched him. Muriel already felt gone from this world. He would be someone else's to raise. As would her daughter. *Elizabeth* . . . Only the stray thought of her little girl, the image dashing across her mind, brought any sense of regret at all. Her Bess. But her eight-year-old daughter had been fathered by her first husband, John Grey, who also had died. With no tie to Thomas, sweet Bess was the only thing she would miss of this world. But, by her father, her precious girl was Lady Lisle, a viscountess. A solid match would be made for her by the king—a suitable guardian found before that. She would have a brilliant life. Pray God, though, that she would not fall in love with her husband.

Muriel closed her eyes, felt death's pull and welcomed it.

Three weeks after the death in childbirth of Muriel Knyvet, and a month after the death at sea of her husband, Mary returned to her apartments from matins and saw the tall, weary-looking man in a soiled green and white seaman's uniform. He stood in silhouette against her window, gazing out across the horizon beyond Greenwich, at the tall ships at anchor on the Thames. Outside, a heavy rain beat against the windowpanes, shaking the fogged glass. Hearing her, he turned. His beard and mustache all but obscured his more tanned, handsome face, yet his eyes had not changed, nor had the look of knowing between them. Without thinking, Mary dashed toward Charles, wrapped her arms around his neck and, overwhelmed by pity and love, began to weep.

Without fear any longer, or concern for the women who watched them, he stood there and held her tightly. His doublet and cape were rain soaked, but she could still feel the warmth of him through the layers of satin.

"I do not know what made me come here like this. I only knew I had to do it," he said huskily.

She touched his face, his beard, his lips. "If you hadn't, I would have come to you the moment I knew you had returned," she whispered into his long, matted hair that smelled of sweat and rain.

The carefree, honeyed richness of his voice, the charming smile were gone. Jane and Lady Guildford appeared at the door, their lips parted in surprise. By his haggard condition, they both could see that he had come straight from his ship. He had not even pulled off his gloves, nor removed his hat with its pale green plume. Rainwater pooled at his feet.

"Leave us," Mary said without turning around.

Joan Guildford took a single step forward and tried to object. "But, my lady—"

"Do as I say."

After they heard the door click and close behind them, Mary drew off his hat and tossed it without thinking onto the floor. Then she ran a hand back through his matted auburn hair.

"It was not your fault," she soothed, framing his bearded face with her small hands.

"I was there, I saw it. That was bad enough."

He dropped his arms from around her as Mary very gently kissed each of his cheeks.

"Thomas was in God's hands. All of you were."

She saw a little vein throb in his temple. She could not have imagined seeing him, of all people, like this. Like the rest of the court, he had been changed by what had happened. Mary kissed his face then with a soft, gentle press of her lips. Charles closed his eyes. Though he did not object, he did not move to take her into his arms again.

"Edward is still out there at sea," he finally said, his deep voice breaking. "He has vowed not to return, not to look upon the king again, until he has avenged Thomas's death."

"How could he expect to do that when the French ship burned right along with his own?"

"He feels responsible, Mary. We both do."

Looking up at him, seeing the desolation in his eyes, rimmed now with gray, Mary tried very hard to hold back her tears.

Suddenly, Charles moved to touch her face. "Don't cry for me," he murmured on a heavy sigh. "I don't deserve it."

"I am crying for us all. So many things were meant to be different."

As he pressed a kiss tenderly onto one cheek and then the other, he felt that the moment and the tenderness bore all of the love in his heart. "If Henry knew I was here now, he would surely have me banished."

"He would likely kill us both. But I don't care," she declared with all of the defiance of a young, untested heart. "You are a brave, honorable, wonderful man, and I want to be with you. . . . I am *meant* to be with you. I know it."

The objection on his tongue dissolved into the echo of her words. This mattered to him. Becoming someone better mattered in the shadow of her young, devoted gaze. Slowly then, a breath at a time, he pulled her close and drew her onto the bed with him. He kissed her once again, although this time neither of them even tried to resist. They were alone, both unmarried, and full of passion for the other. Mary opened her mouth to him, his tongue like fire as he trailed a path down from her throat to where the straight edge of lace met the rise of her breasts, and she wound her arms around him. Skillfully, he continued to arouse her with his mouth and fingers, caressing upward from her thigh. And she yielded, wanting this, wanting him. She did not realize for a moment then that he had lifted his head, arching over her, in a sudden attempt to stop himself.

"You are not one to be used like this," he declared on a ragged breath.

"Why do you not let me be the judge?"

"I must judge for us both," he countered, then turned onto his back and closed his eyes.

He was telling her it was too soon. And though she did not want to believe it, he knew that Mary believed it too. They lay together like that, a powerful intimacy begun between them. Mary laced her fingers with his and inhaled the scent of him. Powerful. Manly. Undeniably sensual. Then she moved a fingertip across the large onyx ring he wore on his finger. She had noticed it before and wondered at it. Bordered by silver, it was flat and round like a mirror.

"That is a magnificent ring."

"It is the only thing I have of my father. When I was a boy and would wear it to think of my father, the king used to say that if I looked very deeply I could see myself reflected back in it. Not just as I was, but as I wished to become."

"That sounds awfully poetic for a man like my father."

He watched her gaze at it in the openly fascinated way of

a little girl, and he bit back a charmed smile. "So what do you see in it?"

"Promise you won't laugh?" Mary looked at him earnestly, her eyes wide. "I see myself . . . and all I wish *you* to become with me."

"That is a great deal to see in such a small thing."

"Perhaps it is because I want very much for it to be there."

Her mind and her tongue were as quick as any adult, but he saw that her spirit and her innocence were still that of such a child. The combination had a powerful effect on his heart. God help him for how completely in love with her he had fallen. Charles began to gaze at the black onyx along with her as if they could conjure the images both of them sought.

"And do you see what my father saw?"

"I see *you* reflected back at me."

He felt foolish—a lovesick boy. This was not how his life was supposed to be. He was meant to be ruthless in order to gain the advantages he still craved. Since Henry had yet to make him a marquess or an earl, the only path to significant riches was still women. He would be expected to marry again soon. No one at court would understand what he and Mary felt, and even if they did they would not respect it. Anything like love between them was still, and always would be, forbidden. Yet in spite of all that, in spite of everything, all that they both fought against and feared had already happened.

He had known it was true, of course. He had only needed to wait for proof. The Earl of Surrey stood stealthily watching Lady Guildford and Mistress Popincourt leave Mary's apartments only moments after Charles Brandon had entered them. His angular face and smooth silver hair had been hidden by the shadows in the curtained alcove at the end of the corridor. He met the Duke of Buckingham there, still his partner in the same cause.

"So then? Is it true?"

"If not yet, it soon shall be," the earl said distastefully, still cautious not to be overheard. *No one likes the man who brings bad news,* Sophocles said, and Thomas Howard lived by that maxim. He believed that absolutely, so he must take the utmost care in this.

"Is it not time that the king was told? Time that both Brandon, and Wolsey for his complicity, support and silence in this sordid affair, were diminished in His Highness's eyes?"

The Earl of Surrey paused suddenly, looking at Buckingham. In spite of the fact that he had even married Buckingham's daughter to enhance his position, the duke had long been Surrey's keenest rival for place and power—the only duke at court. No matter how they joined in this, Surrey must never forget that. "Your Grace trusts me enough suddenly to plan an ambush with you?" he sneered.

"I trusted you with my daughter, did I not?"

Thomas Howard shook his head. "Ambition does make odd bedfellows."

"Not so much ambition, Thomas, as self-defense," Buckingham corrected with a strangely complicitous nod. "If we do not tell the king, and he discovers it some other way, we may look as guilty as Wolsey is about to."

It had not been a social invitation. Charles knew that well enough as he sat in one of his uncle's exceedingly uncomfortable tapestry-covered chairs in a room equally designed to make him uncomfortable. Nevertheless, when Thomas Brandon issued his nephew a summons, his appearance was nonnegotiable, for all of the times Charles had gone there, hat in his hand. There was always Anne and her welfare to be concerned about, no matter what else. As usual, Thomas kept him waiting. Charles knew, of course, that his uncle did this to set him off his game. But this time Charles was determined not to be unnerved by whatever the old snake felt it necessary to say in person.

Ten days after his return to court from sea duty, Charles looked up casually as Thomas Brandon came with labored steps, leaning heavily on a silver-tipped walking stick, into the room at last. He was purposefully imposing, in a costume of claret-colored velvet with black slashings and a heavy jewel-studded neck chain. Stiff-backed and stone-faced, his uncle sank into the chair facing Charles. He drew up a waiting goblet of wine, drank from it, then at last spoke.

"Well, then, to the point, shall we?"

"The sooner the better," Charles replied blandly.

"It does not do the family name at all well for you to be making so indelible a mark at court these days and continue on with no title whatsoever."

"Difficult for me to do otherwise when *you* acquired everything of value in the family, Uncle." The sounds of servants walking past in the corridor beyond the door filled the sudden, awkward silence as Thomas Brandon's stare went cold.

"I also acquired power enough, Charles, to see to the offer of a wardship for you and with it the potential use of a title all your own."

Charles struggled not to show his surprise. Thomas Brandon had never done anything for anyone without there being strings attached. Everyone at court knew about the death of Sir John Grey, Viscount Lisle, and the subsequent passing of the little girl's mother, Muriel Knyvet, in childbirth. The daughter had therefore inherited a title and fortune. A great unease began to snake its way up Charles's spine. There had been enough jockeying for the acquisition of her guardianship since his return to set court tongues wagging.

"Elizabeth Grey?"

"The very same. And I have it on good authority that His Highness will grant it."

Charles involuntarily sprung from his chair. "I do not wish that particular title."

Thomas arched a single silvery brow in surprise. "You are too good to be Viscount Lisle, are you?"

"To access the title I must become betrothed to her."

"That *is* how it customarily works."

"Lady Grey is but eight years old!"

"At least you shall not need to question her experience." Thomas Brandon was delighting in this predicament, Charles could see by his indelicate sneer and the finger he placed beside his chin. "You seem rather unappreciative, my boy, for one with few similar options."

That much, he realized, was true. While his company was well favored by the king, Charles was still the poor relation among the most intimate circle, and no number of positions Henry bestowed upon him changed that fact. In spite of all he had obtained in the last few years, this opportunity was not to be matched.

"And, after all, it is only a wardship we are acquiring for now. Not a wife."

Charles studied him for a moment. There was not a single thing he actually liked about his uncle. "We?"

"You know my policy well enough. Of course it shall be a loan for the time being. But with John Grey's sizeable fortune stuffed into your coffers you shall at last be able to return to me everything you and Anne owe me, and then some."

"My own uncle charging me interest?"

"Let us not forget that I took pity on you, boy, back when there was no one else. If not for my kindness all these years, you would be tending hogs in Cheapside, and that sister of yours would be begging in the streets with a mask over her poor scarred face."

Charles was unsure if he felt more revulsion or anger at that particular moment. This key opportunity was more like a deal with the devil. "I must have time to think."

"Considering other options?" Thomas asked pointedly because he knew well enough there were no other options available. He let the question hang there for a moment, then he lowered his gaze to add, "Do not confuse my goodwill with affection, Charles. You may be my brother's son, but he is my brother long dead. Since another Brandon is to remain at court in the company of the king, he shall do so appropriately titled, and not as my poor relation. In your current state you are an embarrassment to me and a drain on my coffers. I shall expect you to take the offer by week's end so that I may submit it to the king's offices for approval."

Thomas Brandon stood with his nephew only then, like a punctuation mark to all he had said, and proceeded toward the door through which he had come. As always, the meeting was terminated without so much as a polite farewell.

"So, then. Tell me all about Mary."

"The princess Mary?"

"The very one you speak about ceaselessly when you are here." His sister sweetly laughed, and then touched his knee. "Yes, the very one."

As he always did after he had seen his uncle, Charles cleansed his heart and his mind by a visit with his sister, Anne. They sat together in the cozy little fire-stoked nook near the door, made comfortable by two padded chairs covered in tapestry fabric, and two goblets of rich Gascony wine.

"Well, let me see. . . . After my accident in the tournament, she and her companion did bring a confection to my chamber. And then we spoke for what seemed an eternity after my return from the sea, until the same lady did draw her from her apartments, she said, for propriety's sake."

"That would be Mistress Popincourt?" Anne chuckled more boldly. Jane's behavior at court was no secret to Brandon and thus his sister knew every detail he knew. "Mary loves her, Anne. So I must also."

She turned back to her brother's gaze. "So then, is Her Grace as caring as she is lovely?"

"Every bit, I am afraid."

"Does she yet know your heart?"

"No, and she shall know nothing beyond my attraction to her. I would not do that to her. Besides, that exercise in futility does not become my court reputation as a profligate at all," he joked. Yet the cavalier tone he had long maintained when Mary was the subject slipped away just a little. Partially, he knew it was because pretense was difficult with Anne. Partially, it was because he was bursting to tell someone his heart and, in all the world, his sister was the only one he trusted fully.

"If my memory serves me," she observed without a judging inflection, "the lady Mary will be seventeen just before Lent. There seems not so much difference between you now."

"No matter what I feel, she is the king's sister. Her age will change, the rest will not."

"Yet are you not his closest friend?"

"I and approximately ten other gentlemen are his closest friends."

"I fear you give yourself too little credit, brother."

"And you give me too much," he declared, drawing up her hand and kissing it tenderly. "Although I love you with every fiber of my being for it, the truth is I have been insufferably self-indulgent these past years. I am a man with a reputation at court. I have done things for my own advancement that most find objectionable at best. No, my lady Mary is not to be sullied by the likes of me. The king trusts me with her and I should like to keep it like that."

"And what if she actually returns your affections, brother? What then?"

"It would mean not a thing more than it does at this moment. You know perfectly well her life is not her own. Nor is her heart. I owe every bit of the favor her brother has shown me for remembering that."

"But if the king does cancel her betrothal to the Prince of Castile, as you believe he may do, what then? Can you just sit idly by and watch His Highness choose a new husband? Can a viscount not ask more rightfully for the hand of a princess than a man with no title at all?"

He sank back in his chair, studying her as a warm autumnal breeze blew in upon them through the window, fluttering the curtains. "Uncle was here?"

"He visits occasionally, yes. News that is of benefit to anyone in our family seems worthy to him for making the trip. So when you are Viscount Lisle can you not more rightfully broach the subject with the king? God knows, if there were ever anyone ambitious enough to do it, it is you."

"Not when she can have a prince, Anne. No, I'm done with marriage for a while. This time I shall be wise. Perhaps by the time my little ward grows up I shall have repaired my reputation and be ready to marry again. But not before then."

It was a declaration delivered so forcefully he nearly believed it himself.

Chapter Ten

Look with favor on a bold beginning.

—Virgil

December 31, 1512, Greenwich Palace

"I am going to approve the petition, granting you the wardship to make you Viscount Lisle." Henry smiled proudly as he sat in his private cabinet, at his leather-topped desk, the walls around him lined with prized maps that he had begun to collect. Beside him, Edward Stafford, the Duke of Buckingham, lingered near the ornamental cage by the window where the king kept two nightingales.

"But most key to what I have arranged for us will happen this spring, when we attack France by ground. I want you with me, Charles, to fight beside me. I shall announce properly at the banquet this evening that, as marshal, you shall be the one to command all the English army."

"After what happened at sea, I am not certain I deserve such an honor. I don't suppose I will ever get over that," he said haltingly. What he meant was that he was not certain he wished to get over it. Sometimes guilt was a good

156

thing. It could strengthen a man. If it did not kill him first.

"Well, you had better try. That was not your fault. Howard was in charge and *he* let me down, not you. He has been right to stay at sea. You are my dearest friend, Charles. I trust you with my life and perhaps I should have trusted you instead of him with the admiral's post. You have proven your loyalty to me again and again. Since you are the only one worthy of the honor, and the responsibility, you are to be appointed High Marshal as we go to war in spring. That is the end of it."

Charles was stunned at Henry's insistence, considering his own youth and inexperience. There was no greater honor, no bigger military responsibility than overseeing the entire English army. But he knew well and understood Henry's passion for the chivalric code and the romance of war, which he had gained from his father. It was in part that legacy that was urging him on, pressing him to attack the French for land that had once belonged to the English.

"But the advancement to viscount. I don't really know if—"

"It is a sound elevation, especially as you go out to command our army. You shall have an annuity of twenty pounds from it as well. I only regret I did not think of it first." He shrugged.

The money would barely cover his clothing bill, and he still owed a small fortune not only to the previous king's estate but to his uncle. "Very well, I do wish the wardship and title, Harry," he said in an intentionally familiar tone. "What fool would not? I just do not wish the wife to go with it."

"Is *that* the problem?" Henry threw back his head and laughed deeply, his eyes lighting. "Well, based on the age of

Lady Grey, my friend, you have time enough to decide about that. Or is it that you have someone else in mind?"

The question surprised him, and for one mad moment, he actually considered answering truthfully. "There is a certain girl of the court. . . ."

"Well, then pursue her, man. Ho, by all means. You are no longer a married man. Of course you will need to seek my approval for a marriage of any sort, but you do have it on sound authority that the King of England has a soft spot in his heart for you."

Henry wrapped his powerful arm across Brandon's shoulder as they strode away from Buckingham, who he could tell had been listening, out of the chamber together and then down the length of the impressively portrait-lined hall. "Besides," Henry remarked, "while the child has suited your purpose up until now, I actually have someone far more spectacular in mind for you myself than young Lady Grey."

"Do you?"

"It would be a rather daring match—even a bit scandalous once I propose it—so we shall just wait and see how things progress?"

"Well, you certainly have my interest."

"Ask me not to identify her now, but if all goes according to plan you will be more powerful and wealthy than Buckingham and Surrey together, once the match is made. Those two are thick as thieves about something lately, and I tell you, I am not amused by it," said Henry with a sly smile.

Charles waited for her outside the chapel after the noon prayers, completely taken up by the unfathomable thought that Henry might actually intend Mary for him. He stood secreted behind a stone column, head pressed back, hands at his sides. There was so much against them that he needed to hear how she felt about them. He must know if it was anything close to his own affection for her. Only then would he know how to find the courage to talk to Henry. Mary came upon him in the same instant as Jane turned away to talk to Lady Guildford.

Mary was preciously alone. He seized the moment, gripping her arm and drawing her with him behind the column. Silently, he took her face into his hands and kissed her deeply. When she looked up at him, he saw a devoted smile that gave him courage.

"I believe I am in love with you, and, wild as it seems, if you return my affection, there just may be a way for us to be together," he said in a deep voice that was just above a whisper. "It is important to me that you know that."

"I have been in love with you since I was a very little girl," Mary said, her own whispered words breaking with pointed, youthful sincerity.

"There is everything against either of us feeling this way."

"Particularly a king."

The truth of it made him smile and Charles kissed her again, tenderly. They were close, wound in one another's arms. "It is a good thing I am going away for a little while."

"How can that ever be good?"

"We need time to consider everything."

"I need consider nothing, Charles. I know where my heart lies—where it ever shall lie."

He smiled at her naive devotion, feeling another even stronger rush of love. "You are still very young but you must trust me. There is a great deal more than two hearts to consider."

"None of it matters."

"All of it matters when you are the king's sister."

And with that, he kissed her quickly once again, then left. Mary closed her eyes, calming her breathing as she stood a minute longer behind the column.

Mary had never liked the Duke of Buckingham, so when he came upon her from behind a separate column she was not surprised to realize he had eavesdropped on their exchange of devotion. Buckingham was too ambitious, far beyond anyone else at court, she had always thought. Even beyond what drove Charles. He had married off his daughter to the Earl of Surrey simply because she would become a Howard, and it had helped his own standing with the king. He did everything with the same single-minded devotion.

"He will never be able to marry you, you know," he said to her now.

Mary gave him a cursory glance. "I have no idea what you are talking about."

"As one who has watched you grow up, I am concerned only for your welfare, my lady Mary. I was not the only one to see you steal away with Brandon as you just did. Would you think the king would not be concerned as well?"

"You know nothing of what is between my brother and I. I do not fear what the gossips may say to him against me," she replied angrily.

"I think it only fair to warn you that this particular gossip has spread through court like wildfire. Brandon is to be made Viscount Lisle, and the only way to do that is to make her not just his ward but to actually become betrothed to Lady Elizabeth Grey, Viscountess Lisle. He has agreed to it, my lady, and your brother has granted it. He was informed of it this morning. As someone who feels the affection of a father for you, I felt you had a right to know what you may be getting into."

Mary faltered and reached out to brace herself on the column. True to form, the duke seemed somehow to want to work this to his advantage, though Mary could not be certain how or why. One was never quite certain of anyone's motives at court, since few were rarely all that they seemed.

"You are mistaken about Charles."

"I heard Sir Thomas Brandon speaking with Wolsey about it myself. Planning, my lady."

Mary sank against the column then. She felt an utter fool. She had believed him. Loved him with her whole heart. *I feel such a fool, chasing after him like a lovesick puppy.*

Seeing the sickened expression and the way the color had drained from her face, Buckingham softened. "You are a girl in bloom of first love, and he is a grown man who should know better, my lady. No one could ever fault you for that," he said, sounding more genuine than even he had expected to be.

Perhaps he is what they say, and not what I have let myself believe him to be. . . .

That harsh thought raced through Mary's mind as, sitting

beside Katherine with Jane Popincourt, Lady Surrey, Lady Monteagle and Lady Guildford, she watched her brother enter the banquet hall in all of the pomp and pageantry to which he had swiftly become accustomed. Henry looked fit and regal in a magnificent green velvet doublet with gold slashes, encrusted with jewels, ornamented by a sweeping gold cape. His muscular legs accentuated by tight green hose beneath his velvet breeches were fashionably padded with horsehair. On his head was a plumed, green velvet beret studded with a great square ruby. Everyone sank into deep curtsies and bows as he strode by with a confident smile.

The court had had little to celebrate since the death of Thomas Knyvet. The subsequent declaration by their friend Edward Howard, that he would not return from sea until Knyvet's death was avenged, had only intensified the somber mood at court. Everyone wore black. Henry had ordered the temporary cessation of his beloved musical consorts, and even music at meals, out of respect for his friends. But that was all over now. It was New Year's Eve, and the king meant to cast off the old for a celebration of the new.

Surprisingly, walking directly behind Henry, with his long, confident stride, Charles entered the hall. He was wearing a costume nearly identical to the king's: green velvet, gold slashings, gold cape. Conceived by Henry, as only it could be, it was a grand statement of not only their brotherhood, but of Brandon's ever-growing power and influence—something Henry clearly wanted everyone to know. As the king approached the queen and bowed ceremoniously to her, Mary saw that Charles had paused to speak to Lady Monteagle's young, pretty daughter, Eleanor. They were laughing, and he was leaning in toward her. Was he even thinking of her? Would he think of her later tonight? Tomorrow? Mary wondered as she watched them, and felt her stomach twist when he did not soon move on.

Hot spiced wine was being brought around in jeweled cups by an army of servants holding them on gleaming silver trays. To Mary, the scent of it suddenly was noxious. She could smell the cinnamon and sugar mingling with candle smoke and burning wood. She could hear the foolish girl giggling at something Charles said. Mary watched her reach out to touch his arm. Lord, why did she have to care so much what he did?

Henry, who stood a few feet away, lifted his cup in a toast and as he did the room fell silent. His voice was commanding in its rich baritone as it echoed through the vast hall. "For his service to me, I command that Charles Brandon is henceforth officially Master of the Horse, which also makes him my esquire, giving him complete control over all of the royal stables. Those of you who know the importance of my horses to me will understand the great significance of this reward to my dearest, most important friend."

Wolsey lifted a jeweled hand to his chin. So I have Surrey, Buckingham *and* now Brandon's ever-growing influence to balance, he said to himself, knowing that the gauntlet and race for Henry's closest favor had effectively just been thrown down to them all. In the face of so multifaceted a challenge, the title of Royal Almoner did not anymore seem enough to sate his own ambition. Like every other courtier, Thomas Wolsey wanted more, and he meant to get it by being just a little bit wiser than the three competitors. Unlike Surrey and

Buckingham, Wolsey believed that he would gain far more by subduing Charles Brandon through friendship than by trying to vanquish him, as the other two were doing. It was a calculated risk, but success took daring as well innovation.

Dancing began and Mary lost Charles amid the turning, bowing and swirling of velvet skirts and the glitter of gold and jewels. Knowing about the wardship had changed everything for her. How could a man like him—one who had known so many women, and used them all—truly care for her? He might covet the princess, but could a man like Charles Brandon ever truly love the girl? If she remained at court, Mary had no doubt what would happen between them. She had seen too much of Jane's own sad story to believe it would be any different for her. She would not be the first virgin he had bedded, or the first woman to whom he would become unfaithful. Even so, she still found herself searching for him through the throng of dancers, through the laughter and the music. She was made dizzy by it all as Wolsey leaned in to speak.

"It appears that Mistress Popincourt could certainly use an escape to the country," he calmly observed of Mary's friend, who was dancing woodenly with the Earl of Surrey's elder son, Thomas. Her face was devoid of emotion or enjoyment as she did. "Perhaps you could as well. Clear your minds. Both of you."

Until then, Mary had been so taken up by watching Charles that she had not even realized Wolsey was sitting beside her, or that the weight of his significant presence was pressing in on her. Mary looked at him then, the kind, full face—the fleshy, slightly veined cheeks and sharp black eyes—which had once seemed like a father's to her and was just now slightly irritating. Mary looked at him fully. "Leave court?"

"Only for a little while. Leave the things at court that trouble you. Give yourself time to consider," he amended.

She paused a moment. "You know, don't you?"

"I have always known, child. And I am here for you anytime you need to speak about him to someone you can trust. Perhaps just have me listen. I am tolerably good at that, as well. There is a lovely house I have just purchased, called Hampton Court, in Herefordshire that needs checking in on. It is, my lady Mary, an earnest offer from a well-meaning friend."

At least he had not said, like so many others, that he felt himself like a father to her. In spite of the fact that she felt closer to Thomas Wolsey than any other of the men at her brother's court, she could not have tolerated the duplicity in that just now. The room was stifling and the dizziness it caused was making her ill. Charles was dancing with Lady Monteagle's daughter, with her long, shimmering golden hair and clear sparkling skin. Was he trying to make her jealous? He seemed to be ignoring her entirely now that he was a man soon betrothed to his ward. What did it mean? The Duke of Buckingham's words, and now Wolsey's as well, swam in what felt like the thickening clot of mud building in her head. Her heart and her fantasy were making everything more than it was. He was committed once again. She was betrothed. There was no future for them, only heartbreak if they were alone and she let him do what she knew he wanted to do. She had only to look upon Jane's history to see that. When Wolsey reached over to squeeze her hand in that familiar gesture of his, Mary closed her eyes. In response, Wolsey smiled to himself but Mary did not see that.

Thomas Wolsey's grand country estate could not be a more perfect destination. He had marked time for days, waiting for just the right moment to step in and offer it to her. It was like one of the king's favorite dances—timing, with each step, was everything and Mary had needed to be at her most vulnerable. Brandon was close to the goal he sought and if Wolsey was to oversee things, he must intervene now. He genuinely liked Brandon. Always had. And, unlike his two opponents, Wolsey was not entirely certain that what was between Brandon and the king's sister could, or would, be stopped simply by the two men wielding their combined power against it. On the contrary, Wolsey knew that by befriending the would-be lovers at a key moment, his loyalty to them above reproach, the three of them could become a triumvirate of power to which neither Buckingham or Surrey could ever come near.

The next morning, he waited near the entrance to Mary's apartments. Like a moth to a flame, he knew Brandon would come as well, and he did. Wolsey closed his prayer book with a little snap and advanced, his red silk shift the only sound as he walked.

"She has gone to Herefordshire, my boy. It was for Jane Popincourt's sake—and for hers as well."

"Did she ask you to wait here and speak to me like this?"

"I care for the princess Mary as if she were my own

daughter. I know her heart. She loves you and you are in love with her."

"It is true."

Wolsey pressed a deliberate hand onto Brandon's shoulder. "Then let her go for now. No good can come of it for the moment. If she is meant to be yours one day, God will light a clear path and I shall help you find it. I know not why, but something tells me the marriage with the Prince of Castile will not happen. But for now, while the king is so set upon it, you press her into an impossible situation when she must do her duty to England."

Charles did not argue further. Wolsey had convinced him that he was right. She must go with Jane. He must go to France. That was all the future there was for Charles and Mary just now. All that there could be until the time was right.

On the eve of Henry's departure for France, on his mission to aid in the Holy Church's recovery of Bordeaux and to gain back for England that which had been lost at the legendary battle of Agincourt a century before, he knelt on cold stone inside the royal chapel. He lowered his head as he received Wolsey's exceedingly reverently delivered Latin blessing, and the melodic sound of the murmured words was a tonic to the fear overwhelming him. Fanciful thoughts, through the mists of time, of Sir Galahad, Lancelot and Henry V, had been replaced with trepidation and even a hint of dread. The French were a powerful force and would not surrender land easily no matter how methodical or powerful was his strategy. But chivalric glory was the only way to win respect with his powerful allies, Maximilian, Pope Julius and Ferdinand, from which his youth and inexperience had so far kept him.

"God grant me the strength and the wisdom of my father, and those who came before us both," he murmured like a prayer. "Let me be half the warrior king that he was."

Piously, he made the sign of the cross, drew in a breath, then stood and went to bid farewell to the queen, who was pregnant again. He found her alone in her bedchamber, a collection of maps of Europe tacked up on the walls. They were similar to his, yet most of these were written over with what looked like routes or directions. There were books lying open on top of her bed—books about war—a large statue of her patron saint, Catherine, and between the maps a large Spanish cross hung. When Katherine came to him, he saw that she was dressed for travel, in a long rose-colored riding jacket over her dress, bulging in front, and a simple unadorned hat. She clutched a pair of fawn brown riding gloves in her clean, jewel-free hand. Her dark eyes glittered with commitment.

"It is impossible, Katherine."

"But I want to go with you, Hal. I know I could actually be a help to you. I have studied naval strategy! I know all about the French. I am the daughter of a warrior queen. You know my heritage. I ache for my chance to prove myself, as you do. Our chance is now! And you were the one who entrusted me with writing the dispatches to Venice. I could advise you as we go along."

He touched her softly rounded belly gently to calm her. "No, *mi amore*. It is not safe for you in your condition. We must both think first of the child."

"My place is by your side. Other aides have gone."

"But not the mother of the next king of England," he reminded her tenderly when he saw too much desperation in her passionate, black Spanish eyes. This was her third pregnancy in four years without a living child, and they both knew how serious it was that she soon produce an heir who could survive. "Besides, you are to be regent here in my absence."

Her intense expression changed quickly to one of marked surprise. "Regent?"

"Who else has studied the situation as you have?"

He could see her overcome with pride, and the disappointment withered beneath it. The proud and wise daughter of Ferdinand and Isabella would finally be called upon to do more than produce a child. Henry valued his wife—he loved her deeply—and he wanted her to know that without doubt. This was his gift to her. Now if only she would give him a son.

Chapter Eleven

The common folk do not go to war of their own accord but are driven to it by the madness of kings.

—Sir Thomas More

August 1513, Lille, France

By late summer on a hot and dry day as Henry sat astride a magnificent white Barbary horse, caparisoned in tooled silver and crimson velvet, gilded stirrups hanging from his saddle, he rode victoriously through the countryside, Charles, as always, right beside him.

The young girls of the town followed behind bearing garlands of flowers. Behind them were attendants and forces that were strung out for miles. Numbering nearly a thousand riders were his courtiers and servants, including six hundred guardsmen, over thirty of his physicians, his pages and his secretaries. He was also accompanied by a personal bowyer, a trumpeter and his own minstrels, then gunners and blacksmiths to keep the weapons working and the camps comfortable. Behind them rode his favorites, the Duke of Buckingham and Thomas Wolsey, brought along for his ability to deal and negotiate with the French. Wolsey's own motivation for coming had been to ensure that Buckingham did not steal too much ground with the king.

"Not at all bad for a summer's work," Brandon leaned over to remark behind a hand, gloved and studded with silver.

Henry smiled, and waved to the crowds surging forward around them. A moment before, just as they passed beneath the city gates, a herald in royal green livery had ridden up beside the king with an urgent dispatch. The news was somber; Edward Howard had been killed at sea, trying to avenge the death of Thomas Knyvet and to revive his honor with the king. But Henry had little time to grieve, especially for a friend he believed had disappointed him.

This was a moment to savor, for which he had waited all of his life. They had challenged the French and they had been victorious. Advised to protect himself by dashing out ahead of the trouble, Henry had refused, enduring instead the entire battle with his soldiers. After fighting in the dust-choked mists, nine standards were taken and dozens of notable French prisoners who would be held for ransom, before the French troops sped hotly into retreat.

Henry had single-handedly changed the world's view of himself, riding bravely before his men, creating a legend of his own—the conquering hero, taking back first Therouanne, then Tournai and five other walled towns that had once belonged to the English. It was not the French crown, which he coveted, but it was a beginning. Now that he had tasted victory, Henry had every intention of returning to France the next spring for a second campaign, and conquering more of the country. The respect he had so craved he had at last received. At the taking of Therouanne, Emperor Maximilian, who had attended the English during their victory, rode at a discreet distance into the town behind Henry. It was a symbolic gesture whose significance was not lost on Henry.

Now forty miles away, just outside the town of Lille, Henry walked into the massive tent erected there, tanned and handsome, amid dozens of candle lamps flickering on crisp white damask. He was weary and still wearing light armor over a doublet of cloth of silver, but at least he had been doused with the scent of ambergris by one of his gentlemen servants and his hair had been combed by another.

He drew in a breath to collect himself, then wrapped a weary arm across Charles Brandon's shoulder. They were comrades in arms as they moved deeper into the huge, magnificently ornamented tent. Their hostess had constructed it in a vast, open meadow surrounded by flaming torches and urns of flowers and plants. Their hostess, Margaret, Regent of the Netherlands and daughter of the emperor, Maximilian, sat now in the center of the tent on a chair, cushioned in purple velvet, to receive them.

She was mildly attractive, Henry thought, seeing her for the first time. For a woman of her age she was remarkably slender and tall, with chestnut hair and green eyes that in this light looked to him slightly exotic. He lifted the glass of heady *vin de Beaune* that was offered to him, and drank deeply from it to help bring back his carefree smile. Then he and Brandon went to her together.

The triumph Henry felt over the day must be balanced with decorum and enough humor to make an impression. It was important to him. While he was politically allied with the emperor against France, the issue of Mary's marriage still lingered unresolved between them. Henry felt desperate to save political face, and to solidify the still uncertain liaison between his sister and Margaret's nephew, Charles of Castile. At the moment, ingratiating himself with the lovely widow before him seemed the most expedient path to achieving that. When she invited him to congratulate him on his victory—and presumably to discuss her nephew's upcoming marriage to Mary—he readily agreed. Watching her eyes follow Brandon, then flicker with interest at his irritatingly handsome friend, a thought occurred to Henry. Margaret stood and curtsied just slightly as Henry took her hand.

"Lady Margaret, it is an honor." He turned to Brandon beside him then. "You will have heard of my dearest friend, Charles Brandon, Viscount Lisle?"

She nodded, smiled. "Your reputation does precede you, Lord Lisle."

"I hope only the better parts."

"Ah, yet those parts would hold little fascination for me."

Her eyes were wide and pretended an innocence that was slightly appealing even to Henry as he watched the exchange.

"Dance with her, Brandon," Henry said impulsively, his smile made wide by the second goblet of wine he had been given. "That is, *if* she will dance with *you*."

Henry watched the slight girlish flush rise onto Margaret's cheeks. Looking at her, a woman of thirty-three now, it was still easy to see she had been lovely once. Her mouth and her eyes wrinkled at the corners, deepening when she smiled, but he liked that about her. It marked a life fully lived, he thought, the bad and the good. He also saw Brandon's charismatic response—that charming smile, a hand easily extended. He always secretly marveled at his friend's unfailing ability with women. He had known Brandon was good—he had not forgotten how good, but it had been a long time since he had seen it played out before him, and never so easily on a woman so influential.

Henry knew the rumor about Brandon and Mary. But he believed the idea that it was anything beyond flirtation was simply a creative fantasy wrought by bored courtiers. Mary knew her duty too well for that. She would marry the emperor's grandson, as she was prepared to do, and that would be the end of it. But was it actually possible that what Buckingham had said was right? Could Brandon have designs on Mary beyond that charming brand of flirtation of his? Henry knew well enough that his friend was ambitious; he certainly had no illusions about that. Yet to think Charles would be foolish enough to covet Henry's most prized possession seemed impossible.

As quickly as he allowed the thought that Buckingham had set in his mind, Henry stubbornly refused it. No, Charles, his dear friend, would never be so great a fool. He was charming and ambitious, not stupid. But if any man had the ability to make an emperor's daughter fall in love with him and face the challenge of convincing that same ruler that a Master of the Horse was a fit partner for his daughter—it was Charles Brandon. Seeing him with her now, Henry was certain of it. A middle-aged widow seemed just vulnerable enough to make such a notion not seem entirely absurd. Binding Brandon to Margaret in order to ensure Mary's marriage at last to the Prince of Castile—now that would be like cream rising to the top of a rich cup of milk. Charles Brandon was probably the only man in the world who could make a lonely widow convince her powerful father that such an arrangement was her idea.

Henry sat comfortably, watching them both with a discerning eye as they made their way across the vast high tent to the area set up for dancing by torchlight on grand Turkish carpets. He allowed the fantasy of it all to blossom fully in his mind. Henry smiled to himself, noticing then that Buckingham, agile and wiry, had been quick to sit beside him, occupying the seat that Wolsey had been lumbering awkwardly forward trying to take. His almoner stood for a moment, chin pressed into his neck, bushy brows fused, staring disgruntled at a row of chairs all taken up before he turned and found a seat several places away. Henry pretended not to notice the silent, all-too-common little power play. There was far too much infighting at court to take any of it. It was his courtiers' problem, not his. Besides, right now he was far too fascinated by the wonderful little possibility of a dual marriage.

"You dance impressively for a commoner, my lord," Henry heard Margaret remark of Charles with a slightly giddy giggle as he bowed to her in time with the music.

"And Your Highness dances even more impressively *with* a commoner. It cannot be easy."

"You make it feel so, my lord."

They turned again, bowed again, and the song was at an end. As they walked together to the dais, Henry greeted them, his youthful smile broad and beaming. As Margaret turned to speak with the Duke of Buckingham, Henry leaned in next to Brandon as he sank into the chair reserved for him at Henry's other side.

"Did you enjoy her?"

"She is a tolerably good dancer."

"She is also a very important widow."

Brandon chuckled at that and took a swallow of his own wine from a goblet waiting for him beside a brimming bowl of fruit. "I have had my fill of widows, Henry, if *you* remember."

"This one is the Regent of the Netherlands, which would be rather a grand step up from your usual prey."

"A step up for whom?" Brandon focused on Henry then, and was silent for a moment amid the strains of another song that had just begun and which masked their conversation.

"I know that look." Henry smiled cleverly.

"A look only of concern, I assure you."

"Why would it be so? You are an unmarried man and a remarkably ambitious one at that."

"Emperors' daughters do not align themselves with knights, or even viscounts."

"Ah, but they *do*, from time to time, align themselves with important dukes."

Brandon sharpened his gaze as he fingered the silver wine goblet. "And do you know of a particular important young duke who is yet unmarried?"

"Your service to me has been invaluable, Charles, as has your friendship. You know that. You deserve an ample reward for this campaign." Henry toyed with the signet ring on his forefinger. "I had planned to announce it when we returned to England, but there is no reason my most trusted friend in the world should not know my intention now."

"You are making a Master of the Horse into a duke?"

"I am seeing my greatest friend in the world made Duke of Suffolk. I say this only by way of telling you that, should you come to have an interest in a certain beautiful princess"— he began to smile broadly until he saw the odd expression that dawned on Charles's face, one almost of surprise—"and if she were to return that interest, you should know that your status would put you within reach of such a liaison."

"Your Highness's faith in me is an honor to which I shall try to be worthy," he only said.

"I have no doubt." Henry smiled. "Because I *do* have the utmost faith in you."

In the semidarkness of dawn, Charles sat hunched, legs sprawled and bare, on the edge of the bed beside a sleeping Margaret, and raked his hands back through his hair. He should be enormously proud of himself, knowing he had not lost his touch. Instead, he was angry and not a little disgusted. He could not look back at her sleeping there peacefully beside him. He could blame what had happened last night on too much of her sweet French wine, or the lateness of the hour. He could try that. . . . He could blame it on the powerful needs of a man like himself, or even on her willingness.

In the night, a servant had slipped in and neatly arranged the regent's dress, her petticoats, her stockings and her small jeweled slippers. But, in a clear, silent statement, his clothing had been left in a pile on the floor as he had discarded them beside her bed. Charles frowned and pushed away the surge of memories filling his mind. Henry had asked him to consider marrying Margaret, not to bed with her. But the only person he wished ever to marry was the one woman he could not have. The same one who had ridden off to Hampton Court without so much as a farewell. That small bit of defiance he could still maintain had taunted him into what had happened last night, and he almost made himself believe it.

"It is a lovely morning," Margaret said on a sigh, her voice slightly honeyed and rich, yet, mercifully, nothing at all like Mary's.

The sound of it brought Charles back to the reality of his life, and his situation, very boldly, as the sun through the windows deepened to pink and gold.

He felt her hands on his shoulders then and her breasts against his back. "Tell me, Charles, what would you like to do on this glorious day?"

Would that I could just see Mary's face instead smiling back at me when I turned around . . . feel her sweet breath moving through my hair . . . know that my day, all of it, would be spent in her company.

"I, of course, must serve at the king's pleasure."

"Has he not an ample supply of courtiers and advisers to call upon for that?"

"For some reason, His Highness considers me indispensable."

"I can see where he would."

Brandon stood and turned back to her, determined to face what he had done by regarding her fully in the broad light of morning. The emperor's daughter lay on her side, her breasts full and her curved hips slender. Her hair, obviously once a rich chestnut brown, now bearing shafts of silver, fell to the side across the spray of pillows behind her. He thought then, cruelly, perhaps, how she had seemed so much more attractive by lamplight. She held out her warm, slim hand, and for a moment he actually considered taking it and letting her draw him back against her. But that would solve nothing, and it would complicate everything. It certainly would not ease the ache battering his heart and closing off his mind to the honor Henry had paid him by offering a dukedom, as well as a regal marriage, and the trust and love that it implied.

She fingered a coil of his tousled hair just above his neck in a seductive way that drew him back to the moment. "Would I embarrass you, Charles, if I told you that you remind me a great deal of my husband?"

Charles stopped for a moment, surprised. He looked at her again, hearing something vulnerable in that. May God forgive me, he thought, but until that moment he had not felt an ounce of compassion for her, or thought of her like the flesh-and-blood woman she was. For any other man in the world, she would be a magnificent partner—a prize. "You would honor me," he finally responded, trying to press away the mounting guilt for how sincere he knew he was sounding to her.

"He was a good man, handsome, just as you are. Perhaps not quite so smart or ambitious, however."

"Ah, yet he captured *you,* which makes him smarter than anyone."

Margaret smiled at that, then said on a sigh, "I do miss him, the easy companionship and the conversation most of all."

Charles knew well of Philibert II, Duke of Savoy, her second husband. He had died, leaving her widowed and childless, in 1504 after three years of marriage. He could see that, for her, the marriage had been more than a political liaison. Charles understood that and felt it himself. His own second wife, Anne, had loved him that way and a part of him, even at a time when he was wildly calculating in his ambition, had loved her in return . . . just not enough.

If it was possible for a man like him to have changed, Charles had.

He would not make that mistake in a wife again.

That evening the vast tent, striped blue and gold silk, was decorated to receive another guest. The Prince of Castile had journeyed to visit his aunt and to meet his now victorious future brother-in-law.

Gossip about marriages and war swirled like a heady perfume around the flickering candles, the crisp linen, the silver and the grand display of food. The first thing Charles saw upon his arrival was Henry, too taken up by the letter he had just been brought from Katherine to see anything else. He stood near the opening of the tent, reading it again. But he had already told Charles what it said.

King James, whom Henry considered a vital ally since marrying his older sister, Margaret, had become a dangerous opportunist, threatening Henry with war on a second front. The Scot knew well that the English were in France and, bargaining on Henry's youth and inexperience, he had chosen this moment to challenge the English king.

Henry had fired back an angry response of warning,

through his ambassador, that had gone unheeded. Now, in a stunning turn of events that had completely shaken him, a messenger stood before him telling him that Katherine, pregnant, but ever the proud daughter of a warrior queen, had elected on her own to be more in this instance to her husband than mere regent.

"*Jésu,* she cannot! She carries the heir of England as she rides into Scotland. And I will *not* lose another." He was raging so loudly that the music ceased. The crowd assembled inside the tent looked up at him and watched him storm, heavy-footed, back outside. Charles quickly followed.

"The queen believes it is her duty, sire," Charles said cautiously.

"It is her duty to at last give me a living child."

"She is just so fiercely loyal to you," Charles said. But Henry had just once again read the words brought by messenger from London. Katherine herself was at the head of a brigade of English soldiers, prepared to attack at the Scottish border.

"What the devil does she believe she can personally gain?"

"Your respect?" offered Charles. "The thing she wants almost as much as a child."

Henry did not answer and stalked back inside, where he and Charles came to the place where Margaret sat costumed as Diana, the goddess of love. She was beckoning Brandon with her easy smile and a raised hand, spotted with jewels. He drew in a breath and exhaled it before he advanced to her, feeling the weight of hypocrisy and guilt.

She began to recite a verse from the romantic tale of Sir

Gawain and the Green Knight, lingering dramatically on each word.

> *"Meeting her gracious, light-hearted gaze, he took the lord's leave and approached the ladies, he greeted the elder with a grand bow, and wrapping the lovelier in a light embrace, he planted a pretty kiss with extravagant praise. . . ."*

In her ideal of courtly romantic entertainment, her guests—women wearing white silk gowns, each embroidered with a different title such as Kindness, Mercy, Constancy, Honour, and the lords, as Nobleness, Devotion, Pleasure and Loyalty, lounged on sprawling pillows covered in brightly colored silk and tassels. There were urns around them spilling over with fat ruby grapes and silver platters heaped with glistening marzipan, nuts and other sweets. Malmsey from Cypress flowed from fountains set up around the tent.

Margaret herself sat on a gold cushion with Charles to one side and a waiting purple cushion, for Henry, on the other. Across from them sat the Duke of Buckingham, Wolsey and Charles of Castile, who had arrived at last to meet the man he still believed to be his future brother-in-law.

Charles was more curious even than Henry to see to whom exactly Mary was being given. Seeing the gawky adolescent now for the first time, his limbs long and his face marked by a rosy flush, thick lips and a smattering of pimples, Brandon felt an instant antagonism. Still a boy, not a man, he thought with proprietary irritation.

Unaware, Margaret lounged beside him smiling, a jeweled hand now casually resting on Brandon's thigh. Amid everything, Charles was trying to smile, push away his anger and drink enough to forget she was not Mary.

On the other side of Margaret, Charles saw that Henry had managed to contain his fury just enough to sink onto the plush, waiting cushions and drink a goblet of deep ruby wine, then another. As she read verse after verse, he could see how Henry was compartmentalizing, as a king must. This evening with the young Prince of Castile was important and he could afford no distraction. To offend his host or her nephew would be to jeopardize an alliance that had been in limbo for years. The great king, his father, in whose shadow he still lived every day of his life, had not managed to bring the match to fruition. It had become a point of honor now with the son. As had this new notion of a second alliance, one with the emperor's daughter. Beside him, she sat playing with the large silver and onyx ring on Brandon's index finger. She was twisting it playfully and gazing at it covetously, laughing and enjoying him, Henry thought.

"Why not offer it to her, Brandon?" Henry suggested nonchalantly as he took a long, casual swallow of wine, and they both watched the musician who strummed something slow and hypnotic on a lute. But the suggestion was far from a casual one. "Beauty seeks beauty. You two are a marvelous representation of that. Let your ring be a symbol for everyone here," he added, plucking a grape from a large gleaming silver urn before him.

Brandon felt shock warm his face as it had earlier when Henry had mentioned him developing an interest in a princess.

"I cannot do that, sire."

Brandon rarely called him that. Beneath his breath for years they were Harry and Charles. Henry tipped his head, irritated at his friend's odd response. "You would deign to insult the emperor's daughter?"

It was important to right his mistake. "On the contrary, I bow at her feet."

Henry smiled. Charles was again behaving as Henry would expect.

"Then offer her a symbol, a gesture of your favor."

"By all means," Buckingham suddenly seconded.

Again, and despite himself, he hesitated. "The ring is dear to me."

"More shall be my tender care of it," Margaret said, hearing the exchange and smiling up at him like a much younger girl than she was.

I see myself and all I wish you to become with me.

Charles felt the full weight of a thing he did not wish to do just then. Yet he understood the consequences of noncompliance. He gazed down at the jewel, seeing Mary. Seeing the memory. Then, with a heavy heart and knowing no other way around it, he drew the ring from his finger and handed it to Margaret. Promptly and with an eager smile she drew from her own finger a small ruby and pearl, and offered it in return to him. It was all so romantic, such a public display, that he felt a wave of nausea.

"In the tradition of courtly affection, here is my token back to you," she proclaimed dramatically, and those on cushions around them all applauded at the charming, if somewhat artificial, display, that so pleased their lady ruler.

In the face of this, Charles ached to see Mary, to hear her laugh. Being in the presence of a woman so entirely different, so like the women from his past—not the future he wished—only intensified that. He was not at all certain if their display had been part of a courtly drama or if Margaret legitimately expected his heart along with the ring. *My heart . . .* He had never in his life offered it fully to anyone until Mary.

They had been away all summer on this campaign and Charles physically ached to return to court, and to her. He had heard that they were still at Wolsey's new manor along the meadows of the river Lugg. He had heard it was an ostentatious estate, especially for someone who would not want to threaten a king. Things had certainly become tense between Wolsey and Buckingham lately, although he had no idea what had caused it. Probably only the rivalry for the second closest place to the king now that he was number one, Charles thought.

"She cares for you, Charles. I can see it. You've got to seize a woman and an opportunity like that one with great fervor!"

Henry and Brandon wrestled, as always, still like overgrown puppies, on thick carpets laid out in another tent erected just for Henry's daily exercise. For a moment, Charles dominated the match, as he usually did, pressing Henry into the carpet.

"She is lonely. I simply flatter her," he declared, without missing a beat.

As if in response, Henry wrapped a powerful thigh and his torso over Brandon's back, gaining leverage, then flipped him over. "Whatever it takes, old friend. Hasn't that always been your motto? I am offering you the chance of a lifetime here."

"I need time to think."

They rolled again, struggled again, both sweating, grunting, all powerful glistening arms and legs. A group of liveried servants stood ready with fresh, folded towels, a basin of water and two goblets of wine, none of them moving as the king and his friend battled.

"Your hesitation is an insult. Not just to Margaret but to me!"

When a bell rang, the timed match was over and they both staggered back to their feet. "I would never insult you. I am simply unsure of the future."

"You bedded with her. You owe her more than that, by God."

They looked at one another in challenge, both of their chests heaving. A moment later, Henry wrapped his arm around Brandon's broad shoulders as he always did, smiled and shrugged. "I don't begrudge you the tumble. I'm only saying that an important match is being offered to you and with someone you do not find wholly objectionable. It would entirely change the course of your life."

"Respectfully, of course, Harry, are we not getting ahead of ourselves? I rather doubt that *I* am what the emperor has in mind for his own daughter."

"She married Philibert to please her father. Should not a lady so tied to courtly love as that sweet, comely woman in the next tent have an opportunity to make a match of the heart?"

They each took a towel and wiped it over their faces.

Charles's fell away slowly as he glanced at the king. "I do not love her."

"You might come to, in time."

"No, Harry. I am reasonably certain that will not occur." He shook his head, bright defensive images of Mary pressing forward in his mind.

Henry's expression very suddenly became a frown as he took the goblet of wine but did not drink. "And how can you be so certain? There is not someone else who has captured your coldly ambitious, talented heart, is there? Perhaps someone so inappropriate that you are driven to keep her a secret from your oldest and dearest friend, and king?"

The question was so coldly spoken, and so startlingly blunt, that Charles felt an overwhelming chill in response. "Of course not," he chuckled blithely, and so believably that he almost convinced himself it was all a joke. "Love and ambition are a noxious brew anyway."

"Excellent. Then if I can arrange it, you shall marry Margaret. You shall be a great power as duke of all Savoy."

"I was just growing accustomed to the notion of a small bit of power as Duke of Suffolk."

"I'm surprised at you, Brandon. And by the way you wrestled just now," said Henry. "You used to be more ruthless than that—on both accounts."

Two days later, Henry received an odd and slightly ghoulish offering from the battlefields of Scotland sent by his wife, who sought so desperately to please him. Enclosed in a covering of black silk and wrapped in white ribbon was the bloody tunic of Scotland's overreaching King James, Henry's own brother-in-law. He had been slain by English troops in a massacre at Flodden, led by the aged Earl of Surrey and his remaining son, Thomas Howard.

That summer, Henry had attained what he wished—respect among other world leaders, squelching of the Scottish threat and the return of the part of England lost to the French long ago. Henry fully planned next summer to return to regain an even larger foothold. But for now he was tired, victorious, and he wanted only to go home.

He had received word the day before, as he had feared, that Katherine's child, another son, had died. And he could not help it. Amidst so much victory, this one failure left him beginning to resent his queen.

Chapter Twelve

Gossip has it that Maximilian's daughter Margaret is to marry that new duke, whom the King has recently turned from a stableboy into a nobleman.

—*Erasmus*

September 1513, Hampton Court

*T*homas Wolsey's estate was magnificent in its stately grandeur. A sprawling redbrick structure on the banks of the Thames, it was eleven miles from London but a world away.

Henry would love it here, Mary thought as she dashed through the maze of buildings and grounds, playing hide-and-seek with the Earl of Surrey's youngest daughter, Agnes, wishing it were Jane. The late summer sun warmed the brick and the echo-filled corridors through which they ran. It had been a long summer, but the king's troops were returning from France, at last, and it was announced that they were coming here to see Wolsey's impressive new investment.

Things had not been the same for Jane since the death of Thomas Knyvet. She was still at her side as the companion Mary long had known, but there was no light in her blue eyes now. She took no joy in anything. She rarely ate and slept little.

Mary knew that Jane felt a sense of guilt over Muriel Knyvet's death in childbirth but they had not spoken of it since that day. Jane had closed herself off and Mary felt that she had lost a friend.

"Pray, tell me a secret," Mary playfully bid Agnes Howard as they fell onto the grass in the little walled courtyard a few feet from the chapel.

"Such as what, my lady Mary?" She seemed to Mary genuinely vexed by the notion of requested gossip or hidden desires.

"Secret lust for a gentleman, perhaps?"

"I am afraid I have none. None worth telling, anyway."

Mary frowned slightly and sat up, her lip turning out in a little pout. Her azure silk skirts belled out around her, the petticoats firm beneath it, causing it to undulate like the sea. "How old are you?"

"Seventeen next November, my lady."

"And never have you yearned for a boy?"

"My father says I am to be respectable and to save myself for marriage."

"As are we all." Mary *humpfed*. "But that bars none of us from the fantasy."

She waited a moment, tipped her head to the side. "My lady toys with me."

Mary fell back into the soft grass with a little groan, rolling her eyes. "I sought only a bit of camaraderie, Agnes. The moment has passed; we shall speak of it no more."

She thought back then to all of the moments she and Jane had shared, too numerous to recall, precious secret moments, midnight conversations with the covers over their heads, muffled giggles—each other's most private thoughts borne out with trust between them. She missed all of that dearly, especially as she longed for Charles's return. No one but Jane knew of that, and so she had not once been able just to speak his name all through the long months of summer that had stretched endlessly beneath the broad blue canvas of sky here. There had seemed little joy in any of it, not the dancing or banqueting or games of cards, without Henry and certainly not without the company of Charles Brandon.

Here in the solitude of the country, over these months, Mary had come to understand that Charles's tie to Elizabeth Grey was a function of business only, a question of his survival at court and not his love. Mary had allowed her heart to rule her good sense by leaving as she had done, without saying good-bye, and she regretted that now. It had been petty and childish. She knew his heart and she believed now that she understood his ambition. Jane would have known that . . . told her that . . . if they had spoken about it. Or about anything.

Later that same afternoon as the sky paled to pewter, Mary stood in her dressing chamber, hands on her hips, studying the selection of dresses laid out before her by the dressers and wardrobe women who attended her. She looked closely at each one in turn. It must be the perfect costume for Henry and Charles's return. Elegant yet seductive, lively yet a complement to her beauty, not a distraction. Most definitely it must be something to make her feel like the mature young woman she wished Charles to see when he returned.

"Well, Jane, surely you have an opinion?" Mary looked at her friend as she stood in a ring of other servants and rustling of dresses, hoping to get something from her besides another wooden reply.

"There is not a poor choice to be made, my lady," she said blandly. "Each is lovelier than the last. Most certainly with you wearing it."

"A reply so rich in its duty, I am left feeling a bit ill," she shot back quickly with irritation. "You of all people know perfectly well, Jane, why this selection matters to me. Can you not, for a moment, draw yourself back into my world and at least a little out of your own?"

"Would that I could find a way out of my own, Mary," she said very softly in French, and the tone of her voice bore an ache that was more profound than anything she ever had heard. Mary stood, pivoted back away from the mirror and touched the line of Jane's jaw very gently.

"I will help you find it. If you will finally permit me."

"I would permit you the world," she replied at last. "No one could be a better friend than you, my lady. I do know that."

They arrived just after sunrise the next morning, a hundred horses' harnesses jangling like bells—hooves thundering, churning the dirt, as they advanced down the long, straight causeway that led to Hampton Court. Riding proudly for England, a vast collection of mud-caked, weary warriors returned victoriously from France in a whirl of road dust and sweat. Mary leaned out the window of her bedchamber, still in her white nightdress and bonnet. Her red-gold hair was long down her back, and her feet were bare. She searched the sea of dirty bearded faces for Charles, but could not see him for all of the churned dust around the horses and their riders. She dashed back to her bed and tried to rouse Jane, who slept deeply for the first time in days in the place beside her own.

With her windows thrown open, she could hear Henry's deep, distinctive and happy laugh and a call to one of the servants in the courtyard below. She had missed her brother as she knew Katherine had. She pitied the queen, who was in Richmond now, in seclusion. The showing of support she had made in Scotland for Henry had been a costly one. The child she had carried had lived only a few hours. That it had been a son had deepened the wound and all suspected a new fissure between husband and wife.

As with Jane's circumstances, there was nothing Mary could do to help. Wolsey had written to Mary in alarm that Henry had refused all of Katherine's letters and her entreaties to reunion with him. He could not yet look upon the queen, Henry had written to Mary himself. He must have time to reflect on the loss. And so must she. And for the first time in a very long time, her brother had referenced Leviticus and said he was haunted by it. *If he has uncovered his brother's nakedness they shall be childless. . . .*

The pounding on the door just then shook the room. Jane shot upright in bed at last, her nightcap tumbling back onto the pillows. Thinking only of Brandon, Mary's heart slammed against her chest. The summer had been so long. But it was not Brandon, rather Henry who came bounding in a moment later, his smile broad, his face tan and marked now by a dusty copper beard, his eyes glittering with victory. He took Mary into his arms, held her tightly and twirled her around until she was dizzy. Then they both began to laugh as he kissed one cheek and then the other.

"*Jésu,* how I have missed that sweet smile of yours!"

"You deserve this victory, Harry. I know what it means to you." Her heart was truly glad to be reunited with her brother.

"*You* better than anyone else know it."

"Father would be proud of you."

His expression became serious. "I would like finally to believe so."

"He was always proud of you. He just could not always show it because of Arthur and how you shone so brightly above him."

"He never made me feel that way."

"He made you strive harder and you are a better king because of it," she said, and it was with conviction and total devotion.

"Do you miss them, Mary?"

"The king and queen?"

"Mother and Father."

"Well, they weren't really like that for us, not really like a normal mother and father. So I don't suppose I miss them in the usual way. Not like you mean, anyway."

"Father always loved you too."

"He valued me because he thought I was pretty."

"Fair enough." Henry chuckled, but the sound was somber. "Still, in his way, he did love you."

"I want more than that. I want more than someone to value me, which is doubtless the only sort of future I shall find in Castile."

"You are meant for something extraordinary, Mary. No marriage of yours will be ordinary."

"This from a man who got what he wanted? The crown of England *and* the wife he chose?"

"Speaking of which, I have glad tidings for you." He walked across the room and sank into a chair. "I met with your betrothed, and I find him a fine young man. I hope it will please you to hear that your marriage date at last has been finalized. In May next year you shall at last become bride to the Prince of Castile—and granddaughter to the powerful Emperor Maximilian. Finally, we shall have what we have worked toward so hard and long."

Mary lowered her eyes, feeling ill. She breathed in, exhaled, unable to quite catch her breath. But she would not let him see that. It would not matter anyway. "I shall do as my lord and king wills me to."

"I had hoped you would be pleased by the news."

"If it pleases you, brother," she forced herself stubbornly to say. "Then I promise you, I am overjoyed."

He had needed to look into her eyes himself when he told her about the marriage in order to set his mind at ease. Now Henry was satisfied. If Mary had any small romantic fantasy of Charles Brandon, it was well hidden behind a mask of obligation that they both had been raised to wear. One thing he had never doubted was Mary's loyalty to him.

Anxious to counsel the king, and to show off his splendid home, Wolsey took Henry on a private tour of Hampton Court later that afternoon, after everyone had had time to bathe and rest. After leaving the private chapel, where Wolsey had heard the king's confession, they ambled through the many corridors and halls. Then they paused in the central courtyard in the silvery amber light of the setting sun. Bordering their path was a knot garden: clipped hedges surrounding sweet herbs, thyme and marjoram. Just beyond, on a brick retaining wall, was a roundel of the Emperor Augustus and beneath that a garden bench. Wearing a casual doublet of blue and yellow satin now with fresh shoes and hose, Henry sank onto it, feeling the weight of their long journey home.

"I only tell Your Highness that I advised you to trust her, and ignore that poison with which Buckingham fills your head. I knew she would not disappoint you with that sort of deception," Wolsey was saying.

"It makes no sense, Thomas. Why would Edward wish to hurt Mary by inferring otherwise?"

For a moment, Wolsey bowed his head contemplatively. "May I be frank with Your Highness?"

"It is what a cleric is there for, is it not?"

"My lord of Buckingham does not so much wish to hurt her as to be free of her competition for your heart and mind. Even more, I believe, he fears some strange collusion between the princess and Brandon."

"You are right, as always, my good counselor. But Mary has never once opposed the marriage before her. Nor has Brandon refused the possibility of his turning away from his ward, Lady Grey, to marry the emperor's daughter. . . ." Henry truly considered what he had said for a moment longer. "If there was some sort of adolescent flirtation on Mary's part, it was clearly only that, and seems well over now."

"Would you have me speak to her, just to make certain?"

Henry looked at him. "I would consider it an enormous favor, Thomas."

"She is nearly as dear to me as is Your Highness. It would be my great honor."

Henry felt a sly smile suddenly, and in it there was a hint, more apparent these days as he had turned twenty-two, of the jaded old warrior king, Henry VII, who haunted everything his son did as king. "You clerics find pleasure in the oddest of ways, Wolsey."

"The good Lord rules me always. Thus, we make great the few earthly pleasures He ordains."

"More is the pity for you," quipped Henry VIII.

"Why has he not come to see me yet, Jane? He has been returned for hours. Here in this same house, near enough, yet not intent."

Mary paced up and down the plank floor of her withdrawing chamber, wringing her hands, near enough to the door to seize upon it herself if Brandon should call. But as the afternoon passed into the pale gray of early evening, he did not.

"I want to be angry but the confusion stops me. He cannot still be angry about the way we left things."

"And yet a great deal has happened," Jane softly countered. "You heard, as did I, that the king now seeks to marry him to Margaret, the emperor's daughter, as a double political match with your own."

"That old mare had better get in line behind the child to which he consigned himself before he left!" she unkindly declared.

Jane's laugh was a stifled giggle that erupted into a deeper joyous snort of pure, mischievous pleasure. It was the first time Mary had heard the joyous sound in a long time and she saw just a glimmer of the old Jane in it. She looked at her friend and smiled too. "Well, it is true. Ah, such a choice he has before him."

"There would be no choice if he could have *you*," Jane said.

The vast great hall, paneled in rich, heavily polished oak, was decorated for a celebration. Rose and ivy garlands were woven through the hammered gold chandeliers and, laced on the tabletops, candles made the gleaming silver platters, salt-cellars and goblets glow with a magical elegance. The room—and the gallery above where the royal musicians played—was strung with green and white Tudor silk banners bearing the emblem of Henry VIII in gold thread sewn above his motto, *True Heart.*

Mary's stylish, elegant dress of white silk and red velvet rustled as she walked, with Jane, Lady Surrey and Lady Guildford, into the hall. She paused for just a calculated moment on the landing. Pearls and rubies glittered from a gold rope across her breastbone. As she always did when she first entered a room, she was searching for Charles. She could not still her heart for how much she wanted to see him after so long. So much had changed. Mary yearned to seem grown to him, a mature woman at last. Inside, she felt like a child for how nervous she was. Candlelight glinted in her long, shining hair unadorned tonight by a headdress, but just a circlet of matching rubies and pearls. Mary cared nothing now for his commitment, or her own. Her face lit when she finally saw him, with those still-shining eyes, longer hair and newly scruffy beard. And seeing him, she instantly forgave him everything—the women, the ambition, his other children and his sordid past.

Seeing Mary as well and without showing a moment of hesitation, Charles turned from Lady Monteagle and made his way steadily through the crowd toward her. As she came to the bottom step he met her there amid the commotion of other guests, music and laughter, rendering the moment wholly private.

"You look stunning," he said in a soft, yet powerful voice.

She felt her mouth begin to tremble. What was it about this moment that made her want to weep? Stay calm, she told herself. Show him you have grown, that you are no longer a little girl.

"Congratulations on your victory in France."

"It was His Highness's victory."

"You command his troops."

"I was at *his* command." He looked down at her, the smallest smile on his face beginning to break through the formality and tension of the moment. "But I did rather surprise myself, at that."

"And did you despise all of the French as much as you thought you would?"

"There are a few with tolerably good form, like Mistress Popincourt," he said with a little note of humor.

It was only then that Mary noticed the distinguished-looking man standing beside Charles. He was tall, slim and extremely elegant, his carriage as formal as if he were posing for a painting. He wore his silver hair brushed away from his face and long against the nape of his neck where it curled up just slightly. He had a neat little silver triangle of a beard on a perfectly shaped chin, and eyes that could be described only as glacial blue.

"Your Highness, may I present one of the king's prisoners, Louis d'Orleans, duc de Longueville."

"No chains? No iron bars?" She bit back a smile. "How very civilized of my brother."

"I am among a few privileged prisoners, Your Highness," he responded smoothly in English, although his deep voice was laced heavily with his country's melodic accent. "We are fortunate enough to be treated as guests in your fine country until my release can be negotiated."

"He has become something of a friend in our time together." Charles smiled, his own eyes gleaming from that clever spirit that he would never lose. He was weary, she could see that, but the Charles Brandon she loved was still magnificently before her.

"And how have you found your accommodations thus far?" The question was a surprise as it came not from Mary, but in French from Jane Popincourt. When Mary looked back at her friend, she saw an expression on her face she had not seen since they were young and Jane had fancied herself in love with Henry. Her smile was girlish and broad and, to Mary's surprise, she was blushing slightly. Even Thomas Knyvet had not brought that out in her.

"They could not be more splendid when I am in proximity of such beauty," he replied, his eyes on her now as they looked at one another as if they were the only two in the room.

Without even asking, yet with a clear sense of knowing, the duc de Longueville extended his hand to Jane as a new song was begun in the carved wood gallery above them. He led her then into the sea of other dancers, leaving Mary and Charles alone again.

"I have missed you more than you will ever know," he said so deeply that the sound of the words took her breath away, and yet his posture was still formal, his smile polite. "The summer has changed you."

"Have I grown while you were away?"

"Into an even more startlingly beautiful woman than you were before." He touched her hand down near her hip. She felt his restraint and his urgency, but the small movement symbolizing so much was hidden by the folds of her skirts. "I must see you privately."

"My wedding date has at last been set."

"I met your bridegroom myself."

"At the same time you met *your* next bride, I hear."

"Word travels with surprising speed."

"Poor Charles." Mary smiled. "So many women to choose from. What will you do? A little viscountess? A foreign regent?"

"Would that it might be you."

"We shall live with what is, and hope that one of us is clever enough to think of something better. What else can we do?"

"Will you meet me later?"

"I will need to wait until Mother Guildford has gone to

bed. She sleeps near my door and Jane always says she can hear a pin drop."

"Or a wayward princess trying to escape?" He smiled with amusement. "Doubtless the king, concerned about his prized sister's chastity, was the one to see to that sleeping arrangement." They both glanced over at Lady Guildford sitting beside a paneled pillar, happy with a full crested goblet in her hand. "And if she enjoys a bit more wine than usual would she not sleep the better for it?"

"What makes me think you are just the candidate to see to the loosening of a woman's defenses?" Mary smiled, not expecting him to respond. "You would need an accomplice since Mother Guildford is very steadfast about what is placed before her."

"Do not tell me she cares how others find her behavior."

"We, none of us, see ourselves quite as others do. Yet I know how I always see myself when I look into your ring. It seems forever since I have done that." She picked up his hand. "It is gone?"

"A casualty, I'm afraid, lost on the battlefield of France," he smoothly lied, because he could, and because she would never understand what had happened at Lille. Yet he was struck by the expression on her face, telling him that his ring had really mattered to her. The guilt he felt, seeing that, was enormous. Charles tried to press it back, an annoyance, as he had always been able to deal with guilt before, slough it off like old skin. But it stayed this time, unmoving, rooted more deeply because of the honesty in her eyes. He tried to turn from the discomfort. "I will wait for you in the alcove just before the landing on the floor beneath your apartments. Come when you are able."

"I don't know when that will be."

"I will wait all night if I must."

"And if we have only a moment?"

"I will take whatever you are able to give to me," Charles said as the Duke of Buckingham approached them.

"Ah, careful, you two! The court is liable to start talking."

"Are *you* not a part of that court?"

"I don't start gossip, my lady. I am far too busy making my own scandals," he said boastfully.

"If you will excuse me." Charles bowed to him perfunctorily on that note and with the slightest scowl. "I am off to see that Lady Guildford has more wine. I see that her cup has been empty for ages."

They met near dawn in a little curtained alcove off the landing. Mary knew she risked everything stealing away like this. The king would forgive neither of them for putting her betrothal, and her chastity, at risk. But her love for Charles was a strong thing. It overwhelmed her heart and her life.

Now as he held her against his broad, flat chest, she thought how one of their first encounters had been in a corridor not unlike this, with her grandmother and mother, years ago. She had not known it then but she had fallen in love with him that day already.

Still, no one knew. Her heart was her own. It was the only thing about her life she could keep, and she would guard it as covetously as any jewel.

Charles pulled her more tightly against him, and she felt his heart pounding as he kissed her tenderly at first, almost as if she might break beneath the weight of his passion for her. But she drank in the musky scent of his skin, wanting him to kiss her again and again, more deeply, as though he would never let her go. The ring . . . the betrothals . . . women and secrets, all were forgotten in the dusky early light with all of the candles and sconces long extinguished. The only sound was the howl of a damp, chilled autumn wind that rattled the leaded windows across the hall. He touched her cheek with the back of his hand, the turn of her neck, then very gently the cleft between her breasts. Again he kissed her with moist, practiced lips. "I am so in love with you," he murmured.

"It is good to know that I am not alone in it."

Henry was on top of the world, and he knew it. At last, he allowed himself to believe that he, not Arthur, had been meant to rule England. Not only had he vanquished the skeptical rulers in Europe, he had respect as a leader himself now from them. He had finally achieved what his father had not—a firm date for Mary's wedding. On top of that he believed he had found an English bridegroom for the emperor's daughter and meant to try to arrange that. A double wedding would bind the two rulers tightly and ensure an eventual victory over France. It was all the more crucial to forge an alliance with Maximilian because Katherine's father, Ferdinand, had made peace with Louis XII.

Things had changed, but one constant with Henry was his devotion to those he loved. Upon his return from France, he had also seen to several elevations of those closest to him.

As had been promised in Lille, Charles was made Duke of Suffolk; Thomas Howard, Earl of Surrey, for his role in Scotland, became Duke of Norfolk; and Wolsey was elevated to Archbishop of York. Henry loved his friends, he believed in them and he wanted to reward them for their loyalty.

Yet thinking of none of that now, only of the pleasure he had earned, Henry slapped the girl's bare behind as she lay beside him, her hair tumbling down her back and across the side of her face. She giggled, then smiled and playfully tossed a pillow at him.

Elizabeth Fitzwalter, sister to the Duke of Buckingham, lady-in-waiting to the queen and frequent royal lover, was not yet acknowledged as the king's formal mistress, but she soon would be if there were more nights like this one, he thought to himself. She was young, beautiful and entirely uncomplicated—all of the things that his wife was not. And for the first time in his married life, Henry felt no guilt for acknowledging that. He loved Katherine and he had been faithful to her for those first five years. But, after all, he was King of England with power and money beyond measure. This sort of thing was expected. To be a ruler, one must behave as one. He smiled to himself, reminded of that, happy at last to have his life . . . and to be in complete control of not only his own destiny but the destinies of those around him.

Jane was smiling broadly again. The change was sudden and profound. The married duc de Longueville was always lingering nearby, whether at dinner, attending entertainments or evening prayers, and it quickly became apparent to Mary that he was the cause of the change. She thought it a mistake for Jane to give her heart, and her body, to anyone else that way after what her affair with Thomas had cost her. Yet Mary understood it because she would have given herself completely to Charles, had her virginity not been so grand a bargaining tool for Henry.

Her wedding was now only six months away. But she refused to think of that. And until she was actually bound to the Prince of Castile by God, she would give Charles Brandon every part of herself that she possibly could, within the confines of her duty to England. Still housed at Hampton Court, as All Saints' Day passed, Mary dashed through the hedge maze as Charles chased her, laughing so hard that she stumbled, then laughed the more, barely escaping him around a turn. It was a crisp autumn day beneath a cloudless sky and the fall of her headdress billowed out behind her neck. Jane and Louis were somewhere here too within these high hedge walls, since she could hear them murmuring in French, and she recognized the soft sounds of seduction. But she could not think of that. The private moments she could steal like this with Charles were as precious as they were dangerous. She and Jane would need to take their own risks.

Finally, Mary turned a corner and ran headlong into Charles. Pressing herself against him, she kissed him as wantonly as a Bankside whore. Charles pulled her closer. A moment later, he drew back, his fists clenching tightly as he tipped his head toward the sky.

"I do believe I will die for want of you," he murmured as she playfully kissed the thick, tanned column of his throat and drew his hand up onto her breast.

His jaw tightened as she guided his hand beneath the

lace edge of her bodice, down to the warm fleshy rise of her breast and the nipple. "Does that please you?"

"It will likely drive me quite mad any moment."

"I would rather it brought you pleasure."

"That, you always do."

This time when he kissed her it was demandingly as he splayed his fingers once again at her spine, thrusting instinctively against her. Mary felt her own body ignite and she swallowed hard, realizing what was happening to him in the moment before he expelled a breath and then sank against her.

"I must go."

"I . . . didn't know," she said, softly, her corseted chest heaving with her own unmet desire.

As he turned to leave her, he glanced back with just the slightest hint of a smile brightening his censorious expression. "Oh, but you have always known what you do to me, my love."

"It risks everything!" Henry bellowed.

"It does indeed, Your Highness," Wolsey observed as the rest of the king's privy council sat mutely at the long, polished table. In the center was a letter from the Holy Roman Emperor, stating his outrage that the English king would even attempt to marry the questionable Duke of Suffolk to his own daughter, the Regent of the Netherlands.

"Respectfully, sire, now that we know this is his response, you would be prudent to say it was a fanciful bit of humor, that you never intended him to seriously consider such a match," offered the aged Thomas Howard, now Duke of Norfolk. "A bit of courtly lovemaking amid too much wine and laughter."

"And if I refuse to deny what actually happened and the marriage I still desire?"

"Then I believe you endanger the princess Mary's fragile betrothal to the emperor's grandson," said Buckingham.

Henry scanned the faces at his table: Norfolk, Wolsey, Buckingham and Norfolk's son Henry Howard, as well as half a dozen others.

"And are you all in agreement on that point?"

Collectively, somberly, his privy councillors nodded. Henry pounded the table in response. "*Jésu Maria!* I thought it had all been arranged so brilliantly. Two marriages . . . a stronger alliance . . . Brandon is a duke now, marshal of my army *and* a war hero. Margaret has been on the market rather a long time for the emperor to see the proposal as some sort of insult."

"Yet your foremost desire is your sister's marriage, is it not?"

"Now that my elder sister Margaret is widowed, perhaps we might look to match her to the King of France and I can turn my nose up at the emperor's manipulations at long last instead. What of our overtures there?"

Thomas Howard, Duke of Norfolk, pressed a finger and thumb against his silver-bearded chin. "Your Highness, the French king has once again refused the Queen of Scots. We just received word this afternoon."

"Is not my sister a preferable notion to another round of attacks next summer?" he belligerently asked.

"Louis tells your ambassador that she is too old to please him well in the marriage bed."

"*She* is too old? Pray, could he even find the marriage bed without his servants, for how ill he is?" he bellowed. "He may be fifty-one, but his portrait reveals a man whose health has made him quite overdue for the grave."

"It is not only that. I am informed that the Queen of Scots . . ." Wolsey drew in a deep breath of hesitation, then let it out. He shot a glance at each of the other councillors before he announced, "Your sister has eloped with the young Earl of Angus."

"What? Ho, that is not possible!"

"I am so very sorry but it is true," Wolsey replied.

"Damn her!" Henry seethed, gripping his forehead. "I cannot believe Margaret would betray me—betray England like that! She knew better, she knew what was expected of us all."

"Indeed."

"Thank the Lord that my precious Mary is not so far beyond my reach and reason! She would *never* betray me like that."

"No, Your Highness," Wolsey confirmed. "The princess Mary is of sterling character."

"Yet no one should exist on too high a pedestal," Buckingham cryptically observed.

Henry arched a brow in irritation. This was not the time for rivalry when his hard-won plan was swiftly crumbling.

"In light of current circumstances," Norfolk cautiously observed, "Your Highness may wish to consider a proxy marriage before the May wedding in order to increase the pressure on the emperor to keep his promise."

"And maintain the date," the Duke of Buckingham artfully chimed.

Henry scratched his bearded chin, considering. "Does insisting on that not show a lack of faith to Maximilian?"

"Better that, sire, than your faith in him betrayed, along with your reputation."

"Wolsey, you have hardly spoken on this matter. What have you to say now?"

"The princess shall be sorely missed. But she is destined to make the marriage you have chosen for her and which God, therefore, has ordained. I agree that the proxy marriage is the best first step toward your goal."

They were right, of course. Henry knew that. He was angry about his sister Margaret's rash actions, and losing the alliance with the French king she might have made. He could have used her for that. But he still had Mary and she would not betray him. He knew he could count on that.

Chapter Thirteen

Friendship is constant in all things Save in the office and affairs of love.

—William Shakespeare

December 1513, Westminster

*I*t was smallpox.

The royal physician confirmed Henry's condition two days after the Christmas festivities came to an end.

Mary's expression was stricken as she stood before Charles. The announcement she made hit him, as it had her, like a blunt force blow. He could not help that the first thing he thought hearing it, however, was not of Henry, but of his Anne. In a single summer's day, the pox had transformed his sister's life and his own.

He understood Mary's fear better than anyone. She had found Charles outside the royal stables, as a damp fog rolled around their ankles, chilling them both. She clung to him like a little girl, tears falling onto her smooth, pale face. Her cry against him was a soft, pained whimper, and he felt the full weight of his love for her descend upon him then. There was nothing in the world he would not do for her.

More than she would ever know, the king's sister bore his heart.

"We must go to him," he said tenderly.

"But the physicians say it is not safe."

Charles ran the back of his hand across her face. "I care only that he has us with him. It will be all right," he gently assured her. "And you alone have the power with Henry to bring him peace. You matter to him more than anyone in the world. It is where you must be no matter the consequences. And I want to be with you."

They sat together near to the fire and warming coal braziers that cast the king's ominously silent bedchamber in a crimson glow. Outside the windows a pale pink began to climb over the gray, tree-lined horizon as dawn approached. Across the vast chamber near the door where they had banished him, a Gentleman of the Chamber sat slumped in a chair, asleep. Mary had been pacing the room for hours and now, weary, she had surrendered to a tapestry-covered chair beside Charles, who took up her hand and kissed it tenderly. There was an odd communion in being alone together like this, the outcome uncertain, the time together and the silence bonding them the more.

"He will recover from this," Charles said softly to her as Henry slept now finally, no longer fitfully stirring.

"How can you be certain?"

"Shall I tell you something of my own life that I have told no one else?"

"I wish you would."

"There was someone else very dear to me who suffered

from this and survived, although not so well as the king shall survive it."

"Who?"

"Her name is Anne, and she is more dear to me than any other woman in the world but you. She is my sister."

"You have a sister? My brother always told me you were orphaned alone, which was why you were brought to live with us."

"That is her wish, not my own. I was brought to court by your father to pay a debt he felt he owed to *my* father. You would not know it to see her now for the scars, but she was lovely once. Our uncle actually thought to make a proper marriage for her. It was the only way, he said, that either of us were ever to rise above the unfortunate circumstances of our father's death."

"I would like to meet her."

"She knows all about you."

"Oh? And what does she know of me?"

"She said all along that you were of the sort of character that made it not absurd to believe you might actually love me."

"I like your Anne already." Mary smiled for the first time all day. "Thank you for trusting me."

"I trust you with my life."

"And you with mine," Mary said, her eyes shining with open devotion.

Henry did survive, and Lord be praised, the queen was once again pregnant. The country's excitement over that knew no bounds. It quickly spread to a frenzy all across England over

Mary's impending marriage. Every detail of the plans was coveted, each element endlessly discussed, debated and eagerly awaited in taverns, shops and country homes alike. Even the design of her wedding dress was a heavily guarded secret. As the date drew near, Henry VIII's ambassadors sent long, laborious letters to Margaret, Regent of the Netherlands, in whose country it was decided the wedding would take place, detailing accommodation requirements, musical selections and even the food.

By April, the court had moved to Lambeth Palace for the king's convalescence. Mary and Charles were daily fixtures in his recovery, which had been rapid since he was young and strong, and he had not been stricken as badly by the illness; nor was he scarred, as Charles's sister had been. They walked with him, ate with him, read to him and protectively watched over him as he slept. Mary was as devoted to her brother as any wife—and Brandon was devoted to Mary. No one saw it as anything, however, but the dedication of the king's sister to His Highness, and the kind attentions as well of his oldest, dearest friend.

They sat together beside him on a gray afternoon, one that still bore a hint of the winter's chill. Henry was stretched out on a long chair and covered with an ermine throw with heavy carpets over his legs to keep him warm. But he was determined to be out in the light and fresh air, not inside surrounded by fire smoke and human odor, perfume, sweat and old food. There, amid the patchwork hedge of boxwood and the conical-shaped yews, they sat together, the three of them; friends, allies, a triumvirate of trust. Today, however, Henry was out of sorts and both of them had seen it from the first.

Even the king's fool had been excused with a dismissive flick of the wrist as a light mist began to fall. Mary pulled her fur-lined cloak around her neck, and exchanged a little glance with Charles.

"Surely, Harry, it is not the company you keep that has you seeming in such a foul temper today when you are so much recovered, and without a single scar to mar your handsome face."

Henry took her hand and kissed it, but the smile that followed was more of a grimace. "Never. You are what brightens all of our days, does she not, Brandon?"

"Like no other," Charles smoothly agreed.

"So then, be honest with us," Mary pressed. "We are here to share your burden if we can."

"It seems there is a sudden plague in Calais."

Again they exchanged a glance, but Henry did not see it. "The emperor and his new ally, my own treacherous father-in-law, seek to postpone the wedding again, blaming it on that."

"But is it not all arranged?" Charles asked with true surprise. "The travel plans? Her dowry? Even the accommodations."

"Done, I suspect, to inflict maximum humiliation. All that I gained in France, the victory and the hard-won honor, is lost. I feel a fool, which I am certain was the intention."

"How does your council advise you?"

He looked at them directly then, at twenty-two, his face sad and older somehow now. "I am advised to terminate your betrothal. Better me, they say, than Maximilian in control of it."

Mary felt the shock of sudden hope then. Unrealistic perhaps, yet as bright and strong as a beacon leading the way to something better. Hearing the recommendation, she tried to steady her heart and not smile like a silly child. She trusted Wolsey, and she loved him. She always had. Perhaps there was more than his prayers at work for them.

After Henry was taken by litter back to his apartments, amid an orchestrated ballet of courtly maneuvering with the cavalcade of servants it took to run his day, Charles took Mary by the hand. He led her down a twisted gravel path that crunched beneath their soft-soled shoes, to the seclusion of a small greenhouse. She was in his arms at once. As he seized her with kisses, wild and frenzied, his fingers traveled over the bodice of her dress, reaching into the pocket between the silk and her breasts. After a moment, he drew in a shuddering breath to collect himself, then rested his chin on the top of her head, closing his eyes. His powerful arms were wrapped tightly around her, almost, she thought, desperately.

"I dare to hope," he murmured, trailing kisses once again down along her throat and to the hollow just above her collarbone. "And that is a dangerous thing."

"It seems to me the Duke of Suffolk does not hope foolishly."

"If wishing could make it so, you would be my wife already."

His touch and the heady way he spoke the words brought such a sensation of arousal that Mary was almost undone by it. "Dare I tell him the truth? Now may be our moment. We have been there for him for months, and I know he is grateful. What is the worst that could happen when he loves us both?"

"His wrath would be dreadful, particularly directed toward me."

"But does it not seem just the slightest bit fated to you? We have waited for so long and he has tried everything to make a different match for me."

The earnest expression on her young face made him almost believe it could be true. Yet the danger in believing still ruled him.

"Let me handle my brother," she said then so sweetly that he could not hear the steely determination within the words. But it was there, a defining part of her. "We have been here for him. He owes us."

"He is a king. He owes me nothing. I am a duke by his grace alone. It is I who owe him everything."

"Very well," she said stubbornly. "Then let it be for my sake that he accepts us."

Mary found it difficult to find a time alone with Henry. He was surrounded by people from the hour of his rising, when he was taken up with the hundreds there to see to his care with great formality. Ushers, stewards, gentlemen-at-arms, yeomen, dressers, tailors, high-ranking gentlemen-of-the-chamber, gentlemen-of-the-body all gathered for his rising ceremony in the privy bedchamber. Once ushered with great ceremony out to the third and final of the connecting presence chambers, he was greeted by a waiting throng of clergy, ambassadors and noblemen from the countryside, all demanding time to meet with him. Even on the hunt, he was followed always by those wanting something from their sovereign, if only a moment in his presence. So her timing must be exact. Mary could afford no error in this.

The next day, as Henry made his way back from the stables following a check of his horses, Mary emerged from prayer in the chapel. Henry's face was flushed and he was happy and distracted as he walked laughing in the company of his new admiral, Thomas Howard, eldest son of the Duke of Norfolk, Edward Guildford and Gawain Carew, with whom he liked best to hunt.

"Would that I might have a private word with Your Highness," she said. Then, along with Jane and Lady Guildford, she dipped into a proper curtsy, their skirts rustling.

He removed his leather gloves and studied her for a moment, his hesitation clear. "Has something happened?"

"Nothing that should make you unhappy. I would like to speak with you about my future."

He laughed and turned back to his companions, from among whom Brandon was noticeably absent. "I was to visit the queen when I returned but you know perfectly well I can refuse you little. And I need to speak with you about the same thing anyway."

It was precisely what Mary was hoping to hear. But she did not say that.

"She wishes to meet you."

"Meet me?" Anne gulped in a breath, then sank stunned back in her chair as her brother's announcement resonated like a church bell through her small country house.

"You are coming to court with me, and it is about time," Charles said with a smile.

"But what on earth has happened?"

"Everything. You made me dare to hope, and now I have."

"You do not mean the marriage to the Prince of Castile?"

His eyes sparkled. "Gone in a blaze of resentment and broken promises."

"And so?"

"And so there is a chance now, small though it is. Yet hope, as they say, does spring eternal."

Anne laughed at that, the joyful way he had said it, and a ray of sunlight through the window cast a shadow across the scars on her young face. "Four years is a long time to wait for a woman, brother."

"I would have waited a lifetime for Mary," Charles Brandon said.

As Anne and her brother Charles rode toward court, installed again at Greenwich, Mary and her own brother had walked back from the stables and now sat together in his presence chamber. It was a grandly elegant room that had once been a favorite of their father. Over the carved mantel hung a grand painting of Henry VII framed in gold leaf. A similar one had been hung in each royal palace, so that they might never forget his enduring influence in both of their lives. He had been painted as strong-faced and serious, the man he had been in life. Dressed in full armor, the image had captured the very essence of a king, gone to dust, yet whose spirit watched over them. Henry had chosen this place intentionally for the obligation he knew it would engender within Mary when he told her what he must. She knew it always weakened him like nothing else to see that wounded expression in her eyes but today was different. He did not bend.

"You cannot seriously have chosen the King of France for me!" she cried as his announcement hung dark and heavy between them.

"It is a splendid future I have set for you."

"And a horrifying one!"

"You were raised all your life to expect this, as I was."

"I beg you, Harry, anyone but Louis XII! He is an old man, and they say a disgustingly ill one! Twice widowed already!"

"And, for it, you shall be a proper queen."

Mary found the shock of it was intense, and the bitterness rose up like bile. "You cannot want that for me! You would not want it for yourself!"

"If it were my duty I would do it without complaint."

Mary's face blanched. She bolted from the chair and began to pace the room, with its wood paneling and rich Flemish tapestries. Her normally well-schooled calm acceptance of her fate began now to crumble like a sand castle because she had allowed herself to believe in something better. Mary wrung her hands, not feeling them, feeling only the shock. Nothing else mattered suddenly beyond that. An old man . . . infirm, wrinkled . . . a widower twice over, used, tired . . . The images swirled in her mind in the echo of her brother's firm announcement. Henry diligently went on to explain the details of the arrangement to her but his words came at her disjointedly. In the shadow of continuing difficulties with Maximilian, he had been negotiating a marriage with Louis XII for months, he admitted. After the line of communication had been opened regarding the ransom for the duc de Longueville, Henry had chosen to consider it. Through a papal nuncio, who negotiated on the French king's behalf, Louis XII would have one last chance to beget a male heir. Henry, for his part, would be able to save face for how he had been strung along by the emperor. There was no way around it. The marriage with the fifty-two-year-old king was essential—and it would take place.

"Harry, I beg you!" She went back to him, her face full of pleading, her hands outstretched as if her horror alone could change his mind. "I felt ready to marry the Prince of Castile. You know that. I was prepared for it for most of my life. . . . But this, now, such an old, sick man . . ."

"We all have our duty."

"You married the woman you chose!"

His expression darkened and his amber brows merged into a heavy frown. "Katherine was my duty once Arthur died. My feelings one way or the other were of no consequence."

"Will it matter to you a bit if I say that with every fiber of my being I do not wish this?"

He lowered his eyes, the brother she knew so well closing off to her then. "In truth, no." He drew in a breath, softening by a degree a moment later with an exhale. He leaned nearer to her. "I have been made a laughingstock by Maximilian. I have been played the fool. Please understand, Mary. I make this choice not *against* you but *for* England."

"You make it for yourself, not England," she countered defiantly, bolting toward the door and pivoting back to face him only once she had reached it. "Even when Arthur was still alive, you got your way. Father's favorite! Always the indulged one, the charmed one, the one that trouble never reached. And you are selfish enough to want everything for yourself. Even your brother's wife!"

"Mary, I warn you, hold your tongue!" His face mottled red with his own fury.

"Or you will what? Bluff King Hal! That is what the people call you for how hardened you have become."

"I command you to stop."

"Or what? Tell me, brother Hal, will you see me tossed into the Tower?"

"Never that. But I *shall* see you made Queen of France, which apparently for some reason will be punishment enough."

"Then you might as well finish me off and kill me, because that is what it will surely do to me anyway."

They had not quarreled since they were children. That, and the reality that her dream of a love match was not ever going to come true, had reduced Mary to tears. After they had prayed together, she wept bitterly into Wolsey's starched crimson cassock, and against the comforting swell of his belly, as light poured into the chapel upon them through the stained glass image of Saint Jerome.

"Tell me what am I to do, Thomas. I cannot ask him now," Mary frantically wept.

"Surely not. For Brandon's sake, at least." He steepled his

hands and leaned back in the chair that faced the small fabric-draped altar. "There is but one small ray of hope."

"Tell me. Since I surely do not see it beneath the weight of the despair I feel just now."

He paused a moment, reflecting. "Is this King of France not an older man, and quite ill as well?"

"Yes, and the thought of it adds to my torment."

"Adds to your torment, child? Or provides you promise of salvation? As with so much of life, this salvation is what you choose to make of it."

She saw the gleam in Wolsey's eye and the thought came to her then. The tears dried on her cheeks and a cautious smile began to brighten her face.

"Does not His Highness wish you to be happy above nearly all other things in this world?" Wolsey asked.

"Except perhaps to use me as a bargaining chip with France."

"Then, when his guilt is at its zenith, why not tell him you will make your peace with his choice, and with him, but at a cost. You alone, my dear, could make that bargain with the king. Forget not that your sister Margaret in Scotland is now married to her own love."

Although twisted and difficult, a pathway out, a plan, became clear to her although she could tell no one else—not even Charles, for what extreme measure he might take to try to prevent her from one day acting on something so bold. She knew that his love for her would drive him to sacrifice her to her duty to England if she told him. Did she have enough power and courage to gain a solid agreement from Henry to let her choose her next husband once the French king died?

She knew Henry did feel enormous guilt for tying her to someone so old and ill but was that enough? Such a promise could not be extracted, and then fulfilled, without cunning, fortitude and sacrifice. But she was a Tudor. She was strong and determined and she was capable of greatness if pressed. In France, her challenge would be to love an aged man as best she could.

"You would not tell anyone about this, would you, Thomas?"

Wolsey's wet mouth stretched into a reassuring little arc of a smile. "Communion with one's confessor is a private and a holy matter," he decreed with sudden reverence. "Your secrets, my child, shall always be safe with me."

Charles had found the vacant chamber quite by accident, but his only desire was to bring Mary here to be alone with her, as their remaining time together was growing swiftly to a close. He had been planning a reunion since the moment they had moved yet again, this time to Lambeth. The chamber was small, a servant's room on the third floor, decorated sparsely with only a pallet bed, a rush-bottom chair, a round table with a white tallow candle, a basin and a prayer book. The window was small and leaded with a little iron latch. It opened onto the entrance courtyard below, so that there was the constant hum of activity and the sound of horses and groomsmen below.

As Charles closed the door behind her, Mary flew into his arms and clung to his neck as if her determination and her love for him alone could chase the future away. He bent his head and kissed her and, as she always did, Mary melted against him, the spiraling sensation taking over within her.

"I want all of you so badly," he murmured into her hair. "It takes the strength of a hundred men just now not to tear your dress away and take what I know you want to give me."

"You know I do not want to go. . . ."

"I know." They crooned tenderly to one another.

His mouth descended on hers again then and, through her whole body, she felt the groan that tore up from his throat as he parted her lips and pressed her onto the little pallet bed that sank beneath their weight.

"I leave you in so short a time," she said sadly as he lay back with her, his full length, rigid thighs and broad chest, wildly aroused against her. "Let us do with one another what we can—our own communion and promise."

Her words were unashamed, an invitation, delivered with wide eyes full of love and trust. She slid her hands down over his hips then and to the codpiece between his legs.

"You must remain innocent," he responded hoarsely.

Freeing him from the fabric codpiece, Mary took him into her hand and Charles reacted powerfully to her touch, his neck arching as his entire body tensed. He moved with her hand then as he kissed her again, a lover's kiss this time, opening his mouth to hers, and Mary drank in the smell of him greedily, the sweat on his neck, and the overwhelming rush of her own desire feeling how much he wanted her. She ached for more, to have him bare against her . . . the solid assurance of him inside of her, but for now pleasing him was enough to join them in a way they had never had.

The sensation of what was happening was more powerful and forbidden than anything she had ever known, and Mary surrendered to it, letting it wash over her like a wave, controlling her, dominating her. She moved, she kissed him in return . . . she tasted the moan in his throat. Then suddenly, she felt him shudder. His heart was slamming against his damp chest as she stopped, then pressed herself against the fabric of his shirt. She closed her eyes, feeling her own heart race.

"I must remain a virgin. I remember nothing about innocence," Mary softly declared as he kissed the tendrils of her hair. "My body may be his, but you alone shall have my soul."

Her hand tucked tightly in the crook of his arm, Charles brought his sister forward in a new dress for which it would take him months to pay. It was sewn of bright blue French silk dotted with tiny pearls, to highlight her eyes and distract from the scars. But the extravagance was worth everything to him to see the small grain of confidence it brought Anne. As they approached, Mary rose swiftly from the table at which she had been playing cards with Jane. She drew forward, smiling, hands extended, as Anne dipped into a deep curtsy.

"Now none of that," Mary said brightly, taking Anne's cold hands and squeezing them. "Not when I feel I know you as well as if we were sisters. Charles has told me all about you."

"As he has told me of Your Highness, and it was with the greatest delight that I always heard his stories."

Charles took a step back, linking his hands behind himself as he proudly watched an encounter he felt he had waited an eternity to see.

"Where are your children? I should like very much to meet them, as well," Mary asked.

Anne looked embarrassed and cast a glance back at Charles, who moved up a pace protectively once again. "They are down in the kitchens eating candied plums, my lady," Anne confessed.

"How delightful," Mary said sweetly. "So we have a bit of time to ourselves. Do come and sit with Jane and me. You as well, Charles. It is warm by the fire and you have had a long ride. A glass of honey wine should warm you both nicely."

Though she did not see it, Charles smiled at Mary, and felt an even more overwhelming surge of love for her in that moment than he had ever known before. It meant the world to him to see them together, Mary so kind and welcoming to a sister whose life these last years had been so difficult.

"If it pleases, my lady Mary, I should like to leave you ladies to yourselves. I feel a bit out of place at the moment."

Anne shot her brother a stricken look, but he smiled at her in reassuring reply, as if to say *You hold one part of my heart . . . and you know that she alone holds the other. It will be fine. You are safe here always with Mary. On that I would stake my life.*

Mary found Charles's sister kind, clever and genuinely sweet—so much like her brother. Their mannerisms, like their noses, and even the shade of their eyes, were the same. And Mary was surprised to find Anne was not so horribly scarred as Charles had claimed. Perhaps when he looked at Anne he saw too much of what she had lost and the pain of being abandoned by her husband. All Mary saw was a kind and pretty young woman. Mary was instantly at ease with her, and felt they were friends. After a few minutes, Anne's hand did not tremble so greatly when she lifted her cup of wine, and she even managed a smile when Jane asked her if court seemed to her as ostentatious as everyone else new there always said.

"I trust Jane with my life," Mary declared. "She knows the circumstances that bring you and I together—as I know the same sort of details of her life. We can speak of anything with her here."

"And will she attend you as one your ladies of honor when you leave for France?"

Her imminent departure was a subject Mary avoided even considering as it drew near. She tried very hard to control her response so that Anne would not believe she had committed an error in asking.

"I could not even think what my life there would be without her," she managed to calmly reply. "She will be my rock in a foreign place I do not wish to go to, and where I pray that the good Lord shall not see me remain long."

"I know that is my brother's prayer as well."

She reached across the table and covered Anne's hand with her own. "I hope you will stay with us a while at court. At least until I must leave for France."

"I had planned to return home tonight, my lady . . . Mary."

Mary smiled sweetly at her, then took up her hands. "Do stay. You must meet the king, of course. And there are several unmarried men I know who dine with us regularly, and who would be nearly as glad for fresh company here as I."

Her face, covered thinly with a very fine layer of Venetian ceruse in an attempt to hide the worst of her scars, gleamed at the invitation. "If you are certain, my lady, I suppose I could ask my brother to allow me to remain."

"As you wish, but I am certain Charles will agree to that which pleases me."

Anne smiled at that in total agreement.

Mary paused at the entrance to the glittering great hall, wearing a dress of olive green velvet threaded with gold, her arm linked with Anne's. "So tell me," she said, "if you were of a mind to dance this evening, of those gentlemen over there, who might you fancy as a partner?"

Anne pressed a finger to her lips in response. Mary saw that she was earnestly surprised by the question. "I shouldn't think any of them would fancy a dance with me—as I am now."

Mary turned to study Anne for a moment amid the swish of dresses, the sparkle of jewels, the music and laughter alive before them. "What you are, Anne, is lovely, with the most extraordinary smile I have ever seen."

She watched Anne's face brighten beneath the sincere compliment. "People did say that once."

Mary wound her arm protectively through Anne's once again, giving her a supportive little squeeze. "And so they shall again. But they must have the opportunity." Mary then drew her progressively forward into the crowd of guests, even as she felt Anne stiffen beside her. She could see Charles watching them casually from across the room. That they should be friends mattered to him, and there was nothing in the world so important to Mary as pleasing Charles. It was the one thing she could give him fully, and she meant to do just that.

"I am not certain I even know how to speak with a man any longer, the clever little conversation one is forced to make."

"Then Gawain Carew will be perfect for you to practice on," Mary chuckled with infectious confidence. "He is accomplished enough at it for both of you."

Just then, they came upon the collection of courtiers. Gawain Carew was young, and not as tall as the others, but he was sharply handsome, with a muscular body, wide-set brown eyes, a tousle of sandy hair and just the right amount of spirit to help a shy woman to the fore. Mary could feel Anne tremble in the men's presence, all so elegantly dressed, teeming with confidence, their smug expressions worn beneath well-groomed mustaches. But in this light, candle lamps flickering all around them, the scars on Anne's face were softened. With the thin layer of paint on her cheeks she really did look like the lovely girl she must have been before her illness.

The men all bowed to Mary first, then each rose, smiling, dressed elegantly in their doublets of rich velvet and silk with fashionably slashed sleeves and broad chains across their chests. Predictably, Carew was the first to speak, and his voice was rich and well schooled.

"How is it that my lady Mary has a companion we all regrettably do not know?" He smiled broadly, a little too confidently, Mary thought, yet full of enough charm to compensate.

"Master Carew, Lord Howard, and Lord Guildford, may I present Lady Shilston?"

Anne curtsied properly to them and, to Mary's surprise, when she rose up, she was still smiling with what almost seemed like joy at what, only a moment before, was daunting courtly attention.

Was it possible that any man ever loved a woman more, Charles wondered from across the room, watching Mary with his sister. It was an odd sensation, the great passion he felt, when they had never fully made love, because he felt as connected to Mary as if she were the other half of him. He felt what she felt, hurt when she hurt . . . loved what she loved. He could still not bear to think of her with a corrupt old man lying with her, touching her, kissing her . . . filling her with himself night after night in the exotic world of the French court. The image in his mind brought a more excruciating pain than anything else he could ever suffer. She was his—heart, mind and soul.

Charles knew she did not want to go, even more than she had not wanted to go to Castile. Yet he reminded himself repeatedly that the life of a king's sister was not her own. As he watched her now move so smoothly through a branle, each step practiced perfection, he asked himself how he had ever deluded himself into thinking there might have been some small chance for them. She had been raised to understand that—just as she had accepted every step of the complicated court dances they did each night.

After observing so protracted an engagement with the emperor's grandson, Charles realized now that he had convinced himself a marriage would never actually occur. He had allowed himself after that first delay so many years ago to fall in love with her then. But not a reason in the world mattered a whit. By this new betrothal, everything in both of their worlds had changed forever. This one would happen. Mary would go away and become the Queen of France.

There was much to be gained by Louis in obtaining such a lovely and desirable English bride, if nothing more than to stop the threat of another English invasion next summer. Charles felt his stomach seize when he could not press from his mind the disturbing images of the ill, gnarled old man with *his* Mary. But he knew there was no way to stop those images from becoming a reality.

"So, tell me, Wolsey, what do you think of the rumors about Brandon and my sister?"

Across the room on a dais framed by an embroidered red tester, Henry balanced his chin on his jeweled hand as he put the question to his friend—a cleric who knew he owed him everything. Before them, a juggler worked his trade until the king made his usual dismissive gesture, then turned his gaze fully on the new Archbishop of York.

"Perhaps a bit of puppy love only, if there was ever anything. Yet lost, I am certain, beneath the pressing weight of my lady's obligation to her king and country." In spite of having put the notion into Mary's head, for love of her, Wolsey could not afford to be found complicit in anything if she decided to act upon it. That must be hers alone to achieve.

"And Brandon? What of his feelings for her?"

Thomas demurred, pushing out his lower lip in a studied pout of consideration. "Ah, well, sire, what man with eyes would not fall a bit in love with your sister?" He shrugged. "But ambition has made the Duke of Suffolk a wise man."

"He is indeed that," Henry concurred, and Wolsey could see his suspicions easing beneath the somber tone of the cleric's earnest assurance. Yet still Wolsey could see his gaze shift casually across the room to where Brandon stood speaking with the Countess of Devonshire. Wolsey knew he was happy to see that his friend was seemingly unaware of Mary, and engaging a new influential woman. It was good to see just now with so much riding on Mary's upcoming marriage.

"Brandon is *too* motivated toward his own elevation, in my view, to risk Your Highness's ire, considering all that is dependent upon this coming marriage, no matter how flattered he might once have been by a young girl's infatuation."

Henry scratched his chin. "But what of her confessions to you, Wolsey? As her friend, if not her personal cleric, you hear them regularly. Do they support your claim?"

Henry did not see Wolsey stiffen, or cast a glance of his own now across the room at Mary, who stood with Brandon's sister, both of them laughing at something said by Carew. It was a convenient circumstance that made it appear Mary had forgotten Brandon altogether, and he thanked the Lord just now for that.

"Your Highness knows that confession is a sacred thing, spoken about only with God."

"And your king! *If* I should will it, Wolsey."

"But of course, sire."

Henry had snapped at him with a glacial fury, which had begun to replace his easy laughter these days with alarming ease. Wolsey knew Henry was not just irritable because of the notion of his sister and his best friend. The once jovial, fun-loving prince was being replaced by a suspicious, moody king because his place among world rulers was once again called into question and, still without an heir, the line of succession was in doubt. After five long years of marriage, Katherine of Aragon had yet to produce a living child. Henry's patience with his wife's tears and the infant burials they continually endured had grown exceedingly thin.

"I am well pleased to hear it, Wolsey," Henry declared, his tone still harsh as he drew a leg of lamb from the gleaming gold plate and a spirited galliard was begun. "Because loyalty is key to me, my dear old friend. And I would not think twice about crushing anyone who might have a notion of betraying me . . . anyone at all."

The Duke of Buckingham had made a career of listening to everything, and betraying nothing. He had been sitting near enough to the king to be well placed, yet not so close that his own subsequent conversation with his old partner in intrigue, the Duke of Norfolk, could be overheard.

"Damn that son of an Ipswich butcher to hell," he growled, using yet another chance to remark on Wolsey's far more humble beginnings than his own. "I heard him lie as boldly as a whore to the king just now and Henry believed him."

"Take care, Edward. Wolsey is, after all, a man of God—which does give him a leg up above the two of us with our very pious sovereign."

"What God in heaven would take a snake like that? Or so gullible a king as he, for that matter."

"His Highness loves deeply and trusts in the same manner."

"Did he not learn his father's maxim to trust no one?"

"It appears he learned little from his father but how to take a mistress."

"Has he, at last?"

"He has been surprisingly unfaithful to that bushy-browed Spaniard—and with impressive frequency."

"Why, Thomas, that sounds suspiciously like envy. Has that daughter of mine not been accommodating enough?"

A bitter little silence sprang up as the lifelong rivals—one father-in-law to the other, when Buckingham's daughter, Elizabeth, had become Surrey's long-suffering wife—broached a subject never spoken about before. Still, it was well known now at court that Thomas Howard had begun a scandalous affair with one of his own wife's servants, and that Buckingham's daughter was unhappy about it.

"Elizabeth deserves better than that, Thomas."

"She was your concern until I married her."

His sharp eyes narrowed. "Yet I am a ruthless man, Norfolk—unhappy when I am crossed. Wolsey is about to discover that soon enough. I advise you not to make the same mistake with me," the Duke of Buckingham declared as the music and laughter swirled around them.

They met this time after midnight. They had chosen a secluded spot on the little gravel path past the croquet lawn, out beyond two clipped junipers standing like sentries as they flanked the top of three wide stone steps. The full moon was bright, shining down on them in a shimmery wash of silver.

"My love," Charles said as he took Mary tightly into his embrace and pressed his head into the turn of her neck. "Every day I think it will not be possible to love you more tomorrow than I do at that moment. Yet I always do."

She touched his face with gentle fingertips, searching each turn and facet; he thought it was as if it could help her remember him more clearly once they were parted. "And when I am in France, another man's wife? Will you still love me then?"

"I cannot bear to think of that."

"Yet we have only two days more. We must both think of it."

"I want every moment to myself of your remaining time. I will be greedy with you here, Mary. I'll not think of him." He kissed her deeply. "You must come to me like this tomorrow night as well. We must walk and talk and just be together."

Tears slid down her cheeks as she clung to him, and he warmed her with his tall, hard body and with the passion he had let her know he felt for her. "I want to give myself to you, my love . . . fully. . . . I want to belong to you before I face my wedding night . . . so that I never really will be his. . . . No one will ever know, I promise."

"But *I* will know," he said on a ragged whisper full of anguish for what every part of his heart, mind and soul wished to do with her and could not. He pressed her back into the wooden vine-covered pergola that had become their nightly sanctuary. The moon cast a shadow along the side of her face and on her smooth hair, which hung beneath her elegant pearl-studded cap. Charles framed her face with both of his hands, then kissed her again. "Never before have I loved a woman whose body I did not fully know, who I had not explored a dozen times and taken all that I could from her."

"You were a barbarian."

"The worst kind there is. I truly did not care about anything but my own pleasure, and advancement. Then I found you."

She kissed one of his cheeks, then the other, and smiled. "Come to think of it, I really should quite dislike you, shouldn't I?"

"It would serve me right if you did. But that you do not has changed me completely. What I see in your eyes is something I had never seen before—and, from the first, I liked it. You alone in this world made me want to be better, Mary." He drew something forth then from a small pocket in his doublet and gave it to her. It was the silver and onyx ring.

"I thought it was lost in France!"

"As did I." He smiled at her. He still could never tell her the truth of how things were when he was not with her—the kind of man he used to be, the things he had done coldly, willingly, for his ambition. But now he craved that innocent devotion that he still saw in her eyes every time she looked at him. That devotion, above all else, had changed him. Other women had always been easily taken in by him; there was no effort in it at all. But he knew that Mary actually believed in the man he could become.

And when she was gone, he would be Duke of Suffolk, wealthy, powerful, handsome . . . and wholly dead inside. But he would not, could not, tell her that. She would have enough to deal with when she arrived in France.

Alone in his private writing cabinet, with its paneled walls and low-beamed ceiling, Charles sank into the chair at his writing table. He drew up the letter once again that he had hidden in a drawer, pressed between two books.

> *Dearest Charles,*
>
> *How I do cherish the time we spent here together. You shall always be my fantasy of courtly love, and were it not for my father's ambitions, you would be my fantasy of a perfect husband to rule with me, as well.*
>
> *I am returning the ring, as I knew from the first, by the look on your face, that it was more dear to you than you were given leave to say. But I have heard the rumors, even here, and I bid you, dear heart, to consider what you do next. If they have come to me, all the way in France, your king has heard them as well.*
>
> *Take care with that. Your Henry is a complicated man.*
>
> *Margaret*

Charles read the words one last time, ran a finger over the cracked red wax seal, then reached over and submitted it all to the golden blaze of the small fire beside him. Margaret was a good woman, with a strong intuition. He smiled to himself as the flames seized the slip of paper consuming it, and then turning it to ash.

"So I am to be your husband," Longueville said on a stifled little laugh as they stood waiting. "Your proxy husband, that is."

Mary did not know Louis d'Orleans well, but in the months he had been at the English court, what she had seen of him she liked. The tall, elegant Frenchman, with prematurely silver hair, had a straightforward manner and an honesty that was all too rare. And, more importantly, he made Jane happy.

They stood now collected in a small chamber at the back of the chapel—Mary, Louis, Charles, his sister, Anne, the French ambassador, Wolsey, Norfolk, Buckingham and Queen Katherine herself. They were waiting only for Henry, whose presence was required to formalize the proxy match. The ceremony would take place at Greenwich as a warm August wind blew through the parted windows and rustled the gold cloth hung to decorate the walls of the small, close room.

Henry VIII had insisted on this symbolic gesture of a proxy marriage. He would take no chances, he said, with the sudden disintegration of this new, fragile alliance. Across the room, standing beside the queen, was Jane, content finally, Mary thought.

"She has been hurt, you know," Mary said quietly to Longueville, interceding for her friend with him as she had once done with Thomas Knyvet, in hopes of softening more blows Jane was destined to take in life if she continued on like this.

"She has told me everything."

"And you will take care with that knowledge once we are all in France?"

"You shall be queen, my lady Mary," he said, smiling with smooth confidence. "I shall do as you command."

"What I shall command is that you take care with her because it is in your own heart, not because it is in mine."

"Then it shall be as easy as breathing to do as I am bid," said the duc de Longueville charmingly. And, in spite of his smile, Mary found that she actually believed him.

Dressed in an elegant purple gown, with a pale gray satin petticoat beneath, Mary stood listening to the duc de Longueville speaking to her. But she did not fully hear the words for the heavy sensation of Charles's eyes upon her from across the room. From the corner of her eye, she saw him run a hand behind his neck and twist uncomfortably. She knew what he was feeling, even what he was thinking, because she was thinking it as well. There was nothing in the world Charles wanted but for life to be different, for it to be him beside her now, for her to be just a woman, and not a royal princess with obligation. . . . What the devil was taking Henry so long? she thought. All she wanted was for this to be over with.

After the little group moved inside the chapel, a High Mass was performed, and after the Archbishop of Canterbury preached a sermon in Latin, vows were exchanged. Through it all, she saw that Charles sat unmoving in the first row beside a proud, unaware Henry. Every time she caught a glimpse of him Mary made herself study every curve and turn of his face, even the shade of his hair. To give her strength for the difficult future that lay ahead, she needed to drink it all in, every nuance, since she knew how quickly she would be gone from these people she loved, especially Charles. Finally, painfully, as Longueville placed the French king's ring on her finger, she turned to see Anne put a hand gently on Charles's shoulder. Mary knew he believed he was losing her. But this was only the beginning. She was determined to see to that.

That night, Mary and Jane lay together in Mary's bed, protected by the tapestry bed curtains drawn around them, and cuddling as they had when they were little girls. Jane's nearness was a comfort when so much around her was changing.

Finally, all of the women who watched her every move, anticipating her needs, had gone to bed, and she had a bit of peace. Beyond the curtains, with only the slightest parting for a shaft of light, Mary's rooms were full of open trunks, paintings down from their mountings, folded gowns, stuffed jewelry caskets, writing supplies, books, all prepared for packing. They were gathering everything she would need to take with her to France.

Even though the hour was late neither she nor Jane could sleep. They had needed to gossip and share, for both of them had stories they could tell to no other, and the evening had been long and humorous. After the proxy wedding, Henry had insisted on the symbolic intimacy between Mary and Longueville, witnessed and duly recorded. With Charles's wounded eyes upon her and in the middle of all of the other attendants, Longueville, with a single bare leg, had joined Mary, in a silk and lace nightdress, in this very bed. With more witnesses than at a royal bear-baiting, he then touched one of Mary's bare legs with his foot in what she found a bizarre, yet required, symbolic act. Only then were they allowed to rise, dress again, try to forget the embarrassment of the moment, and attend a wedding banquet.

"What is it like to actually make love?" Mary finally asked Jane on a whisper, looking up into the darkened canopy, her eyelids finally heavy with a need to sleep.

"It hurts at first. Then, before you know it, it is the most wonderful thing there is in the world."

"And do you love Longueville?"

Jane looked at her, silent for a moment. "He is married with children back in France. But, yes, he makes me happier than I ever thought I could be again. I thank God every day that he will be returning with us, and that we can steal a bit of time together there."

"You do not care if you are never made a wife?"

"Not if I have him beside me, no. Oh, do you think me awful, Mary? I'm sorry, but it is the truth."

"I think you want love, and you have found it—albeit in an inconvenient place, yet you've found it nonetheless."

"As you have."

"As I have." She kissed Jane's smooth cheek then and let out a heavy sigh. "What would I do without you in France to confide in, to share with me? I accept my life there with an old and sick husband, but I certainly could not bear it without you."

Jane laughed softly. *"Moi aussi,"* she said, then lifted Mary's hand to study the black onyx and silver ring newly on her forefinger. "From him?"

"How did you know?"

"By the way you look at it, as if it is the Duke of Suffolk himself you are gazing at."

Now Mary laughed. "I admired it long ago, and he said he wanted me to have something with me always so that I would never forget him."

"We are not the sort of women who could ever do that. Is there no reasoning with the king? Perhaps asking him to include the Duke of Suffolk in your train who will accompany us? That at least might soften the blow for you both."

"I was told by Wolsey that my brother leaves for London at first light. He says it is business, but I suspect he does not wish to risk any argument with me until I am safely on the ship at England's shore. He and Katherine have promised to meet me at Dover to bid me farewell."

"Poor Katherine—it is little wonder that she would want to be there for you. She knows well enough about leaving her home, and all that she loves, to do the duty to which she was born."

"That she does." Mary looked over at her friend then, both of their faces cast in shadow and light as a small, genuine smile began to turn her mouth into a little mirthful half-moon. "In spite of the risks, I really am so glad you will return to see France again, and with Longueville, although if I am ever asked, I will deny to the death that I ever said so scandalous a thing."

Jane was still smiling, which was a sight Mary would never take for granted again. *"Merci, ma meilleure amie.* And something good for you will come of this marriage. I know it."

"By the look of his face in the portrait he sent, the best I can hope for is that my husband's illness prevents him from most things," said Mary as her own brave smile began very swiftly to fade. "But I suspect it will not prevent him from it all."

"What is this? We leave within the hour and you're not even dressed," Mary exclaimed, hands on her hips, as Jane sat curled in the window seat, knees to her chest.

"There has been a change of plans."

"Whose?"

"The French king has spoken with your brother. I am unwelcome in France. It seems my behavior with a certain duke has scandalized even the French court and I am no longer considered a suitable companion for a virginal English bride."

"That is preposterous! I will go to Harry myself. I will make him see that without you—"

"You waste your breath. I have just spoken with His Highness myself. It seems some part of his fond childhood memories are not entirely cut off to me, thus he did me the courtesy of informing me himself. Your future husband's words apparently were rather to the point: he would rather see me burned alive than there to serve his queen."

The harshness in that surprised Mary and made her despise Louis already. What a vile man he must be to judge Jane . . . to punish Mary when Jane alone would have brought her comfort in a foreign place. It was a foul thing to be a princess, not to have a life of one's own.

Mary went to Jane and sank onto the window seat beside her. They both gazed down then onto the mist-shrouded, undulating countryside, dotted with sheep and poplar trees. It was a vista, Mary realized then, she was not likely to see again for a very long time.

"I cannot bear the thought that I will not have Charles or you any longer in my life."

"You shall be without your Charles and I shall be without my own Louis. We shall be bonded forever by our misfortune and unhappiness in that, no matter where we are."

Mary kissed Jane's cheek. But she spoke no more words. This was not their safe little storybook haven at Eltham. They were little girls no longer. Duty, obligation, that was what lay ahead. Both of them were being made to know that well enough indeed.

Mary and the retinue assigned to accompany her made their way toward the Dover shore, an impressive collection of over one hundred noble ladies-in-waiting, gentlewomen of the chamber, chaplains, her almoner, her own yeomen grooms, everyone she could have wished—but the two she cared about most. She had left Greenwich Palace in a litter, sealing herself up tightly behind the tapestry curtains as if to hide, without saying good-bye to Charles or to Jane because the pain of it would have been almost unbearable. Their final moments, and that last conversation with his sister, Anne, moved through her mind, snaking down over her wounded heart, as Mary stepped down from the litter and onto the dock, wind blowing her hair.

"Take care of him, will you?"

"I will watch over him, always, as he does me. You know,

of course, that it will not be the same. There will never be an-other you *for Charles."*

"He is all that is my heart, or ever shall be."

She felt like a child now, uncertain, afraid, angry . . . so many things as they finally neared the shoreline. Mostly what she felt was desperation for the familiar, for the England behind her, when she turned toward the ink-black stormy water and saw the king's newly completed ship, the *Mary Rose*, bobbing in the harbor awaiting them. Her brother awaited her too and as she joined him she saw tears shining in his eyes. Katherine stood a pace away, arms wrapped around her waist. His sorrow was a surprise to Mary; she had not seen her brother show anything near to sorrow since they were small.

"I told you one day I would name a ship after you."

"You told me a great many things. Like you would never want the two of us parted."

"You will make a splendid queen," he finally said in a voice that broke, as they walked alone together the final few paces out onto the bobbing wharf. "Forgive me, my Mary. But it is right for England and for France."

Yet it is not right for me. . . . She longed to say that but there was no point in it. It was her duty. She would do it. She was proud. A Tudor. Charles knew that and understood it as well as she did. Still, the seed of an idea planted by Wolsey had grown to an obsession now in Mary's mind. Queen or not, this could not be the sum of her life. Her father had made two daughters who were far too determined for that. Suddenly, Mary wished more than anything that she could speak with her sister, Margaret, whom she had not seen since she was seven years old. Mary longed for her counsel, and had sought it in so many others at court; Lady Guildford, Jane, even Charles's sister, Anne. Yet Margaret alone would know how she might smoothly bring about a second marriage of her own choosing after a sacrifice made for England.

"Do not look at me like that, Mary. This must happen," Henry declared, a guilt she could hear bleeding through his every word. "You must understand. It is not a question of what *I* would want. It is what England requires!"

"And I am your loyal servant. Yet, grant me one favor and you will ease the burden upon my heart."

He half smiled, and she realized he must be a little relieved by the idea that he could do something to lighten the burden of guilt he felt.

"I will go to France and marry the old King Louis. But if I am widowed, I ask only one small thing: allow me to make my future my own. After I have been useful to you, permit me to choose my own path."

"But you are a princess, a king's sister. Without Margaret now, I may well have need—"

"Do this for me, Harry. I bid you for all of our little remembered moments, for what we have always meant to one another. . . . Give me this one small gift to hold on to. . . . Allow a young woman with dreams to feel that my life is not entirely lost already. Let me hope, girlish and silly as it is, for happiness and love one day before my death."

"Are you not a trifle young to be considering your death?" Henry asked.

"Tell that to our brother, Arthur."

He was silent for a moment. His half smile became a

frown. "If I agree to this you will go to France? And you'll not make me feel more guilt, as only you have the power to do?"

"Willingly and without complaint."

"Then it is promised by us both," said Henry VIII, the grudging half smile returning as tears slid onto his bearded chin.

Mary could hardly believe what she had heard, what she had got him to promise. Yes, Wolsey had put the notion into her head but she had never actually believed in her heart that Henry would agree to something like that, especially after what Margaret had done to him. Now, just when things seemed the darkest, Mary actually felt she suddenly had something to give her strength. Something at least to hope for.

"Then I will wait with all patience and hope for what my brother promised," she said.

"Yes, yes . . ." He swatted the air with a dismissive gesture, tired of the cold, the rain, and anxious to get back to his mistress now that this was resolved. "I did promise. One day, if you are widowed, you may have your way in it."

He held her close then and, in that single fleeting moment, she could feel a desperation in their connection. "Godspeed, my Mary," Henry whispered.

God speed me back to England, Mary was thinking. *And pray God, Charles waits for me because he knows nothing at all of any of this.*

Chapter Fourteen

On the twenty-second of September 1514, King Louis 12th, very old and feeble, left Paris, to go to meet his young wife, Queen Mary.

—Louise de Savoy, from her journal

September 1514, Abbeville, France

They met in a town along the silvery, snaking Somme River. The wedding would take place not in Paris but amid the lush beauty of the French countryside. The ambassador explained that Louis wished to meet his bride without the delay of the long trip further on to Paris. Mary knew it was an old man wanting to make his best impression first on a beautiful young bride. So far it was succeeding, she thought, as she rode in her open litter down the long tree-lined causeway toward the grand and elegant brick Hotel de la Gruthuse. She could already see that France was a completely different world from that which she had left behind. The trees, the sounds, even the fragrances of the flowers were different. An arc of plane trees, and a border of blood-red poppies and pink delphiniums, lined the gravel path that twisted and swayed in the warming late summer breeze.

Mary laid her head back against the cushion, closed her

eyes and tried very hard not to see an image of Charles in her mind. This was survival now, and to do that she must not think of him, nor could she acknowledge her longing even to herself. She must be more clever than her heart by half if she were to achieve her hopes. She withdrew from the litter with help from Lady Guildford and Elizabeth, Duchess of Norfolk, who was Buckingham's daughter. Also chosen to accompany her, from a long list considered, were Mary's familiar companion Lady Oxford, who was Norfolk's daughter, and her friend Lady Monteagle. Elizabeth dutifully arranged Mary's headdress, then straightened her thick silk skirts. The Duke of Norfolk, also selected for the journey, stood stoic and fatherly beside her litter, waiting. Mary's legs were stiff from the journey, and she was still weak from the seasickness she had suffered on the crossing. Mary had eaten little since she had left England. But, nevertheless, she was a striking figure in cloth of gold on crimson, with tight English-style sleeves, and a head-dress of matching crimson silk. She gave a defiant toss of her head, determined absolutely not to show the complexity of feeling behind her false smile. She meant with every part of herself to be the most remarkable queen possible and, pray God, the queen of shortest duration in France.

Before her, across a gravel-covered courtyard and past a grand stone fountain, a small delegation was waiting to greet her. Oh, how she missed Jane at this moment! Jane . . . who would have smoothed the way for her and made this first moment even the tiniest bit less awkward.

In the center of the well-dressed men, in their brocade doublets and fashionably padded trunk hose, jewels and chains, stood one much taller than the others—a chestnut-haired man with a regal air. That cannot be the king, Mary thought smugly; he is not nearly old or sickly enough. She bit back a smile as he came forward, hands clasped behind his back, chin lifted to an arrogant tilt and his amber-colored eyes glittering beneath heavy lids and long dark lashes.

"Your Highness," he said in French, making her a reverent bow and sweeping a jeweled hand dramatically before him. "I welcome you to Abbeville. I am Francois d'Angouleme, duc de Valois, His Majesty's son-in-law and heir."

The last word left his lips on a slight note of challenge, just as his eyes met hers. Of course, she thought, the opportunistic son of Louise de Savoy, husband of Louis XII's daughter. On the stormy trip from Dover, the duc de Longueville had told her all about them, and how Louise had made it her life's work to see her son one day on the French throne. *He certainly cannot welcome me here, the potential mother of the child who would unseat him.* No matter how ingratiatingly he smiled now, Francois could never be a friend. Mary made a proper curtsy in return, then met his eyes fully, almost in a challenge of her own.

"I trust your journey was a pleasant one," he added.

Pleasant as death, leaving behind those I love. "Pleasant enough."

"You are even lovelier than I was told."

"And you are even more clever than they said."

"Your Highness's French is very good."

"I have spoken it all of my life, so there are few things that will get past me here."

Francois bit back a smile and nodded to her, his match having been well and quickly met in this proud little English girl before him. "I am certain you are anxious to meet your husband."

"Most anxious, especially knowing how many others are looking forward to witnessing it."

"Indeed they are. How did you know?"

"Everyone likes a good show, monsieur. I suspect your king and I are about to give them one which everyone will be speaking about for many years to come."

So the arrogant heir is to be my true challenge here, she thought ruefully as Francois began to lead her, and her ladies, up the sweeping outdoor staircase and into the palace in a flurry and rustle of silk and petticoats. He did not speak further as they entered the palace and he led them up a second grand curved flight of stairs to the king's private apartments. But there was nothing positive he might have said to alter her impression. She did not like him.

They moved through a vast presence chamber decorated with massive Flemish tapestries, the ceiling painted azure and studded with gold fleurs-de-lys. It was stuffed with petitioners and ambassadors who had been waiting for hours to ask for favors or to do business with the king. They were silenced instantly by Mary as she passed, and she felt their eyes rooted on her. And she could not help but notice their manner. The French court was obviously an entirely different place from the English court she had thought of as glamorous. Now suddenly she felt out of place, that even her loveliest gowns would appear common. She also felt as if they were whispering as she passed, judging her. Imagine an English girl, she heard them say, the foreign princess pretending to be a proper French queen.

"Lift your chin, *ma fille*," she heard the duc de Valois say behind her. "The king prefers an abundance of confidence in those who surround him . . . that is, in all but his heir. Me, he wants gone from his life. Ah, but then again, it is no different from what I wish of him."

The way he said it made her stifle a laugh. Could she have misjudged him so quickly? Could someone dripping with such arrogance possibly understand from just their brief meeting the fear she felt, the bitterly homesick sensation and the sense of longing for all that she had left behind? Dressed up, painted, full of loyalty and duty, yet still she fought the urge to turn and run from her future.

The halls and corridors through which Francois led her seemed a maze and never ending. Paintings, statues, thick marble columns, frescoes and the cold echo of formality. Henry's court was warm and inviting by comparison to this quiet grandeur. But perhaps that was because she had been a part of it. Queen to be or not, here she was a stranger.

When they finally arrived in the third and last of the presence chambers, Mary felt a little intake of breath freeze her throat as she paused on the threshold of open, paneled double doors. Louis was suddenly before her, seated on a gilded throne with a thick purple silk cushion beneath him and matching tester above. His veined hands were hooked over the chair arms and he was slumped as if he were not quite conscious. He did not seem aware of her even as she approached and heard her name announced.

Around the king hovered a collection of ambassadors, aides, gentlemen and courtiers, not one of them breaking a welcoming smile in response to her arrival. Mary thought of them then as a circle of crows on the parapets of the Tower back in London, all waiting, watching expectantly to see her show her weakness.

Am I actually meant to bed with him?

That thought had been clattering around in her mind for hours as she anticipated their meeting, yet it pressed now like a cough wanting to burst forth as Mary stood for the first time facing the stoop-shouldered man, made elderly looking by lengthy and repeated illness, she was about to marry. Even in the shimmering golden candle- and firelight his gray parchment-colored skin hung from the bones of his face and hands like paint peeling from a wall.

Finally, Francois cleared his throat, which seemed to startle the king, who looked up and opened his eyes. "Ah. So you have arrived then."

His tone and lilting French were clotted and rheumy from his various illnesses, but Mary heard the definite note of sincere welcome behind it, the first since she had set foot in France. The king faltered to stand as she advanced, falling into a deep, respectful curtsy when she reached the throne. The censure she heard muttered behind a hand from one of the courtiers was remarkably clear.

"For an English princess, she is actually prettier than I expected."

"Pretty perhaps, but for all of the extravagance and bother they used getting her here, the style of her dress tells all. English fashion is really so unrefined."

Entirely taken with her beauty and not the nasty exchange, Louis held out a hand that trembled slightly as he waited for Mary to take it. The odor of camphor swirled around him and she fought a grimace. A door closed and the sound echoed in the silence. More whispers followed. Louis smiled expectantly at her and Mary felt her knees weaken as she forced herself to regard the man with whom she would do her duty to link England and France. Louis XII's patchy, untamable hair, in color, matched the long white satin shift edged in gold thread that he wore to hide the press of bones against his thin flesh. She had been told by Longueville that the king, once a handsome warrior who had actively fought in several battles, was now worn down by years of crippling gout, bouts of smallpox, and a debilitating heart condition, all of which had weakened him to the point of him appearing a much older man. The continuous pain from his ailments could be seen in his every move. She had been told that Louis was fifty-two, but to Mary the ravages of illness made him look as old as time.

He was her duty, they both knew that, and duty was a powerful thing. But the French, all so smug and judgmental, had no idea yet with whom they were dealing. Determinedly, she pushed another sudden bright image of Charles from her mind. She could not have him here now. That was over. She was on her own. How she handled this meeting, and these next few days, she knew, would determine the rest of her life. Now, a long way from Henry or his wishes for her, Mary was absolutely determined to play this part of her life, at last, entirely by her own rules.

"Your Majesty, it is an honor," she said in impeccable French, slowly rising from her curtsy in a cool and dignified manner and meeting the king's gaze.

"I would prefer our meeting were a pleasure to my queen. But I am too old and gouty a king to expect that."

"I assure Your Majesty, the pleasure follows the honor closely."

He smiled at that and Mary saw that, in contrast to the magnificent robe edged to the floor in ermine, his teeth were brown and uneven. Still there was something eager and surprisingly boyish in the expression he made. "Are you weary from your long journey? A rest first, perhaps?"

"Will Your Majesty walk with me?" Mary asked with a sweet smile.

"If we walk slowly. That would indeed be *my* great pleasure."

So he appeared to be a kind and gentle man. Mary had not bargained on that, she thought as she met his dottering pace and they went outside within a little garden, where she could smell the sweet heady fragrance of roses and hear the bees as they buried themselves deep into the fat red blossoms all around her. He leaned heavily on a polished onyx-tipped stick as they walked, showing his weakened condition, and he told her of the exquisite palaces that were her many homes now, and that in each he was eager to have her feminine counsel. He wished their palaces to reflect her taste and desires as much as his own.

"I am happy that you are here at last," he said to her almost shyly. "And I want you to be happy in France, Mary . . . as happy as a beautiful young woman can be with an old king."

"You are not old," she protested with a convincing smile as they sank together onto a stone bench. He groaned with the movement and Mary pressed a gentle hand onto his knee.

"And you are not a consummate liar. It is all right, though. Really it is. Knowing one's limitations and strengths is the mark of a good leader. Surely you learned that from your brother."

"We learned a great many things from one another, sire."

"Louis, please, when we are alone, *ma chérie*." He smiled, showing his brown teeth again. He touched a strand of her hair then, as if not quite believing she was real, or that he was about to make someone so extraordinary his very own wife. "So beautiful . . . Ah, I wish you had known me when I was a young man. I think I might rather have pleased you then."

"You please me now."

"I have not yet," he chuckled, which brought a little cough. "But I plan to do my best."

He drew forth from his robe then a diamond that was as large as an egg, set in gleaming silver. "It is called the Mirror of Naples for its size and flawlessness."

"It is exquisite," Mary gasped, trying to hide behind her back the other ring that she had always thought of as a real mirror, the one in which she would forever see Charles Brandon's face.

"A wedding gift, my *Marie*," he said, speaking her name elegantly, in the French manner. "Old men must be mindful to give beautiful young women better gifts than the handsome young men do, by half." His self-deprecating humor softened her. There were many things she had not expected of Louis, or France. That she might not totally despise him was certainly among them.

"When I was a young man, I still would have given this to you, but I was handsome then. And you would have flung your arms about my neck, and I would have taken you riding on a magnificent white palfrey to see all of the sights of Abbe-ville." Shifting on the bench, Louis let out a low groan once again.

"Are you all right, sire?"

"Dearest girl . . ." He sighed. "Nothing a few decades shaved away would not help. But tell me, does my gift please you?"

"Like no other jewel I have ever seen," she replied, twist-ing Charles Brandon's ring around so it was hidden at that moment in the palm of her hand.

"Then you shall make me very happy when you wear it tomorrow on our wedding day."

"Indeed I shall wear it proudly," she replied, almost meaning it.

He looked up at the sky and let out a sigh. "This court shall be a very different place now that you are here, bright and alive once again," he said with a smile. Then, as an after-thought he added, "One other thing. I know he is far more handsome than I, and far more clever, but do take care with my daughter's husband, Francois. He is ruthlessly ambitious and he quite believes this kingdom, and everything in it, is already his for the taking."

"It shall not be his at all if I give you a son," she said, uncertain why she wanted to comfort this ill, older man who still was nearly a stranger.

"It is that upon which I am staking my life, *ma belle*," he said with an intelligent, half-rakish smile.

There was much she had not expected here in her future husband: Louis' genuine kindness or his sophisticated wit, his ability to make fun of his own age and infirmities. Perhaps, she thought, it just might not be so dreadful being Queen of France after all.

Mary was glad to be shown her apartments at last, just as the sun began to set. In a dressing room facing the courtyard, she stood limp as a rag doll as she was stripped of her dress, her layers of petticoats, stockings and her linen shift. The rooms of the Hotel de la Gruthuse were grand, with soaring ceilings frescoed delicately with biblical themes, rather than beamed as so many of them were in England. The style of furnishings was delicate as well. The carpets, like the frescoes, were complex and detailed rather than bright and bold.

She looked across the room, drawn to a sweepingly elegant gown that had been arranged on a tabletop, and a young dark-haired girl who stood combing the fur-trimmed collar with a brush. The dress was heavy gold brocade, trimmed with ermine, clearly in the French design.

Mary realized the girl, who could not have been more than ten years old, was to be part of her court.

"What is that?"

"It is Your Highness's wedding dress for tomorrow," the girl said shyly in French, with just a telltale hint of an English accent.

"But of course I have brought my wedding dress with me."

Glances were exchanged by the diverse collection of women, both French and English, who cluttered the room in a rival collection of English and French fashion. In the silence, Mary looked to Lady Guildford first, who simply shook her head, as if to say she had no idea. Then her glance moved to the plump and pretty Duchess of Norfolk, whose expression was blank. Finally, it was Claude, the king's stocky, awkward fifteen-year-old daughter and new bride to the heir, Francois, who moved toward her. "His Majesty felt a French queen should begin her reign in French fashions."

"And did the king wonder perhaps what I felt on the subject? No, I see from your face he did not." *Any more than he cared what I felt about not having my dearest friend in the world here with me. Thank God I still have Lady Guildford and Lady Oxford to keep me from being too lonely,* Mary thought, her newborn fondness for the king quickly evaporating in the face of these reminders of how little control she had over her own life.

"It really is a most exquisite gown that shall be the talk of all the world," the dark-haired girl shyly said, yet with a hint of her own charisma shining through in it. Mary saw the spark, and heard it—there was a hint of herself in the tone. She moved toward the dress. It really was an exquisite thing, intricately sewn and quilted, then studded with tiny rubies.

"Are you to be in my company from now on?"

"If it please Your Highness," the girl replied, making a proper little curtsy.

"I suspect it will please me since I cannot have my Jane. You are English after all."

"You could tell?" She sounded disappointed.

Mary leaned forward sweetly. She recognized now that this girl must be from a noble family sent to the French court to be raised in style, as so many English girls were. Her words came in a tone just above a whisper. "An Englishwoman can always tell another Englishwoman. What is your name, girl?"

"My uncle is the Duke of Norfolk, Your Highness. I am called Anne Boleyn."

The grand banquet in Mary's honor that evening was a turbulent sea of introductions into which she was plunged, body against body—all nodding, bowing, dancing, dripping candle wax, fireplace smoke, laughter and endless tales of life in France. Before their official wedding the following morning, Louis wanted to present his beautiful young bride properly to everyone, and he wished his entire court to hear and see the lovely young girl who was about to become Queen of France and make an old man young again. Unlike in England, where she was admired and envied, here she was an oddity, someone about whom to gossip and stare. She was so uncomfortable that she was relieved when Francois requested her partnership in a branle. He stood before her, eyes flashing along with his smile. When the music began he extended his hand and bowed, as if refusal were not an option. Mary took his hand with great dignity.

"I was told you were pretty," he said, his amber eyes glinting mischievously at her. "I am pleased to know that was an understatement."

She shivered beneath his gaze. But he did not see that. "I am many things, monsieur. But I hope always a surprise."

"Oh, I have little doubt of that. A pity it is to be wasted on one unable to fully appreciate the pleasure of it."

She laughed at him for how absurdly obvious his flirtation was. Mary grabbed his arm, as the danced dictated, and let him turn her. Before she knew it, the song was at an end. He bowed. She curtsied, then took his arm again.

"I am thirsty," Mary said. "Perhaps you could fetch me some wine."

"I would give you far more than that if you would take it."

Mary wanted to laugh aloud, but she only smiled. What a world away this was from England.

"For now the wine will do nicely," Mary said.

The wedding took place in the chapel of the king's residence at the Hotel de la Gruthuse. Lady Guildford wept, and the plaintive sound echoed up from the front row of the cavernous stone chapel as Mary recited vows that were her duty to the stranger who held her hand. Determination pushed her. It took her to another place. *Henry would be proud. My mother too. I am a Tudor like all the other Tudors before me. I know my duty. I also know my heart. This will not break me.*

Mary felt as if she were somewhere else during the entire ceremony, not quite a part of her own body. As the Mass was spoken, the songs sung in Latin and French, she stood regally still, attired in the French gown selected for her, that cloth of gold, trimmed in ermine, and studded with diamond clasps. In her hair a coronet of sapphires and rubies glittered.

She saw by a sideways glance at Louis that a surprising wellspring of tears was glistening in his sad, tired eyes as the archbishop droned in Latin. How complex a man was he, to weep for a girl he did not know? Mary softened toward him again and took up his cold hand between the folds of her heavy gown and his elegant doublet, barring the gesture. He turned to her briefly and their eyes met, just before he turned away.

She felt him tremble, then falter against her. She squeezed

his hand to steady him. His court must not see a weakened king on his wedding day. Nor must the duc de Valois see it. Something about the French heir reminded her of Charles Brandon long ago—yet without the heart or strength of character to soften him. She felt a painful little wrench in her heart as the comparison came to her . . . until she realized she had allowed a memory in. *Charles . . . my heart . . . my life . . .* The image of him took hold like a flame, flared brightly in her mind, then burned and faded as Louis took her other hand and, vows repeated, slipped the small gold ring onto her finger, replacing the proxy band, and officially making her Mary, Queen of France.

The king and queen stood framing the royal black oak bed with its intricately turned posts and soaring purple satin canopy, fringed in gold thread and stamped with gold fleurs-de-lys. Around them were French courtiers, nobility and ambassadors from England and France, opulently layered in rich velvet doublets and heavy chains. The noblewomen among them wore gowns with slashed sleeves and tight-fitting bodices, their bare breastbones strung with gold and pearls.

For all of the elegance, the noxious odor of ambergris, civet and sweat permeated the vast, tapestry-lined chamber. Most of those around them were drunk and swaying, making Mary weak, making it all seem so much worse. Louis XII gazed at her, his white silk nightshirt showing through the robe, as dozens of long white tapers burned and the flames danced around them. *I must endure a moment of disgust in order to please my brother . . . my dearest friend—but it is the*

necessary first step toward the happiness I seek, the sacrifice that
will be rewarded with my greatest dream. . . .

Her own resolve helped to ease the worst of the disgust
rising up so powerfully within her. Her new husband smiled
back, brown teeth glistening at her. Someone cleared his
throat but she did not see who as she watched the bed linen
being sprinkled with rose water. Mary and Louis lowered
their heads dutifully then for the bishop's blessing of the holy
marriage bed. She was glad to have Lady Guildford there
beside her, with her fleshy face and kind, pale blue eyes. Yet
she would always miss Jane . . . so dear a friend. It was hard
to feel more than pity for Louis at this crucial moment, knowing how he had prevented Jane from attending her in France
with the others. Whore, he had called Jane for the impure
things she had done. They were the very same things Mary
would have done with Charles in a heartbeat if he would
only have agreed. *Thank the sweet Lord,* she thought then,
that my husband knows nothing of the thoughts that steal
through my mind even now!

After the blessing, Mary took a step back and lifted her
head. Her shimmering red-gold hair was long and loose upon
her shoulders, and topped at the crown with a different coronet, this one simply of pearls hooked to a thin veil. She wore
a delicate, flowing nightdress of Burgundian lace, with tight,
fitted sleeves that were also dotted with pearls. She looked,
she knew, far more angelic than she felt.

Beside Louis, Francois stood tall and commanding in
a doublet of garnet silk. The expression on his face was a seductive smile, accented with a spark of expectation. It was
the expression he always wore when he regarded Mary. *Does*

he truly believe he shall be next in my bed when my aged, ailing husband expires? Mary had wondered more than once.

Francois' young bride, Claude, had escorted Mary to the bedchamber, along with Anne Boleyn; Anne's younger sister, Mary Boleyn; Lady Guildford; Elizabeth, Duchess of Norfolk. But Mary saw that her new stepdaughter's kind smile and doleful gaze were downcast. Poor Claude, an adolescent bride, had no idea that her husband had been pursuing Mary with his every look and gesture since she had set foot in France. And why should she worry? Mary knew that the overtures were made in order one day to accuse her of infidelity so that a son's paternity—and thus the succession—could be challenged.

Louis reached out to her then, bringing the aroma of perspiration, ambergris and his own specially noxious hint of camphor. As he did, Mary's thoughts ceased, pushed back behind the unease. A huge ruby set in silver flashed on his veined, liver-spotted hand. The moment was near. There would be no avoiding it.

Dear Lord, grant me strength, Mary thought as her heart began again to pound. *And more than a little bit of blindness!*

She had one choice, and one choice only. She could not escape the duty that lay before her this night. The only way out must therefore be for her to give a feeble man all that he craved, and amply, and let God decide the outcome. Could anyone truly fault her or think her hideous, after all, if she simply did her duty to her amorous husband? Her body and her love was what he wished. She would give him only that.

The king drew her to him then, and they stood together

at the foot of the bed, her warm trembling hand linked with his cold one. Their faces were both lit by dozens of long, glowing tapers as he lifted her hand and kissed the knuckles with large wet lips. Mary watched a bit of color rise onto his gaunt cheeks. Mercifully, their audience filed from the room then, shuffling through the arched doorway and past the royal guards, posted on the other side. Only the king's senior-most *gentilhomme de la chambre* remained, yet far from the couple, near the door that had just been closed. Mary blew out one of the candles but Louis stopped her at the next one.

"Ah, my *Marie* . . . ," he said softly in melodic French, but his voice retained that tremor of an old man.

"Whatever your heart's desire, I wish to please Your Majesty," she replied as humbly as she had been trained all of her life to do.

This alliance meant the world to Henry. It was more than a marriage. It was England securing her place in the great triumvirate of Spain, France and the Holy Roman Empire. It was power. Mary would not jeopardize it for him. She must say that to herself again and again, until she heard nothing else. With staunch resolve, she kissed Louis fully then, her lips opening so that he might open his own, nearly choking her at needing to do so. But kissing a man with seduction in mind was something she had already done.

Another moment passed as he lifted his hand to her breast and it stilled there. She thought of Charles yet again . . . of all the moments between them that had brought her to this place. All the things that had made her not his wife but Queen of France.

"I know you shall please me well," he murmured.

"You are my husband."

"And you are my queen."

May the good Lord save me, she thought, *but I am.* While she had played at lovemaking with Charles in the maze at Richmond, Mary was going to her wedding bed a maiden. So it was a blessing, she believed, that she was a Tudor, and she was every bit her father's daughter. For surely she needed the courage of a warrior to face what lay before her.

Louis pressed another kiss, this one wet and amorous, onto her cheek just then, yet he did so with surprising tenderness before he buried his face in her hair. She felt his hot, sour breath at the turn of her neck. Revulsion rose up once again. He still held her hand to draw her forth as he blew out the last remaining candles. But the effort of doing so led him into a fit of coughing. The sound was rheumy and very unpleasant. Candle smoke snaked and swirled around them, wax dripping onto the cold, inlaid tile floor.

When the coughing did not cease, a servant, dressed in plush blue and red livery, with neatly combed chin-length hair, stoically advanced. He led Louis, shuffling in his slashed and decorated slippers, through a small private door. Mary knew that the passage did not lead into the vast, formal corridor where the court would be waiting. They would assume for the rest of the night that nothing had even for a moment parted the couple.

Promising her, with a nod and a reassuring half smile, that he would return in a moment's time, Louis and his gentleman disappeared into the adjoining room with a click of the door handle, leaving a still lingering scent of camphor.

Mary sank onto the end of the bed, the enormity of the day descending on her fully only then as flames in the massive fireplace hearth dried the tears on her cheeks. The new smooth gold band on her finger still felt an annoyance, something she had nervously twisted with her thumb since the moment Louis had placed it there. The Mirror of Naples had taken the place of Charles's ring on her other hand. There had been no other choice. She could have no symbol of him, no constant reminder.

When her husband did not return, Mary rose and went into the adjoining dressing chamber where her things for morning had been meticulously laid out along with anything else personal she might desire. Beside her hairbrush lay an ivory-handled mirror, a jar of her favorite balm of Mecca and a small silver jewelry casket. Beside that lay her journal, bound in red leather and stamped in gold with her brother's crest—a Tudor rose topped by a gold crown. She waited, still turning the gold band around on her finger, wondering when Louis might return . . . or if he even meant to come to her at all, and not caring at this moment, either way.

Much was made the next morning as the *gentilhomme de la chambre* pulled back the doors and the waiting courtiers flooded into the bedchamber to find king and queen asleep in the same bed. Seeing them around her, Mary rose, avoiding their gaze and ignoring the snickering laughter. She drew on a waiting velvet robe from Lady Guildford and withdrew quickly from the room. As she passed into the dressing chamber and a collection of waiting women surged protectively around her, she heard Louis happily, vulgarly boast, beyond the doors.

"Ah, gentlemen. It is done. I did indeed cross the river thrice last night and would have done more had I chosen."

A little spasm of contempt worked its way up in her throat. She alone knew the truth. Louis had not returned to her through the little private door until dawn and then he had done so with the huffing groans of an old man. He had crawled into bed beside her, rolled onto his side, seemingly relieved that she appeared to be asleep. That was how they had been found an hour later, as the sun rose, Mary on her back, gazing up at the canopy, Louis asleep beside her. *Charles . . . I miss you . . . ,* she was thinking.

That afternoon, a collection of jewels was laid out meticulously on a strip of crimson velvet for her selection: a diamond and emerald choker, several pearl necklaces, a sapphire bracelet and a cabochon ruby necklace, an overwhelming selection. Nearby lay yards of fabric: blue silk woven with gold, lavender silk edged in silver, and extravagant black and ivory velvet. Louis meant to spoil her with these gifts, perhaps to control her as well—and to make amends for their wedding night. But she would not think of that just now. Not when she was trying to find her way and feel just a little bit less of the pain that loss and love and homesickness had brought to her. She fingered the cabochon rubies. Henry had sent her to France with an impressive collection of English jewelry, but there was nothing like this.

She looked over at the young girl, Norfolk's raven-haired niece, and paused for a moment. Mary took her chin in her hand so their gazes met. "Tell me, Anne. Which one would you choose for me to wear today?"

The girl examined the selection of jewels glittering before her. As Mary had done, she put a finger to her chin, in consideration. "Definitely not the ruby. It does not suit your hair."

Mary looked at her, the raven-black tresses falling long over her shoulders beneath a pearl-studded cap, wide blue eyes, lethal in their innocence. "Yet it does suit yours. So you may try it on."

"Your Majesty," she had the good grace to gasp, "I could not."

Mary thought Anne too poised to be truly humbled. There was something about her, an odd confidence, too marked for that. Mary picked up the jewel, reached behind the girl's slim neck and clasped it there. Even though she was still a child, as she had suspected, it did suit her perfectly.

Mary smiled with years of confidence the girl did not yet have. "How does it feel?"

"As if an angel himself were caressing my throat, Your Majesty."

As the ladies around her chuckled with varying notes of condescension, Anne Boleyn reached up very gently to touch the jewel, her eyes wide as saucers now as her sister, Mary, stood silently near the door. "May I look?"

"I bid you, do."

She stood for what felt a long time admiring herself in the gold-framed looking glass set out on the queen's dressing table. Mary could hear two of the French gentlewomen whispering as the reflection she saw seemed to transform the child into something she found almost regal. A moment later, when she still had not made a move to return it, Lady Guildford advanced.

"That shall be enough, child," she directed in a clipped tone. "You are to put away the others once the queen has chosen, not hope to try them all."

The crescendo of laughter broke through the girl's hauteur and, for a moment, seemed to chasten her. Then Mary saw a little willful spark reignite in her eyes. "My uncle is the Duke of Norfolk, my lady, and he would not be pleased to have you chiding me."

"I do not suppose he would be overly pleased to know his young relation showed such arrogance in the presence of the queen! One wonders, when he put you here to be of service, which would anger him the more."

Experience had triumphed over youth, and Anne Boleyn lowered her eyes.

"I shall wear the pear-shaped diamond," Mary announced to warm the chill that had fallen suddenly upon them all. She adored Mother Guildford, but Mary was struck by this girl, who seemed somehow different from any other little girls she had ever known.

That evening, there was a theme to the banquet. The new queen and her court were attired as Virtues and Vices for the benefit of the citizens of Abbeville, who would be allowed to witness the extravagant festivities as they advanced to the great hall across a path symbolically strewn with roses and lilies. Mary danced with a blinding succession of French nobility, then Francois, duc de Valois, in a rich velvet doublet of teal blue silk and brown velvet, slashed with gold. But with him she danced only reluctantly. His sloe-eyed gaze was always upon her, expectantly, slyly, as if she were prey to be marked for the future. As the dance brought them together, so did his hands. A brief touch to the part of her gown where her thigh pressed against the layers of linen, lace, silk and velvet, the curve of her hip, a skim of his hand to her breast. As heir to the throne of France, he was aware of his power at the French court and took full advantage of it. Mary disliked him immensely but she also realized fully that he was someone with whom to be cautious now that she was trapped here. Still, she could not entirely control her clever tongue.

"Your Majesty's beauty this evening is matchless," he said too smoothly, offering the flatterery as they danced.

"And your flattery, monsieur, is as dull as dirt."

There was a faint gleam of malice in his twisted smile amid the flicker of candle lamps and fire glow. As the dancers moved around them Francois turned, then bowed. "Ah, I have often heard it said that it is best not to burn one's bridges too quickly with ingratitude, madame."

"The same people advise one not to burn one's bridges by coveting another man's wife, no doubt."

"Which shall prove true first, one wonders, my platitude or yours?"

"Clearly a risk on both sides, monsieur le duc," Mary said.

The Duke of Norfolk had watched the dance and heard the exchange. Poor little fool, he thought to himself. Mary really was out of her league with a Gallic snake like that. And it certainly took one to know one, he thought with his own twisted little smile. What set him apart was that no one, except perhaps Buckingham—who was not nearly so skilled at hiding his motivations—knew Thomas Howard for the reptilian self-server he was. And he meant to keep it that way.

It was so warm with this press of bodies and all of this fabric that he was perspiring—and he hated how he appeared when he was glistening with sweat. He knew it took away the aura of easy grace he had spent a lifetime cultivating. Norfolk had seen the expression of panic on Mary's face as the heir had approached her. But she must come to believe she could meet the challenge. A contented and confident Mary was one who would remain in France and happily out of his way back in England. She had too much influence on her brother, and he had worked too hard to go on sharing it on too many fronts. He still had Brandon to contend with, as well as Buckingham and Wolsey. But having been given the extreme honor of a dukedom had rekindled his enthusiasm for the battle of place. Buckingham still believed himself to have some ancient claim to the throne, so Henry would never trust him. Wolsey was only a cleric, who could never fully advise a king on the challenges of a man. If he could next somehow convince Henry that Brandon had lied treasonously about his feelings for Mary, Norfolk's place beside the king would at last be unchallenged.

But each change began with one small step.

With that in mind, he dotted the perspiration from his upper lip and advanced toward the new queen just when the song was at an end.

"A dance, Your Majesty?"

"Thank you, Thomas," she sighed, bowing to Francois, then turning fully toward him, almost, he thought, falling against his chest in relief. "I am now in your debt."

"I am here in France to serve Your Majesty," he skillfully replied.

"Just remind me of home from time to time, Thomas. I assure you, that shall be enough to serve me. I am so desperately homesick for England already."

That night, as Mary sat beside her husband's bed, having Lady Guildford brush out her hair in long, even strokes, Louis came into the room through the little side door he had used the night before. He nodded to his gentleman, who bowed, then silently saw himself out. But unlike their wedding night, there was no further ceremony, no audience, no protestations of prowess.

Lady Guildford looked up and gave a motherly little grunt of disapproval that Mary was glad only she saw. She stubbornly made no move to leave. Anne Boleyn was pushing a warming pan between the bedsheets and Lady Oxford had sprinkled the crisp linen lightly with rose water.

Louis lingered near the door for a moment before he began to scowl at Lady Guildford.

"You had better leave us," Mary said to her softly in English.

"Are you certain, my sweet?"

"He is my husband before God. It is your duty, and mine."

She grunted again, struggling to stand as the moment of her kind expression faded. Then she helped Mary into bed.

She did so, though, without ever once meeting Louis' reproachful stare. Anne Boleyn lingered near as well, still holding the warming pan as Mother Guildford leaned over, gently smoothed the hair back from Mary's forehead and kissed her there.

Finally, after they had all gone, Louis blew out each of the white wax candles until they were in darkness. She could feel him climb silently into the bed beside her and she was instantly aware that he was naked. He reached out and found one of her breasts with rough, trembling fingers. They stilled there for a moment as he moved himself nearer, his leg wrapping over hers. She could feel him hesitate until she reached up to his shoulder, inviting him closer. For a man twice married, he seemed oddly uncertain.

He searched for her lips in the darkness and she met him by the sheer force of her will to do now, tonight, what she must. As he probed her mouth with his tongue, at last becoming excited enough that she could taste his moan and feel his hardness against her thigh, Louis pressed a hand forcefully up between her legs. Her mind spun. *Do it now and be done with it,* she thought, pushing back the press of panic. *So that I may sleep . . . so that I may dream. . . .*

The next sensation was sharp, a mix of pain and surprise, so sudden and yet so brief that Mary had not a moment to cry out or to resist it. Once, twice, his chest against her, now awash with perspiration. Then as quickly, he drew himself from her, rolled onto his back, gave a grand sigh and was still. Only the deep snoring that followed told her he had not just expired entirely from the exertion.

It was a duty, she reminded herself yet again, as if to

convince herself yet again. She was fine. She had done it and she was glad. She lay very still watching him sleep as the sun slowly rose. And then the odd thought came to her. At least one day, when it came, the King of France would die a happy man. *May God forgive me,* her mind pressed in the thought, *but may that be sooner, much sooner, than later.*

The king came eagerly to her bedchamber every night after that. Rarely were his amorous intentions met with the success he intended. In spite of the groping, grunting and perspiring, he was usually unable to completely make love to his wife. Yet he would lie with her anyway in the pearl gray light of early morning, hold her hand, and whisper to her about his plans for their future. When it came time to ride toward her coronation outside of Paris, he explained to her that he wanted her to exercise a right of the queen that would endear her to the French people. As they passed into each town, one after the other, she must free all of the prisoners, a show of the new queen's generosity and compassion. When he spoke of such things she heard the excited tremor of a boy, mixed with the exultant timbre of a completely happy man.

Each day, Louis would dress elegantly for her pleasure alone, he would tell her, and they would attend matins together. As they sat in stoic silence, surrounded by the spoken rhythmic elegance and the echo of Latin prayers, Louis would take her small hand and squeeze it in a way that no one would see. Then afterward, they would stroll slowly through the vast gardens that linked the private chapel and the Hotel de la Gruthuse, Louis pointing out to her his favorite flowers and plants. Marriage had transformed him, the duc de

Longueville, Jane Popincourt's love, told Mary one afternoon as the king sought to play a round of *jeu de paume* in order to impress his vibrant young bride. She sat with Longueville beneath a fluttering canopy, also with her collection of ladies, both English and French, all there to watch the king. Mary felt a little burst of triumph hearing it.

"People here were certainly skeptical at first. But no one at court has seen His Majesty behave like this for a decade or more."

She smiled serenely, as she had seen her mother so often do. "It is a blessing to know a husband is well pleased by his wife."

"And is the wife equally pleased?" There was just the smallest glimmer of sarcasm in the words and Mary looked up at him in response with a little frown. "Do not inquire about my heart, Longueville, and I shall not inquire about yours."

"Oh, I spoke not of Your Majesty's heart." He threw back his silver-haired head, hiding a devilish, thin-lipped smile. His laugh was good-natured as his eyes crinkled at the corners, and she found herself wondering if so fun-loving an opportunist, returned now to his reality, truly was capable of missing Jane. How long could any man miss a woman once she had gone from his life? Even her brother Henry did not seem capable of real fidelity, in spite of his protestations of love for Katherine. Could Charles really be any different? Perhaps *forever* was something best left to the pages of the great romances. She had something solid now. Something sure. She was Mary, Queen of France. At least, as she watched the old man before her struggle with a gaming racket, that was what she tried her very best to convince herself.

As Louis came away from the field carried on a litter, looking ever more battered and weakened by his pervasive heart condition and the host of other illnesses that had aged him beyond his years, Norfolk met up with him. He bowed overly ceremoniously. "Your Majesty was brilliant. I could not have played a better round myself."

"You are as old as I am, Norfolk," he countered irritably, still trying to catch his breath, as a page held out a large silver basin and Louis splashed his face, trying to revive himself with water. In spite of his mood, Norfolk had ingratiated himself as skillfully with Louis as he had with Henry back in England, and Norfolk had managed very swiftly to become something of a confidant.

"As an Englishman of Henry's court, I know that you know her well, you are accustomed to her behavior, so tell me, did the queen see me? Was she watching? That is really all that matters."

"I'm afraid I only saw the duc de Longueville speaking with her. But Lady Guildford could not take her eyes from Your Majesty. That at least is something."

"The old crone was not watching me, Norfolk. She was judging me, as always, since the day she set foot in France."

Norfolk shook his balding head. "I never did understand Wolsey's agreement with Henry in sending her over here. She is far too old for such a vivacious young queen, and far too judgmental," he remarked, accustomed to making trouble and thus elevating himself everywhere he could. "But my lord of York, as he is called, now that he has found himself a title as archbishop, still clings to the notion that he knows better than our English king. I believe Lady Guildford sends him dispatches, reporting on anything he asks. Their affection for one another is of long standing. But perhaps I have said too much."

"I always thought Wolsey a better judge of character than to allow the sort of woman to come here in my wife's train to become a virtual spy in my own household against me."

"I would have thought so once as well, sire. But ambition changes a man. Even a man of God."

Louis' eyes narrowed with irritation. "And has it changed you, Norfolk?"

He bowed deeply. "I like to believe I am the same man I have always been, Your Majesty."

Two days later, Mary stood before Louis, her smooth face white with rage. Anger and panic were a potent brew seizing her throat, her heart and her ability to reason. Her hands were on her hips, covered now in a magnificent gown of ecru silk studded with tiny pearls, and the chain she wore jangled at her waist as she moved. "When did you plan to tell *me* what you had done?"

He shifted from one leg to the other and she saw the grimace of pain harden his face. "Certainly before we left for Fontainebleau."

"In two days' time? Yet you have told Lady Guildford and the Countess of Oxford that they are to return to England with Norfolk tomorrow?"

Mary did not remember ever being so angry. She forced

herself to focus on the words that were swirling around in her mind, driven into a jumble by how she believed she had been duped. Forcing her to leave Jane behind had been horrid. But this was worse because she knew Louis now, and had even trusted him a little.

"They are no longer suitable for my court or yours," he said curtly. "It really is that simple, *ma chèrie*. Make no more of it than that."

Such hubris. Louis pretended to care what pleased her, yet he would do as he pleased, even with the things that mattered to her. "But have they done something?" she asked, unable to keep the pleading from her question because she could not imagine herself here, entirely cut off from everything, and now everyone, who had brought her some bit of comfort. "Perhaps you did not know it, but Lady Guildford is like a mother to me, Louis."

"I am aware of that. And to be frank, that is the very reason Lady Guildford is ever the more unwelcome by a husband. Her constant presence, her expressions of distaste, compromise the intimacy between us, and I will not have that."

"And her absence compromises *my* happiness. I need her with me, Louis! I thought you wished me to be happy here!"

"I wish for *us* to be happy. Apparently, we can have one or the other."

"I bid you, do not take them all away from me!"

"It is not all. I have chosen to allow your almoner, your personal physician, the Marquess of Dorset's brother, Lord

Grey, to remain, and grudgingly, even two Englishwomen to attend your bedchamber."

"Those you name are nothing to me! They bring me no peace at all. I am going to write to my brother. I am going to tell him everything!"

"A wife is to cleave to her husband, not to her childhood friends—or her brother. Even if he is a king." His bloodless mouth tightened and he stared at her, unmoved by her pleading. "I have seen that you cannot be the Queen of France I desire you to be if they remain. You are too tied to England with them here to remind you of your other life all of the time."

"You wish to cut me off from all that I hold dear, then fence me in as if I were some sort of animal?"

"I thought you might hold your king dear, if not your husband."

Mary felt ill suddenly. Betrayed. Trapped. "I deserve better than this, Louis."

"Better than being Queen of France, *chère Marie*?" He arched a challenging snowy brow, then gave her a cold little shrug. "There is a price to be paid for all gifts with which the good Lord blesses us. You are young, so I shall forgive you a small bit of your self-indulgence. But one way or another, it is a lesson you shall learn well soon enough."

Mary stood at the windows inside her bedchamber late that night, unmoving as she gazed down into the darkness of the vast gardens. Louis had been seized earlier by another attack of gout and would not come to her tonight. The announcement from one of his liveried grooms was a blessing, Lady Guild-ford knew. Tonight Mary could not have conjured the smile and encouragement he required, no matter how she might have tried.

"Dear heart," she said soothingly to her young charge, touching her shoulder. "I have been entrusted with a letter. The gentleman who sent it knew I would see it safely to you."

The revelation was soft, almost whispered. They had never once spoken of Charles Brandon in more than a pass-ing way, yet it was clear Mary knew instantly that it was he whom she meant. Lady Guildford then held out a letter sealed with the familiar crimson wax letter *B*. The pain in the girl's heart at that moment was impossible to witness.

"Toss it into the fire. You must leave no trace of it."

"But you have not yet even—"

"You heard me well enough." Mary turned away and gazed into the fire, purposefully pinching a piece of lace at the edge of her sleeve until she felt in control of herself again. She drew in a deep breath, willing her heart to slow. Finally, she turned back, having pressed the tears back from her eyes. This was her life, her expression clearly said. She was a woman, a wife, a queen. There was no room for girlish fantasy now. She was not abandoning her dream, never that. But for the moment, with a husband, and duty, she could not afford to think of it.

"It will make me sad, and I cannot afford to be sad just now, Mother Guildford, with you leaving me as well."

"Dearest child," she said soothingly, her own round face touched by the same sadness as Mary's, as she gently brushed the smooth plane of Mary's cheek. "Life is long. Circumstances do change."

"If I read his words, any of them, I would hear his voice in my head again, I would feel his arms around me, and to be a good wife, a good queen, to another man—I could not bear that."

Knowing well enough the stubborn streak that ran through every Tudor vein, Joan Guildford nodded compliantly, then dutifully surrendered the letter to the flames. Perhaps it was just as well, she thought as they stood together watching it turn to ash. Although she would never say it, she did not believe Charles Brandon was the marrying sort. Certainly not the seriously marrying sort for a matter of the heart. And Mary's heart had been far too tied up with his for too long. Of course she had always known, because she was old and she understood about first love. From that first adoring, wide-eyed gaze up at him, when Mary was no older than that young Anne Boleyn, to that final heart-wrenching glance between them before she left for Dover, Mother Guildford had known it all. She too feared leaving Mary stranded here. She had seen enough of Louise de Savoy and her ambitious son to know that, if Louis died, Mary would not be treated well by the new king. Leaving her now was like abandoning her own daughter. "You know that I have no wish to go, child."

Mary took Lady Guildford's warm, plump hand and squeezed it, fighting valiantly against the tears that only a moment ago she had all but vanquished. The light and shadow cast from the fire moved and danced between them. "I do know that."

"You are as dear to me as a daughter, Mary."

"You have always been more than a mother to me," Mary said, losing the struggle finally not to weep. She buried herself deep in Lady Guildford's full, cushioning embrace, wishing in that moment that, like a mother, she could keep her child like that forever.

My good brother,

As heartily as I can recommend myself to your good Grace, I marvel much that I have not heard from you since my departure so often as I have written to you. Now am I left alone, for my Chamberlain and all my other menservants were discharged and likewise my mother Guildford, with other of my women except those I care nothing about. I beseech you, if it may be by any means possible, I humbly request you to have Mother Guildford returned to me again.

I marvel much that my good Lord of Norfolk would so lightly grant everything else requested here but this. . . . I wish my lord of York, our dear Wolsey, had come and were here with me instead of Norfolk as I would have had much more ease of heart than I can possibly have now.

Thus I bid Your Grace, farewell.

By your loving sister, Mary Queen of France

"Well, what the deuce am I to do for her, Wolsey? She's his wife now and I'll not jeopardize relations with France because of a little case of homesickness!"

Red-faced and fuming, Henry faced Wolsey, who had

just read aloud Mary's pleading letter, which had been addressed to "The King's Grace my kind and loving brother." As Wolsey lowered the missive, Henry began to stalk the full length of his magnificently beamed great hall, ornamented by a new map from the Venetian ambassador. Katherine, stoutly pregnant now, sat across the room near the fire observing them.

Wolsey exchanged a cautious little glance with the queen. "Respectfully, sire, Francois is an ambitious young man and I agree that, in combination with his mother, he is quite lethal. Mary could well be at some risk were the king to die and she was left there entirely alone."

"And so?"

"And so, allow me to write a letter to the king explaining the benefit to retaining Lady Guildford."

Henry quirked a smile. "Ever the diplomat, hmm, Wolsey?"

"That *is* what you wish of me, sire."

"Very well, write your letter," Henry grumbled with a little swat of his hand, feeling suddenly like a man still too under the thumb of a controlling father. "But in it, say nothing that will endanger England's relation with France."

"On my life, sire. I shall take the utmost care."

On All Saints' Day, the Duke of Norfolk bowed deeply before the new young queen, and pressed away the distaste at having to do so. But image, he reminded himself, was everything. Then he kept an even pace with her as they walked across the gravel path in the garden. Lady Guildford had already been taken to Calais, and waited there only for final word on whether Henry VIII would intercede regarding her return to England. Mary was so angry with Louis that she had refused to go immediately with him to Paris for her own coronation. She knew that by waiting she was sacrificing the very public tradition of freeing prisoners, and thus an opportunity with the French people, but she was so upset she did not care.

Guildford's dismissal was a complication Norfolk had not bargained on when he decided to be so exceedingly kind to Mary. She was trying to find a way to maneuver around the will of her own husband. But if Joan Guildford did remain in France, the soft old woman would surely find some way to encourage a renewal of things between Mary and Brandon. If that happened, there was no telling how long it would take them to return to England and resume power, because between the two of them their influence over Henry would be unmatched. So he had planted a seed with the French king. It had taken hold with more speed than he had thought possible. Norfolk knew there was little he could do about it now— even if he had been inclined to. Yet he also knew that Mary, the spoiled twit, meant to ask him anyway when he was summoned by her. He had struggled and fought for everything he had. And all that was required of her was to maintain her beauty, he thought, as she walked beside him now in her vulgarly expensive gown, the collar and long bell cuffs of which were trimmed with rare marten fur.

"Thomas, my dear friend," she began beneath an autumn sky full of heavy gray clouds, "I do so need your help. I have no one else to ask."

"If I can, Your Majesty, anything," he lied.

"My husband favors you."

"I have been graced by his pleasure in me, yes."

"Then stop him from sending my Mother Guildford back to England. You alone can reason with him at this point. I have written to both Henry and Wolsey, but to no avail."

They stopped walking as the cool wind blew the fur at her collar and flushed her pale cheeks. He let out a heavy sigh as though he were about to express real regret. "Oh, Your Majesty, I cannot."

"And why not?"

"Because I do not disagree with him. He is your king after all."

"Would you tell that beautiful little niece of yours, Anne Boleyn, the same thing if she asked you?"

"I would even tell a daughter of mine the same thing, yes, Your Majesty."

"Then I pity her and I am glad you are leaving France," she said in an angry staccato retort. "I thought you were my friend, Thomas. I have always thought that."

"Ah, Your Majesty should take care with illusions. Few people in life shall ever be for you what they seem," Thomas Howard calmly countered.

Since she was meant to be praying, Mary lowered her head, but her thoughts moved away from the memorized words and toward her strongest memories. They were always the same. England . . . Eltham. The laughter. Jane . . . Charles. Happy times. Pulling her. Beckoning her to be remembered.

Dear Lord . . . help me . . . keep me. . . . I am alone here now. Afraid. I despise France . . . I detest my life. But it is not my life. Not truly. It all still feels like it belongs to someone else.

She shot to her feet, stubbornly determined not to be undone by her heart. She would not, could not, give in to this. Survival was the thing. Norfolk, Lady Guildford, all of them had left her now. Mary made the sign of the cross, genuflected and very swiftly left the chapel. She then went up the twisted staircase to her apartments. Francois' wife, Claude, was waiting for her there. Willful little Anne Boleyn was beside her.

"Your Majesty," the stout, awkward young duc's wife said as she fell into a proper curtsy.

"See that my things are readied," Mary said. "It is time to rejoin the king. Send word that I will join him in Paris in plenty of time for my coronation."

As the late autumn wind blew a warm breeze, Charles Brandon and Wolsey met in Canterbury, where Brandon had gone to, at last, meet his young ward. Safely away from the prying eyes and open ears of an ambitious court, they sat together in a house belonging now to him, through his title as Lord Lisle, a stately home with soaring paneled walls and costly Italian paintings framed in gold leaf. They sat at his long table for dinner, with the young Elizabeth Grey and her governess at one end, and Wolsey and Brandon at the other.

"I believe having Lady Guildford and the others returned is Norfolk's cleverly malicious doing," Wolsey said, confiding in Brandon, to whom he was like a kind old uncle, as he was to Mary and Henry. "But why should Norfolk wish to cut the queen off from those who give her comfort?"

"It seems a small price to pay to elevate himself—and undermine the two of us."

Charles felt his heart seize. He had believed Mary in good hands in France, with Lady Guildford at least to comfort her, and her friend Lady Monteagle as well. He was glad Norfolk was being forced to return to England, along with his wife and daughter, even if it meant Mary was alone, because none of that trio had ever had her best interest at heart.

"I must go to France."

"You?" Wolsey whispered in surprise. "Then Henry will know for certain what has always been between you. You risk too much, my son."

"I would risk anything for her." He pushed the piece of lamb, untouched, around on his plate. "Why should I not simply request that I head the delegation to attend Her Majesty's coronation? With all of the others now returning from France, there really must be an English representation. Henry cannot dispute that." His mind whirled with plausible scenarios, pressing away the burst of panic at the thought that she was alone and that Norfolk had cruelly orchestrated this. He had seen Norfolk enough in his dealings with Buckingham to know how deadly he could be. This threat to Mary was not to be taken lightly. "I could take Dorset as my companion, and then to joust with the French king's heir at the celebrations. I hear Francois is a tolerably good athlete whom Harry will want to match in kind."

"Hmm. He shall want to make a good showing of English for that," Wolsey cautiously agreed as he stroked his beardless, doubled chin. "You could check on her that way.

I worry only of what the two of you risk. Putting you together, now especially, is the most incendiary combination of which I can think."

"I must make certain she is all right, Wolsey. This is as good an excuse as any. That is why you came to me about this anyway, is it not? You knew I alone could be trusted to see that your policies would not be tampered with again."

"I thought you might advise me. Not offer to go there in my stead."

Charles laughed. "Then you do not know me as well as I thought, old friend. Since I have been looking for a reason to go to France since the day Mary left England."

Chapter Fifteen

Wives are young men's mistresses, companions for middle age, and old men's nurses.

—Francis Bacon

November 1514, St. Denis

"*Jésu*, you are going to kill me!" Louis chuckled as he tumbled onto the tall canopy bed, bringing Mary with him, letting her ply him with kisses and a gentle touch that instantly excited him. They were reunited just before her coronation in Beauvais, fifty miles outside of Paris. "Yet I would have it no other way in the world."

Recovered enough from his last bout of illness to be a husband to her again, since their reunion Louis had showered his queen with affection, attention and gifts. Each day he strained to do his best to walk with her, dine with her, and even dance with her, to the amazement of a court who believed all of those days were behind him. They even began to whisper that there might well be an heir to show for it, after all.

"Tell me, how am I different from your two other queens," she bid him teasingly late one night as she lay against his thin chest, its rise and fall now actually something of a comfort to her in this place where she had been isolated enough that she now considered Louis her only ally.

"Ah, but a comparison would be impossible since there is no one, and never will be anyone, like you," he answered, reveling in her, the luxuriant profusion of hair, wild across her shoulders, and spilling onto his chest, her full young breasts touching, exciting him the more.

Mary liked the way he said things like that, whether they were true or not. She was alone here now, but for the few distant English servants he had allowed to remain, and she was totally at his mercy. Perhaps he realized that, wanted that. . . . He pushed her back and arched over her now himself, his mouth on her throat.

"Take care," she whispered. "You have only just recovered."

"I meant what I said," he murmured into her hair. "I would have things between us no other way."

The next morning, Louis was again too ill to attend matins with the queen, but he sent word to her through the duc de Longueville that His Majesty had every intention of attending the dinner banquet with her later that afternoon.

"He said that he shall not be gotten rid of quite so easily."

Mary looked up in surprise from her embroidery hoop, and the intricate fleur-de-lys she had been sewing there in the little glass-covered outbuilding from across the dormant garden. Claude looked up absently, as if she had not quite heard, while Mary stifled a smile. "His words?"

"Each and every one, Your Majesty."

Mary liked Claude, yet they were wary of one another. Louis was Claude's father. Mary was her much more beautiful stepmother, her husband's rival, and her own rival in becoming Queen of France. Still, there was an oddly strong kinship between the two young women. Each in her own way was alone. Mary had been given over to France. Claude had been given over to a husband who did not love her, and who had followed their recent marriage with a sudden and blinding series of infidelities.

"Merci bien," Mary said in perfect French, and nodded to Longueville in a courtly gesture that masked the more intimate things they knew of one another.

Seeing him, she always longed to speak to him of Jane and England, of things they both knew, experiences shared. But she never did. Instead, she always reminded herself that he was home now, returned to his wife—and she was home as well. After he had gone, Claude began her embroidery again, pulling the needle rhythmically through the white linen, framed and posed on a stand. Beyond the glass, a chill wind blew.

"Take care with him, *Marie*," Claude said, absently saying her name in the French manner. She did not look up, yet the words were taut with meaning. "My father is very dear to me."

"I like to think I am taking the utmost care of the king."

"He is happy, I do see that. But my father is not a well man, nor a young one. Surely you are aware of that. In his current circumstances, it seems quite possible to me that you would be capable of loving His Majesty quite to death."

Mary set down her embroidery needle and leaned back in her chair to gaze at Claude. Madame d'Aumont, the dour,

silver-haired gentlewoman who had replaced Lady Guildford, silently withdrew, taking along Anne Boleyn so that the
queen and the king's daughter might speak privately.

"What on earth would I have to gain from that? I would
then be powerless and stranded, dowager queen at the mercy
of your husband, his mother and you. Powerless, stranded."

"I did not believe you had thought it through quite so
well."

"I assure you, I think of nothing in this world quite so
much as the future."

Claude's round young face in this light was full of contra-
dictions: smooth skin, full lips and small dark eyes full of
worry.

"Tell me something. Did you love your husband when
you married?" Mary asked.

"I knew him not enough to think about him any way
at all."

"But still you keep to your duty without complaint."

"It is simply the best way for women as we are."

"All I ask is that you allow me to keep to *my* duty. That
way we can stay the best of friends. At least I hope that,"
Mary said.

They wrestled like boys again, brothers. But Charles was
mindful now always to allow the king to win, even as he gave
Henry the brawling struggle he craved. He knew the king
was distracted. Katherine had discovered Henry's affair with
Buckingham's sister, Lady Fitzwalter, and in anger she had
seen the too beautiful young attendant banished to a convent. The battle between them that had followed had been

the gossip of Richmond Palace every day since. Still not a father, Henry had become angry and bitter. Disinclined toward sympathy for his wife, he had shown her no mercy for what was his own betrayal, and certainly no remorse. He had actually upbraided his wife for having interfered.

Henry hurled him powerfully onto his back, then hovered over him. "Had enough?"

"More than enough," Charles laughed, playing along with the scene that had him incapable of besting the fit, young sovereign. And in truth, he was not certain that he could have been victorious any longer because he wisely never pushed himself, or Henry, that far. They both got to their feet and took towels from two waiting young pages standing off to the side of the wrestling floor.

"So tell me, have you considered my proposal?"

"Send you to France?" Henry asked on an incredulous little chuckle, his chest still heaving from the exertion, and his face mottled red beneath his neatly cropped amber-colored beard.

"Send me to head the delegation. There should be a proper show for Mary's sake. And now that I am Duke of Suffolk, I would hope you would find me a suitable enough candidate to represent you."

"The thing is—" Lowering the towel slowly, Henry looked at his friend. He handed the damp towel back to the page without regarding him and began to walk. Charles dutifully followed. "There was some talk . . . wild though it seems, before Mary left for France."

Charles took a breath, exhaled. He was absolutely calm. Believable. "Gossip?"

"It was said that you and the Queen of France had . . . very well, I shall just say it then—that you had feelings for one another that extended beyond the childhood affection we all three shall ever bear for one another."

Having prepared for this moment since the day he fell in love with the king's sister, Charles tipped his head back and laughed boldly. He would do whatever it took to get to France. "Rumors really are ridiculous."

Henry looked at him then, copper brows arched. "So that was all they were? Rumors?"

"Just that," Charles replied, lying so believably that he nearly convinced himself. "And I was hoping to take Dorset with me. He is nearly as strong at the joust as am I, and I do believe we are the only two who can best anyone they may put forth, in a great show for England."

"Best even the duc de Valois? I am told that Louis' rather arrogant heir is a strong competitor who does not suffer defeat well."

"When I represent Your Highness, he shall need to get in line behind *me*, I'm afraid."

There was a moment of silent consideration as they walked. Charles could feel his heart quicken. "Very well, then, Charles. Go to France. And give Mary a hug for me, will you?"

"Of course I will," he replied, hiding his relief, and his excitement, behind an exceedingly practiced smile.

❖

On the fifth of November, amid a chill wind and beneath a slate-colored sky, the citizens of St. Denis pressed forward in a crowd, hoping to catch just a glimpse of their new, young queen, gowned in gold brocade dotted with pearls. A huge diamond, with a great pearl suspended from it, was at her throat. Merchants mingled with monks, soldiers and women, some of them holding children on their shoulders, others shoving one another onto the cobbled stones, to see her atop a tall, sleek palfrey leading a snaking train of nobles, ambassadors and royalty. Ahead of her, the dukes of Longueville, Alçncon and Bourbon rode in great elegance, amid bursts of cheering from the crowd.

She could not even speak to Claude, who rode beside her, for the crescendo of cheers and shouts coming from the hordes along the processional route as they passed into the ancient walled city. Beyond the gates, great vivid banners pinned on giant scaffolds bore the painted images of the king and queen, and they saw a huge ship bearing the live figures of Bacchus and Ceres, and a collection of sailors being battered about as the Four Winds blew air into the sails. It was a fanciful allegorical display that had been organized for the queen. The pageantry was magnificent. The cobbled streets over which they rode were strewn with roses and lilies—the symbolic joining of England and France. As they moved on, there was a second display, the Three Graces dancing around a grand fountain full of the same silk roses and lilies.

Leaving her horse, Mary walked a somber cadence beneath a stone carving of the Holy Trinity above the door as she entered the Cathedral of St. Denis, a rich crimson velvet cloak trailing behind her on the ancient stone floor. Jewels at her fingers and throat flashed brilliantly in the light through the long, stained glass windows depicting the life of Christ as she made her way through a packed sanctuary to the altar, where a throne had been erected. There she was to be solemnly anointed by the Bishop of Bayeux.

As he placed the sacred ring on her finger amid the hauntingly chanted *Te Deum,* and she was ceremoniously handed her scepter and the rod of justice, the heir, Francois, came forward, in sweeping lengths of velvet and fur, to formally crown her. Yet, rather than place it fully on her head, Francois symbolically held the weighty crown above her. The real purpose, rather than simply a symbolic show of compassion, was not lost upon Mary. He intended to be ruler of France, not have the honor go to her son if she bore one, and he meant for the world to know it.

As she tried to surrender herself to the Mass that followed, and not to the ever deepening loneliness that held her, she glanced out at the crowd. The shock of recognition was sharp. Charles Brandon, looking magnificently statesmanlike, shifted in his seat between the duc de Longueville and the duc de Bourbon, directly behind the king. She stared at him, unbelieving—as if he were an apparition that would disappear the moment she blinked her eyes.

It cannot be, her mind taunted. *It cannot . . .*

As the bishop droned on, Mary felt her eyes fill with tears she could not press away, until she could see nothing but colors and shapes. She had not dared to hope and yet she knew . . . yes, she knew, somehow he would find a way to her, and he had.

She stood still in her dressing chamber, amid elegant dresses of moiré silk and velvet, hats, French hoods, fur and petticoats—and more ladies than she would ever need, all milling around her as her coronation gown was removed with great ceremony and discussion, and another equally extravagant gown replaced it. Spindly, harsh Madame d'Aumont brushed out her hair, as Mother Guildford had always done, and Mary cringed at the sensation that something so reassuringly intimate had become a stranger's duty. Then her newly brushed tresses were freshly tamed once again into a new coronet of diamonds and pearls.

Mary had lost sight of Charles after the coronation, though she had frantically tried not to as she was pressed with well-wishers and spirited at the same time away from the cathedral. She rode atop her palfrey in absolute silence after that, stunned by seeing him again, here, especially now. The king was unwell, Madame d'Aumont informed her, and had requested her attendance in his apartments. Sight of her was certain to restore him so that he might accompany his beautiful bride to her banquet, a state occasion, that evening. She complied without comment, yet wanting only to be with Charles, to fly into his arms, ask how he had managed such a thing and never let him go.

She found Louis a quarter of an hour later, pale and reclining on a tapestry-covered couch, clothed in a white linen dressing gown and long claret-colored robe fringed in shimmering silver thread. Mary was always startled to see how ill and frail he looked without the trappings of wealth and royalty, the jewels and cloth of gold that helped to mask the pallor of his skin and distract from his nearly constant tremor. She sank onto the edge of the couch beside him, took his hand and smiled.

"How are you feeling?"

"I am feeling my age, *ma chèrie*. And *seeing* your youth." He smiled grimly. "It really is a rather distasteful combination."

If it were only springtime, she thought, and the weather was warm and restorative. They could go to the country and sit in the garden. He could feel the sun on his face, gain back some of his color and put some of that warmth he needed back into his bones.

"Forgive me about Lady Guildford?" he asked so suddenly, and in such a low, uneasy voice that at first it did not register with her. "I am afraid that the threatened old man in me overcame the good sense of a husband who wished to make his young wife happy."

"But how could the powerful king possibly ever feel threatened by a sweet old woman like Mother Guildford?" she asked, trying to press back the revival of her anger. "She only ever loved me, Louis, and sought to keep me company."

"It was precisely that, I suppose." He laid his head back against the velvet pillow and sighed. For a moment, his eyes rolled to a close. When he opened them, he added, "I saw the way she looked at me whenever I entered your chamber. *Foolish old man,* her eyes always said. *You can push yourself into her bed but someone like you will never find a way into her heart.* Truthful as that may be"—he coughed suddenly—"I could not bear being reminded of it every evening when I sought your company."

Mary squeezed his hand then, feeling another surge of genuine compassion for a man who had only the misfortune of having been born a few decades too early for the life and love he wished to have now.

"I hope with all of my heart you do not remain angry with me for too long. I have sought to make amends, at least in part, by inviting an old friend of yours from the English court to visit with us for a while here this afternoon."

He could not possibly mean he was to have Charles here as a guest! Her heart began to pound until it felt as if it would come up her throat. What did Louis know? Had he heard something? She wanted desperately to see Charles, to be with him. But not here, with her husband so near, and watching. All of those thoughts skittered through her mind then like mice. She sat back more stiffly as Louis nodded and the liveried servants at the other end of the room drew back the carved double doors. Mary glanced up and felt her heart in her throat at the anticipation. Her husband and the love of her life in the same room, and she forced to look pleased? She struggled to remain calm. No matter how she had matured, composure at this moment was a challenge.

Charles swept into the room as she knew he would, a dazzling confident smile lighting his face, and the youthful vigor in his stride restrained just enough not to insult an ailing sovereign—one who must welcome his guest lying down. Had Louis ever looked like that? Mary wondered as her heart pounded in her chest. Tan, lean, incredibly fit and still so unspeakably handsome?

With Louis' assessing eyes upon him, she could see that Charles was wise enough to spare Mary only a cursory glance before he bowed to her, then bowed deeply to the king.

"Your Majesty, it is an honor," he said, sweeping a hand before his doublet, and the glittering gold chest chain there.

"I have heard much of you, Suffolk," Louis responded,

and Mary felt her pounding heart suddenly seize. Guilt made her fear the worst, and she almost could not breathe.

"I hope what Your Majesty has heard has not been too displeasing."

"You were a great military leader on the battlefield against us last summer, and a loyal servant to my peer, King Henry." He quirked a sudden smile that Mary saw from the corner of her eye. "Fortunately for you, he is now my brother-in-law. All of that is forgiven."

Charles bowed again. "I am greatly relieved to hear it."

"Military success is a thing to be respected, even in one's enemies. I learned that well enough in my own youth. Sit down, Suffolk. You make me uncomfortable towering over me as you do."

As if the king had willed it by the mere mention, a chair was swiftly produced and placed beside Mary. He lowered himself onto it formally and waited to be spoken to again.

Mary struggled for courage and for calm as she turned to Charles. "So tell me, have you a private message from my good brother?"

"It is King Henry's greatest wish that I return to England with an agreement that the two of you, not only your ambassadors, meet next summer, and that he will be welcomed here in France for that purpose."

"So long as he does not come at the head of another great army," Louis affably parried, "the gesture is something I shall consider."

"His Majesty asks for no more."

"I am told you plan to joust for the three days of the tournament," Louis said.

"That is my king's wish, Your Majesty."

"And you are to be matched against the duc de Valois?"

"So I was told."

"He is a vicious competitor in sport, as he is with women."

"He has not yet been matched with me in either—respectfully, Your Majesty."

"Yes, well, it shall make for an interesting next few days," said the King of France, as he reached out to take Mary's hand.

In the vast banqueting hall, glittering with flickering light cast from huge candle chandeliers, the walls adorned with allegorical frescoes, Mary paused at the door. There was expectation, and a bit of judgment, pulsing through the room that she could feel. She was still, and always would be, English. She drew in a calming breath, tipped up her head proudly nevertheless and made her first entrance beside Louis as official Queen of France.

Both of them wore lavish gold and white brocade, their sleeves studded with diamonds, as they nodded and smiled to the packed room. The duc de Longueville and the duc de Valois were the first in line at the head of a bevy of noble guests who had assembled there for her.

"She still looks English, even in French clothes." Francois grinned nastily as they watched her advance.

"Knowing her as I do, I believe she would take that as a compliment. I think she looks amazingly confident as she is," Longueville countered.

A courtly galliard was begun amid the swirl of dresses,

feathered hats and beaded headdresses, and the pungent mingling of ambergris and rose water.

"Yes, well," Francois sniffed, "I would rather she looked a bit less confident. Makes me worry there might be a little heir to be had from that old coxcomb after all."

"She is a beauty. If anyone could make him do it, she could," Longueville observed as she smiled and nodded and drew steadily nearer.

"If I had my way, she would be *my* mistress and then the paternity of any child she might have would assuredly be mine."

Charles, standing just behind them, in elegant gray velvet, heard the exchange. He fought the overwhelming urge to wrestle the arrogant bastard, future king or not, to the floor right then and there. He could not wait now to joust against him tomorrow.

He glanced up again at Mary, whose regal countenance and serene smile surprised him. Her confidence had outshone her beauty here in France, which seemed impossible to him not long ago. Especially when he remembered the little girl who once only eavesdropped and pouted and smiled to win her way.

As Mary neared, nodding and greeting, the light catching the diamonds on her sleeves each time she lifted a hand, she paused very suddenly directly in front of him.

He bowed deeply to her in response. "Your Majesty."

"My lord of Suffolk." Her smile, and her nod, were restrained.

"Your brother sends his warmest congratulations tonight," he replied with a skilled smile, nothing at all that would ever give away what was between them.

Charles chose not to tell her that Henry had sanctioned an embrace between them. He hoped there would be a time for that later. But all of the promise of seeing her faded beneath the reality of her duty now. He watched the king's gnarled hand go gently to the small of Mary's back—a controlled movement to press her forward, but an intimacy as well. Charles felt the swell of revulsion that his heart would not let him press away as she moved past him and curtsied deeply to a blinding line of French noblemen.

The evening after that was long, the banquet hall quickly made unbearably hot by the enormous press of bodies. As Mary went around the room with the king for more introductions, he leaned a little too heavily on her for support. She surprised herself when she began to feel a proprietary concern for him take precedence over the bowing, nodding and idle chatter that filled the next hour. It was a virtual sea of dukes and lords, faces she would likely never see again, all smiling at her, all expecting her to know them, and to have something witty to say. Until she came to a couple standing a pace away from everyone else but who, by his smile at them, Louis seemed to know well. The girl was young, but beautiful in a disarming and classic way. Her hair was sleek and golden, her skin was flawless and there was a depth of experience in her crystal blue eyes for one who had not left her adolescence. She was unique enough that Mary paused of her own accord for the introduction. Like the king, the woman's husband was much older, silver-haired, not nearly so tall as she, portly and slightly stoop-shouldered.

"Your Majesty," she said, speaking in a voice that was smooth and deeper than Mary had expected as she curtsied low and respectfully.

"I am afraid you have me at a disadvantage, madame," Mary replied.

"Forgive me, Your Majesty. I am Diane de Poitiers, comtesse de Brézé. May I present my husband, Louis, comte de Brézé?"

Mary smiled at her then, feeling an odd instant kinship, although she had absolutely no idea why. It was definitely more than that they were both young with husbands far older than they were. "Tell me, madame, how do you find it having an English queen?"

"Truthfully, Your Majesty, we find it refreshingly courageous of our king to cast away predictability." She leaned forward slightly. "I am afraid you shall not hear the duc de Valois say that, however."

Mary would have laughed but she knew that Louis expected something more restrained from her in public. Looking at Diane de Poitiers, she thought of Jane. Last night she had dreamed yet again of her dearest friend—of skipping through the meadow out behind Eltham Palace, the two of them trying to catch butterflies. Now Charles was here, and so was this surprisingly interesting young woman who reminded her of Jane.

"Thank you, madame. If you are to remain at court a while, I should like to invite you sit with me at the tournament tomorrow."

"It would be my honor, Your Majesty," Diane replied with courtly aplomb.

Mary felt Louis falter beside her. When she looked over, she saw that he had gone quite ashen. One glance at the servant who lingered just behind them, and he advanced, as he had been instructed to do.

"Should you sit down?" Mary leaned in to ask in a way that no one else could hear.

Louis tried to smile, the lines in his face seeming more deeply etched, the gray circles beneath his eyes more pronounced. "If you do not mind too much, *mon amour,* I believe I am going to leave you to the evening on your own."

"I will come with you," she declared, meaning it.

"Ah, no. This is your evening to shine, *chérie.* Please."

After he had been led away, Mary turned back toward the elegant, parted throngs still assembled before her in their crush of velvet and jewels, all made to bow and curtsy ceremoniously to her by even her absent glance. She bit back a smile for the first time, now knowing the power Henry felt— king, master over all he surveyed. And she was queen. A little shiver blossomed up her spine, blooming on her face. Pride made her bite back a smile as she greeted the duc de Vendome with skilled reserve, and she let him bow to her. No matter her heart, or the secrets she kept there, she truly was Mary, Queen of France, now, and there must be some way to make her life, and her circumstances, work to her advantage, and to make her peace about being here.

That night, a powerfully frigid wind battered the windows and the cold it brought bled through the stone walls of the palace of Les Tournelles, as the longing moved through Charles with what felt like the same force. She had been a beautiful child who had grown into a magnificent woman. A queen. He had wanted to come to France. He believed entirely that it was the right thing to do. To be here, for Mary. But seeing her brought an ache, rather than reassurance. It made him question every decision he had made for a very long time. She was not his. Foolish as it sounded, even in his mind, Charles had actually questioned that before he had arrived here. But seeing the king made her loss real. He tossed and turned beneath the bedcovers, trying to remember a prayer that might bring him some sort of peace. And if not that, relief at least.

He thought then of the true price he had paid for the reputation that his ambition and carelessness with women had brought him. Perhaps if he had led a wiser, more pious life, like Wolsey, instead of trying so hard to be Henry's friend, he would have gained a dukedom sooner. He would have been a stronger candidate for Mary when the contract with Charles of Castile was nullified. He tossed and turned again, awash in perspiration and frustration. This was a situation of his own making. He believed that now. In life, with each gain there was a loss. Losing Mary, seeing her with the French king, protectively at his side, was like a small death. Worst of all, Louis had been genuinely welcoming to him. It made the guilt worse. Yet, God help him, it did not lessen his resolve to have Mary. That obsession now was well beyond his control.

The tournament commenced and then continued for the next three days. Lying on a couch, the king attended the contest only briefly each day in order to make a proper appearance. Mary was relieved each time he retired to his apartments, since it meant she would not have to fear every noise she made or every gesture toward Brandon giving her away to a besotted husband. While she did not love Louis, nor could she, in the days since their marriage she had grown fond of him, and she had no wish to hurt him. Mary reveled in the skepticism turned to admiration of the French people. Each day before the contest began she stood to receive the welcome of the 305 challengers entering the lists as well as the thunderous applause of the crowds. Each time it happened, she thought, *I am a woman in my own right now, a wife and a queen, no longer just the sister of Henry VIII. I have power . . . control, and I like it.*

On the second day of the tournament, amid air that was less frigid as it moved through the stands, the contest turned to hand combat. Francois had been injured the first day in his battle with Charles, and his pride had suffered. Today, in an attempt to impress Mary, Francois made a stylishly grand entrance, then sat near her, garbed in velvet of Tudor green and white. It irritated him the more after his defeat, that she did not even deign to acknowledge his effort. He sat now near the queen and her companion, his wife, Claude, and Madame d'Aumont and Louis de Brézé's very young wife, Diane. Still they were not so near that they heard his exchange with the sly and discreet Claude de Lorraine.

"There is something about Suffolk," Francois said, with a hand casually across his mouth. "He is rather too arrogant for my taste."

"You say that only because he beat you in the joust yesterday. And he *is* rather vulgarly handsome for an Englishman."

"I say it because there is something I don't trust about him, striding around like this, as if he were absolutely unbeatable in everything."

"Perhaps he is."

"Not if I have anything to say on the matter," Francois quickly shot back, his own self-important smile beginning to broaden beneath his long, prominent nose. "Today, he shall face a challenger of *my* choosing and then we shall see how smugly victorious he remains."

From the royal viewing stands, they watched the matches silently until Charles entered the field in a flash of silver, his chest plate stamped boldly with the red cross of Saint George. Francois glanced at the queen and saw the same thing he always did when Suffolk appeared. A broad smile lit her face, like a spark—no more than a flash really—then she stiffened and the smile disappeared as the initial response was pressed back and well hidden. Now it was clear. The foolish chit had feelings for Suffolk!

So that was why she so unwisely chose to rebuff his own advances. No matter, Francois arrogantly thought, touching the point of his small, neat chestnut-colored beard with thumb and jeweled forefinger. That sorry English braggart would return to England soon enough, and the old lion being helped back to his apartments now once again would be dead not long after. That scenario could not play out soon enough for Francois' taste. Then he would see how eager the queen—widowed and replaced by Claude—was to reject the man with all the power! The vulnerable dowager queen would need him then, by God! Alone in a foreign land, and there would be no one here to rescue her when that happened!

Down on the field today, Suffolk faced the opponent of Francois' choosing. He was a gigantic Almain ominously garbed and hooded, in black, his clothing designed to be as intimidating as he himself was. Francois heard the crowd gasp and glanced over the row of guests beside him and could not resist a smile as he watched the queen's face blanch. Sheer delight! The combatants began on horseback, but as Francois watched, it was Suffolk, not his secret giant weapon, who managed to fell his opponent quickly, strike him with the butt of his spear and begin the ferocious ground combat. He resisted every urge in his own body to spring to his feet and shout down at the field as the opponents baited one other, then wrestled like great bears amid the wind and the fluttering banners and the deafening roar of the crowd. In a swirl of dust, loud grunts and the clink of armor, the giant Almain then grabbed a waiting blunt-edged sword and they began to trade savage blows.

Mary glanced to the panel of judges as the two men thrust and struck, then tumbled, waiting in a panic for them to drop the rail and end the contest. But the judges sat watching in stony silence, allowing it to continue for what felt to her an eternity. The young Diane de Poitiers placed a comforting hand on Mary's shoulder then, which brought her back to the stands.

"The opponent may be big, but Suffolk is quick," she said encouragingly.

Mary could not look at her. She could not draw her eyes from Charles, who seemed now to be fighting for his life in what was meant to be a game.

They tumbled again and struggled on. The heavy swords flashed in the daylight as they swung and thrust in a contest of sinewy muscle and glinting steel. Suddenly Charles, who had spent his youth wrestling with Henry VIII, took the advantage, grabbing the opponent by the neck and battering his head with a blinding volley of blows so savage that blood sprayed out in an arc from his nose and he collapsed onto the field, giving Suffolk the victory the dauphin had meant for the other man.

Mary sprang to her feet, unable to resist any longer, in an ovation of her own as Charles dropped his sword, lifted his visor and strode magnificently toward the stands where she stood above him, the fur at her collar fluttering in the breeze. In a gesture lost to no one there, he then made her a sweeping, courtly bow and she smiled broadly at him in response. Francois d'Angouleme cursed beneath his breath and dashed alone out of the stands the moment he saw the exchange.

A quarter of an hour later, Mary sank onto the edge of the bed beside Louis, her smile full of genuine concern as she took up his cold hand. "Are you well?"

"Better, now that you have come. I am told Suffolk made quite a masterful showing today."

"He was impressive."

"Would that I could be so masterful for you," he said on a regretful sigh.

"You are King of France—quite masterful in your own way."

Louis smiled at that and pulled her on top of him, kissing her neck and face in a way that told her what he wished for next. "I was hoping you would say that," he said with a faint chuckle. "Ah, how the King of France does adore his queen!"

Chapter Sixteen

They brought an Almain and put him to my Lord of Suffolk to have put us to shame, but advantage they got none of us, rather the contrary. . . . The Queen continues her goodness and wisdom and increases in the favour of her husband the Privy Council. She has said to my Lord of Suffolk and me that the King her husband said to her that my Lord of Suffolk and I did shame all France and that we should carry the prize into England.

—*A letter from the Marquess of Dorset in France to Henry VIII in England*

December 1514, Les Tournelles

The crowd assembled to see Mary enter the banquet hall this time had swollen to enormous size and was to her a little frightening. They yelled out and called to her, pushing and shoving and surging forth over barriers like a giant wave until, in their fervor, they blocked the queen's path outside of the castle. Francois was at her side and grasped her upper arm in what felt a protective gesture.

"They mean well," he called to her through the noise. "But we mustn't take any chances."

A few words exchanged with the duc de Longueville and they altered their course, moving away from the main entrance to the palace, and instead entering through a side door and up a narrow, far less elegant staircase inside a turret. Mary was grateful for the glass of sweet French wine handed to her the moment she reached the top of the stairs. But Francois, it seemed, dressed in a stunning purple velvet doublet with silver slashing, had forgotten to let go of her arm. For just a moment, she was aware of how awkward that felt. Then, almost as quickly, she was distracted by her introduction to a round little man, his hair a simple skein pressed over the dome of his head, who bowed so vigorously, smiled and happily chattered on so that she could think of little else.

"Her Majesty must greet her other guests now," Francois announced with a proprietary snarl and again pulled her by the arm.

The gesture embarrassed Mary, and yet she was relieved, since the mayor of Paris was quite likely the dullest man she had ever met. The dauphin irritated her at times, and could quickly frighten her at others. But he always seemed to know just exactly what to do, and when. But mostly his constant presence in her life made her wish every day that Louis were well enough at least to be a buffer for her at these events, if not a true partner at them.

She moved among the guests with Francois still beside her, seemingly uninterested in leaving her side. That fact did not bother her overly, with all of the activity—the music and the swirl of elegant gowns and jewels all around her—until she saw a flash of Claude's sad young face amid the crowd as they passed her together. Francois could not have missed her doleful eyes, an expression full of betrayal on her young face.

Yet Francois neglected even to acknowledge her as his wife as they went by her. Beneath all of the French charm, he had such a cruel streak, Mary thought.

Only then did Mary realize that he seemed to be leading her not into the crowd of waiting guests, but through them and with another goal entirely. She tried to stop but he drew her skillfully, introducing her as they moved so that there was no way to turn from him, no moment to object. Ducs, viscomtes, comtes. Velvet, silk, rubies flashing. Smiles. Flattery. An overabundance of bows and curtsies. A blinding repetition of it all, and then they turned a corner and, as she feared, Mary was alone with him. Two studded leather chairs and a table with a burning candle lamp between them were framed by swags of fringed gold and forest green brocade drapery, making it a small and seductive alcove framed by heavy stone columns.

"I thought you might like to catch your breath," he said in a slow, deep voice with which she had not heard him speak before.

Mary looked up at him as he leaned against one of the columns, crossing his arms and one leg casually over the other. "I was actually enjoying greeting my guests, Francois. That is my role here, after all, is it not?" She had tried to insert a challenging tone into the question but the voice she heard echo back at her sounded defensive amid her rising sense of panic.

He reached out then and cupped a hand beneath her chin, then pressed himself closer. She did not want this man, who clearly had convinced himself otherwise. She tried to move away but there was nowhere to go between the chair and the column.

"We really must get back to the king's guests."

"Would you say that if Suffolk were standing here with you right now and not me?"

"The Duke of Suffolk," she tried to chuckle blithely, as if she were not becoming terrified. "What has he to do with this?"

"Why do you not tell me?"

His expression was one of bitterness, his eyebrows raised in challenge. The tone of his question had sounded almost menacing to Mary. She tried to turn away but he brought her chin back around with a hand too powerful to resist.

"I would like to return to my guests now."

"Not before I see if what they say is true, that an English rose has no thorns at all if you simply know how to hold it."

As he pressed his mouth onto hers greedily then, she sensed as much anger as lust in his kiss. But Mary felt him suddenly being jerked back so forcefully that it shook the heavy brocade draperies that hid them on their iron rod. It was not, however, a man who had rescued her, but rather a woman in stiff black silk and a silver chain: Louise de Savoy, the dauphin's own mother. Behind her stood Claude, her sad eyes filled with tears.

"Miserable fool!" Louise charged, not at Mary but at her own son, each word cold and severe. "Can you for once conduct yourself by your brain and not your ballocks!"

He shook his arm free of her hand with one hard snap. "You understand nothing, Mother!"

"At least wait until the old lion is dead before you go chasing his quarry, or you could ruin everything for which you have struggled and worked!"

He arched a dark brow, then cast a glance at his wife, but there was nothing of sympathy in it. He looked back at Louise. "Everything for which *I* have worked? Do you not mean *you*, Mother? It has been your dream, your obsession, to make me King of France since the moment I drew my first breath!"

"And you would jeopardize something so grand for a woman when you are finally this close? Woman after woman, Francois, truly. If your ambition does not lead you any longer, can you not at least be led by a dose of guilt? Think of your poor wife and how you insult her in this continually if nothing else!"

"You care nothing for Claude, *Maman*," he charged back at her, as if they were the only two there. "She has been a means to an end for us both, and you well know it!"

"That is a vulgar thing to say!" Mary cried, hands shooting onto her hips when she was unable to contain her anger at the paralyzing cruelty of their words. Before her were two people quite brutally unraveling the heart of the poor young woman with them, whom neither even seemed to notice. For Mary, that thought took the place of what had almost happened in the alcove with the heir to the throne of France.

Later, when Louise and Francois had both gone back to their guests, Mary remained behind with Claude. Now Mary stroked Claude's hair as she wept, and tried to gain her own bearings about what had happened.

"The funny thing is," Claude sniffed as she pressed Mary's proffered handkerchief against one eye and then the other, "I don't even want to be queen. I was foolish to actually believe, when we were nearly perfect strangers, that he loved me as well, and that was what mattered to me when I married him."

"It is easy enough to be misled by your heart," Mary said soothingly, thinking of poor Jane back in England, with Knyvet and Longueville, and of Katherine as well, who loved Henry still, in spite of how his attention had begun increasingly to wander.

"No matter whether you could ever love my father or not, I am glad you are his wife," Claude said on a sniffle, dabbing at her eyes again.

"Thank you for that."

"And do be cautious with my husband. He really does not lose well at all."

"I will consider myself warned," she said, rising back to her feet and lingering a moment over Claude, who had not moved from the leather chair in which she had first sat curled, knees to her chest.

Mary was tired now and miserable without Charles. Miserable in France. Knowing he was somewhere within the walls of this same great French palace, yet knowing they were apart, was its own kind of torture.

The risk was great but she had no other choice. Mary had decided to enlist the aid of Diane de Poitiers, who she discerned was not so much at the French court that her alliances there would be overly strong. Like herself, Diane had been given over to a strategic marriage with a powerful, much older man. Mary was not entirely certain this beautiful young woman could be trusted, but as the time grew short she needed to rely on someone. There really was no one else. And she had felt a indefinable kinship between them from that first introduction.

In elegant pale blue silk with a pearl-studded headdress, Diane came forward that evening into Mary's private withdrawing chamber. The room was lit to a warm, golden glow by the blazing fire within the carved stone hearth. Louis' symbol, the porcupine, prominently adorned the mantel. Above it was a painting of the king in full battle armor, much as her father had once kept back in England, of himself, astride a great warrior bay, designed to remind his wife of the glory of his youth, and hopefully to impress her. With the painting looming before them, Mary directed Diane to sit beside her near the fire. Then she excused Madame d'Aumont, who had been teaching Anne Boleyn how to play cards at a small cloth-draped table across the room.

"I have need of a favor and, perhaps by the king's own design, there is no one left to me at the court that I can ask."

"How may I serve Your Majesty?" asked Diane, her voice rich with sincerity, her smile a half-moon.

Mary drew in a breath, feeling suddenly that she was in the very midst of one of those great games with Henry that they used to play, where she was about to gamble everything to win. She must do it all, say it all. Now would be her only opportunity. "You must seek out the duc de Longueville at once because he knows this old palace well. Tell him the queen has need of a private sanctuary within these walls, a little-known place where I may be alone and not be discovered. Once he has told you, you are to return to me with the information as quickly as you can, and you are to tell no one. Your discretion in this is of the utmost importance to me."

"Of course, Your Majesty. I understand. My discretion goes without saying."

"And finally—when you find him, you are to let no one see you give him this." She drew forth a small folded missive and held it up, feeling the full weight now of all she risked. "It is to be given by Longueville directly to the Duke of Suffolk and no other." There was an awkward little silence before Mary added, "His Grace returns to England tomorrow and it is he who my brother, King Henry, bade should bring him word of circumstances with the King of France, so I need time to advise him."

Diane curtsied deeply but her eyes never left Mary's hopeful gaze, saying within it that she hoped with all her heart that she had chosen well. "It will be an honor, Your Majesty, to serve both you and the Duke of Suffolk with my fidelity and my discretion. I know the duc de Longueville will feel the same."

Mary studied her a moment longer. Diane's was a kind face . . . sincere . . . intelligent . . . meant for so much more than the life she had. Mary was afraid to trust someone so completely with what was so dear. But there was no other choice. The risk had been taken. Now she had only to wait, and hope that she had gambled well.

The king lay in his grand tester bed, his left leg, the one that pained him most severely, elevated on a stack of velvet pillows, and the ever present scent of camphor strong around him. Glowing candle lamps dotted the vast room and sent shadows onto the walls.

"Did you send for the queen?" he asked his groom, who approached the great bed, bowing deeply.

"The Grande Seneschale de Normandie was just emerging from Her Majesty's bedchamber when I arrived," the servant dutifully reported. "I was informed that the queen had gone to sleep with a headache. Does Your Majesty wish me to have her woken and brought to you?"

Louis let out a heavy sigh and, for a moment, closed his eyes. He thought of nothing but Mary, his bright, precious treasure. He wished for her . . . longed for her . . . and craved mainly the youth that her nearness brought. *She might have come to bid me good night,* he thought, pressing back the disappointment that made him feel more old and foolish than he already did. *There is no fool quite like an old fool,* he thought. *Especially one who dares to yearn for a young and beautiful wife. . . .*

Mary sank against his chest and buried her face against his broad shoulder, wanting to melt into the very core of Charles Brandon as he held her tightly. The garret room up a staircase in the three-story tower was small, servants' quarters somewhere so high up beneath the eaves of the palace of Les Tournelles, beyond a maze of stairs and corridors, that Mary was not certain she could find her way back down.

But she did not care. Nothing in the world mattered but this. And him.

"I know not how you did it," he murmured into her hair, "but you are truly amazing."

"I could not let you leave France tomorrow without seeing you like this."

"You risk a great deal."

"I risk everything for you—and do it gladly."

She gasped as his mouth came down onto hers and he pressed the full length of himself, hard and wanting, against her. He glanced at the small bed with its simple Fustian linen and the single table and lamp beside it. There was no fireplace here, and the room was forbiddingly cold, so he embraced her more tightly. He held her face in his hands as if she were a very delicate thing. "Are you absolutely certain this is what you want?"

Mary twined her arms around his neck. "Never more certain of anything in my life."

"You will be going against God, my love."

"I did my duty to him. I came chaste to France, and here I shall remain as Louis' queen. But no God could be so cruel as to deny me one night with you whom I have loved my whole life."

She lay back onto the small bed and he braced himself over her. His eyes, as he gazed down, glittered full of not only passion, but complete devotion to her. They had come such a long way and it was nearly over between them now before it had really begun. Both of them felt it. The one thing in the world each of them wanted was the thing they could not have, so they would take what little they could here, in this place made private by the night, and she refused to feel any guilt at all about that.

"Open your eyes," he bid her on a ragged breath just then. "My sweet Mary."

Charles covered her face and neck then with feathery kisses and she ran her hands greedily down the broad expanse of his back. As his touch grew more demanding, Mary felt herself shudder. The sensation of his sensual touch was nothing like it was with Louis. He moved his fingertips deftly over the column of her neck, over her breasts, across her abdomen, then along the inside of her thighs, after he had loosened her dressing gown and pushed it away from her skin. She gasped when he touched her there, but she did not care. This was her own secret piece of heaven with Charles. *Let me remember every moment . . . every touch . . . for the winter and the next and the next shall be long and cold without him. . . .* His tongue trailed onto her nipple. Her fingers dug into the skin of his back.

Mary wanted everything now with him, the future and the consequences be damned. They had waited for so long. Once he had helped her remove her clothes, and his own, he moved down onto her forcefully, and Mary closed her eyes, her heart pounding so wildly that she could not breathe. As Charles pressed into her she wrapped her legs around him, pulling him deeper. Mary could feel his breath against her ear and the pounding of his own heart against her breasts. But the ripples of pleasure that moved through her and seemed to have no end as he thrust and rocked swiftly became the only thing. She gasped, then heard herself cry out his name as his taut, muscular body jerked and then shuddered. As he sagged against her, then stroked the hair back from her face with aching tenderness, Mary realized that she was weeping.

"I love you, Charles," she whispered. *Henry's promise. He will keep it . . . one day. He must,* she was thinking.

Chapter Seventeen

*The Queen has hitherto conducted herself, and still does
every day, towards me, in such a manner that I cannot
but be delighted with her, and love and honour her more
and more each day; and you may be assured that I do,
and ever shall, so treat her, as to give both her and you
perfect satisfaction.*

—*A letter from Louis XII to Henry VIII*

December 1514, Paris

The winter of 1514 in France was unusually harsh.
Mary kept busy by planning the Christmas celebrations to
raise Louis' spirits, if not renew his steadily declining health.
After the coronation, the court had moved to the palace of
Blois, Louis' childhood home, tucked into the lush forest of
the Loire valley. But no matter how continually the fires in
all the great hearths were stoked, the chill seemed to seep
through every thick stone wall, and move right through the
bones of every courtier and guard.

Mary spent her afternoons and the early hours of the evening in Louis' private bedchamber with him as he conva-
lesced, either playing cards or reading to him in the English
he hoped to improve. Everyone knew he was nursing an ill-

ness that was steadily growing worse, yet no one was allowed to speak of it, particularly not Mary, whom he would take hunting, he said, the first moment he was able.

"How is our great king?" Francois inquired of Mary as she left Louis' apartments one bleak, cold afternoon.

He had fallen asleep and she found herself desperate for a bit of crisp winter air chilling her face, and some relief from the monotony of camphor and the king's continual rheumy cough. Francois, it seemed, had come out of no-where to walk beside her now down the length of the three connecting presence chambers that led eventually to the corridor, and a bank of uncovered windows, through which gray winter light poured. Mary felt a little ominous shudder at the tall, daunting presence beside her, but she pressed it back. It had occurred to her after Charles and the English delegation left a month ago now that, with Louis' condition swiftly declining, she truly could not afford to antagonize his presumptive heir, no matter how she had stubbornly pressed it with him before. Francois was just arrogant and handsome enough to assume there was not a woman at the French court who would not desire him, given a bit of se-ductive prodding. To protect herself, she must not allow him to believe differently.

"My husband is improving each day."

"That is not what I heard."

Mary forced back the clever retort that rose to her lips. "And what is it that you have heard?"

"That I shall be king soon enough."

"If it is God's will, then France shall bow to a new sover-eign, and I along with it."

"You, Mary?" He stopped suddenly, forcing her to stop along with him as his question hung between them. Once again she faced his charming sneer. "You will bow down to me? A man you love to hate?"

"I shall do as I am bid by my king."

"Ah, now there is a promise worth fantasizing over."

He reached out and ran a finger down the length of her puffed ivory silk sleeve, edged with tiny emeralds. "A lovely cloth. But I prefer you rather more boldly in claret red velvet with a spray of diamonds around your throat. That is, after you are finished wearing your widow's weeds." He lowered his hand then, but his eyes stayed rooted on her, his smile never changing from the clever one full of expectation.

"I shall pray each day that it is a very long time indeed before I must don anything sewn in the color white."

"And yet, one is forced to wonder how that can be so, you so young and desirable, full of life, and with desires of your own—and our poor old king, trying his best to keep up with you, dining later now, dancing, drinking too much . . . making love a bit too often."

By my faith, he is vulgar! And an expert at baiting a woman of whom he knows so little, she thought. Mary steeled herself against the sensation of rage. Instead, she tipped up her chin as she had become adept at doing, and forced a controlled smile onto her face.

"I do my duty to my husband in all things, and he seems pleased enough with me."

Francois surprised her by laughing. "Pleased, yes, most assuredly, he is that. Made well, highly unlikely, with a young bride like you who will surely be the death of her ailing husband."

"Well, I suppose we shall see about that." She began to walk again, but he did not follow her. Instead Francois left her words to echo in the air between them as thoughts of Charles Brandon, and his rescuing her, at that moment seemed very far away.

"Come to bed," Louis bid her with a smile and an outstretched hand.

After the dining and the dancing that evening, only a small portion of which he had been able to attend, the king had sent for Mary. It was Christmas Eve and the court had returned from Blois to Les Tournelles in Paris for the holiday. A light snow fell like feathers past the windows, blanketing the dark and gritty capital city in a fresh powder. Mary forced herself not to see the sickly man steadily weakening before her, but rather the king who desired her and showered her each day with gifts and adoration she knew she did not deserve.

She sank onto the bed beside him and he leaned over to embrace her. "I have missed you," he murmured. "Missed us."

She knew what he wanted. "But you are unwell, Louis."

"I am well enough." He smiled at her and took a bit of her long hair into his hand, then pressed it against his cheek. "I have always delighted in the scent of your hair . . . the feel of your skin, so like silk. . . . You really are so very perfect."

"I do not think you should—"

"Touch me," he bade her, refusing her gentle warning and trailing his fingers down her breasts.

Mary sighed and opened her dressing gown. It was her duty to give him an heir if she could. The prospect, however unlikely, would secure her future and legacy in France, so long as the king survived. If he died and she were pregnant, Mary would be in the most grave danger, and she knew it.

Chapter Eighteen

And I thank you for the good service while he was here of the Duke of Suffolk. I beg you to believe that independent of the place that I know he holds with you, and the love you bear him, his virtues, manners, politeness and good condition, deserve that he should be received with even greater honor.

—From Louis XII's final letter,
December 28, 1514, sent to Henry VIII

December 30, 1514, Westminster Palace

*I*n elegant brown leather slashed with gold silk, Charles Brandon sprinted down the length of the corridor leading to Henry VIII's private apartments, the heels of his kidskin boots echoing across the smooth inlaid wood floor. It was five days after Christmas, and the announcement had just arrived from Paris.

"The king must see me! I have news!" he shouted breathlessly, pressing past the guards and the crowd gathered and awaiting admittance. His Highness' dresser, various Gentlemen of the Chamber, guards and ambassadors who lingered near the door tried to object but he would not be stopped. Charles pulled back the bed draperies with a single snap.

"The King of France is dead!" he announced before he

saw that the naked girl wound around Henry, crow black hair splayed across his chest, was not Katherine but Elizabeth Blount, one of the queen's own ladies-in-waiting. Charles bowed, trying not to look at her, as Henry lifted his head from the pillow and struggled to open his eyes.

"Could you not have knocked, Brandon?" he asked on an irritated sigh. But he accepted Charles here in his midst like the brother he had become, and made no effort to have him removed.

"Louis is dead, and Mary now is widowed by it!"

"That is customarily how it works," he said drolly. As he rolled onto his back he slapped his new mistress's bottom, and she gave a little groan. "Get dressed," he ordered her as he sat up and reached for his own dressing gown lying in a crimson silk pile at the foot of the massive bed. Charles lingered over them, not watching as the young girl slipped from the covers, plucked up her dress, petticoat and shoes and disappeared silently through a small door beside the fireplace hearth.

"All of those years to see her married to someone proper, and it is over in three months' time?" Henry sighed, heading for the velvet-covered closed stool beside the bed and urinating into it as if there was no one else in the room.

"I am not certain she is safe there now, though. The dauphin—now King Francois—has a reputation and it was no secret when I was there that he had designs on Mary."

"Mistress to the King of France was not exactly what I had in mind next for her."

His grooms approached with a selection of ensembles for him to consider. He nodded at a blue velvet with gold slashes, and the others were swiftly withdrawn as a cup of wine was brought on a silver tray.

"Nor is that Mary's desire, I think I am safe in saying," Charles said, and Henry shot him a glance. "I mean only that he is an arrogant sort and the queen is far too proud to serve anyone as a convenience."

"Yes, that would be my sister."

"A delegation should go to France for the funeral."

Henry smiled, then sipped his wine. "And to support her in her grief?"

"She should be supported, even if it was never a love match."

"Of course. She will be vulnerable now no matter what, as Katherine was here after Arthur died, and there should be someone there to look out for her just now." The dresser silently drew a pair of gold-colored hose up over Henry's muscled legs and a thin linen shirt over his chest. "You are rather fond of Mary, are you not, Charles?"

"I have known her since we were children. She is like a sister to me."

Charles stood still, betraying nothing as Henry seemed suddenly to study his expression and, quite likely, his sincerity. "You have been there before. You know the various players. If Mary is in any sort of danger now I would trust you to assess it for me."

He had said the word "trust" with more than a little insinuation. A warning, yet unspoken.

"I feel her loss too, Charles. Her light, that sparkle here at my court is sorely missed. By everyone, me especially."

"You do not write to her often."

He sighed. "It would be difficult for me with her life there now, as Margaret's is in Scotland. I knew I needed to let them go, both to their destinies, and not soften about that."

"Go to France with me, Harry. See her."

"I could not, without a grand undertaking, an entourage as big as my army and months of planning. For what it would cost England to present myself to my new brother, I could finance a war," he chuckled, amusing himself suddenly. But Charles heard the note of regret in his voice as well. "No. You go to France for me, Charles. You will make certain our Mary is safe. You will handle things there exactly as I would. Whatever you do, however, you must not antagonize Francois. We are too in need of the French alliance, no matter how arrogant he is, or how he might bait you."

"He may be powerful, but you are the only sovereign who has power over me."

"He has our Mary, though, until negotiations for her return and the remittance of her dowry can be finalized. We must not forget that. I have heard how that young wolf covets all the beauties at his court, especially since there is no one there any longer powerful enough to object. No doubt you will seem a white knight to her now that Louis is dead and she no longer has his protection."

"I will do nothing to disappoint Your Highness."

"You have changed and matured a great deal, Charles, since those wild days with Margaret Mortimer," Henry declared on a sly smile, yet with a gaze full of commitment, friendship and the many shared years between them. "I trust no other so much as you."

After Charles had bowed and gone, Henry called for Wolsey, who entered the king's apartments in a swirl of scarlet cassock and cap. A heavy gold pectoral cross hung from a gold chain at his chest as he stood before the king. Henry turned back from the fireplace hearth and looked at him. "Have you heard everything?"

"Indeed, sire."

"And do you concur with the thinking, or has he a personal reason to go to France?"

"I do not believe the new king will let our Mary leave, even if she is not pregnant, but especially if she is," Wolsey said. "She is too valuable a bargaining chip now. I am told that he would happily marry her to the noble Claude de Lorraine so that he may keep her there at the French court for himself."

"So Brandon told no lie in that."

"Not from what my sources say, sire. And if she *is* pregnant, by some chance, she could be in grave danger. Francois will not want competition for his highly coveted crown now that he has already had his first taste of life as king." They both knew that her child, if it were a boy, would supercede Francois automatically in the line of succession. Unless some untimely accident prevented his birth.

"Then I am right to send Charles to see that she is safe, and perhaps even to bring her back if he can. The Prince of Castile had wished to renew his suit in the event of Louis' death. Perhaps, considering our options, that would be a good match after all."

"Did Your Highness not promise your sister the freedom to select her own next husband?"

"I would have said anything to get her on that ship, Wolsey, you know that. Besides, I am king. Obviously I can decide something like that far better than a woman! The Prince of Castile was a sound choice for her then and he would be an even better choice for her now. I want you to write a letter to Mary. She will take it better, coming from you, and I know you have the greatest ability to be judicious."

He nodded. "As you wish, sire."

"Tell her that she is to do nothing impetuous, and that she must take great care with my French brother. I do not trust Francois, but he is the king, and at the moment, we need his alliance."

Dear as their friendship was, they both had known Charles Brandon for a long time. No one, Henry thought privately, changed that much when they had led the wily, self-indulgent youth that Brandon had. It was better to let Wolsey handle this. He trusted the cleric completely in all things.

An hour later, Wolsey stood before two of his friars, who had been summoned to his apartments. "You are to personally deliver the king's letter to his sister, the Queen of France. And then you are to speak privately with Her Majesty. Warn her. Tell her that King Henry seeks to arrange her marriage to the emperor's grandson after all."

To be forewarned is to be forearmed in any good war, he thought. But he did not tell the friars that.

Eighty-two days and nights of wishing Louis XII did not even exist, so that she could return to England, and to Brandon's powerful, reassuring arms. Now Louis was dead. Mary, who was called La Reine Blanche already, stood alone in stark white robes, a black cap and veil, gazing at his waxen body lying in state, in the great hall at Les Tournelles. Ringed around his bier were monks softly chanting low monotonous requiem prayers. Louis had been garbed in a crimson velvet robe, crown and gold scepter across his still chest. She saw his pride, even in death. *If only you had known me when I was younger,* he had so often said. Her eyes were filled with tears for a man who had made an unlikely friend in a marriage that had lasted such a short time.

"You mourn as if you actually cared for him," Louise de Savoy imperiously remarked as she came up beside Mary in the irritatingly stealthy manner her son always used. "Lovely show."

Mary shot her an angry stare as a throng of mourners and eager spectators was kept at bay, huddled silently back a distance near the door.

"You have no idea what I felt for His Majesty."

"True." She gave a small shrug standing in a sweeping black dress, edged extravagantly with satin and pearls. "I am rather good with my imagination. And I still cannot envision any sort of true, shall we say, receptivity toward an old man as he was, from you."

"Ah, of course. You are afraid I am pregnant with the king's child," Mary exclaimed. "That would ruin everything for you. Now, when you lasted through his former two queens."

"Unless you are very certain Louis was capable of a miracle, I would advise you to contain Your Majesty's insolence with me." Louise's expression went very tight just then, anger seething from every part of it. "After all, after your period of mourning, if you are not very clearly pregnant by the king, it shall be my son, not yours, who shall be formally crowned King of France, and you shall be useless once more, a dowager without children." She fingered the large ruby suspended from a gold chain at her throat. "An ugly word, 'dowager.' " Louise de Savoy repeated it with more emphasis and a slightly wrinkled nose, as if she had tasted something sour. "Speak the truth, *ma fille*. If there is a chance you were made pregnant—perhaps not with Louis' child—then with some bastard you mean to hold up as—"

"Cease this, I bid you!" Claude cried out, her skin gray now and etched with sorrow, her voice echoing across the silent chasm.

Mary touched Claude's shoulder in response. She did not believe she was pregnant by the king. From the time of her last courses, Louis had been unable to fully do his duty to her in a way that would make that likely. Neither, in his brief time in France, did she think it probable that she could be carrying Charles's child. Even so, she knew when it came to that, that nothing was entirely impossible, and she must remain cautious.

Gazing into the face of such an embittered woman as Louise de Savoy, whose ambition had aged her well before her time, announcing a pregnancy from either man who would still unseat her son might almost have been worth the undertaking of such a ruse.

For the moment, though, Mary would not protest too much. Not until she knew for certain whether she carried either man's child.

The Hotel de Cluny, on the rue des Mathurins St. Jacques overlooking the Seine, with its turrets, beige stone and gray roof, had once been a Benedictine abbey. Stark now and forbidding, it was the customary royal palace used for mourning. There, the law dictated, Mary must spend a full month's time in isolation, heavy black draperies covering all of her windows to blot out any light or fresh air. She lay atop the bed, face to the ceiling, feeling as if she could actually suffocate, and with no earthly idea how she would survive the next twenty-eight days treated like a virtual prisoner.

As footsteps passed in the corridor beyond the heavily sealed door, she took up the letter from Wolsey once again and pressed it against her chest. His words had brought tears when she first had read them an hour ago for how much she missed her dear Thomas, his counsel and his friendship. She knew he was not well liked. His reputation, even here in France, had become one of a cleric bitten by wild ambition, greed and a raging desire to become pope, no matter the sacrifice.

> . . . *move with great care in all that you do and say.*
> *And if any motions of marriage be made unto you, do*
> *not listen or heed them*. . . .

Great irony, she thought bitterly. The only man she had
ever loved or wanted to marry was a country away—a world
beyond her once again. An impossible dream. Light from the
candles flickered endlessly across the folds of her thick white
robes in the blackness of midday. Flames cast odd shadows
around her. She was angry at Wolsey's words, the presump-
tion in them. Angry at her circumstances. A wasted life.
Someday, she thought, *I must speak with Katherine, tell her
that there is someone who understands. I hurt for her now in a
way I did not, nor could I, before. I wish I had tried to understand better then. She deserves someone's understanding, the
way I deserve it now.*

She missed Charles . . . Jane . . . and especially Henry. . . .
Why did her brother not write her some encouragement?

Her French secretary, a mouselike man with protruding
teeth and small eyes, sat before her at an inlaid writing table
topped with ink pot, sand and paper. His poised hand and
nails were stained black. He dipped and waited for her words
of reply, his face, like hers, illuminated by the dancing candlelight.

> *I trust the king, my brother, and you will not see
> in me such childishness. I trust that I have conducted
> myself well since I came to France and to the utmost
> honor of the King. . . .*

She paused, feeling tears push at the back of her eyes,
missing so dearly a time of her life that could never be
again.

*. . . and if there is anything I may do for you, I would
gladly do it. . . .*

Mary brushed away tears she could not contain and drew
in a breath, trying to steady herself, trying to remain, in manner, royal. "Yes, send that. Only that. They know me. They will
both understand that I have been faithful to His Majesty's will
in spite of my desire to do everything to the contrary."

At the very moment when Wolsey bowed to the king in England, Mary curtsied fully to the new sovereign, Francois
across the Channel in France. She rose slowly in the dark of
the shadows and flickering light of her mourning chamber,
her world for the month that seemed to stretch endlessly before her. There was no youthful smile lighting her flawless
face any longer, no blush adorning her cheeks. No music
lightening the somber rooms. Only silence, and the crack
and snap of the wood blazing away in the hearth. Her skin, it
seemed, matched her starkly sewn and unadorned snow white
gown.

Louis had been dead for nine days, and the whispers, even
at the Hotel de Cluny, had reached a crescendo. Was the queen
with child? Would the dauphin ever be crowned or was he to
be replaced by the son of an English queen? Servants lingered
silently in the corner as Francois now advanced toward her in a
sweep of elegant black velvet.

"You are well, I trust?" Francois asked, casually glancing
around with a little sniff of disapproval at the spartan surroundings, and the darkness.

"As well as can be expected."

"Is it mourning sickness that plagues Your Majesty, perhaps?"

"Perhaps. But not at all likely," she replied with a taunting calm. "That is why you have come, I assume?"

Francois smiled slyly in response as he sank into one of the collection of brocade-covered chairs near the fire. "Will you not offer me a cup of wine for my trouble in coming?"

"I need offer Your Majesty nothing. You are King of France. You may take what you desire." She leveled her eyes on him as the civility in her tone slipped by a degree. She hovered near his chair, declining to sit with him, as it would be, she believed, too familiar. They both knew what she meant.

"A king uncrowned is really the same as no king at all," he said.

"Just as a queen without a king beside her is only a dowager?" Mary parried.

Francois sighed, shrugging his shoulders as he accepted a silver cup of wine from Madame d'Aumont, who had heard them, accommodating him in a swift sweep across the floor, her gown rustling in the silence.

"The physicians who examined me said the very thing I told Your Majesty just now. The possibility that I might be with child by the late king is very small."

Francois balanced an elbow on the chair arm and rested his chin on his hand as he studied her then, his smile smug and overly confident. "And so whatever is to be done with you, until we know for certain?"

"We do know."

"Ah, but how desperately I do want to believe you, *ma*

belle-mère." He reached out so suddenly then to take her hand that she could not resist or pull away. She stood stone still above him, firelight playing off the stark white silk of her mourning gown. "It is so inescapably dreary in here. I truly would like nothing better than to cut short your mourning and free you from this perpetual night, ushering you like a beautiful bird back into the daylight."

"There shall be no challenger to Your Majesty's rightful place on the throne."

"But were you not a wife to him in every way?"

"He was not able to be a husband to *me* in every way. Not since Abbeville."

"That was two months ago."

"Yes, it was."

He tightened his grip until she could feel her hand begin to throb. "Will you swear this?"

"With the utmost sincerity."

"I find that I am satisfied with your assurances. So when I return from Rheims, it shall please me greatly to terminate your period of mourning, so that you may attend me, and see what a *true* French court should be like." Francois finally set down his goblet and ran his other hand caressingly from her waist up to her breast. His fingers stilled there for only a moment as he looked up, daring her to push it away—daring her to reject him again now that he was king. "What a waste of such loveliness."

"I have not felt a waste in France. Only ever well cared for."

"Splendid to know." He was still smiling, but his expression had darkened to one that held an ominous offer. "Your good brother the King of England seeks the return of your dowry—or you—which he no doubt will soon find someone suitable to offer for. Yet it would appear that, with you and your dowry still here in France, I hold all of the cards in that particular game. Would you not agree?"

Mary nodded, seeing fully how well, by his ruthlessly ambitious mother, he had been taught to play, and feeling well out of her league in it. Francois would make a formidable opponent for Henry, on any battlefield or council chamber. Mary knew she was likely to become a marriageable bargaining chip once again. This time, however, it would be for both sides. If Francois could successfully marry her off to a French candidate—and the ambitious and wealthy Claude de Lorraine had been whispered about since before Louis' death—she would be forced to remain in France, as would her substantial dowry. If Henry successfully negotiated her remarriage to some other powerful prince, she would lose all hope of returning to England—and to Charles. She was so isolated from any English companions, even from daylight, that she could think of little else but what mystery fate had in store for her. But she was smarter than that, too determined to succumb. She had spent her early years watching how the game was played. Henry, like Francois, had become a master. No matter the pressure, she would not be undone by it now.

"I want you, Mary, and I mean to have you. Not now, when the risk of a pregnancy is great. But after." He touched her cheek. *"Oui, apres.* You and I shall have our day."

"Your Majesty cannot mean that."

"I never say anything I do not mean." He looked at her with sharp eyes, then drew her against him, his face meeting her breasts, his hands tightening at her small waist. "You shall remain in France, either as my mistress, or as the wife of my noble associate Claude de Lorraine, or perhaps . . . if you are very good, as my queen."

She despised his gaze. His touch like this was worse. But she was trapped, and he meant to keep her that way. For now, he had all of the power and he knew it. However much she dealt with the denial in it, the prospect of seeing daylight and freedom a little sooner was worth the risk of not rejecting him fully. She would tell this new king anything he wanted to hear in order to have the warmth of sunlight on her face. She may not be in control of her life, but Mary was a far more worthy opponent than Francois had bargained for. And being a Tudor meant she knew how to get what she wanted. . . . Yes, eventually she would.

From the luxury of the jumbled satin bedding strewn across his massive tester bed, the heraldic symbol sewn into the silk behind them, Jane Popincourt watched the movements of his magnificent bare body. Tanned and fit, he strode like a lion past a mural depicting the life of Saint John.

God, she thought, but Henry VIII was a beautiful man. Finally, she was with him in the way she had believed for nearly all of her life that she wanted. Small moments between them had convinced her at a very young age that one day he might actually love her. That fantasy had colored and changed her entire life. She knew about his affair with Bessie Blount, and about Elizabeth Fitzwalter before her. Like the other two girls, Jane attended Queen Katherine every day. But none of them had mattered an hour ago. Jane realized now she had used Thomas Knyvet only in order to hurt Henry. She had used Louis d'Orleans to hurt herself. She had no excuse for what she had just done with the King of England.

Like some great bubble that had burst before her, Jane saw now with a raw clarity she had never had before that Henry did not love her. In all likelihood, he did not even actually like her. The only place in his heart for that depth of enduring sentiment had been with Mary. Not even his wife but only ever Mary. He did not even seem aware of Jane now as he picked up a stack of letters and began to leaf through them, his bare back to her, as if she were not even there.

The rumor was that Bessie Blount was pregnant with the king's child. He would not have as much use for a pregnant mistress, Jane had reasoned in the tense moments after he had sent for her unexpectedly. She had walked, trembling with every step, surrounded by a coterie of his guards, toward the royal bedchamber, as a willing, fresh conquest. The queen had only recently been delivered of yet another stillborn child—this one the much needed son, so that the king could barely look at her. He dined with her only on state occasions now, or when she absolutely would not be avoided.

It was a little world, this place, a microcosm called the English court. Here, gossip was so rampant that everyone knew everything eventually, Jane thought, watching Henry's every sinewy muscle, every move of his broad, bare body, and trying not to feel the depth of his indifference. Oddly, watching Henry, she thought of Longueville instead. Like Henry and Knyvet, he was a completely unacceptable man for her— noble, important, married. Yet no one had made a more indelible impression on her heart. And then last month, Mary had written that his wife had died in childbirth. The fantasy of Longueville, as it once had with Henry, had increased ever since. This distasteful event with the king had been a tying off, a completion. She had thought she wanted it. Now she was grateful to be done with it.

As if somehow sensing her distraction, he set down the papers and came back to her then, not bothering to cover himself before her, nor she before him. Henry touched her pale, freckled cheek with a tanned finger. Without a word, he pressed his lips against hers and drew her tongue into his mouth. Helpless to stop him, or the story nearly played out at last between them, Jane let the King of England lead her silently back to his bed.

"Very well, you have my ear, Norfolk. Say what you mean to."

"Pray, forgive me, Your Majesty, I know of the love you bear for both of them. But I am afraid I do not trust either Wolsey or Suffolk."

The Duke of Norfolk, slightly hunched now, more silver than bronze in his hair, sat at the end of the council table alone with Henry VIII after all of the other members had gone. Frigid winter cold still bled through the walls of Richmond Palace, and a heavy rain beat against the leaded windows that rattled them nearby. "I believe there is something between them well beyond friendship. Something to do with the Dowager Queen of France, though I have no real proof of it."

"Not that again! Are there not enough real problems to contend ourselves with?" Henry moaned, slumping more deeply into his leather-back chair, weary of Jane . . . of

Katherine . . . of Bessie . . . of the complications of them all. "Charles assured me there was nothing between him and Mary beyond our childhood alliance. No rumors have come from France to the contrary in the meantime, have they?"

Norfolk was cautious. Each word meticulously chosen, each enemy—Buckingham, Wolsey, Brandon—more vulnerable to his desire for power than they would ever know. "If it please Your Majesty, allow me to say that I have it on sound authority that Wolsey writes to the queen daily, counseling her and—"

"His Eminence is like an uncle to us both. I would expect nothing less," Henry interjected, but Norfolk would not miss an opportunity alone with the king, as there were so few of them these days. Now with rumors of Buckingham's potential renewed claim to the throne as a descendant of Edward III, the discontented duke would take care of himself. Norfolk's greatest obstacle remained the team of Wolsey and Brandon. To vanquish them both, he had but to prove that they could not be trusted. But how to convince the king what he already knew? That Wolsey had known all along about Mary and Brandon and even assisted in their deception.

"And, sire, he then speaks privately to Suffolk almost immediately afterward."

"The two are related?"

"One could make that inference."

Henry pounded a fist onto the table. At his feet, his two favorite greyhounds passively lifted their heads. "Facts, Norfolk. By God, I can do nothing at all without facts!"

He had precious few of those. Only what rumors he

longed to believe, and a heavy dose of ambition to bind them. He was many things, but a foolish man Norfolk was not. There was something between Mary and Brandon. Henry could feel it, down to the very marrow of his bones. Now, if only he could prove it, their betrayal—and Wolsey's complicity, the stage, and the power, would be his entirely. And after all, was not the sovereign owed fidelity from those he trusted? And did he not have the opportunity to punish those who betrayed that trust?

"Perhaps I cannot yet prove it, sire. But there is one way to find out."

Henry leaned forward, his red-gold brows merging.

"Since the death of the French king, the Prince of Castile has renewed his suit for the hand of your sister."

"So have several others, Norfolk. What of it?"

Norfolk could see Henry was swiftly growing impatient. Norfolk supposed the king wished to return to Mistress Blount or whoever his newest mistress was. Pleasure now, most of the time, was the only thing. The duke had little time. There must be an impact made with each and every sharp, clear word.

"So have you a plan to entrap my two friends . . . as well as a most beloved sister?"

"The Prince of Castile is older now, a better candidate by far than he was before, but still the same man you and your father before you thought of as suitable for a princess. Send His Grace, the Duke of Suffolk, to inform your sister of that. If there has been anything untoward between them, the announcement of the new marriage shall be like a closing off. If Brandon cannot or will not tell her, you shall have your answer as proof. Then you may send me to finish the job by informing Mary myself."

"Brandon has already offered to head up the delegation to France," Henry revealed with a suddenly uneasy tone.

Norfolk could see as the words left his lips that Henry's mind fought reaching the same inevitable conclusion the duke already had long ago accepted about Mary and the king's best friend. Henry scratched his neat beard, remembering how fervently Charles Brandon had offered to return to France, though he did not reveal that to Norfolk. *If I do this for you . . . do you promise I can choose my next husband? . . .* No, Mary, his Mary, would not take matters into her own hands. They were far too close as brother and sister for her to betray him like that. He had not really meant she could marry *anyone*, best friend or not. And of course she knew that. She was a princess of the blood. He arched a brow in a show of irritation. In life sometimes there were things one simply did not wish to know. But as sovereign, Henry did not often have that luxury. Even if it involved betrayal of the most horrible kind.

"You are playing with fire in this, Norfolk," said Henry at last. "You know that, I hope."

"It shall be worth the risk if I honor Your Highness's trust in me."

"And if you are wrong about all of it . . . what then, Norfolk?"

Freed from the Hotel de Cluny, yet attired still in unadorned white silk, Mary stood before the new French king, Francois, as he had instructed her to do. Her place was beside him, next to the throne of Queen Claude. His mother, Louise de Savoy, was as resplendently attired now as her daughter-in-law, in gold and green brocade and glittering emerald jewels. Mary had thought it an odd arrangement until the entrance of the delegation was announced. She should have known, she thought, that there would be a reason. The shock of hearing his name squeezed her heart.

"Representing His Gracious Majesty Henry VIII, King of England, His Grace the Duke of Suffolk, attended by Sir Nicholas West and Sir Richard Wingfield."

He had returned! Hearing his name now, Mary had the overwhelming urge to run to him, fling herself into his arms. But she was not that little girl anymore. Instead, she held herself with the greatest dignity now. Still she nearly forgot to breathe as Charles, Wingfield and West advanced and all three bowed deeply to the new, young French king.

"It is pleasing to see you again, Suffolk," said Francois. "Though in sad circumstances. But the late king, our good father, was fond of you, so it is a pleasure to receive you nonetheless."

"My thanks, Your Majesty." Brandon nodded. This time when he looked up, his gaze met Mary's. In the fleeting exchange she saw everything: concern, love and longing. She felt herself tremble. But she steeled herself solidly against that. His beard was longer, his smile slightly weary, his eyes held not quite the same youthful sparkle as they crinkled at the corners a little more now. "His Highness, King Henry, sends his greatest love and congratulations to you on your coronation."

"It is a pity you missed the event. It was all such a magnificent spectacle." Suddenly, Mary felt the king's hand go around her waist and tighten with an odd familiarity. "Sadly, Her Majesty, the dowager queen, was required to miss it as well, due to her period of mourning." Francois then glanced over at her with what was calculated to look like a great intimacy between them. "Of course, *ma belle-mère* was as much there in all of our thoughts as if she had been right beside me, as she is now." His jeweled hand moved down to her hip just enough to ensure that Charles could not miss the small, important liberty, which Queen Claude, in her position on the other side, would be spared viewing.

Mary watched Charles's jaw tighten. But he gave nothing else away. Francois was boldly baiting him, knowing that between the two men, he possessed the power, and never quite forgiving him entirely for what had happened at Mary's coronation tournament.

"I assume," Francois said, still not taking his hand from her hip, "that your delegation has come not only to offer congratulations and condolences, but to offer a proposal?"

"If it pleases Your Majesty, I have been authorized to discuss that with you."

"Excellent." Francois smiled disingenuously when he undoubtedly saw, as Mary did, Charles's hands clench and then open at his sides. "Longueville!" the new king called out to the slim, silver-haired French duke who stood at the foot of the dais, along with a collection of other elegantly garbed French nobles. "See these gentlemen to their accommodations. I am sure they are weary after the long journey. But I invite you all, personally, to dine with us this evening once you have had a chance to rest and don more suitable attire." He made a little sneer then as he spoke the last few words, inferring unkindly, Mary thought, as the French always did, that the English had a boorish sense of style not appropriate for the sophisticated French court.

After the men had gone, Mary was dismissed from Francois' presence as well, her usefulness, for the moment, at an end. She had not been returned to her own apartments for more than a few moments, when Anne Boleyn, in crimson silk slippers and a scurrying gait, brought her a small folded note, curtsied to her and withdrew. There were only four words written down. The note was unsigned but Mary recognized the small tight script as belonging to the duc de Longueville.

Third floor, second door.

By design, Charles had viewed the lecherous glance, the uninvited groping. It was meant as a taunting from one man to the other and, in it, was an open challenge. He stalked the length of the grand room, elegantly furnished, facing down onto the peaceful inner courtyard of Les Tournelles and the patchy snow-covered ground. He could not press the ugly moment from his mind. He wanted Mary, he physically ached for her, he loved her still. That would have been clear to any man, whether or not Henry had ordered him not to jeopardize relations in France upon his return. Even the well-being of the vulnerable dowager queen.

I should have killed him in that tournament when I had the chance, as he lay in the dirt, his eyes spiked not with rivalry but with fear, he thought with a building rage now. Whether or not, in his absence, the notoriously womanizing monarch had taken his pleasure with her was the only question. Mary had been like a hostage here. She would have had no choice. His mind understood that, even if his heart did not. *I love you, wildly and forever,* he thought. *No matter what you have been forced to do in my absence. . . . I am returned now, returned for you. . . .* He longed to say that to her, and so much more.

Charles stood at the long window and braced himself with both arms extended against the casement. And then he wondered, because he could not stop himself, if there would be a part of Mary now, one who had spent her company with, and been adored by, kings these past months, that would prevent her from going back again to a mere duke with scant lineage and little else to offer. She certainly deserved better. He could never fault her for wanting that. Mary was everything to him, and if that had changed for her, then he would accept it. He must accept it.

She did not knock a moment later but let herself into his room silently. He heard the click of the lock, pivoted back and saw her standing near the door. The days, months separating them disappeared. The doubt dissolved with it. He went to her silently and drew her up very tightly into his arms. She smelled so sweet, freshly washed. There was the fragrance of sweet spring roses.

"It feels like an eternity," Charles said gently into the soft red-gold hair that hung against the slim column of her neck.

"You know not the half of it," she whispered against his mouth.

"But I do plan to spend the rest of what time we have entirely with you." Her touch had told him what he had needed to know. The separation had only strengthened what was between them. He smiled at her, touched her face very tenderly and then kissed her.

"In this world, there is more against us than you know."

"For the resourceful sister of the most clever Henry VIII?" He bit back a teasing smile, more happy to be this close to her again than even he thought possible before this moment. "Now, since you are no longer another man's wife, or in need of your chastity, just for a little while, do show me how clever *you* can be," Charles Brandon said, answering his own question before she could even respond.

"Yes, they are together clandestinely, Your Majesty," Claude de Lorraine dutifully reported, standing, hands linked behind his back, just outside the king's chapel in the moments after matins had concluded. They stood beneath the carved eaves and pillars that ringed the inner courtyard of Les Tournelles.

Hearing the confirmation, Francois swatted at the air to send his mother and Queen Claude on ahead as he stopped and faced the sleek, blond Lorraine. "Then she is the whore I believed she was. He is nothing but a pitiful duke."

"It would appear so, sire."

"Dieu! I could kill him with my bare hands! I meant to have Mary from the first moment I saw her!"

"Forgive me, Your Majesty, but I thought that you intended the dowager queen for me."

"In name only, *bien sur!"* he said dismissively. "You would not have made the right match for a firebrand like her in any other way!"

They stood still as the clerics began to file out behind them. Francois sighed heavily. "So now what?"

"Well, if the rumors from England are true, and the Duke of Suffolk is serious about Her Majesty, and King Henry knows of it, and has sent Suffolk to France to proceed with his suit for her hand, sanctioning it, Your Majesty's . . ." His words trailed off as he drew in a breath, considering more carefully how he meant to finish his sentence. "Your Majesty's advances could conceivably jeopardize relations, and cause the English to attack again."

"They would not dare. Old Louis was a very different king than the one I mean to be, and my good English cousin could not believe he would fare so well next time, since he would be going up against the court of Francois I."

Lorraine tipped his head, shrugged. "They say Henry VIII is a bold ruler, sire, driven to match his father's thirst for French land. Pressing that point could be troublesome to our own interests."

"Oh, very well," he growled. In spite of the bravado, Francois was a new and untested ruler, without the same lineage of warfare and the experience Henry had, and he knew it. "Then what the devil would you advise me to do about Suffolk and the dowager queen?"

"Perhaps you should confront him directly. If his intention is marriage, and the English king has indeed agreed to it, he will not deny it but boast to you of his good fortune. Then at least you shall know how to proceed with Her Majesty."

When Charles woke, Mary was sitting curled in the window embrasure, a blanket over her shoulders, knees to her chest. The sunrise was a pale, shimmering pink on the horizon, heralding another dreary winter day. He went to her and saw that there were tears in her eyes. He could see by how she could not catch her breath and her face was patched red that she had been crying for some time. He sank down beside her and drew her tenderly against him.

"There now, my love. What is this? It is not exactly the response a man hopes for after a night like that."

It was a moment more before she turned her tear-stained face up to him. "You have come to take me home for Harry, haven't you? You are his best friend, so he trusts you. He has at last worked out my marriage to the Prince of Castile and has sent you to break the news to me."

Charles laughed softly and brushed away her tears with his thumbs. "Where would you get a wild notion like that?"

"Wolsey's men. He sent two friars to prepare me. By my faith, Charles, I cannot bear the thought! And if I do not comply, if I try to remain here hoping my brother will change his mind, remembering his promise to me as we stood on the dock at Dover, Francois will see me married to Claude de Lorraine in the interim! And that, only so that he can make me his own mistress!"

"You know that?"

"He told me so himself."

She was weeping again now, her slim body wracked with sobs. "All my life I have done what I have been told to do! You are a princess, they said! A Tudor, they said! You have a duty! You must comply! Well, enough, I say!" She bolted to her feet, wrapping the blanket and her arms around herself, her face crimson with a mix of anger and despair. "I tell you this, Charles Brandon: I would rather be torn to pieces than *ever* comply with either of those foul plans. I would truly rather be out of this world, dead and buried, and I mean to tell Harry every word of that!"

In all of the years he had known her, he had never seen such absolute conviction. She may be near hysteria, tears still washing onto her wet face, her shoulders still jerking, yet he could see that behind it was a coldly determined woman. For a moment, a dark, forbidding instant, he actually had a vision of her taking her own life rather than giving in one day more to the will of others. She had done her duty—difficult, objectionable duty, with her youth and her virginity. She would not do it again. He knew she meant every word exactly, because he knew her.

"Marry me, Charles!" she bid him, and the words came so suddenly and full of such anguished pleading that, for a moment, he felt as if his heart had actually stopped beating. "Take me away from Paris, and far away from France, as your wife now before it is too late!"

"You know it is what I want more than anything . . . you *know* it. But something so dangerous dare not be rushed. Besides, I promised Harry I would do nothing unexpected while I was here. And he trusts me."

"I trusted him too, Charles, and look where it got me! Widowed, alone and in danger of the gracious Lord knows what sort of second marriage alliance!" She crossed the room away from him and stood by the remains of the small red glowing blaze that they had lit themselves. Again she wrapped her arms around herself, then lowered her head.

She would not stop weeping, and Charles felt himself undone by it.

"I'll not do it, Charles. Not again." She shook her head. "Harry promised me my own choice the next time I marry, and I mean to keep him to his word, even if I need to press him to the wall to do it!"

"You cannot ask me to go against him, Mary! He made me promise before I left England! I am not his beloved Mary, with the single key to his heart. Only you have that power!"

"I am meant to be your wife!" Suddenly she spun back around, hands dropping rigidly down to her sides, all of the conviction and Tudor fire coming alive on her face at that moment in the bedchamber of an apartment that held them both between two worlds.

"What are you asking me?"

"Choose, Charles. There must be an end to it! Either you agree to marry me, here and now in Paris—or I do swear to you, by all that is holy, that I will disappear into a French convent and spend the rest of my life there, because I'll *not* spend the rest of the nights of my life growing old with another man like Louis! I'll not do more than what I have already done for the sake of England!"

Outside there were footsteps. French spoken softly. In the echo of her ultimatum, Mary took up her dress, petticoats, shoes, and slipped from the room without another word. A moment later, a liveried servant stood before him.

"I come from the king, Your Grace. His Majesty wishes to speak immediately with you."

The black oak table was long, highly polished, and forbidding. Charles sat alone at one end. The king, in black and silver, was at the other. The distance between them was intentional. Charles was made exceedingly uncomfortable as he sank formally onto the edge of the leather chair to which he had been directed. The whole scenario reminded him of the command visits to his uncle.

"Your Majesty wished to see me."

Francois' expression was stony as he took a long swallow from a goblet with rich gilt decoration. Charles could hear the rhythm of his own heart beating as the king settled the goblet back onto the table with a little clink. There could be no possible advantage to a sudden and private summons like this. Francois finally leaned forward, steepling his hands. "So then. You have come to France with the traitorous intention of marrying the dowager queen without the permission of my good cousin in England, nor my own, have you not?"

"I assure Your Majesty, I came to France with no such intention," he replied honestly. That much he could say and mean with absolute conviction. Of the many accusations he had anticipated in the long walk to this room, that was not among them.

"Surely my lord of Suffolk knows that a king has spies."

Charles listened to the tick of the clock on the wall behind him. It seemed to match the rapid thud of his heart. There was much he was here to do. Rescuing Mary, and perhaps risking his life to do so, was but a nuance of the greater plan. Before he left London, Henry and Wolsey had instructed him to ingratiate himself enough to the new French king so that he would have leave to bargain. Henry knew that Francois wished the return of Tournai, which he had so powerfully taken from Louis. In exchange for its return now, he demanded all of the jewelry, silverplate and anything else of value that Louis XII had given to his wife. Ironically, Henry had believed that, just because Charles had met Francois before, he would be in a position to negotiate with this lecherous king, one who wished to retain the great love of his life in France for himself.

Betray Henry's expectation of his promise and he could lose his life. Betray Mary now and he would lose that heart forever.

"Then tell me, why have you come?"

"At the pleasure of my king only, Your Majesty, to discuss diplomacy and Tournai. Certainly not matrimony."

Francois fingered his own short beard with thumb and forefinger. The silence seemed to stretch on forever as Francois studied him with a cold, discerning stare. "And the dowager queen? What would she say if asked the same thing?"

"Her Majesty would tell you the truth—that I had no intention to engage in such a dangerous folly as to come into a foreign realm and marry its queen without the authority of my master."

"It would seem the ring she suddenly and permanently wears in place of the king's wedding band—the one into which she gazes as if a mirror would tell a different tale than your own, my lord of Suffolk?"

Mary would never have divulged something to Francois so private and precious as his gift of the onyx ring. And spies were everywhere. Charles felt his anger flare again amid his defense of Mary, but he drew in deep breaths to press it back. They could both find themselves in grave danger if Francois was not convinced.

"Surely you would not look at me, here at my private table, and try to tell me there is nothing of the heart between the two of you. A man in love is a difficult thing to conceal."

Everything raced through his mind.

Mary . . . *You have a choice, Charles.* . . . Henry . . . *I want your word, Charles, that you will do nothing.* . . . Anne . . . *She belongs to you.* . . .

"Very well then, yes. Fate be damned—I do love her." The declaration was firm. Unyielding. From inside of his mind it sounded to Charles like someone else's voice. "Our history is a long one. But I did not come to France to act upon that, or in any way to betray Your Majesty or my own king in it."

"Is it your desire to marry her?"

"As I have told Your Majesty most emphatically, I would never have come to France with that in mind."

"But in your heart?"

"I am a duke. She is a queen."

"I was a duke, who now is a king," he said, shrugging with a sly, slightly thawed smile. "From my own perspective, Suffolk, nothing is impossible. Tell me this: Do you believe she would marry you if it were your desire as well?"

"I believe she would, yes."

"Well, then." He leaned back, paused. "There is no reason I cannot aid and guide the course of true love."

"As I said, I promised my master I would do nothing without his approval."

Francois fingered the medallion at his chest. "Why not write to your Cardinal Wolsey, explain things as they are? Explain that you have the best wishes of the King of France in your endeavor. That should suffice initially to smooth the way and at least prepare my good cousin for what quite likely is inevitable between his sister and you."

It seemed a logical step, a way out of his predicament, but Charles knew well he must avoid a potential trap. There was nothing in the world he wanted so much as to marry her but he must be cautious in every step now.

"Your Majesty's kindness is an honor to me."

"Write to Wolsey, then," he said, in what sounded almost like a command.

The next silence extended out for what felt like an eternity to someone with everything to lose—one who had come to manhood and power led by blind ambition and prevarication, one who had just taken what felt like the greatest gamble of his life in his honesty now. He hated being at this foreign sovereign's mercy but there was no choice.

"I find that I like you, Brandon," Francois magnanimously declared. "I will do all that I can for the sake of that rare thing that is between you and the dowager queen, as that which is so like what I possess with my own queen, my Claude."

Across the room, Lorraine put a finger over his lips. Hearing those false words, it was then, from his place near the door, that the duc de Lorraine knew that the King of France had something very different in mind than a genuine desire to help Charles Brandon and Mary find a way to be together.

After Suffolk had thanked him with irritating profusion and had gone from the chamber, the duc de Longueville and

Claude de Lorraine advanced in a blur of silver thread and silver chest chains, from the place where they had stood together nearly unnoticed, beside the door.

"Do you believe from what you heard that, with my tacit approval offered up, Brandon shall now find the courage to ask for her hand?"

"It is my understanding, Your Majesty, that the dowager queen has already asked *him*. My spies tell me that her ultimatum was delivered rather boldly this morning and with a rain of tears so abundant that she could be heard down the length of the corridor."

"Ah, women and their tears. They do know how to use them." Francois' smile broadened. His teeth flashed. "Feisty English rose . . . what a dreadful waste she shall be on a scoundrel like Suffolk, who could not begin to know how to nurture her as I could."

"Your Majesty has offered the bait with perfection," flattered the duc de Lorraine. "Now we must wait to see if he has more ardor or good sense." He was smiling with complicity.

"I'm not certain I understand Your Majesty's decision," Longueville dared to say.

"Well, obviously, she is not going to agree to marry Lorraine here," Francois declared with a flash of irritation. "And she is apparently not going to become my mistress—not with a man who looks like Suffolk so close at her heel. Nor do I want that sly fox in England to win this by marrying off so beautiful a sister to the emperor's grandson, after all these years."

"It does make France far too vulnerable for anyone's liking."

"And so Your Majesty has an alternate plan?" asked Longueville.

"Always, Louis. A prudent king must always have that. After all, is it not you who always says power is like a game of chess and one must always consider not only the move at hand but the next move, and the next?"

"No, sire. That was Lorraine," replied the man whose own heart had remained in England.

Mary waited all afternoon, full of faith, hoping that Charles would find her and tell her there was nothing so much in all the world he wanted as to marry her now when, at last, they were both free to do so. As she sat beside the queen watching a masque performance in the garden, he did not come. Nor did she see him at the concert that followed. Perhaps he did not believe her when she'd said, with all the conviction in her heart, that she would without hesitation escape to a convent rather than submit to another man out of duty and not love. The truth was, Mary had never meant anything so much in all her life. Everything they had endured, everything she had become, had brought them both down to this single, defining moment.

The queen listened intently to the music and the Italian singer standing before them, but Mary would have given anything in the world to jump up and run very far away right now. Patience had never been a great virtue of hers, and it seemed less so now. Marriage had been a great deal to ask of any man. She knew that. Yet there it was. His choice. When Claude glanced over at her, Mary forced herself to smile and nod but she had not heard a single note sung right in front of her.

Charles sank to his knees onto the claret velvet–covered prie-dieu and lowered his head. He was in the small chapel at the Hotel de Cluny. Mary was upstairs, and what he did next would affect not only his own life, but perhaps history. She might be meant to marry another king . . . beget a great dynasty . . . he could be taking a destiny from her far greater than a common life with him. . . . Charles missed Anne so keenly just then, the trusted counsel of a sister, her honesty and humor. At this moment, he even missed Henry, whose raw clarity in things never wavered. If he could see the king's face, as he always had—read his expression—he would know far better what to do.

As the French king advised, he had written to Wolsey and explained the situation, but of course the letter could not possibly arrive in London in time. The sound of Mary's weeping still echoed through his mind, haunting him with thoughts of all he stood to lose. *If I should wait . . . and lose her love because of it . . . if she should be married off to another because I paused for too long . . .* He closed his eyes. *Heavenly Father, I am at a crossroads. I know not what to do. . . . She is my love, my heart . . . but he is my king. . . . I cannot think how I am to honor one and betray the other.*

When he went to her chamber a quarter of an hour later, he knew what scrutiny he would face from the French ladies there. There would be no turning back from the gossip it would cause. Whatever they decided to do, soon the world would know their secret and the cocoon of secrecy in which they had always lived would be gone forever. But he realized, only by seeing her one more time would he know the right path to take. He owed both of them that. When he could put it off no longer, he rose, made the sign of the cross and began the long walk to where Mary, and destiny, waited.

Chapter Nineteen

Destiny waits alike for the free man as well as for him enslaved by another's might.

—*Aeschylus*

March 1515, Paris

"*I* tell Your Grace the truth, she has already gone."

Charles pressed back the panic and pushed his way past Madame d'Aumont and into Mary's French apartments. His movements were rushed and a little frightening to the ladies who sat playing a card game of imperial. "Surely a queen does not simply disappear!"

"That one certainly has," she countered ruefully. "Her Grace has done as she wished."

In all of her life, there had only been one night that Mary had ever done precisely as she wished, Charles thought, and he had been there. But he did not say that as he moved from room to room, opening the heavy carved and painted doors with one powerful thrust after another. She could not have gone through with it—escaped to a French convent. It was not meant to end like this between them, unresolved, unanswered. The impulsive side of her that had so drawn him four years earlier, now made him angry. But just as swiftly the anger changed, flipped to regret. She could not do this.

As he moved in heavy-legged strides back toward the door, a young woman with smooth blond hair and remarkably wide blue eyes stepped before him. Surprised by her boldness, he stopped and looked at her.

"Perhaps if Your Grace took a moment for reflection, you would find the peace you seek in the private chapel below," she offered with a kind smile and in a very low voice meant for only Charles to hear.

"I was only just there, and I was alone."

"Perhaps Your Grace should consider looking again," Diane de Poitiers suggested calmly. Not thinking, only feeling, Charles took the curved stone stairs two at a time, his heart thundering through his chest. He found Mary a moment later, alone on her knees on the very same wooden priedieu before the altar at the front of the chapel where he had knelt. Mary's head was lowered against her steepled hands, and he could hear her whispered prayers as he came up behind her. He could see that she was dressed for travel, with a white satin jacket lined with white marten fur over her white mourning dress. Her hat was black felt. He knew only then, in that moment as he watched her, that he had never needed Henry or Anne—their approval or their reproach. He would promise her anything, give her anything, so that she would not leave. His answer came as clearly as a broad summer sky as he gazed up at an ancient gold-leaf panel of the Annunciation behind the altar. It felt to Charles as if God himself had sanctioned his decision.

When he placed a firm hand on her shoulder, Mary did not jump. Nor did she seem surprised that he had come. She merely made the sign of the cross in a firm triangle from her forehead and then across her chest, stood and turned to face him. Her expression alone was the thing that surprised him. He had already seen that she had changed here in France. But now those changes were marked. There was nothing of the child left on her face, in her bearing or in the tone of her voice. There was nothing uncertain left about her either.

"My horse waits in the courtyard. A single moment more and I would have been gone."

"Then thanks to God for my impeccable sense of timing," he countered, but she did not even smile. "Forgive me for not returning sooner, but I know what I want now."

"I have known it all along."

"I do not deserve your devotion."

"That's a pity," she stubbornly countered. "Because I most definitely deserve yours."

He took her into his arms then, not caring at all who might see. He pressed a kiss onto her forehead, each of her cheeks, and then onto her lips. "You are my life, Mary. All of it."

It felt as if he were being swept up by a swiftly moving tide, carried along toward something very dangerous. But Charles Brandon no longer wished to free himself. He would live or die, and at peace, by whatever happened next.

The wedding ceremony was performed that same evening in absolute secrecy, in the same little stone chapel at the Hotel de Cluny where each of them had prayed about the other.

Flames flickered atop dozens of long white tapers and set the nave aglow, along with the faces of their witnesses. The king, queen, Louise de Savoy, the duc of Longueville and Claude de Lorraine, as well as Diane de Poitiers and her husband, all sat silently bathed in warm amber light. No one English was present besides the bride and groom. Francois had insisted because he felt that until Henry could be informed, the risk was too great. When Charles suggested a delay to pursue Henry's permission, Claude de Lorraine had countered that, since His French Majesty's graciousness had been offered, that should well be enough. It seemed too great a risk then to insult their host. They knelt together at the altar, all decorated now in white, the frontal embroidered with a Tudor rose. Their hands linked under a silk bridal canopy, prayers and blessings were spoken by Cardinal de Tournon. After a Mass was said, at last, Mary and Charles exchanged vows. Then finally, the wedding ring was blessed. And in deep, reverent French, Charles was instructed by the cardinal.

"Place it now upon her thumb, as you speak the words, *In the name of the Father.* Then move it upon her second finger and say, *In the name of the Son.* Upon her third finger as you say, *And of the Holy Ghost . . .*"

Charles's eyes glowed with love and admiration for her and Mary was awed by that as he trembled just slightly, pressing the ring fully onto her finger. She leaned her head over onto his shoulder then as the cardinal pronounced that they were *mariés.* When he kissed her, she made certain not to close her eyes just in case when she opened them, she would find that tonight had all been nothing more than an exquisite, fleeting dream.

As they walked together back down the aisle toward the chapel doors, Charles gripped her hand and whispered to her, "Would you really have joined a convent?"

"Thank God, we shall never need to find out," Mary replied, happier at that moment than she had ever been in her life.

Wolsey had not wanted to tell him, yet there was no one else brave enough. As always, he had simply needed to plunge into the sea of Henry's fury and try his best to swim through it. It was how he had survived. How he had just last month fulfilled a lifelong dream, having been made cardinal. At Windsor Castle, he walked with Henry through the dormant privy garden, doing his best to keep up with a king who now stalked down the brick path, his face mottled red, not noticing the cold or the damp of the howling winter wind.

"How dare he? Brandon is a traitor to me!"

"Your Highness knows your sister. Stubborn to the core when it is something she desires."

"After all these years, he owed me his loyalty! He gave me his word, for all that was apparently ever worth!"

Wolsey must pace himself, he knew that well enough. Timing and a calm response were critical, not only for Charles and Mary's sake, but for his own. "Love is a difficult thing to contain, sire. It makes one do impulsive things."

"Love?!" Henry barked on a deep and icy chuckle. "The only thing Charles Brandon has ever loved is himself! If he were in England right now, his head would be on the block before he could even think about consummating this insult of a marriage!"

"Our Mary has written to you of the circumstances as well. Perhaps if you read her words, the two of you—"

"The devil I will! My sister is every bit as guilty of deceit in this as Brandon! Can she say anything to alter the reality of *that*?"

"Not alter, but perhaps explain."

He stopped, pivoted back, his expression softened. "Tell me, Wolsey, was I not good to them both?"

"Your Highness's goodness was beyond compare."

"Charles was like my own brother, and I always treated him as such."

"You have shown the greatest brotherhood to both of them," Wolsey believably flattered.

Wolsey drew in a breath, glanced up at the bare, spiny oak ahead of them, prepared to exhibit his most apostolic posture: hands steepled, head slightly lowered reflectively. "And yet, it does seem that perhaps, because of the familiarity with which the three of you have grown to adulthood, this trust was the consequence rather than an insult to you."

"Whose side are you on?" Henry angrily asked in a voice that was becoming deeper and more booming every day.

"Your Highness's of course." He wisely bowed.

Wolsey saw that his familiar expression and tone were something of a balm, and beneath it, Henry softened. "She was my favorite in all the world. She knew that, and she used it against me to get her way."

"She wants your love, Henry. They both do. They want to come home. They want to serve you here."

"Never! It is too late for that now. They shall remain in

France and see how tolerant and loving my good French brother will be to them over time."

"You wish them to remain forever in France?"

"What other use is she to me now? No, she will go straight to the gallows here! As will he!"

Wolsey knew that Henry did not mean that, but he must continue to move with caution. Norfolk was just waiting for an opening to supplant him in the king's mind and heart, as he had worked against Brandon and Buckingham.

The wind picked up then and blew the rich marten fur at both their necks. Wolsey felt himself shiver against the sudden chill but did not dare to break his gaze from the king's. "Her Majesty's friendship is more dear to you than any other. I have heard you say so myself. That shall not have changed between you."

"And the loyalty in that friendship, Wolsey? How could I ever forgive her for abandoning that?"

Wolsey could not answer now. The wound was too new, too raw. But in time, Henry would remember that there was no one in the world like his Mary. How he would help the king realize that, Cardinal Wolsey yet had no earthly idea. That, perhaps, might best be put before God.

Finally—yes, finally—after seven years of disappointment, Katherine had given the King of England a living child, who had remained so for more than a scant few days like the others. The fact that the baby girl had survived a month already seemed something of a miracle to be celebrated. Just before the death of Louis XII, Henry had named her Mary, after his sister. That choice seemed a bitter pill now when Henry felt so betrayed, he thought, as he gazed down at the little cradle, lined with the smoothest white silk and linen. Her sweet little head was peeking out over a mound of bedding and the intricate lace coverlet sent from the queen's father for his first grandchild. The queen was too old now for him to expect miracles, Henry realized, but a living child meant there was still a small ray of hope that she might yet be able to give him a son and heir after all. As they stood together before the tiny bed in the royal nursery, Henry put an arm gently over the shoulder of her stout body.

"Are you pleased with her, Hal?" Katherine tentatively asked, her English still thick with her Spanish roots in spite of her many years in England.

"I shall be more pleased when you give me a son."

She tensed ever so slightly beneath his arm in response. It was a nuance, yet he felt it—and he also felt the guilt. He should not have said what he felt quite so directly, knowing how hard she had tried these past long years to do her duty— and what it meant to her that she had been unable to. The fact that Bessie Blount had given him the son he craved had been an excruciating indignity for Katherine—yet one she suffered silently. He no longer loved her, yet still she was his queen. The emotion did compete with his affection for Bessie's son, a beautiful boy, bastard or not, whom Henry had immediately christened Henry Fitzroy. He had also bestowed upon the infant the vaunted title Duke of Richmond, according him his own household and staff. By virtue of his birth, the world now knew that the problem of conception lay with Katherine of

Aragon alone. The fact, along with his frustration, made it difficult for those barbs not to slip across his tongue.

Still, softened by the little royal child before him now, Henry reached over and kissed his wife very gently on the cheek. "She looks like my mother."

"She is dark, Hal. Her hair is like ink. So are her eyes."

"But her essence—that is my mother, and strictly Tudor." He smiled proudly. "Mary shall be a fine princess. The emperor has already offered another of his grandsons."

Katherine shot him a glare and a gasp. "She is not yet two months old."

"You know as well as I that it is never too soon to look toward those critical alliances for England, and with my sisters both disappointments to me and unavailable now, I must look to our daughter."

"Have you written to Mary since her—"

He gritted his teeth. "Since her secret marriage? God's bones, woman! Why must you destroy every rare moment that is between us these days with something unpleasant?"

"Because I love you, Hal. And I love your sister, as you do. She and Charles wish to return to us."

"Did Wolsey tell you that? Infernal man is as meddlesome as you are!"

"We both care about you. Do you not want her back? Not a day goes by you do not think of her. It was never right for Mary to be in France. She is too much a companion and helpmate to you. You need her."

"Well, my beloved helpmate seems to have cared more for herself than for me! How can I ever take her back now,

Kate? I would be the laughingstock of all the world! I would be that foolish English king ruled by his own sister, the secret bride! Just think of it!"

"If I were you," she calmly countered (because she had known him for so long she still knew how to reach him that way, he thought), "I would think only of how I miss her. And Charles Brandon, for that matter."

"There must be some penalty for betrayal, even for Mary! I cannot take them back," Henry declared. "That is the end of it!"

As Charles knew it would be, the marriage was everything. Perfect. Precious. He wanted nothing more in the world than what they had found at last. Perhaps to go home one day, but Wolsey in his letter made that sound an unlikely happening. Other than that, as they lay wound in one another, deep beneath the bedcovers of her poster bed in the Hotel de Cluny, more happiness for one man was not possible.

His kisses were deep and languorous. Charles murmured as his hands moved deftly again down the length of the curves and hollows which he had come to know well these past long two weeks as husband and wife. Threading his fingers through her own small delicate ones, he rolled his eyes closed. He was sated, replete. Finally happy.

"I wish we could just stay here like this forever." He sighed deeply. "But we must plan for our future now—decide what we mean to do with the rest of our lives."

She looked up earnestly, her eyes shining. "I want to go home, Charles."

"Perhaps we should have thought of that before we married. No matter what I say, Wolsey says Harry will not forgive me. And I suppose I don't really blame him. I really did wound him at the core."

"That very masculine chivalric code of yours."

"Don't laugh. It means something to a man."

"Then why did you agree to marry me?" she asked, with a tiny hint of irritation.

"Because you meant more. A great deal more."

He watched the tears that had been pressing at the back of her eyes flood onto her cheeks. She missed Henry so dearly, he knew. Katherine . . . Jane . . . Mother Guildford. He believed she was happier than she had ever been but that longing would never change. In spite of how it had occurred, they should all be sharing her joy. Charles kissed her sad, wet face then and drew her back against him. "We shall find a way with Harry. Somehow together. There must be a way. I cannot believe he will want to live the rest of his life without you."

Two weeks after their last letter from Wolsey arrived in Paris, and six weeks after their secret marriage, Charles rode a magnificent steel-colored bay beside the duc de Longueville's silver-clad horse, both thundering through the forested countryside beyond the palace of Fontainebleau. Ahead of them, hooves churning leaves and pine needles, the king led a party of other nobles on the hunt. It was an early spring day, cool but invigorating, no longer wet and frigid. The French forest was different from the lush English ones in which he had grown to manhood riding. Sunlight streaked through new, lacy branches like shimmering fingers, and a thick carpet of leaves and pine needles crunched beneath their horses' hooves.

"Still no response?" Longueville, once his captive but now a friend, casually asked.

"Wolsey's last response was that my king was still livid. I expected that. And I deserve it as well."

To the jangle of harnesses, they rode more slowly as the royal scouts pinpointed a stag. "Well, he cannot stay angry at so dear a friend forever."

"Ah, you do not know the king. He has a long memory and a toughened heart for those who disappoint him. His own wife has discovered that well enough."

Poor Katherine. The parade of women through the king's bedchamber door was increasing daily. The French gossiped about poor Mistress Blount, who had given the king the one thing he desired more than anything else, and lost him as a consequence.

"He was not always like that," Charles said as they watched Francois do the ceremonial honors of killing the captured stag. "Not so long ago, he seemed confounded by women and only Katherine's attentions would do, no matter how many lovely girls threw themselves at him."

"One does wonder how history might be changed if the poor Spaniard had given him a son."

"Apparently we shall never know. It is said back in England that she is quickly becoming too old to bear more children, and all of his interest anyway lies with that Boleyn girl."

They dismounted, then stood amid the collection of

other courtiers, both of them removing their gloves. "A thought occurs to me."

Charles cast a glance at him as the stag was hoisted up by a rope pulley into a tree to be gutted beside a strong, new fire. "What if my master, the French king, were to write to King Henry on your behalf speaking of pleasure at your ability to . . . negotiate? Would Henry not find you irreplaceable then and perhaps it could defuse the wildest portion of his anger?"

"How the devil would I ever get Francois to do a thing like that? He has despised me since Mary's coronation."

"One powerful king would not wish to make an enemy of another. Did you not tell me he tried nearly every day she was here before you married, to make the dowager queen his mistress, and rather aggressively?"

"True."

"The only thing that might anger Henry more than what you have done would be to know what a married sovereign had tried to do."

Charles looked at Francois, his long straight nose like a punctuation mark on an otherwise young and handsome face, chin tipped up, that air of entitlement swirling around him as he observed the stag's disemboweling. His arrogance was such a palpable thing it might be amusing to find his way back to Henry's good graces by knocking Francois down a peg or two if he could.

"I suppose it *is* worth a try. I shall speak with him at the banquet tonight. And, if it works, Louis, I shall owe you more than I could ever repay."

"Just send Jane Popincourt here to France when you return," he replied unexpectedly as they tethered their horses to the same tree. "And that shall be more than payment enough."

Jane . . . So Louis actually did care for her after all. This day really was quite full of surprises, Charles thought as they moved toward the dead stag.

Waving off his Yeomen of the Guard with irritation, Henry walked the length of the long gallery, with a view into the gardens, his hands then linking behind his back. Yet it was not a strolling pace his favorite spaniels and greyhounds followed. They were long, stalking strides he took and with which the Duke of Norfolk struggled to keep up.

"Loath as I am to admit it, sire, I find that in this circumstance I do agree with Buckingham. A penalty needs to be paid."

Henry shot the older man an angry stare. "Which one then, Norfolk? Murder Brandon as Buckingham recommended or simply imprison him?"

Henry knew that pain would be shooting up through Norfolk's spine at the king's breakneck pace down the interminably long gallery, which, with his gout, it was nearly impossible to match. Henry could tell he was trying not to huff but he could barely catch his breath. His glory days of war, or even hunting, were long over. "All I am saying is that there must be a price for his treasonous—even treacherous—act wrought against Your Highness. He married a princess of the blood without royal consent, after all."

"I know better than anyone what he did," Henry growled, shaking his head.

"If Charles Brandon is to return to England, then he must also be made to pay a price. Respectfully, sire, you could not possibly act differently on this. A punishment simply must happen."

Katherine was approaching them in unadorned black silk and a tight gabled hood hiding her swiftly graying hair. Her hands held a small prayer book and her expression was somber, with Dona Elvira and Maria de Salinas flanking her in equally plain dark dresses, each with a crucifix bobbing at her chest. When they met, the queen dipped into a deep curtsy to her husband, and her ladies followed.

"Would my husband grant me a private word?" Katherine asked in a low, perfunctory voice still heavily accented with Spanish, which once long ago Henry had found charming.

Before Henry could respond, Norfolk bowed to her, then to the king, and excused himself, along with Katherine's two ladies.

She wasted no time in coming to her point. "Do not let them do it, Hal, I bid you. I hope I am in time to stop you. If I have a shred of influence left on your heart, do not let the dukes of Buckingham and Norfolk convince you to punish them."

"I never liked Mary's eavesdropping, and I sure the devil do not find favor in it from you," he shot irritably. "How would you have a clue what Norfolk and I were speaking about?"

"Because I know Norfolk and I know *you*. You may not

love me anymore, Hal. But there was a time when you trusted my opinion. You even made me your regent, and what a glorious day that was for me, full of so much promise. You know I have always put this country and you ahead of everything else!"

Looking past the sallow skin and the age lines that defined her face now, and into dark eyes that mirrored their years together, the joys, the love and the losses, Henry softened. "I know that."

"Then if you do know it, you must welcome your sister and her husband back to England with the greatest forbearance."

"Reward them for their treason?"

"They only fell in love. That does not go against you, or England. Any more than what we once felt was treason toward your father. You remember that feeling . . . we both do. And there was a time, long ago now perhaps but which, to my heart still, feels like yesterday, a time when you as well would have done anything to marry me—and you did just that." She moved a little nearer, but she made no attempt to cross the chasm of their estrangement. Katherine knew it was too late for that. "Remember it, Hal, how we met in secret, the plans we made, the vows . . . and know that they did nothing more or less than you and I."

From the corner of his eye, he saw the two women and Norfolk lingering beneath the window, Norfolk stroking one of the greyhounds, yet doubtless having heard every word. Henry did not love Katherine any longer, but he would always trust her. Yet he trusted Norfolk as well. There was a choice to be made. Clear, cold and distinct. He saw that. Henry simply was not certain if it was one he was yet prepared to make, even for his Mary.

An hour later, Henry flipped his opponent over and forced him, with a single powerful thrust, to hit the rush mat. The sound was a whacking thud. They were both out of breath and their white linen shirts were drenched in sweat and pressed against the taut curves of their chests. Gawain Carew, new at court and full of enough ambition to challenge the king, tried to pull his twisted arm from a hold that was steadily and painfully being screwed up the length of his back.

"Ahhh!" he hollered out in pain.

"Oh, Carew, why must you make this so tediously simple?" Henry's voice in response boomed out the question to the young man with more than a passing interest in Charles Brandon's sister, Anne, as he let go the arm with an irritated, whipping flourish. Then he made it back to his feet to the roar of applause from the ingratiating nobles who had insisted on watching the king wrestle. Adore the attention though he did, it lost something without Brandon. Charles had always been the only one brave enough to actually try to beat him. He missed that. Fool bastard! Letting his prick lead him instead of his sense. Or, at the very least, that deplorable ambition of his.

Henry splashed water on his face from a basin held by a stony-faced boy with red hair like his own, and a dusting of freckles across the bridge of his nose. "The water is revoltingly warm! Did your master not tell you it must be very, very cold?"

The boy's face went crimson with horrified embarrassment.

"Another basin!" the steward near him called out. It was called out three times, an echo down a line of liveried servants before the king growled temperamentally, "Oh, never mind!" Then he tossed the towel onto the mat and stalked out of the great hall, followed by a collection of stunned servants and ambassadors, who knew better than to utter a word.

Perhaps I should hunt, he thought. *Feel the wind in my hair, the breeze on my face.*

But those thoughts, as with wrestling, tethered him back to Brandon, and to his own anger at the betrayal. Wolsey was waiting for him in his private dressing chamber, sitting in a high-back tapestry-covered chair, as Henry held his arms up and his sweat-stained shirt was removed for him by servants.

"What the devil have you come to plague me about? More pleadings from that miscreant?"

Wolsey silently extended the letter across his scarlet silk–draped girth, the red wax seal broken, a bit of black ribbon suspended from it. "Actually, it is from the King of France, sire," he replied evenly. "He wishes you to know of his great pleasure in the diplomatic work of the Duke of Suffolk. He speaks long and glowingly of His Grace's negotiating skills and of His Majesty's wish that, through Suffolk, your two countries may stay strongly allied."

"Don't look at me like that, Thomas," he said acidly. "I can see your thoughts right through that shiny, bald head of yours."

"Surely Your Highness knows I have only your happiness,

and the safety of England, inside of my head—as well as my heart."

"Too flowery even for you, Thomas. We've known each other far too long for that. Shall we not call a spade a spade and just admit that you have been on their side in this underhanded venture almost from the start?"

"Mary and Charles are both dear to me, as they are to you, Harry," he chose to say. "They have been meant for a very long time to be together. That much I will acknowledge."

"Honesty becomes the cleric in you. It is a novel approach you really should try to use more often."

Wolsey nodded almost to a bow. "Forgive me, Your Highness, if I have shown anything to you but the greatest, most humble, respect."

Once Henry had changed his costume, they walked together out into the long hall with its wall of windows and length of rich Persian carpet. When they were entirely alone, Henry's tone softened. "Look, Thomas, I would like this resolved as well, but it seems an insurmountable task. If I took them back now, after how they deceived me, the world would think me a weak ruler, something I have spent my reign struggling against."

"Yet perhaps there is a way."

"If you truly could find me a path out of this quagmire, Wolsey, I would think you a genius, and the most important person in all the world. . . . The second most important," Henry said, smiling.

Wolsey knew that he was right. The impulsivity of their

marrying in secret had cost them both dearly regardless of the fact that Henry had already promised his sister the right to select again. Clearly, it was a promise he chose not to remember. While he had always known Henry might battle her on her selection of a politically unimportant figure like Brandon, Wolsey also had great confidence in his own negotiating skills. They were about to be put to the test right now as Henry softened enough to listen to a compromise.

"I did not last very long being angry at her, did I? At least not as long as I meant to," the king said of his sister.

"Well, Your Highness, even a hardened old cleric such as I would acknowledge there really was never anyone at this court quite like your Mary."

Chapter Twenty

I was contented to conform myself to your said motion, so that if I should fortune to survive the late king, I might with good will marry myself at my liberty without your displeasure. Whereunto, good brother, ye condescended and granted, as ye well know.

—*Mary Tudor, in a letter to Henry VIII.*

May 1515, Hotel de Cluny

The second week in May, Mary felt the desperation to return home so profoundly that she wrote a pleading letter to her brother in a scribbled shorthand, full of corrections and changes. Charles, as well, and even Queen Claude, who had become a friend, wrote to Henry VIII on their behalf. Mary was not sorry; she could never be that. But she would sound contrite, if it helped Henry to forgive them and allow her and Charles to return home to England as husband and wife.

The eventual response from London, with Wolsey's handprint clearly on the design of it, was cold, sharp and very clear. After a period of ten days in which they were left to consider their crime, if there was forgiveness to be had, the vast sum of four thousand pounds must be paid to Henry. In addition, the great diplomat, the Duke of Suffolk, must find a way to convince Francois I to return to England the vast fortune of gold, jewels and silver Mary had brought in her dowry to France. Since the betrothal had been immediately canceled upon his marriage, Brandon would also forfeit the lucrative wardship of Elizabeth Grey. They were harsh terms that would be difficult to arrange, and to abide by. As far as Henry's pride was concerned, the more difficult the terms the better. The sum would reduce what Mary had to live well on for the rest of her life and, at that moment, that indignity suited her angry brother well.

Mary and Charles sat together on a stone bench beneath a wooden pergola surrounded by new spring vines. His arm was around her, and she sank against him as if he could shelter her not just from the cool breeze, but from everything else that was harsh in the world.

"It is what we had hoped for," Charles said cautiously of the letter, which he had only just received. "A way home again."

"But a punishment as well, when he promised me himself that I could marry who I wished," Mary stubbornly countered.

Charles smiled and ran a hand down along the line of her jaw, seeing for the first time since they had come to France the little girl in her he had long known. "Now, now, my heart. He deserves some way to save face, and a bit of our humbling ourselves before him. He *is* the king, after all."

"He is also my brother, and he gave me his word."

"He did not mean that we could take that to the extreme."

He kissed her cheek tenderly, still charmed by her irascible nature, then he pressed his mouth onto hers. "Come now, let's give him what he asks for, be glad we still have our heads . . . and let us go home, hmm?" He smiled that charming Brandon smile. "After all, you go as my wife, and he does not ask for that to change, which is something . . . would you not agree?"

❈

Ten days later, Mary stood on the dock before the *Mary Rose*, which had been sent from England for their return, a damp mist swirling around them, and her dress fluttering in the breeze up off the briny water. She held tightly to Claude, who had become a dear friend. The young French queen had never blamed Mary for her own husband's attraction to her, and every day she had spent in France she had only ever treated her with kindness. Francois' mother, who stood beside her daughter-in-law in the courtyard of Fontainebleau, liked Mary less. Yet she still managed a chilled, slight smile of farewell as Mary moved to stand before her.

"You have made it memorable," Mary said to her so sincerely that the innuendo was lost on all but the cunning Louise de Savoy.

"As you have for France, *ma chère*. Trust that no one here shall soon forget you and the drama in which you have embroiled us all."

Mary was glad to have Charles's tall, reassuring presence beside her, and his powerful hand at the small of her back, pressing her then toward the duc de Longueville, whom she stood before next. She waited as Charles embraced him first, then she took up his offered hand. Into it he pressed a small slip of paper, then closed her fingers around it.

"See it to Mistress Popincourt for me, will you?"

Mary smiled at him. "I will, Louis," she said with a gentle complicity. "And I shall remind her that France is lovely this time of year. She will have forgotten that."

They then said farewell to Diane de Poitiers and her husband, Louis de Brézé, Mary embracing Diane tenderly and with great affection as she had Claude. "Thank you," Mary said, remembering her role in their union. "For *everything*."

"I envy you a true romantic love, Mary. It is between you very like the one in my favorite poem, *Le Roman de la Rose*."

"I know it well."

"Hold on to that with all of your heart," Diane said. Their eyes met. There was far more in them than even what her words had implied. Mary glanced at de Brézé, older, tired, someone who did not seem a romantic match for his dynamic, much younger wife, and she wondered what might be in store for her one day.

"I shall remember that," Mary said, meaning it with all her heart. "And I promise, I shall ever remember you."

The *Mary Rose* docked at Dover seven months after the king's ship had first taken Mary to France to become a queen. She was returning to England a duchess. She stood now on the ship's deck filled with dread for how desperately she had at first wanted to return home. The details had been worked out through emissaries at last and yet still, she must face Henry. His eyes, she knew, would hold his disappointment in her most brightly.

As she walked a step ahead of Charles down the gangway, Mary saw her brother standing there, surrounded by a huge retinue of courtiers, jewels glistening in the afternoon sunlight off the water. Her brother, the King of England, had come to Dover, yet he was not about to make this easy on her, Mary thought with a smile. No slipping back into England quietly. Ah, but then this was her Harry, and she could expect no less. She had missed him so dearly—the camaraderie, and even the battling, more than she thought. Pressing back a nervous tremor she refused to let her brother see, Mary lifted her chin, taking comfort and gaining strength from Charles's hand in support at the small of her back. She let her mouth tighten and she gripped the railing, as the wind and sea spray tossed her unbound hair.

"Ready?" Charles whispered as they made a tentative path down the long, narrow gangway.

"Ready as I shall ever be."

Mary knew that, no matter what he said now, her brother had indulged her romantic heart as well as her deception. Before him she made a grand, dramatic curtsy. Charles bowed along with her. There was only silence for a long time, and the sound of the gulls. She steeled herself, prepared now to pay any price her brother had in mind for his forgiveness. Still, it was good—so good—to be home.

When she rose up, it was unmistakable. Henry VIII, King of England, did not embrace her, or swing her around as once he would have. Nor did he laugh and welcome her. But he did have tears shining brightly in his glittering green eyes. "Only for you, my Mary . . . I swear it, only you," was all he said.

Epilogue

Time eases all things.
                                                    —Sophocles

July 1529, Westhorpe

"**P**apa! Papa! You are home!"

The young girl's giggle was infectious as she raced to be first down to the barge at dockside of their little tributary, amid the long grass and rushes that bent in the warm summer breeze. Mary and her two older children, Henry and Frances, both began to laugh as ten-year-old Eleanor stumbled toward her father, who had been away from them for a full month. She flew into his arms and nearly toppled him. Charles had been visiting the king and his new mistress, Anne Boleyn. They had been at Hampton Court, once the jewel in Cardinal Wolsey's vast and magnificent crown, but given to the king and Katherine in a desperate bid to keep His Highness's favor. It had done little, and in the end, the forces that had been working against him for all of those years succeeded, and the man who had been a fatherly influence to both Henry and Mary was replaced by Thomas Cromwell, a ruthless man far more clever at telling Henry VIII what he wished to hear.

Eleanor had been ill when he left and not fit to travel, so Mary had remained at their ivy-covered brick country estate, where sheep dotted the fields. Charles had not wanted to leave his wife, but attending the king, and reminding him ever of their friendship, was essential.

"Tell me about court, Papa! Do tell me everything!" Eleanor begged, now fully back to health, rosy-cheeked, chattering, and sounding like her mother as a child. "Tell me about that Boleyn girl and Uncle Harry. Is she as beautiful as they say she is?"

Yes, so like me, Mary thought with a contented smile as she watched them. Of her three children, it was Eleanor who possessed not only the clever tongue but the courage with which to use it. They moved down the embankment and Charles came up to his wife then, embracing her heartily beneath the warming midday sun. He kissed her cheek, then smiled.

"Yes, my heart, do tell us. Is my brother's mistress more lovely than when she waited on me, drew my bath and slipped the warming pan between my sheets?" Mary teased.

He tipped his head back and laughed, then kissed her again. "Not anywhere near so lovely as your mother, Eleanor," he replied. He kissed his daughter's forehead and drew his wife closer. "I've missed you desperately," he whispered into Mary's hair.

She smiled up at him. "That was my sincere hope."

Charles turned and embraced his other waiting daughter, then his son—their first child, a boy named Henry, after the king. Thirteen now and tall like his father, Hal, as they called him, would break as many hearts as his father at court when it was time to install him in a position there. For that, Mary could wait, living happily here in their safe little haven.

"How was she really, Father?" Hal leaned over to ask with a devilish smirk.

"Devastatingly beautiful and horribly obnoxious. I only know what I hear, since the king no longer confides in me as he once did. But they also say he means to marry her no matter what response comes from Rome about a divorce from Aunt Katherine."

Dear Kate, Mary thought, hearing that. All she had ever done was accept her fate twice, as she herself had only ever had the fortitude to do once. Katherine had tried her best to be a good wife to two brothers. Mary was glad she had not gone to court this time—glad she had not seen that little vixen, with her raven hair and glittering black eyes, sitting haughtily in the queen's chair beside Henry. One day soon she would need to go, as Charles had. She must protect not only her own place in England, but that of their three children. They were worth everything to her and for that she would even pay court to a whore who sought to replace the queen.

"I actually felt a little sorry for him," Charles said. "He is not the same Harry we knew growing up. The Boleyn whore has changed him and, in my view, not for the better."

"At least your sister is well."

"Anne and Gawain Carew will be married in the autumn. He has loved her forever and finally, after all of these years, managed to convince her of that."

As they walked slowly back up the grassy incline to the Suffolk estate on the hill, Charles wrapped his arm around his wife's waist, as she did around his. Their pace was easy as they watched their children running happily up ahead. *Joy,* Mary thought. *Even his griefs are a joy long after to one that remembers all that he wrought and endured.* . . . She had always liked that passage from Homer. It really did define this part of her life. The very best part.

"I received a letter from Jane last week," Mary said as they walked through the garden, white iris and rosemary flanking their path.

"Is she still happy in France?"

"Happy that Louis is there, with her."

"They always did belong together," Charles remarked with a smile as he reached over to kiss her cheek again. "As do two other people I know rather well."

When Mary looked up at him, she saw the sun highlighting his face, lined now, distinguished by years, battles, struggles, losses and victories. But it still was the most magnificent face she had ever seen. Being his wife was worth everything. Images of court life, the frenetic pace—the balls, masques and endless banquets—moved through her mind then, with her husband so newly returned from there. Jewels. Gowns. Gossip. Opulence. . . . And she wondered if there had ever been another woman in history so happy not to be a part of that—*not* to be a queen.

Author's Note

$\mathcal{A}$s with each novel I write, while this is a work of fiction, great care was taken to recount the historical events as they occurred. Naturally various subplots and the motivations of some of the secondary characters, where necessary, were fictionally enhanced, such as the details of the romances of Jane Popincourt, about whom history has told us precious little. While her affair in England with the duc de Longueville was documented and commented upon by Louis XII as the novel purports, and both figures did actually return to France to spend their remaining days, the details of precisely what happened have been lost to time. Also, while Gawain Carew did marry Charles Brandon's sister, Anne, the marriage occurred much later. Letters in the novel, with the exception of the private missive from Margaret of Austria to Charles Brandon, are real.

Regarding dates, since scholars differ between 1495 and

1496 as the year of Mary Tudor's birth, for the purposes of this work I have accepted 1495. Similarly, Anne Boleyn's birth is disputed ranging from 1501 to 1507. I have accepted the earlier date, making her thirteen at the time Mary Tudor became Queen of France, as it seems implausible to me that Anne would have been utilized in the French household in 1514 at the age of seven. And, finally, the actual year of birth of Henry VIII's daughter Mary was 1516.

The long and extraordinary love story between Mary Tudor and Charles Brandon, and all that they endured to be together, is true. Mary died in June 1533 at the age of thirty-eight after an illness, having borne three children: Henry, Frances and Eleanor. At the time of her death Mary Tudor was still happily married to the one great love of her life. Charles Brandon married for a fourth and final time in 1534. He died twelve years after Mary, in 1545.

The
Secret Bride

DIANE HAEGER

QUESTIONS
FOR DISCUSSION

1. What do you think of the relationship between Henry VIII and his sister Mary? History tells us they were close as brother and sister, and yet do you think their sibling relationship was as open and loving as one might be today? How do you think it might have been different because they were royals? How does the death of Arthur impact Mary specifically? How do you think her relationship with Henry changed through the years?

2. What specific role in Mary Tudor's life, beyond mere companion, does Jane play? How might the relationship between two young girls like that, one from royalty, the other from a humble background, be different or the same in today's world?

3. In what ways do Mary's strict mother and grandmother influence, both positively and negatively, Mary's life and

her decisions as she matures? How does it differ from the role Lady Guildford plays concurrently in her life? In chapter 2, Lady Guildford is referred to as "tender-hearted." Is it more than that which makes her indispensable to Mary? Do you think Mary had any true confidantes or friends in her life?

4. What are the things, both positive and negative, about Charles Brandon that first capture a young Mary's attention when there are so many other handsome courtiers always around her brother? At what point does Mary begin to see more in him than just the roguish flirt that others see? Is she wise to see those things in him?

5. Charles Brandon is portrayed as single-mindedly ambitious. All his actions and decisions seem designed to further his personal position and power at court. Do you think that makes him an unsympathetic person? Or do you think it means he was smart and practical?

6. Do you believe that Charles's feelings for Mary were pure from the beginning or do you feel that they were based more on her beauty, or perhaps her status as sister to Henry VIII?

7. Mary determines to take some control of her future by extracting a promise from Henry without telling him her plans. Discuss whether you found her plan to have been

admirable in its personal strength or underhanded, considering her position at court and her duty to England.

8. Discuss Wolsey's influence over Henry, Mary and Charles Brandon. To whom do you believe he felt true allegiance, if anyone? Why?

9. Henry VIII had a famous temper. Where do you imagine that it would have come from? How and why was Mary never a victim of that, yet his wives were?

10. Prior to reading *The Secret Bride,* what if anything did you know about Mary Tudor? What about her surprised you? Knowing what you know of the fate of her brother's wives, did you expect her life with Charles Brandon to end happily as it did?

Photo by Brystan Studios

Diane Haeger is the author of several novels of historical and women's fiction. She has a degree in English literature and an advanced degree in clinical psychology, which she credits with helping her bring to life complicated characters and their relationships. She lives in Newport Beach with her husband and children.